FALL OF A SPARROW

Bresciano's first case

SAM BENADY & MARY CHIAPPE

HKB Press

ISBN 978-0-9561443-0-0

Bound and printed by **P&R GRAFIS s.a.**

HKB Press

Also by S. Benady

Sherlock Holmes in Gibraltar
The Keys of the City
General Sir George Don: a Biography
Civil Hospital and Epidemics in Gibraltar

Diary of an Epidemic (with L.A. Sawchuk)
Passing through the Fever (with L.A. Sawchuk and S.D.A. Burke)

Also by M. Chiappe

The Grapes of Warmth
Cabbages and Kings
A Handful of Poems

By S. Benady and M. Chiappe

The Murder in Whirligig Lane

ACKNOWLEDGEMENTS

The authors wish to thank kind friends on whom they inflicted early drafts of the book for their suggestions and support. Special thanks to Ilana Benady, Dorothy Prior, Gaby Chiappe and Jennifer Ballantine Perera.

PLAN OF GIBRALTAR

MEDITERRANEAN SEA

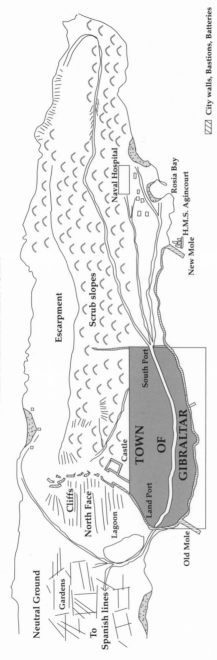

Neutral Ground

Gardens

To
Spanish lines

Cliffs

North Face

Lagoon

Castle

Escarpment

Scrub slopes

Naval Hospital

Rosia Bay

H.M.S. Agincourt

New Mole

South Port

TOWN

OF

GIBRALTAR

Land Port

Old Mole

BAY OF GIBRALTAR

City walls, Bastions, Batteries

Scale
1 Mile

PLAN OF THE TOWN

1. Bresciano's house
2. Bianca's tavern
3. Capt. Weston's quarter
4. Blue Barracks
5. Emiliana
6. Hargrave's Parade and whipping post
7. Abraham Hassam's house
8. Bianca's Room
9. Dr Coll
10. Debtor's Prison
11. Mermaid Tavern
12. Better tavern
13. Bomb House Lane
14. Water Port - gates
15. Princess Caroline's Battery
16. Casemates
///// City walls and fortifications

Charles V Wall

To New Mole

To Naval Hospital

South Port

The old stables

Southport Street

The Convent
(Governor's residence)

Governor's garden

Church Street

King's Bastion

BAY OF GIBRALTAR

Cave

Batteries

Willis's

Temporary camp

Cliffs

15

Castle

Land Port

To Spain

Buena Vista

Green Market

Waterport Street

Irish Town

4

5

3

9

1

2

8

16

14

Lime Wall

10

Old Mole

11

12

13

7

6

FALL OF A SPARROW
Cast of Characters

*Names in **bold** are of real historical personalities.
The others are no less real to us.*

LOCALS

Giovanni Bresciano	*An idealistic and very raw recruit*
Giancarlo Bresciano	*His father, a volatile Genoese*
Eleanor Bresciano, née Snowe	*His level-headed English mother*
Lucia	*His little sister*
Nonna Lucrezia	*His adoptive grandmother, given to drama*
'Aunt Maria'	*The Nonna's daughter, given to palpitations*
Bianca	*An alluring barmaid who gives young Bresciano palpitations*
Carmela	*Another barmaid, more voluptuous and more available*
Emiliana	*Bianca's slatternly mother, no better than she ought to be*
Lola	*A maid*
Dr Coll	*A loquacious GP*
Mrs Coll	*His wife*
***Abraham Hassan**	*The first Gibraltarian recruit*
Antonio	*A small hungry boy bringing bad news*
An angry Barbary macaque	*Himself*

THE GARRISON

OFFICERS

General Sir George Augustus Eliott	*Governor of Gibraltar*
Lieutenant John Drinkwater	*Diarist of the Siege. An avid reader*
Lieutenant Holloway	*Aide to the Chief Engineer*
Captain Weston	*Irascible, perhaps because of....*
Mrs Weston	*who may be carrying on with....*
Lieutenant Black	*Literary and susceptible (to Mrs Weston)*
An orderly	*To Captain Weston*
Captain Lord Manners, RN	*An overbearing naval officer*

| **Dr Arthur Baines** | The Principal Medical Officer |
| Dr Rogers | His assistant |

THE ARTIFICERS

Sergeant Connor	A hard man
Jamie Macfarlane ('Sparrow')	The simple-minded victim.
Corporal Jones	Wants to whisk Bianca off to the Welsh mountains
Private Murch (Fat Murch)	A greedy drunk
Private Tom Tennant	His uncouth friend, no better than him
Malone, Talbot etc	More artificers
Cookie-Will (Corporal Warner)	Kind-hearted and devious
Angel	Cookie's dog
Mrs Bickerstaff	Captain Weston's guard dog
Assorted sergeants, privates etc	Literary fodder

THE WALLOONS

Robert de la Tour	A charmer
Pascal	A quiet man
Jean Pierre	A quieter man

OTHER CHARACTERS MENTIONED

General Boyd	The Lieutenant Governor
Sir William Green	The Chief Engineer
Mrs Miriam Green	His wife, who also wrote a diary of the Siege
Father Messa	Roman Catholic priest
Rabbi Almosnino	Head of the Hebrew community
Baron von Munchausen	A German madman
Admiral Barceló	Spanish Admiral in charge of the naval blockade
João	A Portuguese bosun who is never there
Old Gavarone	A poor substitute for João

*Abraham Hassan was the first cousin five times removed of one of the authors. He was, in fact, the only Gibraltarian to volunteer for the regular army during the Great Siege.

a type
of gun

FALL OF A SPARROW

CHAPTER I

12th July 1779

The first casualty of the siege occurred before a single shot had been fired by the enemy.

"It's Jamie Macfarlane, Sergeant. I think he's dead! There's blood everywhere and he's not moving!" a young private reported breathlessly to Sergeant Connor.

There were those who would later blame the Sergeant for what happened to Jamie Macfarlane, as the Sergeant was not a popular man, but could he or anyone else have known that the musket he had issued to Jamie would turn out to be defective?

Jamie survived, but when his musket exploded, it left him with a damaged left hand and a childlike mind that wandered and seemed to work only by fits and starts. He was, nevertheless, kept on by the Artificers to run errands and perform simple duties around the garrison town. *armd forces*

And as the Spanish forces settled down round the Bay of Gibraltar and just beyond the peninsula that housed the town and garrison, Jamie helped to alleviate one of the *spread* worst of the enemies within – boredom. There was little enough to distract the men now that several thousand civilians, encouraged by Governor Eliott, had left the blockaded town. So it was that Jamie's accounts of what he claimed to have seen and heard *making claims* gave rise to apocryphal tales, scurrilous gossip and bawdy *dealing with sexual* humour in the regiment, for Jamie's stories, *believed to be* sometimes lucid, were, at other times, the stuff of wild imagination. He gave his *matter funny way*

army

3

accounts in all innocence, encouraged by men grown weary of inactivity, sick of the salt meat and bread that was their staple diet, and drunk enough on blackstrap – that fiery mixture of wines that they could purchase cheaply at any of the many taverns in the town – to become a little reckless in their talk at the end of the day.

"So what was it today, Jamie?"

"Heard anything new?" *a town full of army troops*

And Jamie, a short, slight figure, a lad of barely eighteen years, would smile vaguely and try to remember what a day spent roaming the garrison had yielded to his confused mind. It was worth his while as the men good-naturedly rewarded him with the occasional penny for the entertainment he offered.

"Ah took the Captain's washing-washing back to his hoose today, and the maid hung it-it out and there were a lot… a lot of pretty things." → *sexual*

This was greeted with ribald comments, as the Captain's wife, a haughty but remarkably pretty woman, fuelled the fantasies of more than one of the listeners.

"Tell us more!"

"Ah dinna ken… Ah only saw when the-the maid, Emiliana, began to, to, to hang those pretty things out to dry and Ah-Ah wanted to stay because she sometimes gives me… she gives me…"

More laughter and innuendo, for the maid had a reputation which she had earned over the years with succeeding regiments. Jamie grinned happily, not understanding. All he knew was that the men, his friends – for to him all were friends – always enjoyed hearing about the Captain's household.

"… she gives me ale, she gives me. Ale. But today I couldn't stay. Lieutenant Black told me to-to get out. He bumped into me when he went into the hoose and he-he was angry and…"

Now this was certainly worth hearing. The Lieutenant and the Captain's wife! Well! It wasn't the first time Jamie had mentioned such a visit. At least, they thought, it would be worthwhile keeping an ear to the ground where the Lieutenant was concerned – him with his airs and graces. They egged Jamie on to find out more.

And Jamie might tell them of the angels down in King's

Chapel who sometimes spoke to him; or he might explain how he was personally responsible for Eliott's safety. It distracted the men. And after more than a year of siege conditions, life had grown harsher and any entertainment was welcome: firewood was scarce; the days had grown cold and wet; there were no fresh provisions; scurvy and smallpox were scourging the town; and only the wealthy or the officers could afford what food came on the occasional ship that managed to evade the Spanish naval blockade at the entrance to the Bay of Gibraltar.

Eliott bought only for the Garrison, but he ordered all other imported foodstuffs to be auctioned publicly, thus making himself unpopular with prominent men who could otherwise have cornered the goods for themselves alone, for it was an age of influence and nepotism. It all added to the tension in the walled town: the efficient Governor was disliked for taking strict measures to enforce what he saw as the interests of the defence of the fortress; and relations between officers of different political persuasions could become acrimonious.

However, for most of those left in the beleaguered town – whether civilians or military men – hunger and disease replaced fear of attack as the main concerns.

The soldiers' rations, albeit monotonous and gradually growing rancid and even rotten, were guaranteed, and it was military inaction and boredom that became a new enemy. So after a hard day of physical labour building and repairing the solid stone defences of walls and bastions, Jamie's amiable presence and daft narratives helped to while away the empty evenings for the rank and file of the Artificers.

* * * *

So eighteen long, hungry months passed since the start of the Spanish blockade and, while the batteries in Gibraltar bombarded the Spanish lines daily to impede the construction of the usual siege approaches, not a shot had been fired from the Spanish lines less than a mile away. There was no need if the garrison, in the time-honoured strategy of sieges, was to be starved into defeat.

And one evening in December 1780 another, but very different, eighteen-year-old was about to become the butt *aiming for protection*

of unwanted humour. It was a Wednesday evening and an idealistic young man, a proud new recruit, walked through the persistent drizzle towards his parents' house in the principal street of the town. He was over six feet tall, a gangling lad with a nose that looked too big for his face, an awkward youth who would one day become a good-looking man.

December had been a month of torrential rains and flooding in the fortress town, a situation that aggravated the acute food shortages as dry provisions grew damp and rotted and rations for the military and food supplies for civilians became ever scarcer – but young Giovanni Bresciano's spirits could not be entirely dampened. He was eighteen, he was proud to be just the second local man to volunteer to serve in the British army. He had joined up to defend Gibraltar in her hour of need and he now dreamt of honour and glory when the time for fighting came, as come it must.

He was also in love, and he told himself that Bianca would surely be impressed when he appeared before her in uniform. The last time he saw her she had been standing behind the slab of wood that did service as a counter at the tavern where she worked. Her dark hair was swept up and held carelessly with a comb so that a few curls escaped, seeming to caress her slender neck. She wore her red dress with its scooped neckline and she greeted him with her lazy smile. The memory of that dress gave Bresciano sleepless nights, enticing him and binding him to her as did the spells that Nonna Lucrezia, his surrogate grandmother, believed unscrupulous women cast *not honest* over men. The tavern had been full of soldiers – of men – and she had treated him as if he had been a boy. But now... now he was one of them. She would see him through different eyes.

not untested

However, even his youthful optimism stopped short at imagining his parents' delight: there would be none. He stood outside their house in Waterport Street, nervously pulling at his lower lip, and braced himself to break the news to them, bolstering his resolution with high-flown arguments and forceful phrases with which he planned – with his newly acquired military fervour – to storm their defences and win the day. *Italian → intense feeling*

He feared his Genoese father's reactions. Giancarlo Bresciano was a man of hot temper – had he not fled Genoa many years before, disowned by his family after a duel, the third in his turbulent young life? He might now be a respectable and successful merchant, but his temper could still erupt volcanically on occasion, and he would not appreciate any talk of duty and patriotism. And Bresciano's English mother, born Eleanor Snowe of Tavistock, would think his sense of duty praiseworthy, but would surely deplore his sense of timing now that his father was complaining of pains in his lower back that made it well-nigh impossible for him to attempt to sail his polacre to Morocco in the hope of obtaining food supplies.

For the first time since he had walked in to see the recruiting officer earlier that day (or had he swaggered in, full of pipe-dream courage and confidence?) Bresciano was faced with the realities of his choice. So he made himself stand ramrod straight, his musket at his side, then pushed the door open and screwed up his courage to face his family.

He stood in the large room that was the centre of family life, but the house seemed empty. There was no little sister, Lucia, eager to greet him; neither Nonna Lucrezia nor her daughter, Aunt Maria, were there; his father was not in his favourite chair by the fire; and even his mother was not there to turn a smiling face towards him. Bresciano's courage rapidly evaporated, evanescent in the absence of conflict, and he turned to leave.

"Is that you, Giovanni? These horrific, appalling rains. Just look at this, after all the care I lavished on them; and to think I watered the wretched things all these past months in order to nurture them!"

She was trying to make light of her loss, but her voice with its gentle Devon burr masked a degree of despair. Her voice came from the large yard at the back of the house where she grew a few vegetables that enabled the family to eat fresh food occasionally. She stood there, a tall woman, haggard after a year of dwindling supplies of food, frowning over a meagre handful of green beans that she had just picked.

"Heavens above!" she brought a horrified hand to her mouth when she saw him. "Oh, my darling! My foolish quixotic darling! What have you done?"

His defences crumbled.

"I've joined up. They said I could join a company of the Artificers." His voice wavered uncertainly. He had wanted to be a line soldier, one who would defend or attack, earn glory, have an opportunity for heroism. He had wanted a uniform with a red jacket and white facings and had had to be satisfied with his own buff coloured trousers and a white jacket grown dingy with use. He had wanted heroism in battle and instead he was to be involved mainly with mundane tasks of building and repairing defences – like a mason or a builder and not at all like a proper soldier. "I wanted the Twelfth Regiment."

"But to do it without saying a word to us. And to do it when your father has set you up in business... and especially now that he has hurt his back and cannot sail the boat."

"But, Mother, he doesn't need me. He's got João."

"He has not. Surely you heard what your father said the other night? He needs a bosun. That is why he was saying that you could help him out. You must have heard him."

But her son had neither listened nor heard. He was used to his father's forceful monologues on the problems he faced and the solutions he proposed and, besides, he had been anxious to get out to see Bianca.

"João is still sick. You cannot have forgotten. And today we heard that he has got smallpox, Lord help us. And your sister, Lucia, was over at his house with his daughter only days ago. I pray she may have escaped contagion; I pray they both have. Oh, it was rash of you to join up, my dear boy. What will your father say when...?"

She did not need to finish the sentence because there he stood behind Bresciano, a powerful, barrel-chested man dwarfed by his lanky son. He must have heard Giovanni's announcement, because his normally ruddy face darkened with anger.

"Your father," he spoke in a rapid mixture of Genoese and English which gained in power what it occasionally lost grammatically, "is a man who is amazed at his fool of a son. An ungrateful son! Why do I set up a business for you? I get you premises in Waterport Street. The best street in Gibraltar. I give you the gift of supplying ships in a port. How do you repay your aged father?"

"You are only fif... fifty!" Bresciano stuttered.

"So, I shall die young. You want me to die young? Yes. You will kill me with this thing you have done. Giovanni! Giovanni! It takes me thirty years to establish myself here and you are going to ruin it in one day? We have a business to run."

"There is no business! We aren't doing any business with this siege. Hardly anything gets into port past the Spanish blockade at Punta Carnero at the entrance to the Bay. And the few ships that do get past are English war ships, or merchantmen with stuff to sell. They don't want to buy anything from me. We have no provisions to sell in any case. You know that – you were saying so only a few days ago."

"*Signió*, give me *pazienza* with this son of mine!" His father's powerful voice boomed out.

"Giancarlo, my love, sit down a moment and listen to the boy. Perhaps he has something to say." Eleanor never contradicted her husband openly, but she always managed to calm him down. "Giovanni, I know you are a responsible boy so tell us why. Your father will hear you out. You will, Giancarlo, won't you?"

"Yes: why? Why you join the army? Do what your mother tells. Tell us your wonderful reasons for destroying all your father's plans and expectations. I wait for what you say." He stuck his jaw out, a man prepared to hear his son out without actually listening to him.

"Mother, Papa..." he pulled at his lip, took a deep breath and began, aware of how futile his fine sentiments would sound to his father, "You know how it's all gone wrong! We opened the shop in May last year and the Spanish blockade began in June. It has been awful. Do you know how much I sold last month? Eleven *reales*, not even five shillings. I do nothing there because there is nothing I can do! And I think... I felt I had to join up because I think the Spanish are bound to launch an attack sooner or later and there is now talk that even the French armies may come and decide to attack one day – and we will be the ones to suffer if they succeed in capturing Gibraltar. Have you seen how they are building up their forces outside our walls? The defences they are throwing up just beyond our lines? Well, I feel I want to be there to help fight them when they do attack. I met Abraham Hassan today. You know he joined up. Why can't I?" He stared down at his feet, miserably aware that all his carefully structured arguments and fine phrases had gone clean out of his mind.

Out of one of the bedrooms, with a shawl over her short, but voluminous figure, came Nonna Lucrezia, roused by the noise. She crossed herself in horror at the sight of Bresciano's uniform and sat down abruptly, threatening spasms which she abandoned when she realised no one was attending to her.

"You think… you feel," Giancarlo mimicked his son. "I, Giancarlo Bresciano, tell you that you are wasting your time, my fool son! The French do not give a fig for their Spanish allies – and the Spanish will not fight: yellow-livered cowards, all of them. They are afraid of our Governor Eliott. There will be no fighting. Pah!" His father spat out the word scornfully. "They just try to starve us, those *desgrassiati*!" _disgust anger_

"Yes. That's something else. The food. You only managed to get across to Morocco twice last year for supplies. And it's now become too dangerous to go at all. So even you, Papa, with your stores, have not enough food for a year for us. Wasn't that what Eliott said each household needed? And I eat a lot and I knew that… if I joined up, the army would feed me, so you and Mother and little Lucia… well, you would be better off without me here."

He found it difficult to speak. He had intended this noble gesture to be an act of silent heroism and it now looked as if he was attempting to earn their gratitude, as if he was blackmailing his father morally into accepting his decision. He felt wretched.

"And what about Nonna Lucrezia?" The old lady now joined the fray with gusto in her guttural Genoese. _harsh persona vijy_ "No food for her? You do not care about me, Giovanni? Eh? Of course. I am not your real Nonna. She died in Genoa and she never even saw you. You would have fed *her*, but I am only the person who took your father in when he arrived in Gibraltar sick with a fever and penniless. I gave him a place to live. I was his second mother, and my poor Beppo – God rest his soul, old villain that he was – was like a father to him. I am not important, eh? eh?" Logic was not the Nonna's strong point.

"I'll make you some camomile, Nonna," said Eleanor soothingly, but automatically; she had long ago grown used to Nonna's love of drama.

"Camomile yes, but no food, please. No food for me, Aie! I could not eat it!"

"Nonna! *Pe' favore*!" Giancarlo raised his hands in supplication. "This is serious. Of course we all love you so do not talk this nonsense about food. But the boy has joined the army. That is not a game. Look at that – he has a gun because if you are in the army, you fight – and if you fight, you can be killed. I don't want that for my son. The army! We are merchants not soldiers, Giovanni. We have been a seafaring family for generations."

"So I should have joined the navy?" Bresciano's angry humour was ill-placed.

"Are you laughing at me, boy?" His voice rose again.

"I'm sorry, Papa," he was helpless in the face of his father's vehement opposition and general lack of rational argument, "but I am grown up now. I can decide what I want to do. I wanted to do something useful for Gibraltar," he spoke passionately, "and I wanted... I wanted to make it... I wanted you to have one less mouth to feed. And you are the one who is always telling me to make decisions and act like a man, so I made my decision. I did what you wanted me to do, didn't I? And all you do is shout at me."

"Now you will listen to me, my boy..." His brow was thunderous.

Bresciano jammed his hat on, ready to stalk out, and turned to them defiantly. "And stop calling me 'boy', all of you. I am not..." he shouted the last words, "I am *not* a little boy."

The family stared at him. There he stood, an alarmingly tall young man, six feet three inches in his socks, now having to stoop as his hat brushed the low ceiling. His father's mood turned suddenly as he echoed his son's words "... not a little boy!" He was proud of having fathered this tall son and he now stood, slapping his thigh and bent over with laughter – which action hurt his lower back and made him at clutch it with his other hand. Eleanor shook her head at her wayward son and her volatile husband⟶ changing rapidly and even Nonna began to smile, abandoning her imaginary grievances at the idea of this gangling giant as a little boy.   ⟶ believing something is wrong

Bresciano's glared, furious and helpless. So much for honour and glory. How could a man grow up... no, that was wrong... how could he grow up to be a man when he was treated as a child?

"You are laughing at Giovanni. Don't laugh at him." Young Lucia had walked in from the street with Aunt Maria and was looking hard at them, "I think he looks very handsome in those clothes. Are you a soldier now?" She smiled at him and his heart went out to her – she was grown so thin in this past year. He was right to leave.

honour

"Yes. I am a soldier. A Military Artificer," he recklessly bestowed royal patronage *→ given* on the humble Artificers – "a Royal Artificer!" Let them laugh. "I am leaving. I will be sleeping in… in the… in the Barracks tonight and I shall return… when I see fit."

horizontal wood on a door

"I don't want you to go away!" Lucia wailed.

"I must. It is my duty as a soldier of the King!" He swept out. His exit was rendered *→ proved* less than effective when the lintel over the front door knocked his hat off. His father's renewed laughter seemed to pursue him down the pitted and rutted street, a street which Eliott had ordered to be dug up. Bresciano thought furiously that Eliott could see the dangers ahead, even if his father didn't – that was why the streets had been cleared of their fine cobblestones, so that any cannonballs fired by the enemy would bury themselves in the soil, and not bounce on to cause further damage.

Of course there would be fighting! His father never listened to him. He found his lower lip trembling and he swallowed convulsively *scared* – if he had not been a man, he would have wept for sheer frustration: his grand gesture in fighting for his birthplace and in trying to ensure that the family's meagre food stores were husbanded had met with mockery. And furthermore, as was usual these days, he was hungry and had just done himself out of whatever meal his mother might prepare for the evening.

So it was that in a stormy mood he went down to the tavern where Bianca worked, dispensing smiles and drink to whoever came in. She, at least, would surely know how to value his actions.

She stood at the counter and smiled at him: "Giovanni, you… a soldier?"

She seemed amused rather than impressed and he made the mistake of claiming glory before he had title to it.

"Yes. I am a private in the Artificers. I serve his Majesty, King George the Third. Give me some blackstrap." He was one of the men now. *→ meat (food)*

"That's powerful stuff, young 'un."

The intervention was kindly meant, but Corporal Jones

→ added extra

of the Artificers – a man of medium height with muscles like whipcord – should not have absently put his arm round Bianca's shapely waist when he spoke. And Bianca did not push him away! Bresciano stiffened and stared at him, then downed the contents of the thick glass in one swallow.

"Give me another!"

Several drinks later he found himself looking glassily at Bianca, who had developed a tendency to move around and double her image. When Corporal Jones left, Bianca had let him kiss her cheek.

"Mushn't do that," Bresciano said severely. "Might give him the… notion that it's…" he stopped, uneasily aware that he couldn't use the expression 'like mother, like daughter' without causing offence.

Her mother, Emiliana, was that Emiliana currently working for an army captain, with her well-earned reputation among the soldiers of the garrison. She had been a careless parent at best, so that Bianca had run wild as a child with Giovanni Bresciano in her wake getting into scrapes with her and feeling a devotion that she had taken for granted, but never returned. They had both lived up at Buena Vista in those days, in tenements overcrowded with immigrants from around the Mediterranean.

Then Bresciano's father, beginning to make good, had moved his young family to the more salubrious and respectable Waterport Street and Bianca, eleven by then, and the skinny nine-year-old Bresciano had gradually grown apart. They had met again since the siege began and Bresciano's old affections had been fanned into a new and more virile feeling which, allied to the jealousy he felt as men ogled her all-too-evident charms in the tavern, needed an outlet. Perversely, he found it in harassing her.

"Shouldn't let him kish you," he said stubbornly and fiercely.

She wiped the counter with a wet cloth, "Mind your own business, Giovanni. What I do is my affair." Then she brought her face close to his, "And you have no right to tell me what to do: you are not my father. And you are certainly not my suitor, are you?"

She had the satisfaction of seeing him blush and she laughed, not unkindly, for she had fond memories of her childhood friend.

"'S not right! 'S disg... disgrusti..." He gave up.

"So? We may all be dead next year – the Spanish may break through, the smallpox might get me, one day a stray shot from an enemy cannon could land on the tavern and kill us all. I say: live now for there may be no tomorrow. And I can look after myself, don't you worry."

A burst of laughter came from a corner of the room where some soldiers, the worse for drink, were urging Jamie on. The young Artificer was clumsily attempting a sprightly Highland dance on uncertain, drunken feet.

Bianca shook her head disapprovingly. She could remember him as he had been before the siege – an eager sixteen-year-old, an innocent in a world of men. Then that musket had exploded in his hands, for even the Artificers, whose normal tools were their saws and hammers, had been issued with weapons of war. And now Jamie, like any village simpleton, was treated with careless kindness or unthinking cruelty by his peers, who viewed him as a source of entertainment. And so it was on this particular evening in the tavern as the men egged Jamie on:

"A claymore! Ah need a claymore," he cried out in some distress, "It's nae good wi'out proper... proper..." His voice trailed off, and he stood there, looking confused.

Bianca went up to him and took his arm firmly, scolding the men at the same time. "Away with you all. You should be ashamed of yourselves! Come along, Sparrow. Yes, you, Jamie; you've been drinking too much. Come with me and meet my friend. You can be friends together."

She led him back to where Bresciano, looking pallid, was leaning heavily on the counter. Jamie staggered and clutched Bresciano, and Bianca, appraising the situation, steered and pushed them both out into the street.

"Go and be sick somewhere else. I'm not cleaning up after you! Now go home, the pair of you."

"I have no home!" Bresciano called angrily after her.

"Ah hae no hame... neither," said Jamie tearfully.

Then, each with an arm around the other, they lurched off into the darkness. And neither had any way of knowing how very brief their friendship would be.

CHAPTER II

Bresciano woke up to a pearly grey dawn with a nagging headache and a foul taste in his mouth – and someone seemed to have gummed his eyelids down. For a brief moment he imagined that he was in his room at home and could not understand what had happened to him. Then the horror of it struck home: it was smallpox! He tried to sit up and call his mother, but when he attempted to move, his head swam sickeningly so he lay back, waiting for relief to come, wretched and confused; and as consciousness returned fully, he saw his jacket on the floor and realised that he was otherwise completely dressed, down to his shoes. He moaned at the shame of it all: he had set off to help defend the fortress and had only succeeded in getting drunk.

Gradually he became aware of the sound of snoring and, turning, saw a huddled figure lying on a bed near him. A shock of red hair poked out from under the rough blanket. Jamie, yes, that was it – 'Sparrow', 'Daft Jamie' the men had called him – had managed to get himself and Bresciano safely back to the huts near Willis's Batteries that served as the Artificers' temporary barracks while they completed work on the defensive walls above the town. Without Daft Jamie's help he would have slept in a gutter: he was worse than the regimental fool.

He couldn't even remember anything of the journey to the huts, but he blushed with embarrassment as images of the scene at the wine-house flooded back. Had Bianca thrown him out? He sat up slowly and buried his face in his hands. Why had she let that corporal, an insignificant little fellow, take *whatever whant (free)*

liberties with her? And it hadn't seemed to worry her. In fact, she had said... what exactly had she said about it? *beating*

He was ripe for a bout of self-pity and self-flagellation, but he had little time to brood on his memories because at that moment the door was flung open and hazy daylight flooded in, momentarily blinding him. *military orgnicatten*

The shattering sound of cannon fire from Grand Battery began just as a large figure stepped into the doorway, a dark silhouette against the light, an avenging demon.

"Show a leg, you lazy blackguards! You're not in the army to sleep, damn your eyes. Get your clothes on! You're on duty at Princess Caroline's Battery. There's a breach in the wall there where a couple of deserters slipped away last week. The Sappers will be repairing it and your job is to guard them! Not that anyone is likely to attack them there, but orders is orders!" Sergeant Connor growled at them.

As Bresciano tumbled out of bed, he glanced at the figure of Jamie who was still happily snoring, and he leaned over to shake him.

"Leave him be!" The Sergeant snapped. "He's no bloody use to man or beast, anyway. And if he fails to go, I can always have him whipped." Then he turned to Bresciano. "What are you gawking there for? Get out of here."

Bresciano looked around in confusion for a weapon with which to guard the Sappers and thanked his lucky star when he saw his musket lying on the floor next to his cot. At least he had not left it at the tavern. There was no need to dress. He scrambled into his jacket, glad that smartness was not insisted on up on the slopes of the Rock and that he did not have to powder his hair with flour – a practice banned months earlier by the Governor because of the food shortage.

"And who might you be?" The Sergeant looked at Bresciano's clumsy haste with contempt.

"I'm Giovanni Bresciano."

"You address me as 'sir' when you speak to me." His voice was like the crack of a musket shot and a startled Bresciano attempted to stand to attention. The Sergeant looked at him scornfully. "And I don't want any of them foreign *descont and angr* names in my company. I shall call you Busyano. Is that clear or are you as big a fool as your friend there?"

"Yes, sir. I mean... no, sir." He managed a salute and

16

waited for worse to come, but Sergeant Connor had gone.

Bresciano swallowed hard and turned to Jamie, shaking him hard and telling him where they were expected to go. He was rewarded by an incoherent muttering, but it was as much as he dared do. He looked around and drew a mug of water from the water-barrel he found in a corner of the hut and drained it avidly, then upended another mug-full over his head. Feeling marginally better, he grabbed his musket and as an afterthought, filled the jug again and threw the contents in Jamie's face before he lurched out of the hut.

The climb up the slope of the Rock was hard on him. He had become used to a sedentary life. Now he shambled awkwardly on the loose shale till he found one of the many goat-tracks that seamed the rock-face, though any goats that were left were jealously guarded and might change hands for as much as twenty pounds in the hungry garrison. Food for those who could afford it – officers and wealthy merchants, Bresciano thought.

He soon arrived breathless at Princess Caroline's Battery to find the Sappers hard at work, ready to berate him for his tardiness. Guard duty was not too bad, he thought as he stood in the shade of an olive tree and watched the men at work repairing the breach in the wall. He scratched his back absently as he looked about him. A pale winter sun was shining, though clouds were rolling in from the south west. The fresh morning breeze helped to clear his head, and after the recent rains his world looked clean and even beautiful, and he was even able to enjoy the view to the north by avoiding looking at the foreground where the Spanish lines were drawn up. Instead he concentrated on the broad expanse of land that was Spain, a land now green and fertile, which spread away until it blended with the distant hills.

Closer to him, across the waters of the Bay, was the small town of Algeciras, sheltered by the hills behind it, clear and sharp in the morning light. To the south, across the Straits of Gibraltar, the less defined but more impressive mountains of Africa appeared to rise straight up from the sea as if they had been flung up capriciously by some sea god. Below where he stood, from the menacing mass of the great castle which had been built all those centuries ago by the Moorish invaders of Spain, the fortress town spilled down the slopes, descending from the poor huddle of houses at Buena Vista towards the more prosperous lower area with some fine properties and several solid limestone barracks; and from there on to the splendidly fortified city walls and the harbour beyond. Sunshine on red and ochre tiled roofs, rushes of light and shadow over the Bay as the clouds scudded overhead, the sound of sparrows in the trees – Bresciano was visited by a deep sense of belonging to this unique, uncomfortable, bleak Rock, and by the knowledge that this was what he sought to protect when he had joined up.

After a while he was surprised when Jamie scampered up nimbly and sat on a rock near him, gnawing at a crust of bread. He offered a piece to Bresciano, who accepted it gratefully.

"Where's your musket, Jamie? Aren't we supposed to be on guard?"

Jamie looked at him blankly.

"Ah use ma een." He held out his callused hands. "An' Ah can see far… Ah can see like Shot and Shell." He mentioned by nickname the two boy soldiers whose keen eyesight was to become legendary during the course of the siege.

Bresciano found it difficult to follow the thick Scottish accent.

"But you need a weapon if you are on guard."

"Sergeant Connor says just to keep leuking and tae – tae use rocks… to heave them."

"That's ridiculous. Why put you on guard duty at all if he won't equip you properly?"

Jamie seemed uninterested. He merely nodded and shrugged and finished the bread slowly, nibbling at it like a rodent. "Dinna get much food, we dinna, do we?" He complained. Food was one thing that could always hold his attention. "*Daonnan arach.*"

"What's that you said?"

"Ah feel hungry always."

Bresciano nodded; lack of food had become a reality over the past eighteen months, for soldier and civilian alike. The itch on his back, which he could barely reach, was irritating him.

"Some f-fowk do all right, they do," Jamie mumbled. "That Private Murch, fat Murch, him-him over there – aye, he gets plenty t' eat, he does. Keeps it under his bed in-in a bag – seen him snea-sneaking out of the cook-house wi' a poke,

18

Ah have, Ah have..." His voice trailed off into an indistinct mumble, and Bresciano saw that Sergeant Connor had moved up behind them unnoticed. He tried to stand rigidly to attention, fearful that the Sergeant had heard his criticisms, but the Sergeant hardly seemed to notice him; he was staring at Jamie; then he turned on his heel and strode away towards the working party where, at the sight of him, the noisy banter of the men ceased abruptly and they began to work harder.

"I'll have enough t' eat, soon, soon enough," Jamie began again. "Cookie sometimes gi'es me – no, I mustn't tell. Cookie said I mustn't tell. But I've got a... *caraid*... a friend an' he said, he said he'd see me richt, he did. He said he'd take me, take me hame wi' him to Scotland, give me work, and lots of, lots of food, I'd be his-his ghillie – go, go hunting wi' him..."

"Is your friend a Scotsman, like you, then?" Bresciano enquired idly, looking at Jamie's animated face.

Jamie suddenly looked confused and shook his head. He became agitated. "No, that's nae richt, is it? He said... Ah wasn't to say, to say... say anything because bad things would-would happen and bad things can happen to Jamie sometimes like the 'splosion. Ma gun blew up. Ah remember the... the 'splosion." He fell silent for a moment, looking down at the ground, and then began to count off on his fingers: "Governor Eliott is ma friend too. Ah have to guard him. And with ma friend, ma ither friend, the angel, he is... he has wings... and the other angels as well. And Cookie, and you are ma friend..."

Bresciano, listening to Jamie's garbled monologue as he rambled on, left it at that. He was finding that most of Jamie's assertions were the product of a confused mind, poor Jamie. At least this human friend, real or imaginary, with his promises of food, sounded more practical than those guardian angels who watched over General Eliott with Jamie's help.

Below them the Sergeant was marching Private Murch and a couple of other men away from the site, and everyone relaxed as they disappeared down the slope.

* * * *

In the afternoon, Bresciano's guard duty ended as the working party broke off for a meal, but before he could join them

→ brupt/shorty

Sergeant Connor came striding up and brusquely ordered him to go to Hargrave's Parade. The Sergeant was a man with clear ideas about how discipline should be imposed and maintained and he wanted this lanky local recruit to learn from the start what he might expect in the service of the King if he failed in his duty.

"Someone else will take over from you up here. And take that daft Jamie with you. You'll both see something to teach you how we deal with scum and shirkers in King George's army!"

Puzzled, Bresciano set off down the slope with Jamie trotting happily at his heels. It was starting to rain and the wind had become blustery. When they arrived at the parade ground, they found themselves among a group of soldiers, mainly Artificers, staring at the scene being enacted in the centre of the parade ground. Private Murch's pale, flabby body, stripped to the waist, was thrown over a wooden block and one of the sergeants stood over him brandishing a cat-o'-nine-tails.

With the cat held high in the air above the prostrate man, the duty sergeant bellowed in stentorian tones:

"This 'ere filth has been stealing your food from the cookhouse, men. He grew fat while you went hungry, and now he's getting his punishment!"

The men growled approval, and the unfortunate Murch, twisting his head from side to side, caught sight of Bresciano and Jamie and shot a venomous look towards them just as the whip came crashing down for the first time on to his back.

The whipping was a formal ceremony. Because Murch had been caught stealing, the nine whip ends were knotted and where they landed on his back they would crush and tear the skin. There was a pause between lashes as the nine tails of 'the cat' were disentangled. The rhythmic crack of the whip was punctuated by the howls of pain from Murch as the crowd watched in silence, too used to the accustomed savagery of flogging to be moved by it, though a horrified Bresciano winced every time the lash came down, even when he eventually closed his eyes.

"Wot can you expect?" said a stolid old campaigner when it was over, "These 'ere officers gets flogged at them fancy schools they goes to, so I 'ear tell, so they 'opes to pass

on th'advantages of their fine eddication to us common folk."
He enjoyed his reputation as the company wit.

As the bleeding, half-conscious soldier was dragged away, the crowd began to disperse and Bresciano caught sight of Abraham Hassan leaving, dressed in the uniform of the 38th Regiment of Foot. It was a regiment with little enough to offer its recruits either in equipment or uniform, but Bresciano envied Abraham Hassan his dull red coat. Abraham, several years older than Bresciano, had been the only other Gibraltar citizen to enlist, and it was partly his example that had fired Bresciano to a fervour of patriotic action. Hurrying, he caught up with him, while Jamie stayed behind staring at the block on which Murch had been flogged. → wiped / beaten

"Abraham, wait for me!"

"Giovanni! My word! I see you have joined up too. Well done! At least I shall no longer be the only local in the army."

"I only got the Artificers, not a proper line regiment like you," said Bresciano resentfully.

"Giovanni, look at me – I spend most of my time as messenger for the clerk of the regiment. Do you know what that involves? I spend most of my day tramping around the town and fortifications delivering and collecting messages and instructions. But when the time comes to fight, I will. And so will you. In the meantime, don't be ashamed of the Artificers; they will have an important part to play if our Rock is to be successfully defended," Hassan replied reassuringly. "If our defences are not strong, the Spaniards might possibly overrun us, however fiercely the regiments oppose them. As one of our songs says – I think it is from the Bible: 'The Rock is the fortress of our salvation', and it's the Artificers who keep it a safe fortress. So take heart!"

"Like mythology? Calling the Rock one of the Pillars of Hercules? But I didn't know Gibraltar was mentioned in the Bible," Bresciano spoke absently, intent on finding a tactful way of phrasing his enquiry. "By the way, how did *you* manage? I mean, your… being Jewish must have made it worse. Like… all that business about not eating pork and things like that and… " he bit his lip. "And what about the family? Did you get much opposition from your family when you joined up?"

He sought reassurance from the quiet and self-possessed

young man beside him.

Abraham Hassan laughed. "Oh, yes: my mother and my sisters cried and cried and my father was furious with me. His main objection was that I would have to eat forbidden food in the Army. He took me to our Chief Rabbi Almosnino to ask him to forbid me to enlist, but the Rabbi told him that in time of danger some rules could be disobeyed, and then he blessed me and my musket!"

"You're lucky with your Chief Rabbi. Perhaps I should have called in Father Messa to help me out, although I doubt whether he would have been as understanding," Bresciano said ruefully. "And, in any case, my father doesn't listen to anyone when he's angry. I'm afraid my father won't really forgive me for a long time."

They had reached Southport Street, and as they passed the Governor's residence, the old Franciscan Convent, and the adjoining King's Chapel, they saw three officers strolling along in deep conversation.

"That's Lieutenant Drinkwater coming towards us. I've had some dealings with him – had to deliver orders to him. He's not a bad fellow at all, and his companions are Lieutenant Holloway – he's an Artificer, like you – and that tall one, looks a bit arrogant, that's Lieutenant Black, I think," Abraham Hassan spoke airily, but with conscious patronage for he was still young enough to want to impress Bresciano with his familiarity with the officers of the Garrison.

Lieutenant Drinkwater, a young man no older than them, looked up as they passed, and called out: "Hassan, my good fellow, perhaps you are the man to help me. I was just telling Black and Holloway here how I get so devilish bored with this blockade – why, there's not even any fighting to break the monotony! – and I'm desperate for good books to read. Your home is in this town, so do you think you could tell me where I might find some reading material? Or might you have any books in your house that you could lend me?"

Abraham shrugged his shoulders apologetically. "I would be delighted to help you, sir, but alas, all the books in my house are in Hebrew! And the only good bookseller I know left Gibraltar when the Siege began."

Bresciano hesitated, then broke in. "Begging your pardon, sir, if I might be of assistance? My mother is a prodigious

22

reader and she has some books in English at home. I'm sure she would be glad to lend them to you."

Lieutenant Drinkwater looked at the lanky, rather unkempt soldier in surprise. "Is your home here, then, lad? I thought Hassan was the only Gibraltar man to volunteer for the Army."

"I joined up yesterday. I'm with the Artificers, sir. I'll give Private Hassan some books for you as soon as I can get home."

"Good lad. And do tell your mother that I will be most grateful for her kindness."

"Yes, sir. Thank you, sir." Bresciano, a smile on his face, stood looking after Lieutenant Drinkwater. At least someone appreciated him.

"Come on, Giovanni, you're in a dream."

The two young men walked down towards Church Street and Abraham said, "Lieutenant Drinkwater is writing a diary of the siege, as many of the other officers are, but he takes it really seriously. He says he wants to have it published as a book one day. So he goes around every day asking all the duty officers whether there were any incidents in the night, and whether any soldier had deserted, and then he writes it all down in a little notebook. I suppose it keeps him busy. Officers complain all the time that they don't have that much to do at the moment." He looked bemused briefly: "They all really want to fight, to go into battle. They like the idea. I don't. I joined up to defend my home and I will fight when the time comes, but I am not looking forward to it."

Bresciano shrugged, uneasily aware of his own dreams of earning glory in action.

They had reached George's Lane, the narrow thoroughfare leading up towards the flanks of the Rock, where the Hassan family lived. Bresciano arranged to see his friend on the following day to give him a couple of books for the Lieutenant, and they parted.

Bresciano continued to walk heavily down the street, now stripped of cobbles, his boots sinking into the damp red sand. Jamie had disappeared and he thought it likely that the boy had made for his favourite haunt, the wine-house in Irish Town where Bianca was employed. It wasn't a good place for Jamie, and the whole of Irish Town, as the area was called, with its mean huddle of houses and unsavoury reputation, was a place Bresciano would normally have avoided if it hadn't been for Bianca. The thought of seeing her again both excited and embarrassed him. He hesitated at the main square and debated whether to go there. No, he decided, he would go to see his family.

When he pushed open the front door, all was silent inside the house. Silent? No. He thought he could hear a quiet sobbing from the kitchen. There he saw his mother sitting in her pride and joy, her large Cotswold chair, with her head in her hands.

"Mother!" he said softly. "What's the matter? Is something wrong?"

She lifted her head and gave him a faint, watery smile of welcome, which disappeared as soon as she began to reply.

"I knew you would be back and – oh, Giovanni, my dear! It is so good to see you." She stretched her hand out to him and, when he took it, he was startled at the nervous strength of her grip. "It's Lucia – she has a fever, and I'm desperately afraid that she may be infected with the smallpox! It's my fault. I should have agreed to let her be inoculated, but General Eliott himself has refused to sanction it, and the fever seemed to come to an end three months ago. I thought we were safe; people said it was over: this would not have happened now if I had had her inoculated."

"Don't say that, Mother. You know what Dr Coll said. He told us that the inoculation kills almost as many as it protects. You are to not blame yourself!"

"Many people are angry that the Governor has not permitted it. Why, I heard a lady in the street, I think it was Mrs Green, the wife of the Chief Engineer, say that the blood of innocent children would be on the Governor's head!"

"Mother, mother, it is not like you to pay attention to such talk. The Governor would not have come to the decision on his own. It must have been based on the advice of the Army doctors. So you see, it isn't just Dr Coll…"

His own doubts, and fear for his sister, caused his reassuring words to trail away, but his mother had gained some strength from them, and sat up a little straighter.

"You're right, of course, Giovanni. In any case, all we can do now is to nurse little Lucia, and pray, and not fret about what might have been."

Bresciano searched for something else to reassure his mother. "But wait a moment; it might be something else. How can she be infected already when she only went to visit her friend... was it yesterday?"

"No. She has been playing with her for the past weeks, and then a few days ago, and again just before João fell ill: and now his poor girl has also fallen sick..."

"It could still be some other fever, perhaps from a flux? Or an ordinary grippe?" → influenza (flue)

Bresciano opened the door of the room Lucia shared with Nonna Lucrezia and Aunt Maria.

"Giovanni, she has just got off to sleep! Please, please don't wake her," his mother warned him.

Bresciano gazed down at the sleeping form of Lucia, lying in a tangle of bedclothes. She looked flushed and sweat beaded her brow. No sign – yet! – of the dreaded pocks. She had always been a sturdy little girl, he thought, but now she looked so thin and frail. She must have more to eat if she was to withstand the infection, he told himself, even if it had to come out of his meagre soldier's rations. He bent over her and softly stroked her cheek, but though she opened her eyes for a brief instant, she did not seem to see him and she did not stir. He left the room, closing the door silently behind him. He was afraid the child might be dying. He knew little of such things, but the memory of two other sisters who had died in infancy had always hung over the household, darkening life.

"Where is Father?" he managed to keep his voice steady.

"He went off to sea this morning, with only João's son for crew. I could not stop him. You know what he is like. He said that he would bring some fish for us – there is little else left to eat. But to go out, when the Spanish ships are attacking any vessel leaving Gibraltar! He promised me he would hug the coastline, but those ships come so close, those gunboats. I've heard how they come close to shore and have even fired at our walls or wait there threatening anything that puts to sea... hunting in packs, like wolves."

"He'll be back soon, safe and sound. He is a good sailor. An excellent sailor. And he won't take any risks." Bresciano spoke firmly enough to convince himself. "And I will come, whenever my duties allow, and I'll bring something for Lucia."

He sat on with his mother, giving her the comfort of his presence. They spoke in low voices. She asked about the army. It was all strange to her, for her parents had been in trade, as had their parents before them. So he told her of his first day as a soldier, telling her he had found a friend and omitting to tell her that he was called Daft Jamie. Then he mentioned Abraham Hassan and Lieutenant Drinkwater, making much of what had been the briefest of exchanges. His narrative improved on what had been a poor enough start to his career as a soldier: he wanted to stop her worrying about him as much as he wanted her to be proud of him. And, before he left, she rose and went to her cupboard and looked through her precious store of books, books she had little enough inclination to read these days.

"I suppose he will have read *Tom Jones*," she said. "But here is another novel by Fielding, *Amelia*. And here is *Gulliver's Travels* – even if he has read that, he may enjoy re-reading it. Take them to him, and tell him that he is welcome to borrow more books when he has finished them. After all," she said with an attempt at cheerfulness, "We must do what we can to help the brave men who are defending us, eh, Giovanni?"

Bresciano kissed his mother, resolutely refusing her offer of a meal, for he knew there was no food to spare. "There's a good meal waiting for me at the Barracks," he lied, "and, anyway," he added as he left, "I must get back to work or the Sergeant will skin me alive!"

*   *   *   *

In the evening, the Artificers ate their frugal meal in the largest of the huts, which served as their mess-hall. As soon as the meal was over, Private Murch, whose whipping had not totally impaired his appetite, got up groaning with pain and hobbled off to the sleeping-huts, followed by a few men too tired to sit around talking.

"He'll be sleeping on his face tonight, and serve him right!" said one of the men, and the rest murmured agreement. Bresciano wondered whether Murch knew that it was Jamie who had given him away and whether he bore the boy a grudge. Certainly Murch's glare had fixed on Jamie when he was being whipped. The men sat around smoking clay

leaving out

pipes, talking, complaining mostly, some more bitterly than others: the eighteen months of siege did not show only in their haggard faces, but also in their short tempers. Men would use their fists over what they would have simply dismissed with an angry word a year before. One man managed to pick a flea off his neck and Bresciano, who had been trying to reach up between his own shoulder blades, realised with dismay that his own itching back was the precursor of what would become a permanent problem. The men talked now while cleaning their muskets, repairing clothes and polishing the buttons of their Sunday uniforms. The subject turned to Jamie, who was sitting in a corner oblivious to the conversation, humming and whittling on a stick.

"He were never the bright spark, but he went real daft after the accident with the musket."

"Accident? That weren't no accident! Sergeant never liked him, and it were Sergeant gave him the musket!" There was violence in the voice.

"G'wan, Tom, Sergeant may be a hard man, but he wouldn't do that, would he? What, spike a gun a purpose so it blew back on one of his own men?"

"Well, I say 't weren't no accident. Sergeant takes a pleasure in making life 'ard for the likes of us. Take Fat Murch there. 'Ow many times 'as 'e been flogged? Answer me that."

"No, no, Tom! That ain't same thing. Murch may be your friend, but truth is he ain't ever got wot he didn't deserve. Like stealing our stores. Taking food from starvin' men."

"We ain't starvin' yet."

"Damn near it, and there's the scurvy too."

"Nothin' to do with what Murch took. It's lemons you need for scurvy an' there's never a lemon to be 'ad for love nor money in this godforsaken place. An' it were Jamie we was talkin' about and no one's going to convince me that it were an accident when the musket blew up in 'is face. It were the Sergeant, I tell you. Who says different?" Tom was spoiling for an argument at least.

"Naw, y'er wrong there." A new voice spoke out, "If anyone would 'ave given our Jamie a musket that'd blow 'im up it would've been that Lieutenant Black, wouldn't it? You told us all about 'im, didn't you, Jamie? Proper stuck-up Romeo, that Lieutenant, 'im and the Cap'n's wife, eh, Jamie? Right goings on with them three! And the Cap'n's goin' round lookin' like he'd kill someone since word leaked out about 'is wife and the love-sick Lieutenant. I say you look there for your man, Tom."

"Wot you talkin' about? Jamie was given that musket long 'afore he told us about the Cap'n. You don't know nothing!" Tom stormed out.

Bresciano was curious to hear more, but at that moment Sergeant Connor stalked in, and the men fell silent. The Sergeant looked around him and his gaze fell on Jamie who had left his corner and was walking out of the door.

"MacFarlane, let's see you make yourself useful for a change! Fetch the lanterns the work party left behind. We won't be doing any work there until morning and I don't want them stolen by them thieving apes!"

"Aye, Sarge," Jamie smiled happily, "Ah'll go right away, shall Ah? And when-when Ah see ma *caraid*... ma-ma friend... I could bring him bring him back here and... no, not here... Ah..." His voice trailed off.

"You and your bloody friends. Just get on with you and don't be all night at it!"

Jamie left and the Sergeant sat himself in a corner, well away from the men, and puffed silently on his pipe. After a short while he rose again, grunted, "This damn small beer – more like dirty water it is, but it gets to a man. Need to piss every five minutes!" and went out of the hut. When he finally returned, buttoning his breeches, he looked around the room.

"Is that daft creature not back yet?"

Jamie had still not returned after half an hour, and the Sergeant turned to Bresciano.

"You, what's-your-name! He's your friend, isn't he? Go and find him. Stupid sod's wandered off somewhere, I'll be bound." He looked on coldly as Bresciano, startled, leapt to his feet and knocked over his tin plate. "You're not much better than him, are you? Wait there. Corporal Jones, you go with him," and turning to Bresciano: "don't want you getting lost, too, now, do we?"

Bresciano went out, trying to ignore Corporal Jones, and strode ahead. The moon blanched the surrounding trees and crags with a pallid light as Bresciano and Jones made their way to Princess Caroline's Battery, where the lanterns had been left. The wind had dropped and the night was silent. There was no sign of Jamie, but he had obviously been there: the lanterns had been collected and were now piled up together near one of the ramparts.

They walked about, calling Jamie's name repeatedly to no avail, and only succeeded in alarming the bats that skittered overhead. Corporal Jones scratched his chin.

"I've known that daft lad to sleep like the dead – a sign of an easy conscience, they say! But it won't do him any good to spend a night out here. It will rain before morning, I'll be bound. Here, lad, you can search that side and I'll do this part and see if we can find him before he catches his death."

Bresciano approached the rampart. Below it was a steep slope dotted with dwarfed and undernourished olive trees, leading to a sheer drop of over a hundred feet. A new thought pulled Bresciano up short: had Jamie got on to the rampart for some reason? Had someone left a lamp just out of his reach? He could have clambered up and slipped in the dark. He tried to reassure himself. No, it was not possible: Jamie climbed easily and confidently. But the thought persisted. What if Jamie had fallen over the wall and down that cliff? He had a vivid image of a body crashing down over a hundred feet onto the rocks below and lying twisted and still – a bloody rag-doll in death. There would be no chance that Jamie could have survived such a fall. His heart was racing as he leaned over uneasily, fearful of heights, and tried to see into the night.

"I can't see any sign of him," he said, relieved, but realised immediately that nothing would be clearly visible in the dark and from this height.

Despairingly, he forced himself to make sense of the darkness beyond the rampart. On the slope immediately below he could make out shrubs and a stunted fig tree clinging tenaciously to the shallow and inhospitable soil. And at the foot of the tree the darkness seemed to thicken. There was a dark mass huddled there.

"My God!" he cried out. "There's something just here. I think it might be a body, but I can't see what it is!"

"Light up one of the lanterns," was the curt reply. "What, no tinder box? Let me light it." Corporal Jones took over competently as Bresciano, holding the lantern in a convulsive grip, continued to stare down, willing it not to be Jamie.

The lantern flared, and Bresciano jerked it above the edge

of the wall.

"Careful, lad! There's a body there right enough," Jones said urgently. "It must be Jamie. Look, that fig tree has stopped him from rolling over the cliff. He may still be alive. We've got to get him up!"

"If he regains his senses and moves –" the thought was too horrible to put into words and Bresciano found himself incapable of rational thought.

"Go! Get a couple of the men and a rope," was the reply. "And make it quick!"

Bresciano raced back to the mess hut and alerted the men, but it was Corporal Jones, brought up in the Welsh mountains, who volunteered to go over the rampart to where the body lay. With the rest of the men holding one end of the rope, he lowered himself over the parapet and was eased down towards the tree where – to Bresciano's horror – Jamie had made a faint groaning noise and might move at any moment. It seemed to take an age, as if time had become perversely sluggish, but it was not long before Jamie's body had been hauled up over the wall. He was still alive, but his breathing was harsh and heavy.

"Take him to the hut. We can look at him better there. The lad must have fallen over in the dark, clumsy fool that he is!"

"He'd have had to climb on to the wall to fall down there. Why do you think he would do that?" Bresciano reverted to his original idea, as puzzled as he was shocked.

"'E may have thought 'e was one of 'is angels and could fly away! 'Oo knows?" one of the men answered. "Don't just stand there gawpin'– lend us a 'and with 'im. Sparrow or not, 'e weighs more'n you'd think and 'im so skinny."

In the hut, with all the lanterns ablaze, the rest of the men crowded round Jamie. There were superficial scratches on his face where he had fallen against the tree. The only other injury was a shallow wound on the back of his neck, the blood still coagulating, already surrounded by an area of purple bruising.

"Look – how did that happen?" Bresciano stared at it in confusion. "He didn't get that injury in the fall. He fell face down."

He shook his head in disbelief and began muttering to himself. "But how? He fell over on his face." He stood, lost in thought, using his hands to explore the movement of Jamie's

30

body as he imagined it falling. "I think... I believe that... someone must have hit him. That's it! No other explanation is possible. Someone knocked him out, and – my God! Someone threw him over! It's just by chance that the tree broke his fall.

"Someone must have attacked Jamie!" The words issued from Bresciano's mouth almost involuntarily. He looked up to find himself the centre of attention as the men stared at him in disbelief.

"You stand there spewing rubbish, swinging your arms like a sodding windmill!" The Sergeant spoke the words furiously. "Who'd want to do that? Daft Jamie wasn't worth the effort. He's just a clumsy fool who stood on the wall – the Lord knows why – and fell, hit his head on the edge and rolled down."

"No, no! I observed him up there this morning and he clambered up the slope with the agility of a monkey." He blurted the words out, contradicting his superior, so anxious to be believed that he forgot who he was and where he was. The more earnest he became, the more pedantic he sounded. "Someone must have attacked him. Perhaps it was an attempt to assassinate him. It's the only rational explanation. I mean, look at him – consider how all the scratches are on his face and a few on his hands. And how did he come by that isolated and substantial wound and bruise on his neck?" He looked anxiously round at the ragged circle of incredulous faces. Already they were losing interest and some of the men were beginning to drift away. He needed something to convince them. "You men have asserted that Jamie said many wild things when he'd had a drink or two – or even when he was cold sober," he was desperate to be believed. "I mean... Murch! Murch could have done it! He would have borne a grudge against him – you had him flogged because of what you heard Jamie say about his stealing, didn't you, Sergeant?"

He had gone too far.

"Are you questioning my judgement?" The Sergeant's voice was too quiet and the men moved back, distancing themselves from Bresciano.

"Oh, no, sir. No. Of course not. No. I know what... I mean... the theft of food... er... especially now with the siege... you had to... he had to be... made an example of... so..." Bresciano knew he was babbling mindlessly, and abruptly he fell silent. It suddenly occurred to him that the Sergeant didn't like Jamie for some reason, so perhaps the Sergeant *had* tried to kill him once before with the faulty musket as that soldier had said, and had might equally have tried to finish him off this evening when he'd stepped out of the hut.

"Couldn't have been Murch, could it, Sarge?" one of the men said scornfully. "He's lying in bed moaning and groaning fit to burst."

"Could 'e be putting it on?" said another.

"You've seen a flogging before, haven't you?" said Sergeant Connor. "He was damn lucky not to pay the death penalty, but he got a good flogging. He won't be fit to move much for days, let alone attack anyone! And you..." he went right up to Bresciano and stood threateningly close. "You with your fancy, jaw-breaking 'assertions' and 'assassinations' and 'substantials'. I don't want another word out of you – either long or short: you had better watch that mouth of yours, Busyano."

"Busyano – that's a good one, Sarge!" There was some sycophantic laughter which grew as the men, released from the scenario Bresciano had called up and now sanctioned by the Sergeant's anger, became abusive with this raw recruit.

"That's enough!" He pointed to Jamie's body, "Take the fool to his hut and put out the lanterns. It's a waste of good oil." The Sergeant had done and he left.

Someone put a cold compress on Jamie's neck and the men carried him to his hut where he was left to sleep off the effects of the fall.

Corporal Jones stood in the hut and carefully looped the rope which had been used to pull Jamie to safety. He hung it on a hook on the wall and turned to Bresciano before leaving. "You'd be well advised to do as the Sergeant says. Last thing we want up here is to start a panic. We have enough to cope with as it is, and no one doing guard duty at night wants to be looking over his shoulder in case one of his mates might attack him."

Bresciano looked sullen: first the Corporal rescued Jamie and now he was dispensing advice. Why didn't he take himself off to his own hut?

"Fancy yourself as an expert in violence, do you, lad? No, don't take offence; you might be right, though I doubt it.

→ runaway soiger

"If anyone did try to kill the poor crazy lad, it must have been a deserter that he came upon tonight. Someone who was trying to get away from the Rock – we get a few of those every week. They want to get to the Spanish lines and they'll risk falling to their deaths to get away from here. Can't understand it myself, but it takes all sorts to make a world."

Bresciano was unresponsive, and the Corporal left Bresciano watching over Jamie, who lay there breathing stertorously, his face deathly pale. Bresciano sat by his side and tried to make sense of the events of the evening. The Sergeant might force him to keep silent, but he couldn't stop him thinking. He recalled how they had stood so close that he had smelt the Sergeant's sweat and felt his breath on his face. He had stared into his face, seen how a small muscle quivered at the corner of his right eye, felt the physical power of the man – as tall as himself, but so much more powerfully built – and he had been afraid. But orders or not, fear or not, Bresciano was convinced that he was right.

Firstly, he was certain that Jamie had been the object of a deadly attack although the soldiers were probably right on one point... Murch was in no condition to commit an assault, but maybe he had a friend among the men. Of course, there was the bellicose Tom, Murch's friend as someone had said, and Tom had pointed the finger at the Sergeant over the affair of the musket that had nearly killed Jamie.

There was also the Sergeant who could have done it when he left the hut that evening. Why, he had almost followed Jamie out. And he had been out a while. He could certainly have had the time to do it, but why? And could this attack be connected with Jamie's earlier 'accident' which the men blamed the Sergeant for? But why should the Sergeant have wanted to kill Jamie in the first place? And while the men treated Jamie with a mixture of mockery and affection, the Sergeant alone was harsh with him.

What about all those people Jamie had apparently told his stories about, like the Captain and his wife, and the seemingly philandering Lieutenant Black... and who knew how many others? → frequently casual sexual relationships

Or perhaps Jamie had met one of his angels, who was no angel, or a friend who was no friend... or a deserter, as Corporal Jones had said.

He didn't know how long he sat, turning the same few facts and speculations over and over in his mind. Then suddenly Bresciano began to smile. What a fool he was to worry pointlessly. For all he knew, Jamie had seen and attempted to flee from his attacker. Tomorrow he could wake up in the morning and be able to name the man. The mystery would be a mystery no longer. In the meantime, he would need to watch over Jamie in case his would-be murderer returned to finish his work. Wearily he rested his head on his hands, ready to keep vigil. → Staying awake

Giovanni Bresciano fell asleep, still sitting by the bed of the unconscious Jamie.

CHAPTER III

Day broke. Bresciano's uneasy dreams were briefly filled with exploding muskets, and he awoke with a startled cry to the sound of a thunderous cannonade from Willis's Batteries. The Garrison artillery had taken up their daily bombardment of the ever-growing Spanish fortifications on the isthmus that separated the besieged Rock from Spain. Not that they had succeeded in deterring the enemy who, despite heavy losses of soldiers, workmen and mules, were doggedly building what became known as the Mill Battery. It was a formidable achievement and the building work went on into the night, as did the gunfire against it. So much activity and yet not a shot fired from the Spanish lines at the garrison itself, not one in all the time the siege had lasted.

Bresciano shook his head and focused his eyes on Jamie, aware that he had failed to keep watch as he had intended, but Jamie's breathing was regular and no further harm had come to him during the night. Bresciano stood up, careful not to disturb his friend, and stretched his cramped limbs, very conscious that he was cold, unkempt, hungry and felt dirty after two nights spent sleeping in his clothes. Life as a soldier was not dangerous – it was a simpler matter of physical misery. He turned back to the bed.

"Hello," Jamie was awake and looking at Bresciano.

There was nothing wrong with him! Now he would be able to give an account of the events of the previous evening's attack: Bresciano sat down beside him, eager to question him.

"How do you feel?"

He grimaced, "Ma neck hurrts."

35

"Of course it does. I think that blow was pretty hard."

"Why did you – you hit me, then?"

"I didn't hit you!"

"All richt," he smiled vacantly.

"Jamie…"

"You know ma name." He seemed to find the fact very gratifying. "What's yours?"

"It's me, Giovanni Bresciano," he looked at Jamie's blank face, "I'm your friend. You must remember me. You must." There was despair in his voice.

"Ma friend? Ma friend is… different… he is-is going to tak' me… *a' dol dhachaigh.* Ah'm tired."

"What does that mean?"

"We… we'll go back hame."

Jamie closed his eyes and Bresciano looked down at him helplessly.

"So how's this fool?"

The Sergeant walked in and Bresciano, alarmed, stood up to attention:

"He says he's tired. I think he… he… I don't… I don't really know," he ended lamely, aware that he was sounding remarkably like Jamie.

"'Course you don't. You and your wild ideas – Murch attacking him, indeed! No, there's not much you do know, is there?"

"No, sir."

He jerked his head towards the bed. "So, has he spoken at all? Said anything about last night?"

Bresciano knew he had been wrong about Fat Murch, but he was on his guard against this much-more-likely murderer. He had to protect Jamie. It would be best to throw the Sergeant off the scent. "Nothing. I think… I think he's lost his memory. He didn't recognise me."

"On some days he wouldn't recognize his own father, if he ever knew him."

Bresciano thought quickly, "Perhaps he should be in hospital?" It was a way of keeping Jamie safe; after all, he himself could not keep a twenty-four hour watch on him. "Maybe a doctor should see him."

"Are you telling me my own business again?" The Sergeant stood, legs apart and head thrust forward.

"No, sir."

"Have you ever been inside the Naval Hospital? If you're not sick when you go in, you get sick just from being there. A death trap, it is. And they've got their hands full. There are men with the pneumonias and fluxes and scurvy and the pox. What has this fool got, eh? A sore head? He can stay where he is. He'll be better off here under my eye."

(ing inflammation)

"But, sir..."

cheeky or impatient person

"Listen, you young jackanapes, and don't start again with any more ideas – I told you before – just you watch that mouth of yours! The only thing wrong with him is a sore head and a few bruises. I've seen cases like this a-plenty. Bang your head and you get what the sawbones call concussion, see? You forget things and they never come back to you..."

"Yes, sir!" It was a relief to hear because in that, thought Bresciano, might lie Jamie's best protection. Without any remembrance of events, he could not accuse nor present a threat to the Sergeant. "Thank you."

"I hadn't finished," the Sergeant snapped. "Sometimes your memory does come back. Knew a man knocked flying when a shell blew a hole in the ground next to him. Remembered nothing. Two months later he began to tell us about it as if it had happened the day before. Not that this fool ever makes that much sense."

Jamie stirred uneasily and Bresciano feared he might wake up. He needed to throw the Sergeant off the scent before Jamie said anything, recalled anything. "He did say one thing," Bresciano improvised desperately, "something about climbing up on the wall."

The Sergeant looked fixedly at Bresciano: "So why did you tell me he didn't say anything?"

"It was only a couple of words. He just mumbled them." Bresciano was humiliated to find his voice shaking.

"I see. Remembered suddenly, have you? Or were you afraid of admitting what an ass you were last night? So he climbed up and took a false step in the dark? Is that what you're saying?"

"Yes, sir, I suppose so."

"Good. That clears that up, wouldn't you say?"

"Yes, sir." He swallowed, feeling his Adam's apple too big for his thin neck.

"Right then – get moving. If you plan to wet-nurse this idiot, you can forget it. There's nothing much wrong with him that a day in bed won't cure, so he can stay there – no loss to us. But you're on duty down at King's Bastion today. There's building materials to be shifted. Now make yourself useful and collect his rations when you get yours. You've got half an hour."

Bresciano looked after him in frustration. That man could easily have sent Jamie to the Naval Hospital. It was clear that the Sergeant truly wanted to 'keep an eye' on the hapless Jamie. And woe betide the lad if ever he did recover his memory. He certainly didn't have the sense to keep his mouth shut, and Connor would kill him without a second thought. He gnawed his lower lip, suddenly conscious that there was an added danger – to himself as Jamie's possible confidant. He felt the hair rising on the back of his neck at the thought. But there was nothing he could do except spread the word that Jamie had said he had climbed the battery wall. And he prayed Jamie would not deny it.

He took his tin can and went to join the queue of men collecting their food from the mess hut. Rations had been cut that month as relief supplies still failed to come from England. Enterprising traders from Minorca had found either the winds against them as they tried to run for Gibraltar's small harbour, or had been taken by the Spanish Admiral Barceló's ships as they rounded the Rock. Bresciano's dreams of taking food to his family faded as he drew his rations. There was a hunk of bread the size of a small loaf; a cupful of oatmeal; and a slice of salt pork that could not have weighed more than three ounces. Little wonder that the men lining up for their rations were sullen and ready to pick a quarrel if they felt anyone else was receiving privileged treatment, even for such appalling food as they received.

Bresciano was served – the salt meat was rank and slimy. He looked into the barrel where little remained of the oatmeal, and he felt his gorge rise: there was movement down there – weevils! He took what was given. There was nothing else he could do, and on his way back to the hut to give Jamie his share, he began to retch, a futile physical reaction on an empty stomach.

"You don't want that? I'll take it off your 'ands, lad. Can't be perticular these days." It was an ingratiating voice, Murch's friend, Tom. "Bloody sight better'n the rotted salt cod we was given in July. Could smell that even in my sleep. You can give me that stuff – turns your stomach, don't it? I'll have it."

He reached out with an eagerness that horrified Bresciano, who shook his head and stumbled away in silence. Back in the hut he looked at the inert figure of Jamie, sleeping like a child. He put the meat to soak in water in the hope that it would make it less repulsive. He could not bear to look at the slowly shifting grain, but perhaps Jamie might want to eat it. So he took the oatmeal, together with Jamie's bread, and put them in his knapsack which he hung from a hook on the stout beam that spanned the ceiling, well away from any rats. Perhaps Jamie might want to eat it when it had been cooked. As for himself, the bread would have to suffice.

"Ye're ma friend." Jamie had woken up and was upright, a little pale and unsteady perhaps, but almost making sense. "You... you were good tae me. You-you dinna like the food. Ah... Ah'll go outside and get some stu-stuff to make it taste better when you, when you come back. Ah saw them apes eating it up the Rock – green stuff it was."

Bresciano smiled encouragingly at him. Perhaps Jamie really was regaining his wits. He would get whatever had really happened out of him in the evening. Maybe Jamie would be safer outside than asleep indoors. And he would eat whatever Jamie gathered outside. If it didn't harm the Rock apes, it wouldn't kill a human – or would it?

"Be careful where you go, Jamie, watch your step. Don't... fall or anything, will you."

"No, Ah–Ah won't, won't... climb on the wall. Ah... Ah climbed on the wall, didn't I? I can't m-mind it... but Ah heard you say it tae the mon who came in."

Bresciano shrugged in despair. The ploy meant for the Sergeant had backfired. At the moment Jamie's wits seem to come and go from minute to minute. Outside the hut he could hear the Sergeant berating the men for being slow to leave the camp. There was no help for it. He would just have to go, and questioning Jamie would have to wait.

He took his mother's books, intending to leave them later at Abraham Hassan's house, and made his way down hurriedly to the King's Bastion to report for duty. It was cold, threatening rain, and he resigned himself to day of hard physical labour or boredom. All his ideas of noble service had already been eroded. Only two days and the ugly reality of his choice faced him starkly. He would have to bear it – after all, he was helping to defend the Rock in a way, he supposed. It just wasn't as he thought it would be, but he was beginning to realise that war is rarely heroic.

Then the rain began to fall, the sort of persistent drizzle that eventually soaked your clothes. With little firewood available to light fires to dry them, he could not afford to get wet. Thank goodness for the solid stone walls of the King's Bastion down along the city walls: at least he would be sheltered, better off than the men still working up at Willis's where they would be exposed to easterly winds and driving rain. He put his head down and ran.

* * * *

By the end of the day he was more tired and hungry than he had ever felt in his short and privileged life. He wanted nothing more than to find a warm room, a bed and, of course, a meal. Some of the men he worked alongside had fantasised about food when they sat down to eat their scant lunch, but Bresciano could not bear to think of wholesome food when he knew the sort of fare that awaited him. Better to forget. Instead he brooded over the attempted murder of Jamie as he ate some of his bread – for murder had certainly been intended. He needed to consult someone he could trust. He trusted his father, but his father didn't listen to him and was too quick to dismiss his ideas. His mother – well, she had enough on her mind and he did not want to alarm her. That left no one.

Wearily he made his way to Abraham Hassan's house with the books for Lieutenant Drinkwater, walking heavily along side-streets that were now thick with mud, the cobbles stacked along the walls of the one-storey houses, waiting for better days when they could once again be laid down. It was just another of the many trials that went with the siege.

He was pleased to meet Abraham as he turned into Church Street.

"You've got the books? Well done! Lieutenant Drinkwater will be delighted. I had to deliver a message at the mess and

40

the officers were complaining that they've not even seen a newspaper since July. Now, what about you – have you settled in?"

Bresciano shrugged. Talking about it would make it worse.

His friend looked at him searchingly, "Come in here with me, you look awful." He indicated a small tavern, one of the many in the town. Inside he asked for a tankard of small ale, which he handed to Bresciano. "What's been happening to you?"

"It's hard, isn't it? The army. And the food is rotting." He gulped down the ale and shuddered.

Hassan nodded. No need for words.

"I hoped to take some of my rations for my sister Lucia: she's ill. She may have smallpox and she needs food."

"The oatmeal is not bad once you pick the weevils out," Hassan spoke pragmatically. "Take her some of that. I would say it's safer than the meat. Keep the bread. Your family can buy bread even if it's rationed, and you'll need to eat something. Have your parents any savings they can spend on food for Lucia?"

"Yes, my parents will do what they can, but the food just isn't there to buy! And when it is, which isn't often, everything costs so much. Last month when the *Sabine* managed to sail in to Gibraltar, my father went to the auction. He was able to buy a cheese and a bag of potatoes. The price was phenomenal! Even the potatoes. He paid one shilling and sixpence a pound for them. Can you believe that? A fortune! And the people at the auction nearly came to blows when they were bidding against each other. Fortunately my mother grows a few vegetables. I know we're lucky: my father is eking out the stores he had in his business, but I'm so worried about Lucia and the possibility of smallpox. And then there's Jamie." He stopped.

"Jamie? Is he a cousin or something? I don't know him, do I?"

"No. I mean the one they call Daft Jamie. He's in the Artificers like me."

"Oh, yes, I've seen him around. Harmless lad. I gather he's full of tall stories of ghosts and heavenly beings! So, what about him?"

41

"Someone tried to kill him last night."

The silence that followed his words felt leaden, but Hassan looked at him in amazement rather than in disbelief and Bresciano realised he had here someone who might take him seriously, certainly someone he could trust, a compatriot with whom to discuss the whole sorry and frightening matter. The tavern was empty as yet, and he poured out his tale into the sympathetic ear of Abraham Hassan. His recital ended and he waited.

"That wound and the bruising at the back of the neck certainly sound suspicious. Was there nothing on that short slope to account for it? No rock? You are certain? Let me see: as it couldn't have been Murch, you suspect either a friend of his – Tom you called him – or the Sergeant? What about that possibility of it having been a deserter?"

Bresciano dismissed it with a wave of his hand. It had been Corporal Jones's suggestion and he didn't want to entertain it.

"It seems reasonable enough. Those deserters are desperate men. If they're caught, they will hang. If Jamie crossed their path they'd have no compunction about dealing with him." He had given Bresciano's narrative his full attention and was bringing a logical mind to bear on it. "But you indicated that there might be others, that Jamie is the source of some scurrilous stories circulating among the garrison and that his unguarded tongue may have earned him enemies. Surely his stories are too far-fetched for anyone to take them seriously. I heard the one about how Governor Eliott invited him to dine at the Convent. Do you honestly believe that sort of thing would give rise to murder?"

"No, not that sort of story. But he does wander round and he may have seen something seriously compromising for someone. Like what happened because of his comments on Murch. I mean – Murch got a flogging, and there may be someone else with much more to lose and much more to hide. But the one I really suspect is the Sergeant. I'm afraid of what he'll do to Jamie."

"Sorry, Giovanni, but as far as I can see the only thing he has done is put a stop to your rather wild accusations last night, and given you good advice about the Hospital. No, listen to me. I've been inside that hospital and I can tell you it's an awful place: no sanitation to speak of, few medicines, not enough staff, and men crowded in on each other with infections rampant and spreading. And if you stop to think about it, you haven't given me one good reason why he should want to kill Jamie in the first place."

"There was the faulty musket he gave him."

"In front of witnesses?"

"I don't know. I suppose so."

"Would you say the Sergeant is a stupid man?"

"No."

"It sounds a very uncertain way of trying to dispose of someone, doesn't it? And what motive could he have had? Why kill a simple soldier?"

"All right, that may have been an accident, but what about last night? He sent Jamie out and then followed him. Well, probably followed him," he amended conscientiously.

"Giovanni, you have to look at all the actual facts carefully. Was anyone else outside at the time?"

"I'm not sure. I think Murch's friend was, and… I can't be sure. I don't know all the rest of the men yet, but…"

"And didn't the Sergeant tell you to go out and look for Jamie when he took so long? And," he raised his hand to stem Bresciano's objections, "didn't he also tell you to collect Jamie's rations this morning? He sounds like any other sergeant I've met so far: they're ordinary men doing a job of work."

"The men don't like him."

"What exactly does that mean? That he gets someone flogged for stealing? That he has no patience with a feeble-minded soldier? No, no, Giovanni. A man can be unpleasant without being a villain. My own sergeant is a bit of a… let us just say that none of the men like him. I don't like him, but he gets the work done – which is what he's paid to do. Consider what you've been telling me. I'm not sure that you have any evidence against anyone. I grant you that that blow to the back of the neck is certainly suspicious, but you have to work things out logically. If I were you I'd start with the deserter. There you have a good motive for murder – to escape detection, to silence Jamie. Motive is important."

"No… It's just an idea someone threw up. Anyway, how can I possibly find out who this imaginary deserter was? "

"Not necessarily 'imaginary', Giovanni. I'll ask Lieutenant

Drinkwater. He notes everything down. I told you so. Whoever deserted two nights ago will be down in his diary. I tell you what: I'll ask him when I give him the books you've brought, and I'll let you know what he says. Remember, you have to approach the thing logically. You're too emotional, Giovanni!"

"And you should be a lawyer."

"And *you* should tread carefully, and I don't mean anyone is going to try to kill *you*, I wouldn't worry about that, but you have made yourself rather unpopular with that sergeant of yours – according to what you've told me – and sergeants can make life very difficult for us rankers when they choose. Just keep your head down and avoid inviting trouble."

They parted company, each liking and respecting the other, but neither too inclined to accept the other's conclusions.

Bresciano turned his steps towards his billet. He must check on Jamie. Perhaps he should have gone up sooner, but it had been such a relief to talk to Abraham, even though his friend had failed to appreciate fully the character of the Sergeant. He trudged along the late evening street where the darkness thickened, many people choosing to close their thick wooden shutters on an uncertain world. Furthermore, Eliott had ordered all lights extinguished by the harbour area after seven in the evening: though the Spanish land batteries might be quiescent, the Spanish had begun to use gunboats that could sneak in under cover of darkness and wreak havoc along a well-lit shoreline. So Bresciano kept his eyes fixed on the uneven ground. Just ahead of him he could see a pair of stout boots, and his eyes travelled up to the well-worn waterproof cape his father always wore in bad weather – unbleached calico treated with linseed oil and then painted black, a sailor's oilskins. He hesitated, remembering how they had parted – with himself as an object of ridicule, but the man ahead of him stopped, his hacking cough forcing him to rest a moment, and Bresciano caught up with him.

"Papa? Are you all right?"

"My son! Ay! This cough. I will stop smoking my pipe one day soon. I will have to. This is all the tobacco left now!" he held up a pouch he had collected from his store, "but for now it is one of my few pleasures." He spoke as if the heated argument of two days before had never happened. "You have seen your mother? You know about Lucia? We hope it will turn out to be influenza, only a bad grippe."

"Yes. There are no spots on her face. Mother told me you went fishing with your bosun's son. That was dangerous: she was very worried."

"I never really went out," he spat in disgust, "And it wasn't João's son. He is sick too. It was Gavarone."

"Is he a proper sailor?"

"Not really, but he needs the money, poor man, and I was safe enough. I had to promise your mother I would stick close to land. As it happened, I had no choice. We hadn't got out more than a few fathoms when one of those damned Spanish gunboats saw us. And I, Giancarlo Bresciano, had to turn like a coward and run for cover!"

"They fired on you?"

"Pah! It was... " he shrugged dismissively. "When they left, we went scrambling below the city walls, among the rocks, looking for crabs and mussels. Nothing! All the places have been cleaned out. And the military here spotted us and forced us to come back up. So we tried further along. It was the same. All we got was a dead cuttlefish that had been washed up. Better than nothing. And I was going to buy some vegetables. Gavarone told me there were a few for sale in the vegetable gardens under the Northern Defences. Near the Spanish lines. When I got there I found those thieving Spaniards had walked across in broad daylight and stolen what there was! And what they couldn't carry they trampled into the ground... *bastardos!* I would have killed them if I had been there." His voice was level. He meant what he said.

"Yes, I can understand that. We had a man in the Artificers flogged yesterday for stealing from our own stores. It was awful, but imagine stealing food from your friends when everyone has so little! It was a despicable act. I hated watching; it was appalling, but he deserved to be punished."

"I know, but there is a difference: those Spaniards are not facing starvation like we are within these walls. I might do something like that Artificer of yours did. I know I would do it for your mother or your sister."

"But not for yourself!"

"Perhaps not, how can I tell? Sometimes a man's belly can swallow up his principles. It is human nature." He patted his son's arm. "Your mother tells me you know Lieutenant...

a name like *Bev'aegua…* "

Bresciano mentally translated the Genoese patois. "Drinkwater."

"That is the name. Well, well – my son and an English lieutenant. Very good. You must make such good friends. And come home, come and see us tomorrow. It is too late now. We go to bed early nowadays, as you know. Sleep is one of our remaining luxuries."

He was gone. He looked tired and defeated and Bresciano did not want to see him like that; he had always been a man of volatile temper, as given to exuberant anger as to delight, but he had seemed invincible. He was the turbulent young Genoese disowned by his family who had gone from wealth to exile, and who had then clawed his way back up from penury to respectability and relative wealth in his new home. To Bresciano, his father had always been a man for certainties and endeavour. Tonight he had seemed vulnerable and… he hesitated, trying to pin down the elusive feeling. It was connected with his attitude to Gavarone, and even with what he had said about Murch. Compassionate! That was the word.

Behind him he heard the sound of slow hoof beats on the sodden ground and he stood aside. A white horse, ghostlike in the moonlight, went by with its rider. With a sense of shock allied to a feeling of familiarity, Bresciano looked at the man's profile with its heavy parrot-beak of a nose and the familiar tricorn worn low on his brow, and sprang to attention. General Eliott was doing his nightly rounds of the garrison, and in the near-distance a voice called out from the city walls, the words drifting in on the easterly breeze, followed by ever fainter calls as the sentries along the walls took up and repeated the cry:

"All's well!"

It was reassuring and Bresciano trudged upwards away from the town feeling the better for having seen the great man and knowing that there was a constant guard kept along the city perimeter. And up at the billet, to his relief, he found Jamie moving slowly, and tentatively feeling the back of his head, but up and about.

In a small unit like theirs, each could be responsible for his own food and Jamie had cooked theirs and carefully set aside Bresciano's share. It was a good sign. If he remembered Bresciano, he might eventually remember the events of the previous night.

"Ah picked oot the-the weevils."

"Good," Bresciano, hungry in a way that was new to him, reached out for the plate: the smell seemed to stab up through his nostrils and he could barely hide his disgust. "Well done. You remember me now, don't you?"

"Ay, you were here this-this morn. Are you ma friend?"

"I was with you at the tavern two days ago, and we were on duty together yesterday. Do you remember?"

"That... that was nice," his guileless face was blank.

Bresciano gave up and sat down, attempting to eat, forcing the food down with great gulps of water, but he soon put down the plate, afraid that what had been swallowed with so much effort was about to make its way back up. He leaned against the wall and closed his eyes till the feeling of nausea grew slightly less. Tomorrow he must try to trade his meat for bread with one of the other soldiers. He would try Tom. It occurred to him that if he made a friend of sorts of him, he might be able to get him talking, to winkle something out of him, because if Murch was a suspect then Tom... no, that was wrong. It was Tom was the suspect and it was important to find... to ask... to try... He nodded off.

"Dinna ye... dinna ye want the food?" Jamie hovered over him hopefully.

"It was fine, Jamie. I'm just tired. You can have it if you like. I shall lie down in a minute."

"Thank you." He spooned it up contentedly. "It dinna smell... sae bad today. And the morn Ah-Ah have," he frowned, "that big mon," he searched vainly for a word to name him," he said... Ah have no... no duty... that's what he said. Ah have no duty and ma heed hurts and-and Ah was crying because... because... Ah was crying... and he said that."

"The Sergeant? He's let you off work?" Bresciano's eyes opened slowly – what was the Sergeant up to?

"The Sairgint...?" Jamie was bemused. "He's ma friend."

While Jamie again began laboriously to enumerate his 'friends', which now included the Captain, his wife and their slatternly housekeeper, Bresciano stripped off his jacket and breeches and fell into bed, too tired to try and consider what the Sergeant's intentions might be. And, even the cannon fire,

47

sixteen shots of it, that greeted the day had no power to rouse him. Jamie had already collected their rations by the time Bresciano struggled into consciousness of the new day of hard labour that awaited him. As he dressed, he attempted to draw Jamie out.

"How does your neck feel today? Can you remember how you hurt it?"

"The big… Sairgint… the big mon… said Ah fell… Ah climbed a wall and fell."

"And what do you remember?"

"I remember he said… Ah climbed a wall. Ah remember."

Jamie could no longer distinguish between what he had been told and what he might have known. Not yet, at least. Perhaps he would eventually recall the truth, but for the present, Bresciano thought, he was safe enough in his ignorance.

"And Ah want to go home… wi' ma friend." Tears rolled down Jamie's face. "He said-he said Ah could gae wi' him and be a-a ghillie. Ah want to go now."

"Who said? Was it the Sergeant?"

Jamie shook his head, looking confused. "Ah… can be his ghillie." Suddenly he smiled at the idea and wiped his nose on his sleeve, his tears gone.

There was that story again. What 'friend' was he talking about? Perhaps Jamie fantasised about Scotland as other men did about food – anything to dream yourself away from the siege. Bresciano abandoned the effort of making sense out of Jamie's disjointed nonsense. For one thing, he didn't have the time, but in the evening, if he wasted no time and came up directly after his stint of duty, he might get some more sense out of Jamie. It was the best he could think of.

Now he had other things that must be done. He took half his bread and stowed it in his tunic. Then he took the meat and went in search of Tom with whom he was able to make an exchange, one more favourable to Tom than to himself, but at least he would be able to take some bread home to his family.

On the track down to the town he bumped into Corporal Jones. Remembering the episode with Bianca, he was about to push past him, but then he considered: apart from Jamie, Jones was the only one of the men who had been halfway civil to him. Courtesy, as his mother always said, cost nothing and

↳ poligtnew

meant much. He stopped and said:

"Jamie seems to have made a good recovery."

"Ay, he's got a thick head, that one. But you want to be careful, lad, with what you say. The Sergeant's not a man to cross."

"Jamie... I find it difficult to understand him – he mumbles, and sometimes he uses strange words – it's as if he were talking a different language."

"It's two different languages he speaks, look you! Usually he speaks Lallands – it's what they speak in the Lowlands of Scotland. It's close enough to English to be understood most of the time, but when he's excited or with friends he goes into his mother tongue – that's Gaelic that they speak in the Highlands. They call that having the two tongues. They also say that the Gaelic is like my Welsh, but I'm blest if I can understand a word of it!"

They parted, and Bresciano quickened his pace. He had to hurry now if he was to stop at the house. There was only time to hand his mother the bread and ask after his sister; time enough to hear that, while Lucia's fever had mounted during the night, her wasted body was still clear of the terrible spots that would identify her illness as smallpox; and just time to hug his mother and feel how thin she too had grown.

The morning spent at King's Bastion was a repetition of the previous day's unremitting labour, but his lunch hour, that short break to eat his bread, he spent differently. Irish Town was only a few minutes' walk away. Bianca was only a few minutes' walk away. He would redeem himself in her eyes. He would swear her to secrecy, of course, but he would tell her how he was the only person who had had the intelligence to see that something was odd about the attack Jamie had suffered. What a coup for him if he did uncover the identity of the man involved! That would make her see him in a new light.

Bianca was there at the tavern, as desirable as ever, even in her poor clothes. She had a way of looking at a man with a slow smile, a smile that reached her eyes, a smile with a tantalising hint of mockery. Unfortunately there were others who had, like Bresciano, come to the tavern with its smell of ale and blackstrap and fug of pipe smoke; its feeling of camaraderie of a sort; its promise of a life beyond the boredom

49

and hunger and hard labour of their days. Some came to see Bianca and others came for the other tavern maid with her crude sexuality and more willing ways.

Bresciano went up to the bar. Bianca looked up from swabbing the boards with a damp and very grubby cloth and met his eye. That smile again. Bresciano gulped and looked around. Perhaps he had better just make conversation at first, then casually lead up to his news, his attempt to impress her. Three men in unfamiliar uniforms were sitting together in the corner.

"Who... who are those men over there? I don't think I've seen them before."

"Oh, they are men who came in from the Spanish lines – imagine that! They are called Walloons, I think. They come from somewhere with something to do with the French. Can you believe it? to desert from the freedom on the other side to come into this, this prison, where there is nothing to eat? They must be mad. But one of them, that good-looking one there – see, he's smiling at us – he said some of them may have been forced to join with the Spanish, but he says *he* never signed any treaty with Spain. 'I'll be damned if I lift a finger against Gibraltar,' he said. He risked his life to get here. Had to get away from the Spanish lines and run the risk of being shot when he reached ours! I call that really mad... and sort of brave."

It was enough to make Bresciano hate all Walloons – whatever they might be. He opened his mouth to tell Bianca about his discoveries, when he was interrupted.

"There 'e is! So what new crimes 'ave you discovered today?" A rough voice called out, "That's our very own genius, that is!" It was Murch. "'E accused me of attacking Daft Jamie! Wot a clever feller 'e is. There woz I, lying in me bed of pain, couldn't move more'n a yard without agony – and in full sight of everyone in the 'ut, mind you – and this 'ere Bloody Busybody tells everyone I woz leapin' around outside akilling that fool."

There was loud laughter and Bresciano's hands tightened into fists. So much for his hopes of impressing Bianca!

"Jes' look at me now – only got 'ere thanks to my good friend Tom as 'elped me 'obble down for a drop o' drink." Murch stood up with difficulty to demonstrate his weakened state of health, and to bleed the situation for all the pathos *pitty* it was worth.

"What have you been up to, Giovanni? It's been the talk of the men for the past day. You and your imagination." Bianca sounded amused.

"It wasn't imagination. Ask your precious Corporal Jones if you don't believe me. He thought it might be a deserter. I suppose you'll believe him rather than me." He turned round defiantly and spoke out, imprudent, rushing his fences. "Someone did try to kill Jamie. The rest of you are too stupid to see the nose in front of your face."

It was an unfortunate expression to have chosen, for Bresciano, grown too tall and too lean in the past two years, had yet to acquire the weight and muscle of the man he would become, and had yet to grow into a nose that would one day look noble, but that was at present an embarrassment to him.

He had thrown out an ill-judged challenge, but the situation was defused by the men's reaction.

"Jamie climbed that wall, you fool. 'E said so hisself, or 'adn't you 'eard?"

"Better call you Daft Busyano!"

"Naw, let the lad be. I mean, talking of noses – 'e really is the man to smell out trouble with that great one o' his!"

Their laughter was cut short as a figure appeared at the door. Officers did not often enter such taverns and the sight of Lieutenant Black effectively silenced the men.

"Where's James Macfarlane? I am told that he frequents this... establishment." His figure was elegant, his voice was terse, his manner threatening.

"Would that be Daft Jamie?"

abrupt "Don't know, Lieutenant Black, sir."

"Yes, 'e's down at North Front."

"No. Sergeant sent 'im up Europa Point."

"Naw, that were yesterday. 'E should be down at King's Bastion."

They spoke seriously, following each other's lead as they closed ranks to protect their own; savouring the Lieutenant's frustration and throwing out a few more conflicting locations till he turned on his heel and stalked out. The Lieutenant might be richer, younger and better fed than they were. He might be enjoying the favours of Captain Weston's wife, but he wouldn't get the better of them or lay into Jamie while they were united. They rejoiced over having routed him. Even Murch, his grievance against Bresciano forgotten, was loud in their self-congratulatory chorus. Bresciano was left isolated, marooned in the no-man's-land he inhabited as a new recruit, a foreigner among them, and a fool to boot.

Bianca pulled at his sleeve: "Well, Giovanni, what else did you want to tell me?"

"I'll tell you another time. Alone. Not here." His eyes asked for her understanding.

"Sunday morning. I still go to church, for all the good it does. God doesn't seem to listen to requests for food, does He?"

"I'll be there."

He walked out, jostling the three Walloons, who were leaving at the same time. One of them, the handsome blond with a devil-may-care air about him, looked back at Bianca and smiled. Bresciano glared impotently and turned towards King's Bastion. As he worked through the afternoon, he turned his thoughts to planning exactly how he would convince her with a clear exposition of what had happened that night, and imagining how she would admire his keen intelligence and perspicacity. And when his work was done, he returned to Willis's, to the hut he shared with Jamie, feeling almost confident that by encouraging Jamie to talk and by careful questioning he could elicit from him the information he wanted.

"Open up, it's me, Bresciano!" The door of the hut was locked, but he could hear Jamie moving around inside. "Come on, it's Giovanni, your friend."

A voice seemed to call out in answer, a faint cry, but the sounds were drowned by cannon fire as the men at Grand Battery sent the last shots of the day towards the Spanish lines. Seven thousand shots since the siege started, so Bresciano had heard. He waited for the explosions to die down.

"Hurry up, it's cold out here."

Nothing but silence greeted his words and he hammered on the door, a little irritated by Jamie's tardiness.

"Come on, Jamie, let me in."

There was an almost imperceptible sound of scuffling inside, then total silence, and for no reason he could imagine, he felt his scalp crawling. Something, he knew, was terribly wrong in the hut.

CHAPTER IV

Instinctively Bresciano flung himself against the locked door, but his frame ran to height rather than weight and the door did not give way. He staggered back clutching his bruised shoulder and only then took time to think. The window! There was a window at the back of the hut. He prayed that Jamie had not closed the wooden shutters. As he raced around to the back, pushing aside the branches of the small trees that impeded his progress, he registered a rustling in the bushes where he must have startled some large creature, surely an ape. The window – thank heaven! The wooden shutters were open wide and he flung himself through, landing in a heap inside the room.

Picking himself up, he looked around, blinking as his eyes accommodated themselves to the gloom inside, and a movement caught his eye. Something was hanging from a rope looped around a beam in the centre of the hut. It was Jamie. Horrified disbelief held Bresciano frozen for seconds, before he stumbled forward with an inarticulate cry and threw his arms around the dangling legs and raised them, hoping to relieve the pressure on Jamie's neck.

What now? He had no knife. If he let go and tried to unfasten the noose around Jamie's neck, Jamie would choke – if he was not dead already. He looked around wildly. No key in the door. On the table, an opened bottle. Some green plants neatly arranged in a cup. A small wooden box, not more than a foot high, was on the floor not far from the hanging body. No knife or anything else that might help. Bresciano filled his lungs and bellowed:

"Help! Help! In here!"

He shouted again, in growing desperation. Would anyone hear? He had seen no one near the hut as he approached it.

"Murder!" He screamed, the word coming unbidden to his lips. Never mind, at least that might bring them running. He shouted it again and again and was rewarded by the sound of someone rattling the door.

"Window!" he shouted desperately, but the sound had stopped. He cursed himself: had they just gone away, thinking that it was just another of the flights of fancy of 'Daft Busyano'? How long would he be able to hold Jamie? He glanced up. Jamie's normally peaceful face was purple and congested and his eyes bulging; he did not appear to be breathing. Bresciano, despairing, found himself screaming incoherently. Just a few more desperate moments and he was rewarded by a mighty crash as the door burst open. Framed in the light that streamed in from a lantern outside he made out Sergeant Connor wielding a sledgehammer, and a couple of men pressing to get in.

The Sergeant took in the situation and, striding forward, drew a knife from his pocket and pulling the box over, he stood on it, reached up and hacked at the rope. Corporal Jones rushed to help Bresciano and eventually the inert figure of Jamie collapsed on to Bresciano, who let go of the legs and cradled his head. There was a faint gasp, and a tiny sound and he leaned forward hopefully: perhaps Jamie was still alive, perhaps he could be saved, perhaps he was trying to speak. But that barely audible gasp was all. He felt not even the warmth of Jamie's breath on his face; and putting his ear to Jamie's chest, Bresciano could hear no heartbeat. He remained cradling the body, willing Jamie to breathe, not wanting to accept the reality. Jamie could not be dead, must not be dead. A long minute passed before he raised his head slowly.

"I think he's gone," he said flatly, and looked up at the Sergeant.

"Why did you shout murder?" The Sergeant spoke coldly, "I thought I had knocked that nonsense on the head, or don't you listen to what you're told? Maybe you need a different sort of lesson, do you?"

"No, sir. I shouted for help and... no one came when I called. I needed someone to come..." he swallowed, "so I shouted 'murder'... to get someone's attention." He remembered Abraham's advice – he must keep his head down – and he repeated, more assertively, "I didn't really think it was murder."

"Of course it wasn't murder! He must have done it himself. Why, the lad was crying on and off this morning," said Jones, "he must have been in a fit of melancholy. Came with us up to Willis's Battery and then wandered off later."

"'E were 'appy enough when I saw 'im this afternoon" said the man with the lantern. "Going to make a salad 'e said! Seemed all right to me."

"I tell you, he was probably melancholic. Made precious little sense when I spoke to him up at the Battery."

The men argued, citing their experience of a Jamie whose mood that day had veered from tears to happiness.

"So he was peculiar all day, right? It goes to show that that fall and the knock on the head... " The Sergeant stared down and shook his head. "More serious than it seemed. Nothing physical, mind you. We've got hard heads, harder'n we think. But this lad was not normal. His skull may have been thick as yours or mine, but his mind had been going for a long time."

The two other men made vague noises of assent and Bresciano sadly noted the irony: Jamie dead had become 'the lad' and 'this lad'; he was no longer 'Daft Jamie' or 'idiot' or 'fool'. The living were fair game, but men were more circumspect in the presence of death.

The Sergeant looked around and picked up the box that now lay a few feet away from where they were standing. He considered it thoughtfully, then took up the thread of his conclusions. "He must have stood on this, put his head in the noose and then kicked the box away. Looks as if he committed suicide, 'while the balance of the mind was disturbed' – that's what they always say. Well, his mind was certainly disturbed – we know that. Aye. It was suicide right enough."

"That's right, Sarge, stood on the box and kicked it away – makes sense."

"Yeh, fancy that, and him all happy when I saw him. You can't never tell, can you?"

"I always said 'e would do 'isself in one day."

"You never said nothing like that!"

56

Bresciano opened his mouth to argue and then changed his mind, uncertain of himself. He wasn't even sure why he had cried 'murder', but he resented the fact that Sergeant Connor was so sure that it was suicide and that all the men had taken up the idea so quickly, even though it did seem the most logical explanation.

"Yes, sir," he said dully.

By this time several other men had arrived, attracted by the commotion. They stared, wide-eyed and open-mouthed at the body of Jamie, still with the halter around his neck.

"Done himself in! Who'da thought it?" one of them said, "He were that happy this afternoon. Said as his friend was coming to see him."

"Friend! We all know about 'is friends!" That was Tom. "Angels and the like. Friends? 'E never 'ad no real friends!"

"I think he was expecting a real friend," insisted the first man. "I mean... I saw young 'Shot' down in town and he said Jamie had sent him to fetch him a bottle o' real wine. Gave him money for it, he did. Look, there it is on the table."

"You know, it won't be the same without him and his tall stories, will it?"

"Now we'll never know what the Captain's wife is up to," muttered one of the men, and this drew an unfeeling laugh from some of the others.

"That's enough, men!" the Sergeant snapped. He indicated the limp body of Jamie. "Pick him up and take him to the Barracks."

Grumbling, the soldiers, who had hoped for time to speculate and argue over Jamie's unexpected death – for it was, after all, the most interesting event of their day – dragged the body out, hoisting it on to a board in order to carry it down to their headquarters at the Blue Barracks, some way down the hill. Without a glance at Bresciano Sergeant Connor followed them out of the hut.

Bresciano remained alone in the gathering darkness and found that he was beginning to shiver uncontrollably: he was quaking, and he dropped down on his bed, his head in his hands, feeling unutterably tired and sick and confused. And there was something else. Something beyond the shock, the regret and even the guilt for what he had failed to prevent. He realised that it was sorrow. He had only known him less than a week, but he felt sad at the death of poor, simple Jamie, his only friend up here. Tears pricked his eyes.

He sat for a long time, rocking back and forth, mourning the death, unable to think clearly. Jamie was – had been – like a child… and barely eighteen… and Jamie was dead.

It was very late that Friday when he lay down, but sleep would not come. Instead he kept recalling the last few days: Jamie smiling vacantly and amiably; scrambling nimbly up the steep path to Willis's Battery; listing his many friends; offering to get the ingredients to make their food more palatable – never meaning any harm to anyone. And there was the memory of Jamie's limp body hauled up from where he had surely been thrown to what should have been his death; and the awful image of that inert weight hanging from the beam in this room.

He sat up with a jerk and shook his head furiously. "Get a hold of yourself, Giovanni!" he said out loud. "Jamie is dead and nothing will change that, but you can still do something about it. Start thinking!"

And as he spoke the words, he knew with an unexpected sense of conviction that he had shouted the word 'murder' for a reason, that there was something at the back of his mind which, mixed up with the turmoil of images both kindly and horrifying, would not let him rest.

He groped around till he found the lantern, lit it and raised his head to look around the hut. On the table was a bowl with some sort of gruel or porridge that Jamie had made with their rations, and the bunch of herbs which Jamie had collected as he had promised. Bresciano picked them up, sad evidence of what Jamie had done in his last hours. He was no expert on plants, but thought that there was fennel there – palatable enough – and wild garlic, which was less appealing. And as he stared at the plants, he recalled clearly his last conversation with Jamie. His friend had certainly been crying in the morning because of his longing for Scotland. There were others who testified to this fact that he himself had witnessed. But had there been any real sadness? Had it been an easy outpouring of tears rather than the weeping that came with deep distress? It reminded him of the tears Nonna Lucrezia often wiped away, tears produced by her eyes, not by her emotions. He pulled thoughtfully at his lip. He would have to ask the men who had seen Jamie, but he felt certain that Jamie had not been disconsolate. He had cried that morning like a child, and had forgotten his sorrow even more quickly than a child.

And the porridge and these plants. They might indeed prove to be evidence! A man about to commit suicide would surely not have taken the trouble to gather these herbs for his and Bresciano's supper, and order a bottle of wine, would he?

Bresciano felt a quickening in his mind, a measure of excitement. Ah, yes, the wine. There was that too. He picked up the bottle. A fine sherry from a vineyard near Jerez. Impossible! He stared at it in amazement. It was an expensive wine at the best of times, and after eighteen months of blockade it was almost unbelievable that it had survived undrunk. It must have cost Jamie a pretty penny – and Jamie had no money. What could a man save on a soldier's wages? And it… why…? Had it been bought in anticipation of the meeting which Jamie was expecting to have with his real or imaginary friend? But there was still the question of money. Jamie could only afford ale or blackstrap. This sherry was heady stuff, and part of the bottle had been drunk; had it been used to dull Jamie's senses? Had that been done to make it easier to hang him? Or had Jamie drunk the wine in order to gather up the courage to hang himself?

Bresciano shook his head, thinking furiously, ideas crowding his mind – forcing him to think. The window! If Jamie had been murdered, whoever had escaped after doing the deed must have gone through it. He remembered the disturbance he had noticed in the bushes when he had rushed to the back of the hut – what if it had not been an ape? It could have been the murderer escaping. Had he just missed him? Who could it have been? Fat Murch with his flayed back and corpulence would never have got through the window – not easily, anyhow – but his friend Tom might have done so. The Sergeant was a big man, but athletic, so he could have done it. How was it that Sergeant Connor had arrived so promptly? Now it seemed to Bresciano that the Sergeant had been suspiciously near at hand when he had called for help. And what about the whereabouts of others who might want to kill Jamie? People like Lieutenant Black who had been out searching for James Macfarlane that very day? Or someone else – perhaps Jamie's friend had not been so imaginary after all – or so friendly? That could have been someone like

59

Captain Weston, who might have heard the rumours Jamie had inadvertently set about, who might have been furious at being called a cuckold behind his back. Yes! He might have pretended to become Jamie's friend, lured him...

Bresciano's mind was racing with the possibilities he could suddenly see, like the door – the door! It had been locked, but the key was not in the lock. He looked around the simple room. There were few places to hide a key. And why would Jamie hide it? Feverishly he searched the small room with its few bits of furniture, but it was nowhere to be found. He stopped. The possibility existed that Jamie could have locked the door, preparatory to committing suicide, and put the key in his pocket. *↙ to prepare*

He mumbled to himself as he went through the actions suicide would have entailed: "Lock the door, fetch the rope, tie the noose..." It made no sense to pocket the key. He would have to make sure – he would need to get down to the Blue Barracks to look through Jamie's pockets. The idea of searching Jamie's dead body made him shudder. It would be a desecration of some sort. But it needed to be done if he was to get at the truth.

There was something else. Something that he could not put his finger on. Something that should have been there, and wasn't. The rope that had been used to save Jamie on the previous night was no longer hanging from the hook on the wall and Bresciano had the sick revelation that it was that very rope which had been used to hang Jamie. But that wasn't it. What was he searching for? Something quite ordinary... possibly important?

The idea, an elusive will o' the wisp, betrayed him into uncertainty. He had nothing but vague conclusions; the others would laugh at him. He could imagine their arguments and began to doubt himself. What if they were right? He forced himself to be devil's advocate, making himself think as they might: it could have been that Jamie had been frustrated by his addled wits, which made him the butt of the other men's derision, frustrated to such a degree that he had decided to end it all... or what if – though in Bresciano's limited experience he had seemed quite contented – the other men who had known him for far longer had recognised a real melancholia? ... or what if it was as the Sergeant said – that Jamie's erratic behaviour that day was evidence that the blow to the back of his head had destroyed what little sense he had? But then there were Jamie's two 'accidents', which seemed to suggest that someone wanted him out of the way. And was there not enough to suggest that the apparent suicide had been staged?

Bresciano closed his eyes, his thoughts going round in circles. 'Think logically,' Abraham Hassan had said. Well, if he set aside his feeling that Jamie had not been suicidal, that his preparations for the evening meal betokened no morbid intention to commit suicide, then it left the key as a concrete fact. The logical thing to do would be to look through Jamie's pockets for it. If the key was there, it made suicide much more likely.

One thing he was clear about: he would not cry wolf again, not till he was sure of his ground. He believed it was not suicide, but others would say otherwise.

Back in bed, exhausted, he fell into an uneasy sleep to awake in the early dawn, before the others were stirring. He rose, packed away his bread together with the fennel Jamie had collected and the food he had made, and slipped away quietly down to the Blue Barracks where he found Jamie's unattended body laid out, still dressed, in a small room in the Barracks infirmary.

In fear he bent over and searched the body with uneasy hands, expecting Jamie to move and accuse him of violating his sleep. He found himself apologising to this dead waxen figure with its smooth face that had been wiped clear of all confusion, all pain, all joy. A child's face that did not reproach him for what he was doing. He persevered in his grim task and eventually straightened up.

The key was not there.

It was not suicide, he thought with satisfaction; he was sure of that now.

He must talk to someone. His mother, a sensible woman, always had good advice for him, but what did she know of murder? His father would tell him not to meddle in the affairs of the English. Abraham Hassan had been sympathetic and helpful, but Abraham had almost as little experience of the Army and its ways as he had, and if the murderer were the Sergeant, or even an officer, he would have no idea how to proceed.

Then Bresciano remembered the books he had given Abraham Hassan for Lieutenant Drinkwater. Now there was a young man who might be hardly older that Bresciano himself, but one surely with a knowledge of how things worked in this military society. He would take him another book, and then try to engage him in conversation. He could ask him about deserters and then they might talk of other things and the conversation could be led around to Jamie and the attempts on his life.

But first he wanted to get home to see his family. He had to see whether Lucia was better, and his mother had looked so tired yesterday. He had the fennel and the remains of his uneaten rations in his bag. At least it was something, but he must find food that was more filling and nutritious for little Lucia.

*   *   *   *

Bresciano's mother met him at the door of the family house. Unusually for her, she looked distraught, and even more exhausted than yesterday.

"Giovanni – Lucia!" She could hardly speak.

"What? What has happened?" Bresciano was filled with dread.

"It is the smallpox. It is certain now – she has come out in spots. Her fever is down a little, I think, but..." She put her hand up to her mouth, not wanting to betray further weakness.

He followed her into the bedroom. In the gloom he saw that Lucia was awake. Her face was covered with raised red spots. There had been other children who had caught smallpox and he had heard how the spots soon filled with clear fluid, which would then turn to pus. It could be the beginning of the end.

With an obvious effort, Lucia raised herself slightly on one elbow and smiled weakly at her brother, a travesty of her usual impish smile. "Thank you for coming, Giovanni. I so wanted to see you."

Bresciano felt a lump in his throat, but forced himself to speak cheerfully. "I couldn't keep away. You are my betrothed, remember?"

She laughed feebly at the old joke that harked back to

when she was barely three and had said that she was going to marry him when she grew up.

"Lie down and rest, my little Lucia. And you must remember not to scratch at those spots. I absolutely forbid it! I don't want the face of my lovely sister marred by scars!"

"But if it is smallpox…" she fixed her eyes on his face.

"No," he lied resolutely, looking carefully at her face, "no. You look exactly like some of the soldiers at the Blue Barracks. I was there earlier this morning and they were covered in spots too, like you: it's…it's just…"

"Chicken pox." His mother supplied the word.

"That's right. Only chicken pox, there's a lot of that about. It's nothing serious."

Bresciano sat at her side and she lay down again and closed her eyes. He remained where he was until her regular breathing showed that she was sleeping and then he joined his mother in the kitchen. Eleanor was sitting at the table and her slumped shoulders spoke eloquently of defeat.

"That was a kind lie, Giovanni, but this is the worst epidemic of smallpox that I can remember. So many people have died, especially children, hundreds of them. Hundreds! And now that it all seemed to have passed and I felt safe. Lucia…"

She choked back a sob, and Bresciano said quickly, trying to give his tone a confidence which he did not feel. "Mother, you have to stay calm. We must not give up hope. Think of all the children who have survived it. Why should Lucia not get well? Lucia will get better, I know it! You are right about the epidemic – it is ending, it is getting weaker so obviously… Lucia will not be as sick as other children who were infected in July and August." He was no medical man and to him it seemed a reasonable assumption to make.

She raised her tear-stained face and Bresciano looked closely at her. The skin of her face looked transparent and there was a fleck of blood on her lips.

"Mother! You are not eating properly, are you? You're giving all the food to Lucia and starving yourself! You mustn't do that – if something happened to you, what would we do? What would become of Lucia?" He watched her wet her lips and his heart sank. "Your mouth is sore, isn't it? You were the one who said that we had to tell you if anything like that

63

happened, if our gums became painful. You are beginning to show signs of scurvy!"

Eleanor smiled wearily. "Lucia has been wasting away and now she is very ill, Giovanni. She is the one who needs the food. Your father has gone out to look for food. Perhaps he will bring something…"

Bresciano remembered the food in his pack. "Mother, here is some bread. It's little enough, I know, but I'll try and bring more when I come again. And here's some fennel from the Rock – didn't you say green things are good for scurvy? It was collected by a friend." He caught himself up on the word. Poor Jamie, who had been his friend for such a short time, was still being his friend, even after his death. And Bresciano felt a fierce desire for justice, even for vengeance: it was up to him to unmask the murderer – because someone, for some reason, had cold-bloodedly done the innocent, harmless Jamie to death.

His thoughts were interrupted by Aunt Maria who came in from the yard where she had been hanging out a meagre wash. Like Eleanor she looked gaunt, with dark shadows under her eyes, large dark eyes that seemed to have sunk deep into their sockets. She sounded exhausted, defeated by life under siege.

"It's impossible to get anything clean with only cold water," her surprisingly deep voice was hoarse, "we need wood or charcoal to make a proper fire. And the clothes inside the house are all spotted with mildew and we can iron nothing without a fire to heat the irons and my nerves won't stand all this! We should have left Gibraltar when the other merchants left. I told Giancarlo. I told him we should leave. Let England fight her own battles. Why should we be involved? And now we shall all starve slowly to death, if the smallpox doesn't get us first. I tell you, we should have gone long ago!"

Her voice rose and trembled and she sat down abruptly, the tears running down her face. Eleanor forced herself over to where Maria sat and gently stroked her head.

"There, there. Things will not look so bleak when you have rested. We none of us got much sleep last night worrying about Lucia. Just sit there and rest. And tomorrow is Sunday and you will go to church: you know what a consolation that is for you. Here, put Nonna's shawl over your shoulders and close your eyes."

She soothed and petted the younger woman and, in doing so, found her own strength and consolation.

Bresciano frowned at her. "But Papa offered to send you all away when the siege began, didn't he? Didn't Aunt Maria refuse to go?" His voice was low.

"He did. He said he himself had to stay to protect the business – heaven knows what would happen to it left unattended. It could have been looted, his stock stolen. And you are right, he offered to send us all away. I couldn't leave him, and Nonna said she would stay and fight the Spaniards if they broke through our defences."

"I thought she said she would throw herself from the top of the Rock rather than be taken."

His mother gave him a watery smile, "She said that too. And Maria, poor woman, who wanted to leave, refused to go away without her. But you must not blame her for today's outburst – it is her daily task, as it has always been, to buy the bread – but it is no longer a simple matter of going to the baker and chatting with friends. Now she has to face hostility from those with barely a penny to buy anything; and there are the children whimpering with hunger as they wait for the baker to open. She finds it harrowing." → destressing

He had to go. It was growing close to the time when he had to be on duty. Seeing Drinkwater would not be possible now. At the thought, he begged a book off his mother and then hurriedly took his leave. Both her state and that of Lucia were deeply worrying. Somehow, he had to find food that would help them fight the scurvy, for Lucia too must be on the verge of it, and she would surely recover from the smallpox more quickly if she were not weakened by scurvy.

He knew that British sailors warded off the disease on long voyages by eating something, what was it? He tried to remember what his mother had said, and it had also been mentioned during the conversation in the hut about Murch's theft of food. Someone had said... lemons, that was it! And now he remembered hearing that Spanish sailors from Seville never contracted scurvy, because their ships always carried the oranges which were so plentiful there. But where could he find fresh fruit in this beleaguered town? But find he would, he promised himself.

Down at the Bastion, the hard physical labour of the morning left him feeling light-headed and he knew that he must force himself to eat what food was available to him. He had told his mother that she must keep her strength up and the same applied to him or he would be of no use to anyone. He took out the tin can he had brought and forced himself to swallow the porridge quickly and even managed some of the meat that he found at the bottom of the can. Jamie had used wild garlic liberally.

It occurred to Bresciano that with the whole town combing the slopes of the Rock for edible plants it must be difficult to find any. Where had Jamie found them? Perhaps if he, Bresciano, could find where Jamie had gone that day, he also could find fresh green plants for Lucia. He closed his eyes and finished off the meat, retching with almost every bite, but determined.

Shouts from his fellow workers stopped him as he prepared for work again. An argument had broken out. Men made irascible by privations and by the monotony and demands of hard physical labour were not inclined to be rational. Accusations, denials and counter-accusations and even blows were being exchanged. The cause of the altercation was the lack of equipment needed to move large blocks of limestone that had been delivered and could not now be unloaded. The wooden ramps available were inadequate. Someone was to blame. No one was admitting to error.

All work came to a standstill and, till matters were set to rights, no further work could be done. Men found a sheltered spot wherever they could and prepared to wait. Someone took out a greasy pack of cards. Bresciano slipped off unnoticed.

Now, how to find Lieutenant Drinkwater? He had forgotten to ask Abraham Hassan where the Manchester Volunteers were billeted. As he hurried down the street, he caught sight of a soldier in the uniform of the Volunteers. It was not Abraham, but he would have to do.

He walked up to the man. "Where can I find your Lieutenant Drinkwater? I have to give him a message." He made it sound important.

"What, Dreamy Drinkwater?" was the disrespectful reply, "If he ain't on duty, you'll surely find him under one of the trees outside the South Port, with his nose in a book!"

Bresciano ran down the street. It was a matter of minutes before he found Drinkwater as his informant had predicted, sitting on a low wall in the shade of a tree just outside South Port, one of the gates that pierced the thick city walls. He was reading a well-thumbed book. He looked up enquiringly as Bresciano approached. Obviously he had not recognised him.

questioning

"It's me, Giovanni Bresciano, sir. I was with Hassan yesterday when you asked about books to read. I already gave him some and I've brought another."

Lieutenant Drinkwater's face cleared. "Oh, yes, dashed good of you, Private Bresh... er Bresciano. Most grateful. I've already made a start on Fielding!" He indicated the book he had been reading.

"This is *Tristam Shandy*." Bresciano reached into his pack and brought out the book. He pointed to a bookmark his mother had placed in the book long ago, "My mother has marked the page where Tristam Shandy's father mentions – or rather, where the author says – that Tristam Shandy's father came to Gibraltar. She was much amused by it."

Drinkwater smiled. "Your mother must be a very well-read lady, Private Bresciano. Tell her that I thank her most sincerely for this – a treat indeed. As for *Gulliver's Travels*, it is always worth reading again, even if one already knows it. I look forward to meeting her when I return these books. She does have others which she could lend me?" he enquired anxiously.

"Oh, yes, sir, she has a number of books." This was the moment, Bresciano thought. "I wonder, sir, if I might ask you for some advice?"

"Advice, Mr Bresciano? What sort of advice?"

"Well, I wanted to ask you whether any men deserted to the enemy in the last two days. I know you keep a diary, and Hassan said ..."

"Curiously enough, Bresciano, though we had eight... no, nine deserters in November, there have been no desertions from the Garrison for over ten days. But, ironically, there have been several deserters from the enemy who have come *into* the fortress. God knows what drives them to desert to a place which is beleaguered and starving, and which their leaders assure them will soon fall! Came in during the past week. Walloons, you know. Aren't French, although they serve in

surronded by foes

67

the French army, even in the Spanish army. They seem to escape to us in Gibraltar for political reasons. Certainly not for any comforts we can offer. But this is information, not advice. There's something else on your mind. Come on, out with it, man!"

This was enough encouragement for Bresciano. Unbidden, he sat down on the wall by the Lieutenant. Drinkwater raised an eyebrow, but said nothing. He listened attentively as Bresciano poured out the whole story of Jamie, his accidents, and finally his death by hanging.

When he had finished, Bresciano looked anxiously at Drinkwater. The young Lieutenant was silent for a moment, then said:

"You have made a persuasive case against the poor fellow's death being suicide, Bresciano, but it is largely based on the door of the hut being locked and the key nowhere to be found – but did you search outside? Could your Jamie not have thrown the key out of the open window? Not the act of a reasonable man, I agree, but he was not a reasonable man, was he? As for the wine – he might have come by some money, saved some, even stolen some. And his other action – collecting herbs – if his mind was so disturbed, and his mood unpredictable, he might have done this and then committed suicide on an impulse. It could still have been suicide."

Bresciano was crestfallen. He tried to say, "Jamie wasn't like that," but Drinkwater interrupted,

"If there's nothing else that you can think of, I'm afraid that suicide is still the most likely possibility. Not murder."

Bresciano rose to leave, deeply disappointed. He visualised the scene at the hut. How had he not thought of the key being thrown out of the window! He was still sure it could not have been suicide, but... wait! He turned back to Drinkwater.

"I *know* it wasn't suicide," he said with conviction.

"Yes?"

"Jamie would have had to get on a chair, or the table, to tie the rope to the beam, and there was no chair near him when I found him."

"But you said there was a box, the one which the Sergeant used, the one he said your Jamie must have kicked away."

"It would have been impossible!"

"What do you mean?"

The will-o-the-wisp thought of the previous night now became a clear physical reality in the light of day and he blurted it out. "There were two chairs at the table and Jamie was a small lad, so it would have been sensible to get a chair and not a stupid box because it was ridiculous to use a box, because even standing on that box he could not have reached to put his head through the noose, and that box would only have been of use to a tall man wanting to force Jamie's head into the noose – because the roof is quite low and a tall man on a chair would have banged his head on the cross beam and lifting Jamie might have been awkward but not impossible for a strong man if Jamie was too drunk to resist or had been knocked out or something like it and I heard scuffling noises – probably him pulling Jamie up before he fled through the window when I arrived!" His voice rose breathlessly and triumphantly.

Drinkwater laughed out loud. "Bresciano, you should be a writer or a captain – you're wasted in the ranks!"

Bresciano shook his head sadly. "I shouldn't be in the Army at all, sir. I should be helping my father. I only joined up to help protect my home and now, instead of that, I find myself mending walls and trying to... avenge the death of a poor fellow who may well have been murdered by one of our own! And I didn't invent what I said."

"If the lad was murdered – and you have nearly convinced me that he might have been, just a possibility, mind you – who do you think could have done it?"

"There's the Sergeant... and Lieutenant..."

Bresciano saw the way that Lieutenant Drinkwater's good-natured expression changed and hardened and he stopped short. He knew he had over-reached himself and expected too much from this young Englishman. Mentally he was floundering as he tried to change tack, "The Sergeant... well, he's not very keen on my ideas and... the Lieutenant..." Invention failed him.

"Hmm," Drinkwater was not deceived. "My advice to you is that you look for further information before you make any accusations. Without proof you should be very, very careful what you say. Is that clear?"

Despite his youth, his voice was severe and Bresciano

shrank back into himself. Drinkwater, ready to take umbrage on behalf of fellow officers, relented. He felt kinship with this eager young man, a man of his own age by the look of it, who seemed likely to put his feet in it – rather large ones he noted. He himself had been in the army since the age of fifteen and was already a seasoned campaigner; he had learnt the value of not antagonising senior officers, and was experiencing the frustration of promotion deferred indefinitely. He could identify with Bresciano.

"Remember what I have said. For everyone's sake, your own included, be circumspect. Nevertheless, if there has been foul play, then justice should be done. But you will need incontrovertible proof."

Bresciano left the Lieutenant to his books. Drinkwater was right: he had to find out more about his suspects. Where could he start? Casting around in his mind, he remembered that Bianca's mother worked in Captain Weston's house. Perhaps she could tell him about the situation there. He hurried back to the King's Bastion, fearful that he had spent longer than he thought away from his work and was relieved to arrive as a supply of stout ropes and new ramps were about to be put into place.

70

CHAPTER V

The working day was over and Bresciano stood uncertainly at the top of the wall of King's Bastion. His hands were filthy and his knuckles bloody where he had scraped them against rough limestone blocks, but he felt a sense of satisfaction. He watched a couple of Spanish gunboats in the distance. Abraham Hassan was probably right; the work he was doing was necessary to keep the enemy from breaking through their defences. An attack by land was on the cards, but no one expected it to succeed – or to succeed without tremendous loss of life on the Spanish side. And any attack by sea would surely be repelled by Gibraltar's sea defences, like this impressive Line Wall from which the Bastion jutted out into the Bay. He felt light of heart. Tomorrow would be an easier day. His duties would involve cleaning his kit and preparing to parade – army discipline – but he would be able to see Bianca as arranged.

Tired and hungry, he turned to make his way up to the hut, but he was stopped by a voice calling to him loudly in Genoese. It was a voice he remembered well from his childhood: Emiliana, Bianca's mother.

She stood in front of him in the narrow lane, barring his way, swaying slightly, a broad, foolish smile on her face. She had once been a handsome woman with an erratic temper who had always treated him with careless affection when, as a child, he had run tame in and out of her small, untidy hut at Buena Vista. The years had not treated her kindly. He noted her dishevelled appearance and was embarrassed to see her dirty shift underneath a low neckline grown lower as a result of the loss of two buttons.

"Gianni!" she used his childhood diminutive, "You are a soldier? My Gianni! You are defending Gibraltar! Oh, you brave man!"

She reached up and took hold of his cheeks between thumb and crooked forefinger and shook them affectionately as she had done to him as a child, then she laughed inordinately, telling a passer-by, a stranger, that she had known the lad since he was a baby, that Giovanni Bresciano was a hero now, and that he was a real man. Then she flung her arms round his neck, embracing him with fervour and Bresciano recoiled involuntarily from the stench of cheap wine on her breath. As usual, she was much the worse for drink.

"You love old Emiliana, don't you, Gianni?" She now had a grip on his arm. "You remember how you used to come to my hut to play with my Bianca? You were a lovely boy. And now, look at you – a fine man! And you can't play with my Bianca now? Eh? Eh?"

She laughed again. She had grown coarse and vulgar with the years and Bresciano was repelled, regretting the loss of the woman he had known in childhood – a generous woman who had been quick to laughter. The years and the desertion of Bianca's father, who had failed to marry her, had left her with a child and the beginning of a reputation, a reputation which had grown worse and better-deserved with time.

"*Sciâ* Emiliana! I'm glad to see you. You are well, I hope? You look well." He felt awkward as he uttered his platitudes.

"Gianni, you are a liar! I look terrible. And I am drunk. What I say is, what's the use of having a daughter in a tavern if she doesn't give her old mother a drink when she needs one? That's what I say. I needed it, you know." She leaned into him with an air of confidentiality and again he smelt the blackstrap on her breath. "Yes, needed it. I can speak to you in confidence for we are old friends. I have been a model of discretion till now. I swear it on the life of my daughter, but I can speak freely to you – that woman! I spit on her," and she suited action to word. "Called me a whore! She said that to me! She is a bigger *putana* than me. *Putana!*" She wept noisily, wiping her eyes with the hem of her skirt.

"Oh." Bresciano was acutely embarrassed. He had no idea what she was talking about. He had meant to speak to her about Captain Weston and his wife, speak to her sober when she might have information to give. Now he wanted to get away, but her grip on his arm was resolute.

"Yes – 'oh!' as you say. You understand me, eh? You are right! She tells me to leave the house and never go back. Me!" She grew briefly tearful again.

"I... I'm so sorry."

She looked at him, her eyes dull and unfocused. "You're a good boy. You worry about Emiliana, eh? Don't worry. Don't you worry." She hiccuped and began to laugh, her maudlin mood forgotten. "I'm not worried. No! Emiliana will go back. That *Scignoa* Güeston will have to take me back. You know her? Her and that young lieutenant – pah! I say she deserved everything she got. A husband has to be master in his own house, that's right, isn't it? So when he asked me, I had to say, didn't I? And he did what he had to do. She deserved it!"

Bresciano stared at her – she was talking of the Westons and of Lieutenant Black. He had wanted to know more about them, but how much could he rely on this disjointed information from someone who was drunk? If he wanted reliable information, he could approach her another day, when she was sober. Nevertheless, he could try now:

"*Scignoa* Weston dismissed you?"

"Yes, but I shall go back. It is the husband who pays me so I shall go back, but I mustn't talk about it because he told me to be... discreet. So I mustn't tell."

"Tell what?" He slipped in the question adroitly.

"About the Lieutenant and his letters and his visits and..." She let go Bresciano's arm and wagged her hands mockingly under Bresciano's nose. "Aha! You want me to tell, but I am like the grave – silent as the grave! I shall say nothing, you hear?"

He took the opportunity to move away before she could lay hold of him again: "That's right. You keep quiet about it. You're a sensible woman. You always were."

"Do you hear that?" she turned round and addressed the darkening street, supporting herself with a hand on the wall, suddenly oblivious of him. "This brave soldier knows that Emiliana can be trusted! He is an intelligent man. He knows me. I told his mother he would be a clever man. I knew him when he was a baby. I have washed his little bottom and I used to sing to him."

She began a lullaby and Bresciano backed off. There would be a better time to get sense out of her. He turned and strode quickly away, her drunken song and reminiscences hanging on the evening air behind him as he crossed the substantial Church Street with its fine two-storey houses with their balconies and solid doors, and turned into the narrower confines of Whirligig Lane where he stopped once he was out of Emiliana's sight.

The lane was lined with humbler dwellings of a single storey. It was known locally as the Street of the Seven Spins, which had puzzled him as a child as there were only two twists to the lane. Then he had learnt that the whirligig that stood at the entrance to the lane was what the 'spins' referred to: a woman convicted as a shrew or charged with immorality would be placed inside the wooden cage which would be spun round viciously. In an age of harsh punishments this simple device was particularly unpleasant, causing the victim to vomit and even defecate and lose all dignity. And though a man might also be placed in the whirligig, it was deemed a particularly suitable punishment for women. It had been removed with the siege when the cobbles had been dug up, but it was surely kept somewhere, and Bresciano wondered if Emiliana had considered that her possibly slanderous comments on Mrs Weston might land her in the whirligig.

In any case, Emiliana had given him something to think about that seemed to confirm the gossip that Jamie's vague ramblings had given rise to. While he was sure of nothing else that she had said, he believed her when she swore on her daughter's life that she had been discreet – certainly till now. Emiliana was superstitious and would believe that a vain oath would bring down disaster on her daughter's head. And now that she had been dismissed and was less than discreet, it seemed clear to him that something had gone on in the Weston household that could have given three people a motive for wishing Jamie dead. If what Emiliana hinted at was true, then there was a husband made to look ridiculous, and a lover and his mistress betrayed. And the word had spread as a result of Jamie's innocent reports of what he had seen.

He felt deeply satisfied at having three more definite suspects, then he realised he was collecting people as Lucia collected pretty religious cards – delighted with any new one that came her way. It was ridiculous. He needed to reduce the number of suspects, not increase them indefinitely. And if potential suspects were going to keep appearing like the plentiful Rock scorpions did when you turned stones over... He grunted as the enormity of his task struck him forcibly. He felt he was battling with an octopus of mythical proportions and with more than eight tentacles: how was he to control everything? It all seemed to be getting more complicated instead of clearer.

He attempted to review the day as he plodded up the rough track that led past the Blue Barracks and on uphill to his hut. He had spent most of it helping to shift several tons of limestone, but he had been able to establish that, though there had been deserters from the Spanish lines *into* Gibraltar, there had been no deserters leaving Gibraltar: no one trying to evade attention and ready to attack Jamie to silence him if he had spotted their flight. So much for Corporal Jones's theory, he thought smugly.

And he had found that Weston, his wife and the Lieutenant could be considered potential suspects. Perhaps not Mrs Weston, for women surely did not commit murder. He had also tracked down the source of his unease about that small box in the hut where a chair would have been needed for little Jamie to stand on if he was to tie the rope to the beam and put his head through the noose. That was the most satisfying deduction of all. It was proof. It was an incontrovertible fact. Jamie had been under five feet tall. Bresciano remembered that first night when he met Jamie. They had left the tavern, each with an arm round the other – Jamie's arm round Bresciano's waist and Bresciano's arm draped over Jamie's shoulders. There was no way that he could have got the rope over the beam and no way he could have put the noose around his neck without standing on something like a chair. Bresciano savoured his deduction: the box which the Sergeant had indicated was surely too small – it must have been a chair – and the two chairs in the hut were by the table at the other side of the room!

It had not been a bad day's work. He hadn't done so badly. Perhaps he had to be patient. Perhaps he should approach it as he did his games of chess when he played with his father. 'The game of the mind, a game for the nobility!' his father used to boast. And, where his father was an occasionally inspired but erratic player, Bresciano, less experienced and consequently more hesitant – took his time to consider the possibilities opened up by new moves. He rubbed the side of his nose and stopped for breath. Yes, he would try for patience.

Ahead of him were the lights of their small encampment. The darkness in his hut brought Jamie's death back to him. Resolutely, he moved to the mess house. He still had to check out Jamie's mood that morning by talking to the men.

The air in the mess house was acrid with the smell of old sweat and unwashed bodies. It mixed in with that of burning tobacco. He plunged in, determined not to show his distaste. This was army life, a life he had willingly embraced, and he had to make the best of it.

"You're a dark 'un an' no mistake, Busyano!" One of the men clapped him good-naturedly on the shoulder as he stepped inside. "You and that Emily cuddling, eh?"

"Not that Emiliana from Weston's house?"

"I tell you; saw them cuddling – with their arms round each other!"

Well! Listen to that, lads! An' our friend 'ere looking such an innercent."

"She's a bit old for you!"

"She's still a cosy armful, I'd say."

"Butter wouldn't melt in your mouth, would it?"

Bresciano blushed and would have denied it hotly, except that it was borne on him that to fall in with them, to accept their joke or suspicions – whichever it was – was to become one of them. It might work to his advantage. So he shrugged and grinned self-consciously before joining them. One of the men had found some wood, a luxury these days on a rocky peninsula denuded of firewood, and they sat round the fire they had built up against the cold.

They continued to make May game of him for a while, tired men with little enough to talk about. Then their desultory talk moved on to this and that.

"Tom never turned up for work today. We tried to cover up for 'im, but Sergeant knew. No getting anything past 'im."

"Not even Murch 'ere knew where 'e was, did you?"

"Tom's a lazy sod, 'e is."

"You're right there. An' we was short-handed what with

Jamie gone – he weren't much good, but it was an extra pair o' hands, like."

"Aye. Fancy 'im topping hisself like that. I'm not surprised, mind you. I seen 'im in the morning, sobbing away. Miserable 'e was. I reckon 'e done hisself in right enough."

"Can't see it meself. Saw 'im in the afternoon and 'e was that 'appy... going on about 'is friend comin' to visit."

"Well, all I say is I saw 'im in a right state in the morning."

"That were the Sergeant." A new voice joined in.

"Wot you talkin' about?"

"Din't you 'ear the Sergeant goin' on at 'im? Jamie went and broke two lanterns, that's all 'e did! I'm telling you, the Sarge was ripe for murder! Gave him a right mouthful, 'e did! Threatened 'im with a flogging if 'e caused any more damage."

"You can't hardly blame the Sarge – 'e's the one 'as got to answer for our stores an' the like."

A chorus of abuse met this defence of a man whose strict control and acid tongue had made him deeply unpopular with men thirsting to blame someone for their harsh living conditions and general discontent.

"Drove Jamie to top hisself, that's wot. Picking on the poor sod like 'e did."

"An' Jamie with no sense in that 'ead of 'is since that musket blew up."

"Balance of 'is mind was disturbed – that's wot 'e said! I know wot I think of that!"

"An' whose fault were that in the first place, eh?"

"I reckon you're right: drove Jamie to top hisself. Might just as well 'ave strung 'im up with 'is own 'ands."

There was a low rumble of agreement from most of the men. Then they moved on, some elaborating on the Sergeant's many sins and others dwelling on how they would love to teach him a lesson he wouldn't forget. Bresciano had heard enough. He went out into the cold darkness outside, unnoticed by the others, and walked reluctantly to his hut.

He struck a light and the flame flickered uncertainly – Jamie was lying on the floor! The light went out and Bresciano felt fear like a hammer-blow to the chest.

Forcing himself into stillness, he waited till his hands had stopped shaking, then struck a light again. There was certainly a body by the table, and the frayed rope still hung from the ceiling, for no one had bothered to return to the hut, but the figure was that of a burly man. Bresciano found the lantern, lit it and held it up. It was Tom lying there snoring quietly, an empty bottle of wine still in his hand.

Bresciano felt a sudden and powerful revulsion. It was not *a* bottle of wine. It was *the* bottle of wine: it was Jamie's bottle of wine, wine bought for some reason he had yet to fathom. He stood, biting his lip, muttering to himself, images of the morning's awful events moving across his mind: Jamie's body hanging, Jamie's body being carried out and men crowding round, staring, held by the fascination of disaster. Tom had not been among them, but Tom had been hovering in the background later when the others had left.

It could mean that he had been inside the hut, killed Jamie, then escaped out of the window and had... had... taken time to hide the key somewhere? It might be pure speculation, Bresciano thought, but it would be gratifying to find himself with another suspect. He pulled himself up short. He was doing it again: collecting pretty pictures like Lucia! Well, Tom might turn out to be a suspect, but perhaps not right now. He began muttering to himself: "More likely to have had his eye on free drink and was waiting for the hut to be empty to creep in and take the wine. Nothing suspicious in that. Tom probably drinks like a fish," he told himself severely.

It was disappointing, but a simple enough explanation. Now all he had to do was get Tom out of the hut. He shook him hard. Nothing. He tried again. Nothing. He put his arms round Tom's inert body and tried to drag him towards the door, grunting with the effort. The wretch was totally drunk. Dead to the world.

That did not make sense! With a start he straightened out, letting go of Tom whose body fell back with a thud. If Tom had come in to steal the wine, it must have been some time after Bresciano had gone to the Barracks. It must also have been before the working day began. He had never turned up for work. That meant that he had taken the wine early in the morning. Did that mean that he had downed the contents of the bottle – over half of it had been left – and then fallen over dead drunk? Impossible! The man must have a hard head. Anyone who regularly drank blackstrap would be immune to the effects of a few glasses of good wine.

He realised with a sense of triumph that there was only one possible explanation: the wine must have been drugged. There had been no need to overpower Jamie physically. Whoever had given him money to buy the wine had drugged it and then killed him – Jamie had been expecting a friend. That's what one of the men had said, that Jamie had been happy that afternoon because he was expecting a friend. It was clear. His friend had done it!

Bresciano groaned. Jamie had seen everyone as his friend, from Eliott to the Sergeant to the angels and probably to Murch, as likely as not. His heart sank – if Tom had drunk the wine, he could not have known it was drugged, hence, he could not have been the murderer. He did not know whether to be delighted with his deduction or annoyed at having lost a prime suspect. However, that still left Murch. It might mean that Murch had done his own dirty work... if he could have got out through the window! Impossible! Murch was still suffering the after-effects of the whipping.

He cast his eyes up in despair and found himself staring at the remains of the rope. He could not leave it there. It was a macabre reminder. Not that he needed reminding of Jamie's death. He looked down at his feet where Tom lay sound asleep. Let him stay where he was and sleep the night out on the floor.

The rope, however, was something he could deal with. Reaching up, he struggled to undo the knots that secured it to the beam. Even with his considerable height he could scarcely reach the beam. He pulled up the box and stood on it. Fishermen's knots – his father had taught him how to tie them – knots with interesting names, knots for different purposes, complex knots that he had delighted in mastering as a boy. He stepped back: knots, he thought grimly, that Jamie with his twisted left hand – a result of the musket explosion – could never have managed to tie. He left the rope where it was. One more fact. Proof again that it had not been suicide. How could anyone doubt that it was murder if he faced them with facts and not wild guesses or vague ideas?

He certainly had a few facts that clearly pointed to murder, but he couldn't go to the Sergeant – a prime suspect – and there was only Lieutenant Drinkwater – who had warned him off making hasty accusations. He thought bitterly that all he needed now, unaided, was to unravel a situation which he felt was beyond him. Abraham might be of help. He would seek him out him tomorrow, after he had seen Bianca... and how was he going to impress her with what was a puzzle to him? It was all demoralising. For the moment there was nothing for him to do, nothing he could do. Everything would have to wait till morning. His narrow bed could hardly be said to beckon, but it held the promise of temporary oblivion.

* * * *

When he awoke, it was still early, and even the guns were quiet this particular morning. He looked around, heavy-eyed, and found that Tom had gone, leaving the empty bottle on the floor, so he closed his eyes again and luxuriated in the silence and the fact that, it being Sunday, his time was his own for a few hours for the first time that week. What had seemed an impossible situation the night before took on a less negative aspect as the sun rose on a cold but bracingly dry day. The north wind might chill you, but it felt better than the sodden days when nothing dried and dressing in damp clothes made life a misery.

The first thing was to wash! He doused himself in cold water, shivering, but alert, using a hard piece of the soap that Nonna made, which was guaranteed to clean everything from floors to faces. He managed to catch and squash several of the bedbugs that were just one more unpleasant aspect of life. Then he shaved as best he could – not that there was much facial hair to deal with. Finally he settled down to clean his musket and then his shoes. All that remained was his crumpled uniform which he shook out vigorously; it was all he could do. With no firewood on which to heat the heavy irons, no one, not even the wives of officers, could afford to iron their clothes, creased after being washed, and washed in cold water at that. He might not look his best, but he would pass muster.

The sound of bells ringing sent him hurrying down to meet Bianca outside the Spanish Church, where he waited, standing erect, hoping his uniform and military bearing might have their effect on Bianca. The Mass had ended and a subdued and small Sunday crowd began to come out of church. Many citizens had moved into makeshift tents away from the town and the possible danger from enemy attack. He searched the crowd eagerly for Bianca, but there was someone who had arrived ahead of him. The Walloon she had favoured at the tavern was now escorting her out of church, his arm crooked so that she could thread her hand through it. "Proper little fop," muttered Bresciano. "Affected fop." He repeated the word with satisfaction. What could she see in such a fellow? Whatever it was, was making her smile and nod and, clearly, enjoy his company. Then she broke out into laughter. A few of the people near her looked at her, surprised – there was little enough to laugh at these days.

Bresciano was not in the mood to wait and he strode up, stuck his chin out, and addressed Bianca, ignoring the smiling Walloon.

"Bianca. Here I am, on the dot." His voice, meant to be light-hearted, came out truculently.

"This is your old friend, I think." The Walloon was ready to charm Bresciano too.

"Yes, I am her friend. Her very old friend. Very old." He knew he was making a fool of himself.

"Then, Miss Bianca, I shall leave you for the moment with your 'very, very old friend'. And I shall hope to see you later."

She slipped her hand off his arm and he took it between his hands, pressed it and raised it to his lips, keeping his eyes on her face till she looked away self-consciously. Then he strolled off, a handsome fellow with a beguiling twinkle in his eye.

"You might as well have kissed in public!" said Bresciano, forcing himself to sound scandalised.

"Giovanni! Don't start that again. First it was Corporal Jones – now there's a nice fellow. And now it's Robert… Robér' de la Tour." She aimed for a French pronunciation and succeeded admirably. "You just let me alone, you hear? It's none of your business. You have no right to tell me what to do – you are not my brother!"

The knowledge that her brother was the last thing he wanted to be held him silent.

"Come on," she took his arm, "stop grousing and tell me what it was you wanted to talk about."

"Come away. There are too many people here and what I have to say is for your ears alone."

She looked amused, but intrigued, and he walked her away from Church Street and into the nearby Bomb House Lane. There he stopped and turned to face her. He would be clear, decisive and impressive:

"Jamie Macfarlane is dead!"

"I know – I heard. Poor Sparrow, poor Jamie. I really had a soft spot for him. Bless him. To kill himself like that. Makes you think – I wish I'd been kinder to him, slipped him the odd free drink when he had no money."

"Jamie didn't commit suicide," he spoke with dramatic deliberation, "he was murdered!"

"What! Not that again! Giovanni, what's wrong with you? Who would want to murder an inoffensive lad like him? The other night you made a right fool of yourself when Jamie fell over that wall. I mean, imagine accusing a man who could barely walk and who had plenty of witnesses swearing he hadn't moved out of their sight. Now you've gone one worse... murder! murder! If that's all you've got to say, I'm leaving."

Her disbelief stung him and he abandoned the grand manner.

"No, Bianca, in truth, you have to believe me. I've got proof now."

"Proof of what? That that old scoundrel, Murch, was helped by one of Jamie's angels?"

"No, no. I know it wasn't Murch. That was a mistake. But I know that this was murder. I can prove it. Just listen to me."

She was moved by his pleading as she had not been by his histrionics, and he hurried into an account of what he had found: the missing key, the knots in the rope, the drugged wine, the absence of a chair and the impossibility of Jamie hanging himself with a noose that hung well out of his reach. She heard him out, not entirely convinced, not even listening too closely to what he said.

"I don't know, Giovanni. I can see what you mean, but there's no reason for it, is there? I mean – who could have a motive for killing him? If anyone had taken against him, they could just have beaten him up or something. Teach him a lesson, but not murder him. That's the way things generally happen here. I've bandaged more than one sore head this past year. This damned siege is making everyone short tempered.

And that chair business – what if someone came in, saw Jamie had hanged himself and got frightened… and locked the door and maybe picked up the chair. It's the kind of thing you do without thinking – straighten things. Then you came along and started banging on the door and the person panicked and got out."

"But…"

"And you're just guessing that the wine was drugged. Knowing Tom, he could've had a skinful before he drank the wine, morning or no morning. I think you're barking up the wrong tree. You should leave well alone, Giovanni. It's a serious business is suicide – or murder. And you certainly shouldn't be making a fuss. As Rober' says," she lingered over the vowels of his name, "'Get over heavy ground lightly.' That's what they do in the cavalry. He was in a cavalry regiment. Says the French don't understand cavalry like the English do. It's funny. There he is, French army, speaking French, and it sounds really nice when he does, and hates the French like poison. It's a bit like some Scots hating the English – that's what he said. Remember when we were small… that soldier we knew… Private… what was his name? Ferguson! He used to say something that made me laugh. Ah, I remember! 'I've taken the King's shilling and if I could, I'd stuff it up the old swine's bum'!"

"Bianca!"

"Don't be so fusty. You used to laugh as well."

"That was then. We're grown up now. I don't like it when you swear."

"I can be a lady when I need to. In fact, Rober' was saying that I'm too refined to work in that tavern. He's seen the world and he mistook me for the owner when he first came in, a week ago it was. Said I was too good for that place. There's a real gentleman for you. And a brave one. Escaping from the Spanish lines and risking his life to get here! All because he was determined to serve under the British flag."

"Yes, I know – you told me before, remember?"

"You should like him, you know. He's also very clever. Look how well he speaks English."

"Yes, yes, yes… very brave, very clever, wonderful fellow."

"There's no talking to you today, is there? What's wrong

with you? Are you jealous of Rober' or something?"

"Me, jealous? Of a little dressed-up fop like him?"

"Grow up, Giovanni – he's well built and… and what's wrong with trying to look smart? He cares how he looks – not like you – he's a man with… presence. He's strong and he's… oh, he's *simpático* and he knows how to treat a lady. And you – you are just being boorish! Being a beanpole and living in Waterport Street with the 'gentry' doesn't make you better than everyone else."

"But, but…"

"And if you're not interested in my opinions or in anything I have to say, I don't know what I'm doing here."

"And you don't believe anything I say. Lieutenant Drinkwater thought I made sense. He was willing to accept my ideas, so why can't you?"

"Maybe because I know you better. You and that imagination of yours. You should let things alone. Jamie, poor lamb, was never too bright and he was plain daft after his accident. And falling off that wall must have knocked what little sense he had straight out of him. And this life we're leading would depress anybody. I can't remember the last time I felt warm and with a really full belly. You people in the army are lucky – you have your rations, but many's the night I've gone to bed on an empty stomach and woken up to a bare food cupboard. But as for Jamie, I wasn't surprised to hear he had killed himself. And he wouldn't be the first one, would he? How many suicides have there been this year, eh? It's this damned siege. Face it. Everyone thinks it's suicide Why do you have to be different?"

Bresciano shrugged. As far as he could see, she was determined not to be convinced. "Fine. Fine. I'll see you back to your house."

"Don't bother. I'm not going there right now." She looked a little self-conscious.

"I suppose you're off to see your wonderful, wonderful Walloon, your 'Robair'." He mocked her pronunciation clumsily.

"And what if I am?" She snapped, "He's better company than you are." And she flounced off.

He stared after her and hit the wall beside him hard with his open hand. All he had to look forward to now was a parade of his company just up the road and round the corner, at the site of the whipping post where Murch had been flogged. The street was almost clear of people. The roads, still muddy from the recent rains, discouraged most people from venturing out. He would go to the parade, then try to see Abraham Hassan. It would be a relief to talk to someone who wouldn't fall over himself describing Robert de la Bloody Tour's many virtues.

It was fortunate that he was free after the parade as Abraham proved hard to find. He had been helping interrogate a Spaniard who had deserted from the Spanish lines a couple of weeks earlier. The man spoke little English and Abraham had acted as interpreter.

Unfortunately, as Bresciano went through his reasons for dismissing the idea of suicide, he got a tepid response. When Bresciano taxed him with inattention, he apologised:

"I have a lot on my mind. I managed to see my family last night as they sat down to the Sabbath meal and it brought home to me how bad things are. They will not, cannot, eat the salted meat available, it's mainly pork, and you know how scarce everything else is. I worry about them all the time. If only a ship could run the blockade and come in laden with beef and mutton. I even dream of it. Or perhaps there will be another opportunity for civilians to leave the Rock."

Bresciano sympathised and realised that his friend was about to move off.

"Wait!" he said, "I want your advice."

But Abraham was little better than Bianca when Bresciano listed his suspects.

"Say something, Abraham. What do you think?" He was finding his friend less than sympathetic.

"I'm not sure. You have given me a number of names of people who might have had a grudge against Jamie, but have you cited a single powerful motive? And you have a vague idea of who might have had the opportunity to kill him, but where is the proof? You will have to find out more about your suspects. And be careful, Giovanni; you had better have some very convincing proof before you accuse anyone of murder, let alone an officer or even a sergeant! This sort of work – uncovering a hidden truth – requires a high degree of skill." He sounded almost smug.

"I know," Bresciano said sombrely. "I have no idea how

I'll find proof, but I will – I must! And if it isn't one of those I have mentioned, who could it be? There is the 'friend' that Jamie said he was going to meet – that doesn't sound quite as if it was one of the people I have mentioned, but knowing Jamie, this 'friend' could have been anyone of those, or anyone else, or may have existed only in his imagination. And in any case, if he was a real friend, why should he want to kill Jamie?"

"Well, I wish you luck in your investigation"

"Abraham, what's wrong with you? You're not really interested, are you? You aren't helping me to think. You're just nodding your head, but your mind is elsewhere."

"I'm sorry, Bresciano. You're right. It's that I have to get back to barracks. It's…" He hesitated. "Just keep this under your hat, all right? This deserter I've been helping with… he's under lock and key because there's a good chance that he may not be…" he hesitated, "…as innocent as at first appeared. For the present we are keeping everything under wraps."

He found it hard to keep the pride out of his voice. He, Abraham Hassan, was engaged on what amounted to a secret mission. He stood up.

"Anyway, you keep on investigating. And I do have one piece of advice: look for a real motive. With this sp… man we have on our hands it seems to have been money. In what my captain called a premeditated crime, there's a reason behind what people do. In a violent crime committed in blind fury it is different. Jamie's killing seems something someone planned, doesn't it? Look for a reason – so far you have only suggested vague ideas as to why your suspects might have wanted Jamie dead, but it is no more than speculation. Remember – be logical. And if I think of anything, I'll let you know. Now I really must get back."

He was gone and Bresciano felt the anger of frustration and envy. Everyone but him was of some importance. Abraham was valuable to the army. That bloody Walloon was important to Bianca. And he was just a standing joke with his fellow Artificers.

"Right, then," he mumbled morosely, "I'll do it alone."

Motive? He had enough motives… hate and revenge seemed good enough to him. The place to start at would be investigating all his suspects and finding out where they had been when Jamie was being murdered. It was unlikely to be

Mrs Weston – unless she turned out to be a veritable Amazon, but she might have egged the Lieutenant on. That left him with four men. At least he'd eliminated Tom, and Murch was looking less and less like a suspect. That would cut down his work. And as for the possible deserter – there had been no deserter.

But there had! There had been three! Deserters worked both ways. Some escaped from the fortress and others sought refuge in the fortress. And look at Abraham's deserter – a spy, no less. What was to stop the Walloons from being spies too?

Even as he framed the thought, he was aware of his ulterior motive in entertaining such a far-fetched idea. After all, why should a possible spy risk his mission – and his life – by murdering the inoffensive Jamie?

He put aside these doubts: he would need to check out all three thoroughly, without arousing their suspicions. He would also have to be very careful. Naturally, he told himself, he would be as logical and objective as possible. He smiled: poor Bianca – it would be dreadful for her if the heroic Robert de la Tour turned out to be just a common murderer!

He set off with a spring to his step.

CHAPTER VI

Bresciano's newfound enthusiasm lasted only as far as Grand Parade, the main square of the town, a handsome open space. He stopped, thunderstruck, as he suddenly remembered that the time for Jamie's funeral had been set for sunrise on that morning – and he had forgotten! He had fully intended to be there to say his last farewells. Once again he had failed Jamie.

He turned off Waterport Street and up Whirligig Lane towards the Blue Barracks; perhaps he would find the chaplain still there, conducting a Sunday service for the men of the Artificers. He knew that Scotsmen followed their own version of the Protestant faith – perhaps there was a Scottish chaplain he could talk to, someone who could tell him more about Jamie. Even as he thought of it he knew that what he wanted was forgiveness for having forgotten poor Jamie.

He was in luck. The chaplain had just finished his service, and Bresciano, slightly out of breath from hurrying up the hill, approached him as the men dispersed. The chaplain was a little man with bristling red hair and bulging eyes that looked permanently startled, giving him the look – Bresciano thought irreverently – of a panic-stricken sea bream.

"What I can do for you, mine man!" His voice boomed, a deep baritone, a voice at odds with his slender frame. "You are late. The service you have missed," he said severely. The accent was thick, but it was not a Scottish brogue; it was distinctly Germanic.

"My friend – Jamie MacFarlane – funeral…" Bresciano tried to catch his breath. "Was he buried by the Scottish minister?"

"Nein, Artificer MacFarlane this morning early I have buried. There is no Scottish minister. No Scottish regiment, so no Scottish minister, yes? I am pastor for Hardenburg's Regiment from Hanover, and I have a good Lutheran funeral given him. So, what you did wish to know?"

This was another dead end, then. With little hope, Bresciano essayed "Then, you did not know him before...?"

"Nein, I did not know him. I asked his commanding officer what was good I could say about him, and he said 'Say that everybody have like him.' The officer said that of no family he knew, but that he of a good friend from Scotland had heard him talk, but who the friend it was he did not know. He said that Macfarlane talked of many friends, but that he was disturbed in his mind and these friends surely in his head only exist. Now, you tell me. Why to mine service have you not come?"

"I am a Roman Catholic. I have just come from the Spanish Church," Bresciano said, stretching the truth only mildly.

The German pastor frowned, but said no more, and Bresciano wandered off. He headed for the room where he had last seen Jamie's body, but it was empty now. He wanted to sit and think, but not in that characterless room where bodies were laid out with no one to mourn them. He walked out heavily and made his way down the passage, past a large room from which came the groans of weakened men, some with the scurvy that was eventually to claim more lives during the siege than did any battle wounds. These were men excused duties, but were not sufficiently ill to be transferred to hospital, yet the very air seemed foetid and he plunged away up the first stairway he found and then through the first doorway he came to.

He found himself in a small room, a store-room by the look of it, which contained only some empty sacks and a stool. Bresciano sat and leaned his head back against the wall. He needed to think, but his mind remained blank. As he stretched his legs, he kicked on one of the sacks: a round object rolled out of it.

Bresciano stared at it. A round yellow object – it was a lemon! His hands shaking, he leaned forward and pulled the sack towards him, and put his hand inside. There were five –

no, six lemons. The peel looked dry, as if they had been there for some time, but they had not rotted. He remembered that a Danish boat had been captured a month earlier, laden with lemons and oranges, which had been commandeered by the Governor and distributed to the regiments to ward off scurvy. This sack must have been one of those allotted to the Artificers and discarded under the impression that it was empty.

Lemons! But this is what his mother needed to make her better – his mother and Lucia. He rose and looked out of the room. There was no one to be seen. He began to slip the lemons into his pack and suddenly his hand stopped in midair: he had just stolen food belonging to the army. If caught, he would receive a flogging if he was lucky, or, he blenched at the thought of the more frightening but definite possibility, he might even be executed for the offence. The fact that he was doing it for his family and not for himself, would not help him: theft was theft. He set his jaw. He had to do this, whatever the consequences, for Lucia's sake and for his mother's. He hefted the pack and walked out of the room, his heart pounding.

He was in luck. There was no one around to be seen or to see him, and he made his way down the hill until he arrived at his home in Waterport Street. He walked straight into the kitchen and unloaded his pack. His mother came out of Lucia's room and her eyes widened when she saw the six lemons on the table.

"Where... how... how did you get those, Giovanni?"

Bresciano should have had a story prepared, but in his exultation at finding the lemons he had neglected to think of one. He hesitated, then stuttered "I – I told one of the officers that my sister was sick and he said I could have them to give to her... Yes. That's what he said."

His mother, clearly disbelieving, opened her mouth to say something, but his father, who had followed her into the kitchen, interrupted,

"Ah, yes, Giovanni, you were telling me yesterday of the officer, Drink... water, was it not? who has befriended you. No doubt he has given you these in exchange for the books, no? It is good to make friends with officers, eh!" He clapped his son on the back and gave him a warning look. Eleanor said no more.

Bresciano recalled his earlier conversation with his father

and what his father had said about stealing food. Something like – 'for your sister and your mother'. Well, perhaps he was more like his father than he cared to believe. At this moment Nonna Lucrezia burst out of Lucia's room, crying out, "She is burning up with fever, poor mite... raving. Oh, oh, I am so afraid for her!" She burst into sobs and Giancarlo led her to the kitchen chair into which she collapsed.

Lucia was writhing around in the bed, her whole body bathed in sweat. Bresciano could see that the pocks on her face and arms had filled with a clear fluid which was already beginning to turn cloudy.

"Her fever should be down by now, so long after the rash came," Eleanor said faintly. "I fear that because of her weakness, she has developed some complication. What are we to do?" She held out her hands to her husband and her son.

Bresciano's heart went out to her. In all his years, she had always been the one to advise him when he was in trouble. Now, she needed him.

"Mother, do not worry." He took her hand, feeling how inadequate such reassurance was. "You must... you should... do what they do in hospital. Make her have one of the lemons, and I think you will see her get better. And have one yourself," he added quickly. "Make her suck it."

"The child cannot suck a lemon, Giovanni! She must be made to drink the juice." His father reprimanded his ignorance, reverting to his usual manner with his son.

Eleanor nodded mutely, and left the room. Giovanni sat by his sister, and bathed her brow with a cloth which Nonna Lucrezia had placed in a bowl of cold water by the bedside. Gradually Lucia calmed down, and opened her eyes.

"Giovanni, is it you, Giovanni? I'm so glad to see you. I feel bad, so tired..." She began to weep quietly.

"None of that, little Lu." He used the pet name which she had had as a baby, and which in later years had always infuriated her when he used it to tease her. "I've left important military duties to come and visit you. I said to Governor Eliott, 'You must manage without me, sir. I have to visit my Lu!' So here I am, a heroic soldier come especially to visit you. I'm afraid I left poor old Governor Eliott in tears, but *you* must not cry!" His nonsense made her smile faintly, and he continued, "Mother has just gone to prepare you a drink which will make you feel better. "It's a magic potion I purchased earlier today."

At this moment Eleanor returned, bearing a cup. "They are quite juicy, those lemons. I squeezed one and mixed it with water and a little honey that we had left."

"Good. If you give me the cup, I will help Lucia to drink it. And Mother, you go back to the kitchen and make the same drink for yourself," Bresciano said firmly. "Do as I say."

Eleanor looked at her gangling son with affection and amusement. He was truly a man now, she thought. "Yes, dear," she said, and left.

"Lemons," Lucia said faintly. "You brought them, didn't you, Giovanni? But that's not a magic potion."

"Of course it is – magic lemons! Now drink up before I turn you into a frog."

She giggled weakly and he brought the cup next to her lips. Slowly she began to sip from it, pulling a face at the tartness of the drink, but making no other protest. When she had finished it, she lay back and closed her eyes. She was calm now, and did not appear to be so hot. Bresciano stayed sitting by her side, watching her.

Gradually his mind began to move over the events of the previous few days as he considered his suspects – and he was brought up against his actions at the Barracks hospital. He felt ashamed. He felt guilty. There had been men in that hospital section still suffering from scurvy, men who needed the lemons he had taken. He had turned thief, however good his reasons: he was no better than Murch.

It made him less inclined to regard Murch in the same light as he had done earlier. In a way, he had acquired a fellow-feeling for the man, for they were both thieves, weren't they? It was true that Murch had been caught pilfering in the past, but a thief was surely very different to a murderer.

His eyes closed, and he dozed off in the chair.

*   *   *   *

When he woke, it was mid-afternoon. Lucia was still sleeping peacefully. His father was smoking his pipe in the kitchen and of his mother there was no sign: perhaps she would now be able to get some much-needed rest. His father looked fixedly at his son.

"Giovanni. I know you. You with your head stuffed with

those stories your mother told you when you were small. King Arthur and knights and *onore e gloria*. Very nice stories. In life it is not always like that, eh? So you don't worry. Listen to your father – those lemons… we say nothing to your mother. Sometimes a man has to do things he does not like. *Sì?*"

Bresciano nodded. On impulse he decided to ask his father's opinion. He chose, nevertheless, to be cautious:

"Papa, there is a… puzzle I wanted to ask you about."

"A good puzzle? What is it?"

"The men were talking about it yesterday… um… let me see if I remember…" he was hesitant as he constructed the supposed puzzle. "It starts with a very poor man… with a withered left hand, who has a rope. He is a short man, a bit taller than Nonna. He is found hanging from a high beam, a high one like the ones in our shop store-room. The rope is secured with fishermen's knots. Beside him, on the ground, is a small box this high," he indicated the height with his hand, "and on a table nearby is… er… some food gathered for a meal. Oh, yes, and a bottle of expensive wine, half drunk."

His father was leaning forward and listening attentively: he too enjoyed puzzles.

"The door is locked, but there is no key in the lock or on the body or anywhere in the room. Now, the men wanted me to guess why the little man had committed suicide. I think they were laughing at me."

Giancarlo drew on his pipe slowly, savouring the challenge. "And was there a noose? Tell me again, slowly."

Bresciano obliged, a little nervously which made him stumble uncertainly.

"My son," Giancarlo leaned back in his chair with an air of satisfaction as he blew out a long column of smoke, "those comrades of yours were doing what they always do to the new young man who joins any group – they were teasing you. Every man has to be made a fool of before he is accepted. You see," he was enjoying scoring over his clever son, "the story they told you does not make sense."

"I wondered about that."

"Listen carefully:" he ticked the points off on his hand, pointing with his pipe, "first is the fact that a man with a withered hand cannot tie complicated knots; and secondly he is too short, even with that box you mentioned, to reach the noose; and also perhaps a man with food and good drink does not, I think, have suicide in mind."

"Of course! And... how can a poor man afford expensive wine?"

Giancarlo slapped his son's knee, "Aha! I missed that one!"

"Thank you, Papa. Oh, I was forgetting. What do you make of the missing key?"

"Why do you lock a door? Because you do not wish to be disturbed. Someone locked the door and took the key away. It cannot be the hanging man. You see? It does not make sense. That is the point of it. You go back to those friends of yours and tell them so."

"Excellent! I shall do so."

He was genuinely grateful to his father for confirming his own suspicions. At last he had had someone listening to him intelligently. However, he noticed something in his father's tone, which, together with a slightly raised eyebrow, made him wonder if Giancarlo had swallowed his tale of a 'puzzle' set by his mates to fool him. Bresciano rose to leave, but his father detained him a few seconds, his hand on his son's arm.

"And about those lemons you brought your mother – you tell none of your companions in the army about them. I know you have no money to buy, and I have seen none for sale. A man keeps his own counsel, do you hear? And be careful, Giovanni, will you?"

Bresciano left the house quietly. His father's complicity served to convince him that he was forgiven for having joined up, and he thought wryly that it had taken a lack of principle to do it. His father accepted the theft of the lemons, but Bresciano could not forgive himself. However, it was done and he could not wish his theft undone if it helped Lucia. Suddenly he found himself smiling: 'a man has to do things.' 'A man keeps his own counsel.' His father had not called him a boy as he so often did. 'A man.' He savoured the moment before setting off at a brisk walk.

He had better make the most of the rest of Sunday, he thought. Tomorrow he would be hard at work in the King's Bastion or at Willis's Batteries and would have little time for investigation, or for anything else.

He made his way to Irish Town, gnawing at the sour

bread he had put in his pack and wondering if he would ever get used to the sickening hollow feeling of hunger. He went directly to the wine-house where Bianca worked. Perhaps he could speak to her and try to repair the damage of the morning. He found her behind the bar. There were only a few soldiers drinking at two of the tables. No one he knew, he was glad to see; he might take jibes against himself, but was in no mood for jokes and innuendos about himself and Emiliana. That would embarrass him vilely with Bianca present – and what of Bianca herself?

He approached her uncertainly, but Bianca was friendly enough, greeting him with one of the open smiles he remembered fondly from his youth, smiles that lit up her face – so unlike the slow, languorous look which she affected nowadays.

"Did you hear, Giovanni? The soldiers are all talking about it. Someone shot at General Eliott!"

"No!" Bresciano was shocked. "Was he...? Is he...?" He could not bring himself to put it into words.

"No, no, he is all right," Bianca hastened to explain. "He was coming out of King's Chapel after the service when a shot was heard. By the greatest good fortune, one of the General's cats ran out of the door of the Convent to greet him at that moment and he bent down to pick it up just as the ball smashed into the wall above his head."

"Thank God!" Giovanni said fervently. "But have they caught the man who did it? Who could it have been?"

"No, they haven't caught him yet. They think it may be a mutinous soldier, or a spy, or a soldier with a grudge. You know how angry people are with General Eliott for refusing to allow soldiers and even their children to be inoculated against smallpox. I know someone in my street who has lost two children. Can you imagine?"

"I know. Our Lucia has got it now. It's terrible."

"I am sorry to hear that." She covered his hand with hers, her eyes full of concern. Then she said angrily, "Eliott is a pig-headed man. He should have let people in the army decide for themselves if they wanted to be inoculated or not. No wonder someone shot at him. I think I would if my children had died."

"So nobody knows who did it?"

"I told you... they just don't know. The Town Major

has determined that the shot was fired from the roof of an empty house in Crooked Billet Lane, a house just opposite the Convent, but by the time they searched the place, there was no one there."

Before Bresciano could enquire further, there was a disturbance as Tom staggered through the door and fell heavily against the wall. He straightened himself with difficulty and lurched to the bar.

"Gi' ush a drink o' rum then." He stared owlishly around, gradually focussing his gaze on Bresciano. "And one for old Bizhi – Busyano here. Gives us plenty of laughs, 'e does. Yeah… gi' old Busyano a drink."

"You show me the colour of your money first," Bianca was used to dealing with such situations.

"Tom's got plenty of… of cash today." He slapped a coin on the counter with an air of triumph.

Rolling her eyes at Bresciano, Bianca put a glass in front of each of them. Bresciano looked at his with distaste and pushed it away: that first night with Jamie had put him off strong drink. Tom turned to Bresciano and breathed fumes of alcohol over him. He had a silver chain around his neck and he now pulled it out, revealing a misshapen lump of metal hanging from it.

"Know what thish is?" he rambled. "It'sh Tom's lucky charm, it is. Ball hit me on the chest – up in Shcotland, it were, when we was clearing out them Jacobite rebels. Shtill a lot of the buggers around, there are. Hit me in the chest, it did, and got buried in the bone, right here" he thumped his chest and was taken by a fit of unpleasantly raw coughing. "Sawbones said it were a bloody miracle I wash shtill alive. A bloody miracle! Took it out and give it to me, he did. 'Tom,' he shaid, 'here'sh your lucky charm'. Sho I put it on a shilver chain – took that off a Highlander I killed, I did – but now Lucky Tom ish goin' to buy drinksh for everyone, an' I'll buy a gold chain for my lucky charm…" His rambling became incoherent, and he slumped over the bar.

Meanwhile, the room had filled up. Sergeant Connor was at the other end of the bar, nursing a mug of ale, and the three Walloons had arrived together, as usual, and came up to talk to Bianca. With a look of disdain at Tom, one of them said to her, "Why you do not get rid of this?" His Spanish was thickly accented.

Bianca looked around. Bresciano was about to say that he would take Tom outside – anything to get back in Bianca's good books – when the Sergeant came up.

"He's one of my men," he growled. "I'll get rid of him for you."

Two slaps on the face restored Tom to a measure of consciousness, and Connor frog-marched him out of the door and disappeared with him.

"I wish I was in the money like this Tom," Robert declared. "Because then I could buy drinks for all you good defenders of this Rock." With a comic look of dismay, he pulled out his empty pockets, and Bianca smiled at his clowning.

"Never mind, Robért, here is a drink for you. You can pay me later, when you have money."

Bresciano saw his chance of a quiet talk with Bianca vanish. He looked at that Rob-air with his infectious smile and dimpled chin. He could not bear to remain in the wine-house any longer. With a curt farewell to Bianca, he left, conscious that he was leaving this wretched Walloon a free field, but unable to do anything about it.

"Deserters!" he muttered. "That's what they are, just deserters! Maybe… maybe this Rob-air is a spy. The spy who tried to kill Eliott! Immediately, he felt foolish for allowing his emotions to run away with him. Just because one of these Walloons was cutting him out with Bianca… why, he might as well suspect Corporal Jones for the same reason! 'Be logical,' Abraham Hassan had said. He walked over to the Line Wall, and sat on the ramparts, looking out towards the Bay.

Who were his suspects now? Murch and Tom did not seem to be likely candidates any longer, so all he had left were Sergeant Connor, Lieutenant Black, and Captain Weston and his wife. And the Walloons, of course.

Why would Sergeant Connor want to kill one of his own men? Bresciano realised that he knew almost nothing about the Sergeant. Perhaps he could engage Corporal Jones in casual conversation; he might know something about his Sergeant's past.

What about Lieutenant Black? Bresciano had seen him only once with his fellow lieutenants and once when he had entered the wine-house looking for Jamie. He certainly had a motive – he appeared to know that Jamie was the source of rumours about his relationship with Mrs Weston, and might well have wanted to silence the little Scotsman to prevent further gossip being spread

And the Westons? Bresciano didn't even know what they looked like. Mrs Weston might have perhaps egged the Lieutenant on to murder in order to conceal their affair; and what about her husband? Perhaps if he felt his honour had been besmirched, he would have been more likely to take it out on the Lieutenant or his wife, rather than attack a simple-minded gossip. But you never knew what a man was capable of, Bresciano thought with his unpleasant new-found knowledge of himself.

What about opportunity? The Sergeant had certainly been at hand when Jamie had taken that potentially fatal fall, and when Jamie had been found dead. But he had no idea whether Lieutenant Black or the Westons could have been anywhere nearby on those two occasions.

Clearly, he would have to find out more about Black and the Westons, but he had no idea how to go about it.

With a sigh, he got up and walked off aimlessly, less than eager to wend his way up the hill towards his temporary billet at Willis's. It was late on this Sunday evening and the streets were silent and deserted. As he reached the Green Market, its stalls closed on the Sunday, he heard a commotion and raised voices on the other side of the street. He turned towards the sound and saw Emiliana leaving one of the grey stone buildings which were officers' quarters, shouting angrily over her shoulder at a woman who was about to close the front door on her. Bresciano recognised her as Lola, another old neighbour from his Buena Vista days. This must be Captain Weston's quarter, and Lola must have replaced Emiliana as their maid. His theory was confirmed by Emiliana's aggrieved tones.

"You are lying, Lola! She is not ill, she just doesn't want to see me, because of what I know! Or you are lying, because you know that if I talk to her she will have to give me my job back! No matter, I will go and find the *Capitán*, and tell him what his wife is up to! Then she will see!"

She stamped off furiously; in her heart of hearts she must know that it was her slatternly ways that had lost her the employment, a fact which, perhaps unsurprisingly, made her all the angrier at Mrs Weston. As she had told Bresciano, she had been discreet in her own way for while she surely hadn't cared what the Captain's wife did or didn't do, she knew she had a regular wage that she could depend on. Now, her wage lost and the chance of new employment being unlikely, she was lashing out at the woman she had served. Bresciano hoped that her drunken ramblings did not come to Captain Weston's ears, or it might be the worse for her. Perhaps he had better warn her. He put out his hand to stop her, but she stormed past him, unseeing, and he set off in pursuit, but ran into another man approaching the quarter.

"Hey, hey. Giovanni. Why are you in such a hurry always?"

Bresciano recognised Dr Coll, the local general practitioner whom his family sometimes consulted in time of illness, and a particularly loquacious man. He cursed under his breath. Emiliana had disappeared into the warren of side streets around the Green Market, and he would never catch up with her now.

"I see you have joined the army, Giovanni. Well done, well done. We must all pull together if we are to withstand this blockade. Look at me: tonight I am serving the army too! I have been asked to see Captain Weston's wife because Dr Baines is too busy in the hospital. It seems that the beautiful Mrs Weston has fallen down the stairs – again! Poor woman!"

"What do you mean 'again'?" Bresciano asked, curious in spite of his haste. "Does she have the falling sickness?"

"No, no, not exactly, Giovanni," the doctor said with a laugh, "But I must say no more – professional discretion, don't you know. Perhaps I should not have said even that." Changing the subject, Dr Coll asked about Bresciano's family. "So, tell me, how is Nonna? Your sister has the smallpox, I hear. Dreadful business. And your mother? How are things with her? Not that anyone is too well in these hard times, eh? My wife, poor woman, spends her life lying down. She cannot keep down the sort of food available to us nowadays. Always was very particular about what she ate. A delicate constitution, except when it comes to sweetmeats!" He laughed. "And look at you! You are too thin, far too thin. We have to eat what we can. Better a bad meal than no meal at all, that's what I say."

He was a man more interested in what he himself had to say than in listening to any replies, but Bresciano broke in, anxious to ask about the lemons which he had acquired for Lucia and his mother.

Dr Coll smiled approval as Giovanni told him that, on his advice, the family had managed to buy a few lemons.

"You should be a doctor, Giovanni. Well done indeed. That is the latest treatment for scurvy, I am told, and though I prefer the old, tried and tested remedies, I must admit that the lemon treatment is often remarkably effective. I know what – I will speak with your father and tell him that I am willing to take you on as an apprentice!" He laughed, much amused by his witticism, "But now, enough talk. You must delay me no further. I must go and see to the unfortunate Mrs Weston!"

He went up to the Westons' quarter and knocked on the door, leaving Bresciano standing there.

By now night was falling and Bresciano continued on his way. He found Willis's almost deserted. Most of the men were probably still in town, getting drunk, and only Corporal Jones was sitting on a stool outside the main hut, smoking his pipe.

"It's a warm night for December, look you," the Corporal said amiably. "Why don't you sit outside for a while with me?"

Bresciano assented. His resentment about Jones cutting him out with Bianca hardly mattered now that it seemed as if that damned Walloon had supplanted Jones in Bianca's affection. And, in any case, he had intended to get some information from the man. He resolved to be careful and not go directly to the subject of Jamie's death.

They sat in silence for a few minutes, the only light coming from the stars and the glow of Jones's pipe.

"Do you smoke, lad? I have a spare pipe if you'd like. It is a capital aid to contemplation. And it makes a man forget his belly."

Bresciano shook his head and then, realising that the Welshman could not see him, said politely, "No, thank you, I have never acquired the habit."

It was Corporal Jones who raised the subject of Jamie. "Sad, it was, the lad dying like that. I've seen death often before, but a man taking his own life – God's gift – it's different. Worse, somehow. A tragic waste. He was your friend, was he not?"

"I'd only known him for a few days," Bresciano replied. "But yes, I think he was my friend." He wanted to add more, but was cautious, and they sat in silence again.

After a while, Bresciano decided to ask about Sergeant Connor. He realised that he could not ask about him directly, so he began, "Tom got beastly drunk in town today and Sergeant had to take him away. Did he bring him up here?"

The glow of Jones's pipe moved sideways as he shook his head. "No one has come back up here yet. It may be that he took him to the Blue Barracks, before going on to the cemetery."

"The cemetery?"

"Aye, Sergeant Connor goes there every Sunday evening to visit his wife's grave."

"I didn't know he'd been married." It was difficult to imagine the Sergeant with his granite face as a loving husband.

"Married late. Never been one for the ladies. Only married for two years. And his wife, a lovely girl she was, died in childbirth, near a year ago. Child died too."

This was an aspect of the Sergeant which Bresciano had not been aware of. As he digested this new information, Jones continued,

"He's always had a temper on him, long as I've known him, but he went quiet and dry and bitter after she died. Like a man carrying something dead inside him. Yes, he became a harder man. Always fair, mind you – in his own way – but harder." He sucked on his pipe, and then added thoughtfully, "Made him a better sergeant, perhaps. More to be feared, at any rate."

"He was hard on Jamie, wasn't he?" Bresciano began tentatively.

"Aye, well, Jamie could try the patience of a saint at times. You never saw Jamie when he was telling the Sergeant to repent and be saved from hell fire, did you? Him and his angels! But, to my way of thinking, Sergeant was always fair with him, fair enough... for all he can't abide Scotsmen."

"He doesn't like Scotsmen?" Bresciano repeated, feeling excitement growing in him. "Why ever not?"

Corporal Jones had settled down to the role of narrator, something respected back in Wales – a land of bards and poets and not like this barren alien place. He was enjoying being the purveyor of information and glad enough to be talking sensibly, away from the bawdy talk in the mess hut and the constant complaints about work and lack of food.

"I've heard tell that it was because of his father, see. He was a sergeant too, under the Duke of Cumberland and General Wade during the Scottish rebellion of '45. He fought at Culloden and it was after the battle of Culloden."

He smiled at Bresciano's imagined incomprehension. "You probably don't know what I'm talking about, do you, lad? Let's see. You've heard of the Scottish rebellion? And Bonnie Prince Charlie? Right, then. Well, he was defeated and had fled and the rebellion was over, or so they thought. Some time after, they say, two of those Highlanders made up to Connor's father. He was seen in their company one night. Liked his drink, I believe. It was the last time he was seen alive. His men found him next morning, cut to bits."

"How could they be so brutal?" Bresciano asked, shocked at the picture the Corporal had conjured up.

"Aye, well, I met a man who had been at Culloden, 'a bloodbath' he called it. The English troops under the Duke, Butcher Cumberland they called him, had slaughtered every Scot – man, woman or child – that they saw after the battle. There's many Scotsmen will bear a grudge against the English to their dying day!

"Our Sarge would only have been a little lad at the time. It could be he saw his father's body. Since then, he's hated Scotsmen. He's a bad man when it comes to holding a grudge. Not like Murch who spews out hate when he's drunk and then falls flat on his face and never does anything. Our Sergeant Connor hates when he's sober – and he drinks but little – a mug or two of ale is the most you'll see him having. Men who hate sober are more dangerous."

Shortly after, the men began to drift back, mostly the worse for drink, and Bresciano went to his hut and lay on his bed. He had much to think about. On the one hand, the Sergeant seemed more human after Jones's disclosures, but on the other, he hated Scotsmen – and Jamie was... had been... a Scotsman. He tossed fitfully in his bed: images of Jamie on the mortuary slab; the Sergeant bursting the door open with a sledge hammer; Lucia with those obscene pocks which might disfigure her face – all gradually gave way to images of Bianca clasped in Robert's arms. Finally he dreamt of a table loaded with the choicest cuts of mutton and beef, fruit and vegetables, and six dry-looking lemons. He awoke with a groan and it was a long time before he fell asleep again.

CHAPTER VII

Monday morning brought with it a damp easterly wind that rapidly swathed the Rock in a heavy levanter cloud. It obscured the craggy barren heights and then moved downwards like a ravening creature to engulf the slopes with their scrubland and stunted trees. The high humidity and low morning temperature were guaranteed to chill to the bone men who were poorly clad in their working clothes – loose tunics and patched breeches. There was much of the usual discontent, lightened by the inevitable banter of soldiers used to making the best they could out of ill fortune. Bresciano collected his rations and went once more to offer the meat to Tom in exchange for his bread as he had done previously.

But Tom, shuffling along ahead of him, suffering the after-effects of the previous night's drinking, was surprisingly offhand.

"You can keep that rubbish. I'm sick o' it. I'll be getting meself something worth eating today, and I'm done with blackstrap an' all. It'll be rum for Tom from now on."

Bresciano shook his head: he would have to take his own bread home and eat the meat himself. He would have to ask his mother for a little of her precious supply of herbs – perhaps even a little of the pepper she still had. You could not eat pepper, but it might help to disguise the taste of the old salt pork. He set it to soak against the evening. In the meantime he had another day of hard labour ahead down at the King's Bastion and he needed to eat something, however unpalatable. At least it would put warmth in his belly. He now understood an old story his father used to tell about a starving man who cooked old pieces of leather to make soup: true or not, it made sense. With a sigh he settled down to pick the weevils out of the porridge oats.

It was a slow business, but while his hands were occupied with the unpleasant task, his mind was busy with ideas. Morning had brought a clearer head than he had had last night as he had lain, sleepless, thinking on everything Corporal Jones had told him. As far as the Sergeant was concerned, he felt his original instinct had not led him astray. The Sergeant was a clear suspect with motive enough – a man with a hatred of the Scots in general, and certainly with a grudge against Jamie in particular for having become a focus of the men's dislike of their sergeant. Many of them blamed him for Jamie's accident with the musket; some even held that it had been no accident. He was a man with little to lose now that his wife and child were dead. He was also a man who had been on the spot both when Jamie had been thrown over the rampart and later when Jamie had been drugged and hanged. And he had refused to send Jamie to hospital where he would have been safe from that fatal second attempt on his life because he had wanted to keep his eye on the poor lad – all too smoky by half!

Bresciano considered his next move. What he needed to establish now was where exactly the Sergeant had been before he had battered open the door of the hut in reply to Bresciano's desperate cries for help. He would do that in the evening when the men all gathered in the mess hut. The men were all too willing to turn the trivia of life into a matter for gossip. Suddenly he grinned. Cunning was needed: he would begin with warm praise of the Sergeant for having come so promptly to his aid… that should stir things up. Some of the men would be quick enough to resent such praise and react to it. It would get them talking better than any direct questions would.

And as for the Westons and Lieutenant Black… he pulled at his lip and wrinkled his brow in thought. The day before he had seen no possible way of getting information about them, but now he began to see avenues of investigation. He began to mutter to himself: "Emiliana knows something… she… can't be hard to get her talking about it… ask her tonight… And Lola too! She can help me now she's working for the Westons… Humph."

He straightened his back, his distasteful task done, and

put the porridge to heat on the small stove with its meagre supply of kindling. He watched it, waiting till it began to simmer and the grey surface erupted into small mouths that popped and made sucking noises before subsiding. He served it. It felt half cooked, but it was hot enough.

He was soon ready to leave and took a slightly different route down past the Green Market. It would take him close to the Westons' quarter.

As chance would have it, early though it was, he saw a woman emerging from the house. He stopped, making much of checking the buttons on his tunic while he looked covertly at her. She was of middling height and slender. All the soldiers agreed that Mrs Weston was beautiful, but there was nothing to tell him whether or not this was so because her features were obscured by a shawl that she had drawn across her face. She walked slowly, with a pronounced limp, like an old woman, but it was surely Mrs Weston. No one had mentioned her lameness and it puzzled him till he remembered that she had fallen down the stairs, apparently more than once. As she drew away from him, the shawl slipped a little and he was treated to the sight of the back of her head – a mass of palest blonde hair swept back into some sort of knot at the nape of her neck.

She went towards the Green Market – there would be little enough for sale unless someone had salvaged a few vegetables from the Neutral Ground near the Spanish lines after the recent raid by the Spanish. Virtually the only vegetables grown locally came from the odd gardens that officers enjoyed or from small patches of land on the rocky slopes where soldiers were encouraged to grow a few vegetables, which they guarded jealously. The Governor, a vegetarian, an oddity among the hearty meat-eaters of the day, would have fared ill if it hadn't been for his Governor's Garden, over an acre of land in the heart of the town. Thinking of gardens reminded Bresciano of the herbs Jamie had collected the day he was murdered. Perhaps it would be possible to find some more to take Lucia. He would try later, once his working day was over.

Ahead of him walked three familiar figures. It was the Walloons, and Bresciano was annoyed to find that they appeared to be going in the same direction as he was. Something remarkably like a sneer replaced his normally good-natured expression. They were just deserters, hangers-on in a beleaguered town that could have done without three more mouths to feed. By contrast, he was a soldier and he had work to do. He strode past them determinedly, acknowledging their presence with a curt nod, but failed to shake them off as Robert hurried to catch up with him, calling to the others in French to follow him.

"Bianca's friend! Giovanni, is it not?" His English, despite its alien intonation, was irritatingly fluent. "Here we all are, bent on the same errand, or so I believe. We too are working for Gibraltar and have been sent to the King's Bastion to join the Artificers in their work. It is good to feel useful."

Bresciano was forced to make some reply and found he was being introduced to the other two – Pascal and Jean Pierre. Pascal spoke passable Spanish and virtually no English but was taciturn and disinclined to talk; Jean Pierre had little enough English; consequently the conversation limped along in poor Spanish, some French phrases and English when Robert took a hand as interpreter. It took Bresciano a while to see beyond his spleen and realise that he was being granted the opportunity of getting to know these men. From these introductions it would be an easy step to investigating their movements over the past week, something he had intended to do. He must exploit their acquaintance.

As he pondered the matter, he avoided the question of motive: why 'Robair'… that was to say… why they – any of the three, naturally – should have wished to kill Jamie was a mystery at present, but, he told himself virtuously, he had to investigate without fear or favour. Jones had been the first to talk about deserters, albeit he had referred to those deserting to Spain. "The principle is the same," Bresciano mumbled to himself, wilfully ignoring the blatant lack of logic that this involved. He was, after all, only eighteen – intelligent without having acquired wisdom; and in love without having developed any of the defences that time might bring.

Work at the Bastion involved fixing some final limestone blocks in place with the use of lime mortar, and clearing the site of all the material that was left as the stone was needed at a breach in the Line Wall defences further to the south. The skilled Artificers got on with their task and the rest began to load the waiting carts.

"Someone, help! – *à mon sécour*! *Ici! À mon sécour* !" There was an edge of panic to the voice.

It was Pascal, tall and powerfully built, who had attempted to hoist a block on the cart on his own and was now in difficulties. Bresciano ran over to him and tried to get a grip on the stone block, but it began to slip down the tailboard of the cart, turning over as it did, trapping Bresciano's right hand and wrenching the wrist painfully so that he cried out.

Someone gave a warning cry, "Watch out there!" and the stone crashed to the ground, barely missing two men who had been standing a little below, and Bresciano was left supporting his forearm with his left hand and gritting his teeth against the pain.

"I might have known it!" The Sergeant was there, shouting at him. "You could have killed those men, you damned incompetent ass. I lose Daft Jamie and get bloody Clumsyano in his place. And don't stand there whingeing like a girl. Let a proper man get on with the work. Get out of my sight! Just get down there and clear the loose rubble. It's all you're fit for. You're not to be trusted with anything else."

Pascal seemed to realise that Bresciano was being blamed and tried to remedy matters, but there was no Robert to translate, for he was at the other end of the Bastion, so all he did was pour out a stream of French aimed at the Sergeant, who told him to keep his damned Froggy language to himself.

Though he tried to follow the Sergeant's instructions, Bresciano was incapable of using his right hand, which felt as if someone was stabbing it through viciously with hot irons. It was bleeding, with the fingers and wrist swelling visibly. He struggled on for a few minutes till one of the Artificers, an older man, took a grubby neckerchief from round his throat and bound Bresciano's wrist up: it was now badly swollen and the abrasions on his fingers still bled sluggishly.

"Don't reckon you'll be able to use that 'and for a few days, lad. For longer if ye've broken any bones. You're not fit for duty 'ere, that's for sure. Don't 'e worry none. I'll tell Sergeant."

And before Bresciano could protest, the matter was out of his hands and he found himself being sent off – the subject of imprecations and insults by Connor – to make himself useful at the Blue Barracks. He stumbled away, miserably aware that his injury, not honourably sustained in battle, would impress no one. He was equally worried by the possibility of having broken his hand. Smarting from the tongue-lashing he had received, he damned the Sergeant to hell as he nursed his arm against his chest. As he walked through the deserted streets, he reflected glumly on his situation. Rather than a heroic battle injury, he had a bruised hand ascribed to clumsiness. He was a labourer, not a soldier, and not a very good labourer at that!

In a spirit of defiance he decided that the Blue Barracks could wait. He turned towards Dr Coll's house and prayed that he would find him at home, where he generally treated his patients.

The alarmed reception he received from Mrs Coll was gratifying. She was actually moved to rise briefly from her daybed and instruct the maid to help him; and he realised how dramatic things looked with blood streaking his forearm and encrusted on his fingers. By the time the doctor came into the kitchen the maid had removed the bloody cloth and washed his hand.

"Broken? Probably not," Doctor Coll cheerfully examined him. "I know you young layabouts – trying to get a few weeks off work, is that it?" He laughed loudly. "Now… can you move your fingers? Splendid! See, there's movement there." Then he pressed each of the fingers in turn with a sharp pin and watched Bresciano flinch. "Excellent. Plenty of sensation there, would you not agree? You'll be right as rain in less than a week. It's nothing but a sprain – a bad one, I grant you, but that's all. Your hand will be black and blue by tonight, but there's to be no malingering, do you hear? Just be sensible and don't try to use that hand for the present."

He strapped the wrist up, put the arm in a sling, and saw Bresciano out.

At the Blue Barracks he tried to report to someone in authority and was eventually directed to Captain Weston. He felt it a stroke of luck without being sure why this was so. At least, it would allow him to meet this hitherto unknown suspect. A captain, he felt, would be an upstanding man, an experienced soldier. What would his ideas of honour be? How would a man like that respond to being thought a cuckold by the world at large?

There was little time for speculation. He stood in the

small quadrangle he had been directed to and saw the Captain ahead of him, issuing orders to a small unit of men. He was a man of middle height with salt and pepper hair pulled back and tied neatly with a dark ribbon; his voice was low and, when he turned round, Bresciano saw how his light eyes, clear glass-grey eyes, bulged slightly, like Nonna's.

"Yes?" He looked at Bresciano, his face expressionless.

"Giovanni Bresciano, sir. Artificer. I was working at King's Bastion and… there was a big block of… it slipped… I…" he held up his hand. "Sergeant Connor sent me here." He found those near-colourless eyes and rigid face disconcerting. "It's not broken. A bad sprain."

"A doctor, are you?"

"No, sir. It was… I saw a friend on my way here, he has medical knowledge," he did not care to say that he had stopped at Dr Coll's house, "and he said…"

"Enough. Light duties. Report here every morning. Back to proper work in four days."

He turned and walked into a small office. Bresciano stood outside, uncertainly waiting for further instructions.

"In here," the voice was cold, "take these documents to…" he paused, "can you read? Good. Then deliver them to the people named on them. I shall need you this afternoon again. These papers have been sealed. If I hear that the seals are tampered with, you will be severely punished. Report back to me when you have done the work."

"Yes, sir."

He attempted a salute and managed to turn smartly on his heels and walk out with a degree of military precision, but the Captain, bent over some papers on his desk, had no further interest in him. It was a strange sensation for Bresciano, as if he had ceased to exist once the Captain stopped looking at him. He shook his head. What a fanciful notion! But it was not fancy: he had felt as if he had been wiped out. Yet the Captain had not been annoyed at him; had no reason to be angry; had not even raised his voice

Bresciano found himself hurrying on his errand and it took him only part of the morning to deliver the papers he had been entrusted with. He felt a sense of relief when he had done and the tension in his body left him. He realised that, while he was embarrassed by the Sergeant's open abuse, he was actually afraid of the Captain's cold disapproval. He decided it was wiser to report back immediately to the Captain than to give the impression that he had dawdled the morning away, but the Captain was not at the Barracks. With some trepidation, Bresciano decided to try his quarter, but drew a blank. The one thing he achieved was establishing contact with Lola, the new maid.

"Giovanni! It is Giovanni, isn't it? I haven't seen you in years. Gibraltar may be a small place, but one loses track of people, is that not so? And you are in the army! What did your father have to say to that? What? No, no, the *capitán* is not at home. You have a message for him? Did he tell you to come? He doesn't like visitors, you know." She sounded concerned. "He did not? Well, you had better leave then and I shall not tell him you were here!"

Over her shoulder he caught a glimpse of Mrs Weston. She was standing rigidly, framed in an open doorway, certainly a beautiful woman as far as he could see, for part of her face was in shadow somehow. Then she raised her hand to her face and turned away just before Lola closed the door.

Bresciano stood stock still for a moment, then moved off thoughtfully. It appeared that the Captain was guarding his wife from further visits by the Lieutenant. It was hardly surprising. And now that he had met the Captain and seen his wife he was none the wiser. She was beautiful. Bianca wasn't beautiful, but her face was full of life and light and Mrs Weston's face was... he stopped. It had not been in shadow and she had raised her hand to cover the darkness he had seen – the left side of her face had been disfigured by a large bruise. The sense that there was something wrong in the house grew on him. Was it possible that Mrs Weston, the beauty being guarded from intruders, had rushed down the stairs and fallen as she ran to open the door to... her lover? Was it like Arthur and Guinevere? An older man and a young wife? A dashing lover? Or was the Lieutenant a cold-blooded seducer taking advantage of an innocent woman?

Emiliana! he thought. She lived a few minutes away and he had time on his hands. He would seek her out and see what answers she could come up with. With renewed purpose he set off and found her sitting on the doorstep of her small and ill-kept two-roomed house well above the Green Market – a disreputable house in a disreputable alleyway.

"Giovanni! You have come to see me? Sit down, my good boy. Sit here with me. Oh, your poor hand!" she patted it and he cried out, pulling it away.

"I'm glad to see you looking... well," he muttered. "I have just come from the Captain Weston's house. I had a message to deliver."

"I do not care about that house! I will never set foot in it again. The *Capitán* has found me better work. Yes, I work with a respectable woman who is older. There is none of that 'business' going on *there*."

"Ah yes, 'business'?" Bresciano made his voices sound knowing.

"You know what I mean," she dug her elbow in his ribs. "But my lips are sealed. Emiliana knows how to keep a secret, especially when it's been made worth her while!" She laughed.

"Oh," Bresciano attempted to match her arch look and tried a stab in the twilight rather than the dark, "you mean about her and that young lieutenant?"

"Shhh!" Emiliana leaned over towards him and lowered her voice. "The *Capitán* is such a jealous man. I promised silence." She covered her lips with her thumb, making a small sign of the cross.

"Absolutely right," he cast around in his mind for the next step and lowered his voice, "but you can't tell me what I don't already know. You see – I was Jamie MacFarlane's friend."

"Ay, ay! Poor Jamie. I always gave him something when he came on a message."

"And he saw things, didn't he? The Lieutenant and the *Scignoa*...?"

She snorted. "That Lieutenant came whenever he thought the husband was out – disgusting! Like a dog round a bitch in heat, he was. And her, with that look of innocence, like a frightened rabbit. Pah!" She spat on the ground. "And the *Capitán* tells me I have to say when the Lieutenant comes. He is right. A man protects what is his. It is not my fault if he..." She stopped and eyed him warily, wondering if she had said too much.

"You mean when the Captain..." his eyes widened. He felt he knew what had happened. "When – she 'fell down the stairs'?"

"You know about that too?" she was relieved. "There it is. What can I say? A man sometimes has to beat a woman. It wasn't my fault, was it? It's natural. She deserved it. Now, my own man, God rest his soul, never laid a finger on me in all our years together, but then – I was a respectable wife."

Bresciano, remembering the epic battles Emiliana and her 'husband' had waged in the past, looked straight at her, unblinking, and nodded his head, not even surprised at her burying a healthy common-law husband who had, in fact, tired of such sport and run away years ago with another man's wife.

"So you saw everything that happened in that house?"

"Everything." Emiliana rolled her eyes.

"And the *Scignoa* was often alone with the Lieutenant? Very often?"

"Yes, I'm sure. All the time. I think she waited for me to leave. The *Capitán* went out a lot. He played cards with his friends. That is what officers do. Sometimes he played all night. And it is a woman's place to stay at home, is it not? She complained. I don't know much English, but I know the words for 'money' and 'gambling'."

For Emiliana, whatever she might have done in her own life, subscribed publicly to the ethos of male dominance established in both the military and the civilian Latin culture of the fortress town. She had, in fact, fought her mate tooth and nail, though she could not now be brought to acknowledge the fact.

She resumed her aggrieved narrative: "They had money and he was spending it. What is wrong with that? They are married. I never grudged my man a penny."

Once more Bresciano nodded in spurious agreement at Emiliana's last outrageous statement. "Of course. Tell me, wasn't he out last Thursday night? Or was it Friday? I think I saw him up near Willis's where I'm living at present."

She thought for a moment. "Yes. I suppose so. I always left early, but I know that both Thursday and Friday he goes up to the Blue Barracks and Saturdays he is with the officers down at South Barracks. Mind you, before I left the house – in disgust at her conduct, and certainly not because I was told to leave, oh no, I just went...'I will not stay in a house where there is immorality,' I said, just like that. And I left. I have my principles, and so I told her." She stared at Bresciano, daring him to challenge her new version of events, and was satisfied with his look of rapt interest. "What was I saying...?"

"You were about to tell me what happened before you left."

"Yes. The *Capitán* told her that she would not be alone much longer."

"What did he mean?"

She shrugged, "Maybe he will get his friends to come to the house to play cards. Or he will stay at home. Or he will pay Lola to stay the night. I do not know. And I do not care. She called me a whore, did you know that?" Her grievances surfaced as they had when she was drunk and it was with difficulty that Bresciano extricated himself from her clutches.

Now he knew there was no King Arthur, though there might be a Guinevere and a Lancelot. He was finding it difficult to accept the idea of an English officer as a man who could beat his wife. It had been common enough among the poor immigrants up at Buena Vista where he had lived as a child, but an officer of His Majesty's forces? Beaten her hard enough to cause those bruises? Perhaps thrown her down the stairs and hurt her sufficiently to cause that limp he had noticed earlier in the day?

It would be wiser to suspend judgement till he could find someone else to confirm what Emiliana had said. He felt that she was hardly a reliable witness. At least he now knew that Captain Weston had been out and about on the two nights in question. He had the motive and the opportunity. And now that he himself had met the Captain, he could see him cold-bloodedly dealing with anyone who stood in his way or earned his hatred. "No!" he admonished himself. "That's pure conjecture... pure imagination... slander..."

He trudged along to his parents' house and found Aunt Maria, who was in full flood about the appalling scenes played out outside the bakery in their neighbourhood. She spoke with a wealth of gesture:

"There was fighting, I tell you. The baker was only open for an hour. Then he said all the day's ration was finished. He should have kept quiet and closed up quickly – there were people there with their money who had got nothing. It was as if they went mad. I had to hide our bread under my shawl or they would have torn it out of my hands. Two men fell to fighting over a couple of pieces of sour bread; their women were screaming and their poor children were crying out for food. It was terrible – and you know how bad my nerves are! And it was as bad in the market. I got these cabbage leaves for five pence! Not even a half a cabbage. And I heard that someone paid nearly a pound for a pig's head. A pound! That's nearly five Spanish dollars. Who can afford those prices? I cannot face these things any more!"

"Enough, Maria." Eleanor soothed her, "We don't want to upset Lucia. She will hear you. It will only be for a little longer. I know how awful it is for you to see these things, but while Lucia is so ill, I cannot leave her. Soon I will do the shopping and you will help to nurse the child. I shall depend on you."

"It is my nerves. You know I am a martyr to them." But she was genuinely distressed.

It was only then that they noticed his bandaged wrist. He was made much of and that, together with his gift of bread, relieved the tension. As he took a few herbs and a little pepper he had begged from his mother, he realised how lucky he was to have a regular ration, however unpleasant the food. His own wage of fourpence ha'penny a day would not go far, but if he saved it, he might be able to get something in a few days. Before leaving he visited his sister's room. It was difficult to tell, but she seemed less distressed, though tired enough for him to cut his visit short. Besides, he was anxious to return to the Barracks. 'This afternoon' was what Weston had said and it was past mid-day. What constituted 'this afternoon'?

But the Captain did not return till past three. He looked at Bresciano's hand.

"Left handed or right handed?" He asked, his voice without inflexion.

"Left, sir."

"Can you write a legible fist?"

"I think so, sir."

"I want an answer – Yes or no?"

"Yes, sir."

"Get down to the stores. I want an inventory of the lanterns, uniforms and bedding we have. I want it written out in duplicate. Take four sheets of paper and a pencil now and make a clean copy in ink later. You will finish by tomorrow evening."

He was already busy with documents on his desk and again Bresciano experienced that sensation of worthlessness. The Captain had not looked him in the face. He hesitated and was startled by the chill, quiet voice:

"When I give orders, Bresciano, they are to be carried out immediately."

*   *   *   *

By the time the light had faded and he could no longer see to write, Bresciano had completed a good deal of the work and he had brought a measure of order to the clothes carelessly piled around and the untidy heaps of blankets. Several times he had found himself looking over his shoulder as if the Captain might descend on him to check out his performance, but no one came down to the stores and he was left in peace. When he went back to the office, he found it closed. He was free to leave. Free to look for Abraham Hassan, because he needed to talk to him, to test his theories on a disinterested party.

But it was Lieutenant Drinkwater that he met.

"Mr Bresciano, well met. I hoped to run across you. I have a friend who has asked if he could read the books you lent me once I have done with them. He has promised he will take the greatest care of them, but I said I first had to ask your consent."

"Yes, sir. I am sure my mother will be glad to help him."

"Splendid. Lieutenant Black will be delighted. He is something of a scholar and to be left without books is for him a severe penance."

A nod and a smile and he was off. Bresciano stared after him. Lieutenant Black, a scholar? It did not tally with his ideas of either a daring lover or a heartless rake. Another idea that had lain dormant at the back of his mind surfaced suddenly: if Captain Weston had been out and about on the past Thursday when an attempt had been made on Jamie's life, and on the Friday when the second attempt had succeeded... he groped to clarify his ideas... if the Captain had been out and Emiliana had left early as she said, then Mrs Weston could equally well have been out and about. He began to see her as a siren. Emiliana had referred to Lieutenant Black as 'young'. Was

Mrs Weston then an older woman, a femme fatale? Had she led on a quiet scholarly young man to perdition? No. It did not square with the woman he had seen so briefly walking painfully towards Green Market and later, her face drained of expression, looking at the door where he had been talking to Lola. Nor did any of it quite fit in with her reputation for haughtiness and with Lieutenant Black – erupting into Bianca's wine house and angrily demanding Jamie's whereabouts.

It seemed to him that the more he uncovered or discovered, the less he knew.

He went wearily up to his hut and did his best to make a palatable supper out of the salt pork, but no amount of pepper could disguise the foul taste. Later, in the mess hut, he heard that Tom had come by meat somehow and had feasted on it before the rest of his colleagues arrived. The smell of fresh meat had lingered in the air and his denials had done him little good. And to add insult to injury, he had drunk the better part of a bottle of rum without offering any to anyone. Even Murch viewed his erstwhile friend with something akin to loathing. Anger was close to the surface these days.

"Well," Bresciano spoke when the complaints against Tom had worn themselves out, "we can at least be thankful for some people who are a help to us when we need them." In order to put his little scheme into operation, he waited till he was sure that enough of the men were listening, "I don't know where he was or how he heard me, but I shall always be grateful to Sergeant Connor for being near at hand and rushing in to help when I found poor Jamie hanging there."

Their reaction was all he could have wanted and by the time their assorted diatribes had ended, he had been called a series of uncomplimentary names for his praise of the Sergeant, but he was in possession of several facts. The Sergeant had not been with any of the men; he had just appeared from nowhere; one man swore he had come from behind the hut. Bresciano, well pleased with the result of his little scheme, was content to listen to the conversations around him. Someone took out a fiddle and began to play a lively air which the men stamped their feet to with enthusiasm as a couple of them stood up to sing the obscene lyrics they had made up for the tune. Bresciano was taken aback: vulgarity was not something he was used to, but the song gave way to sentimental ballads and he leaned back against the wall and thought about his position.

The next day would be easy enough. He knew he could finish the work at the Barracks in a few hours. He found his next idea alarming; Weston was not a man to be crossed lightly, but he decided he would only present his completed inventory lists at the end of the afternoon. That would leave him much of the day free to see Abraham and to get back to Pascal, who would surely be eager to oblige with information, either out of gratitude to Bresciano for shielding him, albeit unwittingly, from the Sergeant's wrath, or out of a sense of guilt. He would need an excuse for getting information... he would have to think of something.

"A concert, is it?" Sergeant Connor walked in and the men fell silent. "Now listen, all of you: we will be leaving this place within a day or two. Work up at Willis's is nearly done and we're needed again down along the Line Wall. We have to raise the level of some defences beyond the city gate at South Port. Have your kit ready to move. I don't want time wasted while some fool goes off looking for stuff he's mislaid. Understood? And you, with the fiddle – Malone, isn't it? – carry on playing. I enjoy a spot of music myself."

A plaintive lament followed, but the spell had been broken and it had grown late. Bresciano began to nod off on the stool. Time to get to bed. As he lay down he remembered his intention of finding fresh vegetables for Lucia. He would make time tomorrow to comb the rocky slopes for edible plants. There were places he had gone to as a boy with Bianca: she always daring him to climb higher, to take risks, mocking his clumsiness and then scrambling away from him, surefooted as the goats that had grazed the slopes in those days. There was a particular ledge which was all but invisible from below. They had discovered it one day when they had run away from Nonna Lucrezia after Bianca had put a mouse up her petticoats. They had had to spend the afternoon roaming the less accessible slopes, chewing on wild asparagus, dandelion and wild leeks. They had found a ledge near the upper town, but almost invisible from below and had lain there in the sun till night had driven them back into a small cave, more like a deep hollow in the rock face, where they had fallen asleep. By the time they awoke feeling cold, it was dark and even the lights in the houses were extinguished. They had huddled together for warmth till the dawn.

The following day they had returned to Buena Vista – to a beating from Giancarlo for Bresciano for scaring the whole household witless by his disappearance, and to nothing much for Bianca, whose parents had been too busy fighting the previous night to notice her absence.

Now as he lay in his cot, tired, his hand aching, he remembered that night, with Bianca's skinny frame against his. He had been the younger one, but so much taller and, in those days, plumper than Bianca – and he had held her in his arms.

It could happen again. He tried to remain awake holding that image in his mind, but perversely he was asleep within minutes.

CHAPTER VIII

Unfortunately, after only two hours Bresciano woke. He was to sleep little that night, roused time and again by the throbbing in his wrist, and kept from dropping off back to sleep by the sound of driving rain and gusts of wind whistling round the north face of the Rock. The Levanter had turned stormy as it occasionally did. He could imagine João, his father's old Portuguese bosun, solemn with borrowed wisdom, quoting one of his favourite pronouncements on the weather: '*Quando com Levanter chove, as pedras move*'. He turned over in his sleepless bed and tried to distract himself by translating the saying into English. Lying there in the dark, he finally achieved a creditable bit of doggerel: 'A rainy Levanter – makes the stones canter.' True enough – rock-falls were common on some of the slopes of the Rock, especially after heavy rain. They could be quite dangerous, too. He could just remember the great storm of 1766 when a terrifying flood of muddy water had poured down the slopes dragging large rocks with it in a wave of destruction. Their little house on the upper outskirts of the town had survived, but others had not, and several people had died. He turned again, easing his aching wrist and fell to wondering on the chances of stones from the cliff above Willis's 'cantering' on to the hut. His eyelids grew heavy... it did not seem to matter, the hut was stoutly built, the roof was... he finally dozed off.

By the morning, the wind had dropped and the rain had been replaced by a fine mist, the kind that would surely be dispelled by the winter sun that was likely to grow almost hot by midday. The sound of some of the other men setting off for a final day's work on the defences at Willis's woke him and he sat up quickly, alarmed at having overslept. Captain Weston was not a man to be kept waiting. As he dressed hurriedly and somewhat awkwardly, he was pleased to notice that his arm had stopped throbbing, and his wrist did not appear to be badly swollen although it was still tender.

He was on the point of leaving when he remembered that he had meant to look for the key to the hut to discover if Jamie had thrown it out of the window before committing suicide.

While Bresciano had the intelligence to resolve the puzzles that Jamie's death faced him with, he had more imagination than organizational skills and his investigation was lurching on from one random idea to the next. He was himself aware of it: he knew he should have looked for the key sooner; he knew he had yet to investigate the connection between the Westons and the Lieutenant; and he felt as he had done once when, as a boy, he had fallen out of his father's boat and, finding himself facing away from it had realised what it meant to be all at sea.

He was determined now to bring method to bear on his investigation. He would do something about the Westons, but first he must search for the key.

If Jamie had thrown it out of the window, it would still be lying out there somewhere behind the hut. The sound of Sergeant Connor's voice outside as he rounded up the last of the artificers who were to go down to the King's Bastion made Bresciano hesitate and he waited till they had left. He would need to hurry. If he looked out of the window the key might be visible.

But the mist made visibility poor and there was no key to be seen. Taking one of the small heavy glasses on the table, he positioned himself opposite the window and threw the glass out, reasoning that if he followed the trajectory it would narrow down the area to be searched. Then he climbed out of the window, found the glass and looked around. No key on the bare ground behind the hut, but as he turned away despondently, he suddenly saw it, wet and glistening, quite close to the side wall of the hut and half-hidden in a tussock of grass. He picked it up and hurried to the front of the hut where he tried it on the battered door. It was definitely the key, but there was no way that it could have landed by the side of the hut if it had been thrown out of the window.

He held up the key in triumph. Well, he had never really doubted that Jamie had been murdered, but his discovery now clearly made the suicide theory even more untenable. The murderer must have pocketed it after locking the door and then, startled by Bresciano's knocking, had left precipitously through the window and had probably dropped it when he raced away from the hut and into the bushes... or perhaps it had fallen out of Sergeant Connor's pocket as he ran in response to Bresciano's frantic calls... if it was the Sergeant, of course. He went back, replaced the key where he had found it and covered it with a small tussock of grass. If the murderer chanced to come looking for it, it would not do to make it obvious that it had been disturbed. Now what remained was to catch the murderer. And once he had done that, Bianca would be forced to acknowledge how she had misjudged him

"I knew I was right!"

The sound of his own voice, loud in the silence, brought him back to earth. There was no one left in the camp. And he had kept Captain Weston waiting!

He ran down to the Blue Barracks, slipping on the wet slope and cursing as he picked himself up painfully. By the time he arrived he was a sorry sight with his uniform now smeared with mud down one leg and his hair plastered down by the rain. The Captain would be angry and rightly so, or more likely, he might be expressionless and correct in exacting his pound of flesh.

But he found the Captain's office empty. Muttering a prayer of thanks he took his lists and hurried away. He had imagined that the Captain normally worked there all morning. Perhaps he had been called away for other duties and had not been to the Barracks yet, had not noticed Bresciano's tardy appearance, and would not put him on some sort of charge for dereliction of duty

Down in the store-room he set to, shifting and recording the remaining stores. After three hours of hard work he put his pencil down and flexed his cramped fingers; his right wrist ached and now his left hand did as well. He had to take a rest from writing. The stores were organised and carefully stacked round the room, and his lists neatly written in his careful hand. All that remained to be done was to make the fair copy.

His good intentions about bringing some sort of order to his investigation proved evanescent in the face of his other good intentions: there was his family to think of. His determination to provide them with fresh food had occupied his mind even as he drew up the lists for Captain Weston. He realised that there was no chance of finding anything eatable in the area of the Barracks or around the camp at Willis's. For that matter, most accessible areas of the Rock must have been thoroughly combed by hungry soldiers and civilians.

Then Bresciano remembered again the place where he and Bianca had sheltered in those younger, happier days. It was almost invisible from below and inaccessible if you did not know the way up to it – a simple enough route, a narrow goat-track leading south from Willis's to the place, but he had noticed that the beginning of the track was now difficult to find. With the passage of years it had become almost obscured by bushes, but there at the end of it he knew he would find the cave with a flat area in front of it with plenty of vegetation. Surely – if no one else had found it – he would be able to find nourishing herbs growing there! He remembered that there had been a small fig tree, though it was far too late in the year for fruit, but there were palmettos too. He had occasionally been given some to eat as a child and he knew that the apes would chew on the roots of this plant, so there must be some food value in them. And who knew what else he might find?

Determined to get away from the Barracks now that his work was almost completed, and well ahead of the deadline the Captain had given him, he deliberately disarranged his tidy lists. Then he moved some of the stores around to give the room an air of work in progress. Finally, satisfied with the reasonable degree of disorder he had created, he hid the last page under a pile of blankets. If the Captain chanced by he would assume Bresciano had stepped out for some reason and would be back to complete his work. And if he met the Captain on his way out, he would pretend to have spoilt one of the precious pages he had been given for the inventory and ask for a new sheet.

His mouth felt dry as he stepped out of the store-room and tried to walk casually along the corridor to the entrance of the Barracks. His heart was pounding and his hands felt clammy. Surely someone would see his tension and guilt. It amazed him that the several men he passed did not notice anything strange. No one stared, no one stopped him, no one questioned him. As he reached the Captain's office ready to edge his way past, he was surprised and relieved to see it still empty.

Striding purposefully uphill, he arrived within minutes at the point where the unsurfaced road to the camp was fringed with overgrown bushes to the right. There was no one to see him as he pushed his way through the tangle of vegetation and on to the narrow track. It was as he remembered it, except that the scrub was denser, and he found himself smiling as he walked the path towards a spot he recalled as idyllic. The path grew narrower and the ground on his right dropped away more steeply the further he went. Always fearful of heights, he now pressed close to the rising ground on his left to avoid looking down, and when he arrived at the ledge, he found that the fig tree was no longer spreading its broad leaves above the track. It had fallen victim to some disease and the trunk was a shell from which a few branches struggled to extract sustenance.

The ledge itself was much smaller and barer than the little paradise that he remembered as a boy, and behind the fig tree creepers had spread downwards obscuring the entrance to his cave. At his feet grew several miserable palmettos: they would have to do. Ironically, what had once been the food of the poor would now be treated as a welcome gift when he took it home, and the palmettos even had fruit, rather wrinkled and tired-looking, for their season was past. But the tight pale orange clusters like oval dates might still be edible.

He felt betrayed by the past as much as by his present dreams as he knelt and began to probe at the earth around the palmettos with his knife. They were quite close to the edge of the ledge, and he avoided looking down. He knew that at this point there was a drop of at least thirty feet to the next ledge below. Bianca had slipped one day, and almost gone over. She had managed to clutch on to a palmetto – the ancestor of one of these he was about to despoil, no doubt – and Giovanni, cold and sweating with terror, had wriggled to the edge and had managed to pull her back. He remembered how they had lain there afterwards, unable to move, trembling in reaction to the incident. No, better not to look down.

The morning mist had cleared and it was warm in the sun so his work was not unpleasant, and the rain had softened the ground. He made slow but steady progress in uncovering the root of the smallest plant, although he was hampered by being unable to put any weight on his aching right wrist. As he worked, he became aware of an unpleasant smell which contrasted sharply with the pleasant odour of wet grass and earth. Perhaps the palmetto root had rotted? The root had a firm hold on the ground and he was wet from both rain and sweat by the time he was able to dig it out. He gouged out a small piece from the bottom of it out with his knife. He sniffed and tasted it. It was tough and almost tasteless, but it was not rotten. Reassured, he continued to dig, but the other roots ran deeper and it felt as if he would never succeed in hauling them out. Eventually he had three mangled palmetto roots, which he cleaned of soil and looked at, dispirited, before putting them in his knapsack. They were not quite the small, tender roots he remembered with their flat pouches filled with some granular substance – the heart of the palmetto. That had been in his childhood, in the spring. These were clearly older plants, tough parents to the easily edible new growth yet to come.

"Better a bad meal than no meal at all," he quoted Dr Coll and looked around to try to supplement his disappointing haul with green plants like the ones which Jamie had collected.

As he turned to go back, he heard a rustling among the creepers. He approached the cave cautiously. Tentatively he put out his hand to pull them aside and was almost overcome by a wave of the unpleasant smell he had noticed earlier. As he recoiled there was an angry scream above the cave as a furry creature leapt out at him, chattering with rage. It was a small rock ape, and it was carrying something that swung and gleamed in the light. Bresciano, who had instinctively stepped back, found himself teetering on the edge and threw himself forward with his left hand stretching out to get whatever purchase he could. His right hand brushed the ape and he landed face down, twisting his hand painfully. As the ape loped away, still screaming its irritation, Bresciano found himself looking at the ape's toy which lay on the ground in front of his face.

It was a bright chain, from which a dull metal lump hung. He recognised it: Tom's lucky bullet. Very gingerly, he pulled himself away from the edge and sat up, turning the lucky bullet over in his hands. The same bullet, which was now hanging from a slim gold chain. How had Tom made good his boast that he would get a gold chain?

A breeze had sprung up and a sudden gust of wind made the creepers sway behind him: there was that smell again!

It came from inside the cave. He pushed the fronds of vegetation aside and looked in. The smell was stronger, easier to identify, unpleasant to identify, but he forced himself to crawl inside. At the back, the sandy floor was coated with a dark substance, and a large stone at the mouth of the cave was covered with the same material. He picked it up and looked at it; the stone was encrusted with blood and with some other material that he preferred not to think about. He dropped the stone as if it were red-hot and wiped his hand on his trousers. He felt sick. So this was how Tom got his fresh meat – he must have found his way here by chance, caught an ape and bludgeoned it to death. And in the struggle with the fierce and desperate animal, he had lost his lucky bullet! Ape meat – this was what Tom had feasted on the night before. It was disgusting, cannibalism almost, but as Bresciano now knew, hunger could drive men to extremes. He looked distastefully around the shallow cave. There was no sign of a body, not even the pelt. Tom must have taken the dead creature away and butchered it elsewhere. No doubt he had it hidden somewhere, probably near Willis's Battery. He put the chain in his pocket, and made his way down. On the way he collected a poor crop of green stuff which he hoped would have some value.

At the Barracks he was able to eat a frugal midday meal, which he gulped down with a desperation new to him and then sat back, exhausted, closing his eyes and listening to the other men. Wooden spoons scraped on tin plates, benches were pushed back, and chatter and complaints grew fewer as they finished and left.

"That's right, take a rest, lad," he opened his eyes to find the cook looking down at him with a kindly smile. "You look right tired. Skinny lad, aren't you? Are you one of the ones that've been up at Willis's? Aye... thought I hadn't seen you around. Cooking your own food, I'll be bound. Ever had to cook before? No wonder you look hungrier than most. 'Ere, come along with me."

"I can't. I have to get back to work. Captain Weston will be looking for me." Bresciano stumbled to his feet, still half asleep.

"'E hasn't turned up today. Less work for me – 'E's that perticular what 'e eats. So don't you worry none. Just listen to old Cookie-Will – that's what they call me – and…"

"You are Jamie's friend, he mentioned you."

"I am that, or I was." He sighed, "You come along. I can see you're new to all this. How long've you been a soldier?

"A week, more or less. Today is Tuesday and I joined up Wednesday last, the day before Jamie Macfarlane was killed… I mean, it happened when he fell and then he…"

"Don't go upsetting yourself. Knew 'im, did you? A friend of 'is? I 'eard all about it. Poor slip of a lad, we used to call him Sparrow – you know, small and chirpy. Used to come here to the kitchen. 'E could always wheedle something out of me! Too soft, that's my problem. But I got to be careful. You remember that, all right?"

Down in the kitchen he took a few cabbage leaves and handed them to Bresciano: "Take this and don't you tell no one about it, see? Eat it raw. Do you good. Now put it away quick."

Free to follow his own pursuits, Bresciano decided to risk a hurried visit home, where his mother opened the door with a faint smile on her face. She patted his cheek affectionately, as she used to do when he was a little boy.

"Lucia is definitely better today; she was delirious all night but very early this morning the fever broke! She woke with almost no fever, and one or two of the pocks are beginning to dry. It's the first sign of healing! And she was able to talk to us quite rationally. I'm certain those lemons you brought have helped, and I feel better too!"

He followed her into the house and gave her the palmetto roots and the other green stuff which he had been able to find. "It looks very tough but perhaps you can make some soup with this?" He was apologetic. It seemed so meagre a contribution.

"Oh, Giovanni, thank you! Why, you have even got the fruit of the palmettos – certainly edible – and inside the root I will find the heart, the tender part that can also be eaten raw. And cabbage leaves too! I can add them to a soup I am making with some greens and potatoes that your father managed to find, heaven knows how!"

They went into Lucia's room, which was still darkened. Lucia lay there with her eyes closed, but as soon as she heard them she called out faintly, "Giovanni! Come and sit with me."

Bresciano sat on the side of the bed and took her hands in his. He studied her face. The rash was certainly no worse, and it did appear that some of the pocks were drying up and crusting.

Lucia smiled at him. "I had such strange dreams in the night, Giovanni. I can't remember most of them, but in one of them I was chasing sparrows to catch and eat them, because I was so hungry, but they all flew away from me – and then I woke up, and I was still hungry!"

Bresciano tried to shake off the memory of Tom and the Rock ape. Even Lucia was having fantasies of eating strange things. "You mustn't think of killing sparrows, my little Lu; they are harmless and happy creatures and there's not much to eat on them anyway! Mother will give you a delicious soup soon with some new magic vegetables which I brought, and you won't be hungry any more."

Lucia glowered. "Don't call me your 'little Lu' – I'm not a baby!" Her voice was weak but firm.

Bresciano smiled. Lucia was recovering both her temper and her appetite. She was definitely getting better. "Very well, big sister; just remember, don't scratch those pocks! Now I'll go and see how that soup is getting on."

In the kitchen, he took the opportunity to study Eleanor as she worked. It was clear that she too was looking better. If he searched that room in the Barracks where he had found the lemons, was there a chance he might find some more?

"The soup will take a while before it is ready, Giovanni. Can you stay and have some?"

He shook his head. "I have already eaten, and I must go back to finish some work for my captain."

As he was leaving the house, he ran into Abraham Hassan on his way with messages to deliver.

"Giovanni, wait, I was looking for you. I have something interesting to tell you about..."

"I can't talk now, Abraham. I have to get back to finish some work for Captain Weston." Bresciano still felt resentful at the way Abraham had refused to entertain his theories.

"But that is precisely who I wanted to tell you about! And whatever you have to do can wait, because Captain Weston won't be taking an interest in your work," he paused dramatically. "He's been arrested! It's all over the town!"

"What?" Bresciano stared at his friend in disbelief. Soldiers might be arrested and soldiers might be flogged and even hanged, but a captain…? "Are you sure? What happened?"

"It seems that the Captain and Lieutenant Black were about to fight a duel. General Eliott got to hear of it and had them both arrested before they could harm each other."

"A duel! What was it all about?"

"Well, no one knows for sure. Both of them refuse to say anything, but there's a rumour among the officers that it was over Mrs Weston, that Black had been paying too much attention to her and the Captain called him out."

Hassan hurried off and Bresciano stood there in the street, thinking. Perhaps it was the other way round and Lieutenant Black had called the Captain out because of his brutality to his wife. In either case, it seemed that emotions were high around the beautiful Mrs Weston. He had to find out more.

He would have to try Emiliana again. Unreliable though she was with her hints and sly winks, she obviously knew something of what had been going on. He had a few pence of his own money and reluctantly decided he had to sacrifice them in the interests of his investigation. Stopping at one of the wine-houses to buy a bottle of their cheapest wine, he hurried up the slope toward her house. She greeted him effusively and was clearly well on the way to inebriation, as the open bottle of wine on the table testified. Bresciano noticed that it was a better wine than the one he had brought. Not that this mattered to Emiliana, who accepted his bottle gratefully, with wine-laden kisses for her 'little Gianni'. But when he tried to broach the subject of the Westons, she became unexpectedly truculent, thrusting out her lower lip with drunken stubbornness.

"As God is my witness, I have never been indiscreet, have I, Gianni? You can vouch for that. Did I tell anyone anything about what happened in that house? No. Not a word has escaped these lips of mine." She stared at Bresciano, suddenly suspicious, "Did you say anything to the *Capitán*?"

He shook his head, "No, no, you told me nothing. 'My lips are sealed,' That is what you said to me. Remember?"

"I did, didn't I? And that's what I told the *Capitán*, and I have kept my word. And then some scandalmonger goes and tells him I've been talking about his wife. Me! All I say is that that woman is mad to call me names like she did. But I say nothing. I tell you this, Gianni, two dollars is not much, is it? Frankly, sometimes it doesn't pay to know too much."

And nothing Bresciano said could coax any more out of her except for a final outburst – that because of her treatment of Emiliana, 'that woman' richly deserved anything that was happening to her.

"She must be mad to treat me as she did after I was so good to her! Putting up with her moods. You have no idea. You are an innocent. And I've been like a mother to her!"

By this time she had finished her bottle of wine and made inroads into the one he had taken her. Nothing she might say now could be trusted to be true. He'd been a fool to give her the wine. He tried to leave, gruffly avoiding her tearful embraces and her offer of 'a little glass of wine for my Gianni', and ended up having to unclasp her arms from round his neck with more force than he intended.

"Come back!" her voice pursued him as he made his bid to escape, "You can't burst into my house without permission and then just turn and leave when it suits you! Come back here!"

With Emiliana unwilling to go too far in giving him information – whether paid off or warned off by Captain Weston, or both – Bresciano was left with only the cheerfully indiscreet Dr Coll as a possible source of information. His wrist presented him with the perfect excuse. He decided that he would go to the doctor's house on the pretext of asking him to look at his wrist, which was in fact aching more now after his exertions of the morning. He was sure that the doctor could be encouraged to tell him something about the Weston household.

The doctor was at home and, with no other patients in sight, he bustled over to attend to Bresciano. With cheerful insensitivity he manhandled Bresciano's wrist, ignoring his winces and occasional yelps of pain.

"Yes, yes, Giovanni, you're doing very well. No infection

there, and certainly no fracture. A couple more days and it will be as good as new! You'll be back to work soon, protecting us from our enemies."

Bresciano played on the doctor's love of gossip: "I'm doing some work for Captain Weston, but when I went to look for him this morning, he wasn't in his office. And do you know why?"

"Tell me!" The doctor looked up expectantly: there was obviously interesting news to come.

Bresciano retailed what he had heard about the aborted duel and the arrest of the Captain and Lieutenant Black. Coll listened avidly, and said, when Bresciano had finished:

"You know, I was expecting something like this. When I went to treat them…"

"Were you treating both of them?" Bresciano asked, surprised. "I know that Mrs Weston was injured when she fell down the stairs, but…"

"Ah, well, there's falling downstairs and falling downstairs, isn't there?"

Bresciano tried to look knowing.

"As I say, 'fell down the stairs.' Funny woman, that. And yes, the Captain did have a few deep scratches on his wrists, which I cleaned and bandaged for him, and a bruise on his forehead. He said the cat had scratched him, but as far as I know they have no cat!"

"Do you mean that…?" Bresciano stopped. He needed more information, he needed facts.

"Now, now, Giovanni, you must be aware that I am not permitted to tell you about my patients – professional ethics, don't you know! But… a duel, eh? Over the fair lady? Do be sure to come back and tell me what happens to Captain Weston, won't you?"

He ushered Bresciano out of the door.

Bresciano stood in the street, undecided about his next move. Already he had cast Captain Weston as the potential villain of the piece. He had been repelled and intimidated by him – a cold, unemotional man – but to beat his wife and throw her down the stairs must show strong ungovernable passions as well as intense cruelty. Bresciano felt a surge of naive anger at the brutality of Captain Weston. He felt sure that Dr Coll had been implying that the Captain had received those scratches as the unfortunate woman tried unavailingly to defend herself.

Poor Mrs Weston, forced to live with this brute! No wonder she had turned for comfort to the more sensitive, intellectual Lieutenant Black. It was probably an innocent friendship. So thought Bresciano in *his* innocence; he could not imagine a lady like that stooping to immorality. But the Captain had clearly put the worst construction on the friendship and he had first attempted to kill his wife, and then challenged his rival to a duel to the death. Such a man could also have murdered poor foolish Jamie to prevent the boy's innocent prattle from impugning the Captain's honour.

He had to find some way of getting into the Weston house. Now that the Captain was out of the picture was the time to find out what was really going on there. Ah, he had it. He would go back to the Barracks and complete the fair copy of the inventory and go to the Weston house on the pretext of delivering it. Once there, he was sure that he might manage to talk Lola into letting him in and perhaps he would even have the chance to speak with Mrs Weston.

He plodded up the hill to the Barracks and spent the next two hours restoring order in the room once more and then making a painstakingly neat copy of the inventory of equipment. The Captain would get to see it eventually, so he had to be sure that it was satisfactory. He sanded the last sheet of paper and folded it carefully with the others, then walked down toward the Green Market. He strode past where some soldiers were lounging about and walked up to Captain Weston's quarter, nervous, because the Captain might well take him to task later for such an intrusion, but prepared to knock firmly on the door. As he raised his hand someone seized his shoulder and pulled him round.

"I will never forgive you, Giovanni. How could you? And to think I trusted you. I thought that, however daft or grand your ideas, you were still a gentleman!"

He found himself facing a Bianca livid with anger.

"What...?"

He got no further. Bianca swung her arm back and delivered a resounding slap that jerked his head violently to the side.

"That's for getting my mother drunk today! And that,"

she hit him again, "is for spreading rumours about her!"

The knot of soldiers, aroused to interest by the unexpected and welcome entertainment being offered, joined in: and while some jeered at Bresciano, the others egged Bianca on with loud words of encouragement. Bresciano's cheeks were burning with shame as much as from the blows as he tried to understand what had happened.

"Two bottles of wine you got her! Don't deny it – she's told me everything. Trying to turn her up sweet after going behind her back and talking about her to Captain Weston and poisoning his mind against her! Aren't you ashamed of yourself? You and your damned scandal-mongering and trouble-making! First it was poor Jamie and now it's the Westons and my mother – as if she didn't have enough problems. No! Don't you dare speak to me!"

She flung away from him and he remained staring after her with his mouth open, the words of defence dying on his lips.

Behind him the soldiers raised a mocking cheer.

CHAPTER IX

It was just not fair! Bresciano thought, looking despairingly after Bianca's shapely form as she swept down the road in a fine fury. He knew from past experience that no apologies or rational words would sweeten her when she had taken umbrage. Not that he had anything to apologise for. He would have to wait till her emotional storm blew over. Damn Emiliana with her lies! And damn Bianca for believing her! And damn him for damning Bianca!

"I never did any of that!" he shouted after her retreating form, choosing to forget the single bottle of wine he had given Emiliana, and was rewarded by a mixed chorus from the soldiers at the corner:

"Course you didn't."

"Yes, he did; shouldn't have done any of that, should you?"

"Can't trust women."

"Don't let her get away with it."

"Naw then, got to treat women right."

And a final urging from one of the older men: "That's right. After her, lad, show her what you're made of – give her something she'll like."

This last innuendo appealed strongly to the rest who broke out into noisy laughter that left Bresciano humiliated and angry. What was only their crude humour, he read as contempt and, swallowing his bile, he stormed away despite his determination to get into the Westons' quarter. What he wanted now was somewhere to hide, and there was nowhere for him to go: Bianca's tavern was out of the question, Abraham had probably been hurrying home to see his family, and he himself had no idea any longer what he should be doing.

What had begun with such certainty about the attempt on Jamie's life had become a tangle that he was incapable of solving; and in the process of what he had been fond of thinking of as his 'investigations' he had become a thief and a laughing stock.

His tendency to run himself down, a trait that would never quite leave him in his long life, took firm hold now. He stood at the side of the street, his hands hanging limply at his sides, feeling ridiculous. Even the uniform he had been glad to wear made him feel foolish – the jacket he had been issued had been cut for the average soldier and the sleeves ended well short of his wrists. He knew he had cut a sorry figure a few minutes earlier in his impotence in the face of Bianca's attack on him.

"Impotent! That's probably how she sees me. Well," he mumbled to himself, "let her prefer the oily blandishments of 'Robair' – who probably doesn't even know the meaning of the word – to my sincere and well-intentioned affection. If she values lust above love, then I... I..."

His imagination failed him at this point and he kicked the nearest wall.

"Watch out, soldier, you'll be knocking that house down before you know it."

It was the roughened voice of Bianca's tavern colleague, a slightly older woman whose low neckline always revealed a generous portion of her ample bosom. "So what has upset a fine good-looking soldier like you?"

Bresciano was all too conscious of his coltish movements, his Roman nose and his protuberant Adam's apple to be comforted by her practised and easy flattery, but the look she gave him was appreciative.

She ran a hand slowly along her neckline: "Come along and cheer yourself up, let's have a drink... and maybe something else?"

Her meaning was clear even to his unpractised mind and he pulled himself up with a semblance of military discipline:

"I fear, madam, that I have an important matter to transact in this vicinity."

He saluted smartly and went back the way he had come,

feeling, surprisingly, less of a fool than before.

And when he saw ahead of him the plump figure of Lola pulling a shawl over her head as she left the Westons', he was glad that he had failed to enter the house earlier. She had already told him that the Captain discouraged visitors and would probably have stopped him from seeing her mistress. He waited till she turned up into Castle Street before going up to the door and knocking gently. Too gently. No one came to open so he rapped hard with his left hand.

"Who is that?" A voice, low-pitched.

"It's only Private Bresciano with some papers for Captain Weston." Now that he had done the deed, he was nervous and his voice wavered.

"Please wait a moment."

He felt vulnerable and exposed standing outside the door. What if someone saw him and reported it to the Captain? If he had been ready to fight a duel with Lieutenant Black, what would he do to Private Bresciano? A man insanely jealous would be unpredictable and vengeful. Bresciano had time enough to create alarming scenarios for himself before he heard bolts being drawn back.

"Please come in."

She stood behind the door so he could not see her, and the house was in near-darkness. Then he felt the door being closed slowly behind him and heard a sigh from the woman he had his back to. He felt his scalp crawl and he swallowed.

"Follow me."

She brushed past him, a slight figure with that mass of fair hair he had seen once. She was dressed in some floating pale material. Her steps were hesitant, but she no longer limped as she led the way down a narrow flagged passage to a small room at the back of the house.

"Emiliana has gone... no, it is Lola... Emiliana is no longer here... it is Lola... and Lola has just left. But she will return... soon. She will be staying here, in this room. I shall not be alone. I shall be safe. But we must get a bed in here. We have to do that. We really must."

She sounded distracted, her speech disjointed; it seemed to Bresciano that she was talking to herself, reassuring herself, rather than speaking to him.

As she spoke in her soft voice, she busied herself with

136

a small tinder-box. She lit a lantern before turning to face Bresciano.

The light from the lantern picked out her hair so that it glowed, a diaphanous halo. He stared at her. She was beautiful: her face a perfect oval, her eyes the colour of dark amber and her skin like magnolia blossom, except where the large bruise spread its darkness round a sick yellow centre, like a cancer. Though she was taller than Bianca, he felt that he towered over her. This woman was neither the Amazon nor the femme fatale of his imagination. His one thought was one of disbelief that anyone could choose to hurt such a lovely and delicate creature. It would be like pulling off a butterfly's wings.

"You have some documents for my husband?" He was aware that he had been standing in front of her with his mouth open and the papers clutched in his hand, and he nodded.

"Some personal papers?" She put her hand to her mouth, as if fearful of his answer.

"No, I'm sorry if I alarmed you." He was convinced she had heard about the duel. "It is merely that I had some work to carry out for Captain Weston and I could not find him at the Barracks. I wanted to assure him that the work was done and to hand him this inventory personally."

She waved the papers away. "You must take them back. Yes. Not here. My husband does not wish you to visit. My husband... you will not find him here till... I am not certain. Some days, but I will be safe with Lola. You must not worry about me. Lola has gone... but 'only a few minutes' she said. She went for... arnica and... and you... you should not be here."

Her face was not animated like Bianca's was; it had the stillness of a painting of the Madonna. All expression rested in her voice which appeared to respond to the concern and sympathy his own face betrayed. He wondered that she had opened the door to him at all.

"Of course." He inclined his head, a bow of respect, not the action of a soldier.

"Now you must leave." She was suddenly agitated. "No, not that way. I don't want them to see. They watch me and they are not to be trusted, but there is a door at the back. Come."

She moved out and opened a heavy door that gave into

a small yard. As she stood there he realised that what she wore was some kind of wrap over her nightdress and that her hair was tumbled and uncombed. She must have been resting when he had knocked.

"I'm afraid I disturbed your rest. I am sorry." He bowed again.

"No, no," she looked down at her wrap as if surprised to see it. "I was coming down to play the harpsichord. Music is so soothing, don't you agree? Now go. Quickly!" Her eyes filled with tears and she left him in the yard, closing the door in his face.

He climbed over the wall of the yard hurriedly, the very action making him feel guilty, and jumped down into a narrow alley at the back. As he moved stealthily away, he realised to his chagrin that he could have used the gate at the end of the wall, a gate he had missed in his haste. And as he skirted the house, the sound of music, very faint in the early evening air, came to him from one open window at the side of the house.

Now that he was able to reflect on what he had seen, he was disturbed at the recollection of the darkness inside. The windows were shuttered and the shutters closed except for that single window, which he had glimpsed as he walked down the passage – and that one was barred with a simple iron grille, one of the local *rejas* that kept homes safe from intruders. The place was more like a fortress than a home, he thought indignantly. And whom was the Captain paying to watch the house? The foolishness of having left via the yard struck him with unpleasant force: if someone had indeed been watching, whoever it was must have seen him go in – and could not have seen him leaving! How would that look to the Captain?

He walked off hastily, biting his lip as he attempted to make sense of what he had experienced. The thought of returning to the Barracks depressed him. Well, there were plenty of taverns in the town and he told himself resentfully that he had no need to go to Bianca's. There was a cleaner, better one opposite the church that would do very well.

Inside were several corporals and even a sergeant major sitting at a table over a bottle of brandy and a game of cards. Definitely a better class of place. Bresciano went up to the bar and asked for small ale, which he downed thirstily. Behind him the conversation turned on serious topics: the government in England that had yet to send supplies to the desperately beleaguered town; the enmity between Governor Eliott and his deputy, General Boyd; Eliott's decisions both popular and unpopular; the failed attempt on his life; and even the rumours about the aborted duel.

For Bresciano it was a relief to be away from the rough comradeship of the camp and the jokes at his expense. While he took no part in the conversation, he listened with pleasure to the kind of rational discussion he had not heard in days. The tension he had been feeling since he climbed the wall of the Westons' yard slowly eased. His father often said that the truth was always best – unless you could come up with a more convincing lie. As far as his flight from that house was concerned, and it had been a flight, he had no lie he could think of. If faced with his departure, he would have to say honestly that he had been shown out the back. He could, with almost equal honesty, claim that he was not sure why – for he had no idea who was acting as the Captain's informant. He had seen no one outside, but there were houses around with windows that presented good vantage points.

"Another small ale, please."

"No offence, lad, but I don't know you. Haven't seen you here before. So show us your money." The tavern keeper waited, holding a large jug of ale poised over the mug.

"Here," Bresciano plunged his hand in his jacket pocket. He groped around to no avail. He tried his trouser pockets before he realised where the money had gone – Emiliana's wine! "I'm afraid... I had some money here... I... I..." His voice petered out.

"I pay for my friend."

The words were in Spanish though the accent was not, and the voice was confident. Bresciano turned with relief to see Pascal behind him.

"Pascal, Thank you. I forgot I had no money left. I'll pay you back."

"¿Qué dice?"

Bresciano laughed with relief and replied in the same tongue. "I forgot that you don't speak English. I'm very grateful to you. I would have looked a proper fool – again!"

"No. It is I who am grateful. You took the weight of the

Sergeant's anger yesterday when it was I who was at fault. And when I saw you come in just now, I tried to catch your attention and meant to buy you a drink by way of thanks, but you looked like a man with much on his mind, and I did not want to intrude."

"I didn't see you."

"I have been sitting over there," he nodded to where a settle with high side-pieces had hidden him from view.

"I've never been here before, but I like this tavern. Sometimes I get tired of the other place. That friend of yours, Robert, is always there." He could not keep the resentment out of his voice.

"Yes. And where Robert goes, Jean Pierre follows. I also like this place. Here it is usually quiet and men talk with sense."

"Oh. Your English must be improving."

"No, no. Just a few words, but you can tell from their voices. That is all."

"My father comes here sometimes and he says there is never any rowdiness. He has seen the landlord knock heads together and throw men out for disturbing the peace!"

Pascal was about to return to the settle when Bresciano stopped him: "May I join you? I am alone tonight, well, I am alone all the time really."

They sat, Bresciano sipping his ale and the normally reserved Pascal nursing a brandy.

"Why did you escape from the Spanish lines to come here?"

Pascal did not reply immediately. He swirled his brandy in the glass before looking up at the honest curiosity in Bresciano's face.

"I joined the army to fight for my country. That was a long time ago."

"But you are not so very much older than me, are you?"

"About a hundred years only."

Bresciano smiled uneasily. "So your country is…?"

"You could say it is Brabant, but the army was French."

"Bianca says that Robert hates the French."

"Robert de la Tour – yes, so he says. I cannot answer for him," his voice was faintly mocking. "You will have to ask him what his reasons were for crossing into Gibraltar."

"Do you hate them too? But why fight for them, then? And why were you with the Spanish forces? I don't understand. Gibraltar is such a small place and I sometimes feel very ignorant, well, stupid."

"It is a long and ugly story. I'll make it simple: I joined the army. My family were honest people, wealthy enough by local standards. Some… French soldiers went to the… farm one day." He was choosing his words slowly, like a man trying to pick out maggots from a lump of meat. "Those men took what they wanted and did what they wanted, drove the livestock off and set fire to the barns. I try not to think what they did in the house… but when they left, only my dog was alive, and they had gouged its eyes out."

Bresciano was staring at Pascal, horrified and mesmerised.

"I was not there when it happened. I only heard about it all much, much later. It was… the pastor who eventually told me. Later I came here to Spain with other fellow countrymen. We had been sent to help at this siege. We were France's gesture of good will towards Spain. I was glad of it." He tossed off the brandy suddenly, "That is why… I took the first opportunity I had to… get into the fortress. You will see. Sooner or later I will have my revenge."

There was silence. Then Pascal called for another brandy, but Bresciano shook his head wordlessly when Pascal pointed to the half-empty mug of ale.

"Now tell me, how is your hand?" The Walloon's brisk question startled Bresciano.

"It was only a sprain." He forced the words out.

"So you are not doing any hard work now, eh? You are a lucky man. We Walloons are working outside the city walls towards the south. Fine defences there. The work is hard. Too much work on too little food, but it is good… very good to be here among the English."

He spoke in a neutral tone of voice; the voice of a man holding a mundane conversation and Bresciano shivered. He was thinking of his own family: little Lucia, Nonna with her love of drama; his strong and gentle mother; Aunt Maria and her nerves – and his mercurial, caring father. He imagined them all dead, butchered. He looked at Pascal who was now sipping his second brandy slowly and asked himself – how could one man hold so much pain in himself? For such a man to have considered Bresciano as, what had he said? 'a man who has much on his mind', a man, no less, was quite... showed a... Bresciano could not put into words what he felt.

"And how are things with you?" Pascal's voice brought him out of his ruminations.

"Bianca is angry with me. She shouted at me and... all that."

"A woman with spirit."

"But she believes... she thinks... and it's all lies. I want to tell her the truth."

"Avoid her – do not seek her out. Make *her* want to see *you*. It will work." His tone was cold and assured.

"I don't know that anything will work. The only one she wants to see is 'Robair'!" he imitated her pronunciation.

"He has charm with fine tales to tell of his adventures. He is heroic, but he is so very modest."

Bresciano replied with dawning knowledge, "Why, you don't like him either!"

"There is nothing to dislike. He is like a pretty picture, and he has painted it himself."

"But Bianca talked and talked about how brave he was to escape into the fortress to help the British, risking his life. She thinks he is so special – I can do no right and he can do no wrong."

"He has a good figure for a uniform and speaks several languages fluently. It is enough for him to work with."

"And I'm only an Artificer and he's been in a cavalry regiment."

"Was he? Interesting. He has the worst seat on a horse I have ever seen."

"But he told her..."

Pascal shrugged. "As I said – he painted the pretty picture himself." He stood up. "I must go. They are moving us down from Willis's into town and I have to clear out what little is left in our hut."

Bresciano was confused. "Willis's? But you have not been there. I haven't seen you there."

"No, not at your temporary camp. We were sent up when we first arrived to a small hut with half the roof fallen in. I think it was used once for *chevres* – goats – yes? It is away from your huts, well above, but the last rains brought a landslide and demolished most of it. In truth, we have nothing left except for part of two of the walls."

He turned to the landlord and paid for their drinks. Bresciano looked around, and saw Sergeant Connor rising from the next alcove. The Sergeant stared at him and at Pascal. Had he been listening? Bresciano was glad that he had not mentioned the murders to Pascal. The Sergeant left without speaking, and Bresciano looked down at the table. The last brandy sat on the table, unfinished. He stared at the remains of the golden liquid, golden, amber – like Mrs Weston's eyes – and when he looked up, Pascal had gone too.

Bresciano made the remains of his ale last as long as he could, then rose reluctantly and set off along Church Street, now dense with shadows. He too needed to be ready to move down, away from the small hut where it had all begun, and he had yet to deliver those blessed lists. Whether or not the Captain was in detention somewhere, once released he would doubtless check precisely when Bresciano had finished the task he had been set. Turning right by the Spanish Church he set off purposefully up towards the Barracks where he would hand the papers and, with luck, might find that there was some sort of meal available. Twice he found himself stopping to catch his breath. He had already noticed how any physical task found him flagging after too short a time: a poor diet took its toll on them all.

Coming out of the Barracks was the welcome figure of Abraham Hassan. "Well met, Giovanni."

Bresciano stared at him, his eyes widening and his mouth falling open.

"Is something wrong? You look as if you had seen a ghost. It's me – Abraham."

"I know! I know! But… I've had a wonderful idea! Wait here, can you? Good. I have something I must consult you about. Don't go away!"

He hurried in and handed the papers to an orderly who now sat in the Captain's office. Outside, Abraham sat on a low wall looking up at the sky.

"Look, Giovanni – a clear sky at last. That is the Great Bear, or the Plough over there. Is it not foolish how we create a complex shape out of a few small points of light? The Plough is the only one that makes sense to me. The best thing about tonight is that the sky heralds good weather for tomorrow. The rabbi's prayers at the Sabbath service have been answered."

He spoke lightly, but, like everyone else in the fortress, he was growing gaunt and there were shadows under his eyes.

"Listen, Abraham, about that man you were helping to interrogate, this deserter you mentioned…"

"I can't talk about it. I'm sorry."

"Oh. But perhaps you can answer a couple of questions? Very simple ones. Please?"

"I'll know when you ask," Hassan said cautiously, feeling he had been too open with his friend before. He had been flushed with importance at helping in a serious matter involving the safety of the fortress and he feared he had been indiscreet.

"Did this man have anything to do with the attempt on Eliott's life?"

"That's simple enough. The answer is: nothing at all. It was a woman, a military wife – would you believe that? A neighbour found her about to drink bleach or something and babbling about what she had done. Apparently she has lost her three children to the smallpox and now her husband is laid low with the scurvy – he is dying. As I heard tell, she has lost her mind. Took her husband's musket and… well, you know the rest. She blamed Eliott for everything that has happened to her, poor woman. She has been placed under restraint to stop her harming herself."

Bresciano expressed his horror with an inarticulate noise and shook his head.

"Life has grown hard, has it not?" Abraham was silent a moment. "What else did you want to know?"

"This man you questioned, has he been released?"

"No."

"He is a spy." It was a statement and he looked at his friend for confirmation.

"I have not said so. If people thought spies could easily come and go, it would create a climate of fear. Fear in a small place. People would begin to mistrust their neighbours. We have enough to deal with as things stand. Do you understand what I'm saying? What I'm asking of you?"

"Of course." He straightened his shoulders. "I am Giovanni *Discrezione* Bresciano. It's my middle name!"

"You are a clown too."

"Listen, Abraham. I am serious now. There were three deserters who came into Gibraltar around the time Jamie MacFarlane was murdered. I have proof that it was murder." He saw his friend's sceptical look, "I'm ready to swear it was murder. Listen to this."

He spoke quickly and convincingly, keeping to the facts and avoiding talking about his suspects, where all was speculation and possibility.

"It was you, Abraham, who told me to be logical. And Lieutenant Drinkwater told me to look for motive. And now I have one: your deserter..." he lowered his voice at the approach of several women who hurried past, "your deserter turns out to be a spy. Why shouldn't mine be spies too? And if Jamie had spotted them nosing around somewhere he would soon have told about them and they killed him to stop his mouth!"

"All three of them? As well as the one being held in the Black Hole? Four spies in a week? Do you think they send them over in platoons?"

"No, but that would explain..." He stopped. It explained nothing, so he began again, "At least one of them has lied about himself and, for a Walloon, he speaks very good English, and other languages as well!"

"Being a linguist is no sin. Even you have a smattering of French and Portuguese."

"But this is a port and my family runs a ship chandlery. We are bound to pick up things like that. Goodness knows where he comes from – and a successful spy, well, it would help him to speak the local language, wouldn't it? He could ingratiate himself with... people."

"So, he's a liar who speaks good English."

"His English is too good!"

"So are you thinking of making well-spoken English an offence? All right, all right! Can you not take a joke? And what about the other two?"

"One is from Brabant and I've been talking to him tonight. I don't know anything about the third," he ended lamely.

"So you do not know much. It's all guesswork again, is it not?"

"Yes, but... that Robert... there is something about him. He's a man who uses his past, or what he claims about his exploits, like having been in the cavalry – and he does not know one end of a horse from the other – and he uses it all to dazzle... people, so everyone likes him. For some reason women seem to accept everything he says as if it was Bible truth."

Abraham took a deep breath and smiled. He knew about his friend's interest in Bianca. "Is he, by chance, to be often found exercising his charms down at the King's Head?"

"I don't know."

"Giovanni?"

"Yes. Yes. He is. Too bloody often."

"No need to swear."

"*You* would if you knew him."

"I never swear."

Bresciano looked away from Abraham. Swearing was something his father did not countenance either, and he knew that in his few days in the Artificers he had sworn more than he ever had done in his life.

"That's beside the point. You've never met the man anyway. You don't know him."

"But do you know him? I mean, really know him? You don't, I am certain. Listen to me. I am ready to admit that you have made a reasonably convincing case for Jamie's murder. I have come to believe that you may be right about that. He was done to death by someone – for whatever reason. You also have a few people whom you suspect might have done it and you have even come up with a number of possible motives, some more convincing than others. What you have not yet found are any facts at all that establish the guilt of a single one of these people. It is all supposition. And you may never find the answer. You do realise that, don't you?" He sounded weary, but his final words were delivered with quiet authority: "Giovanni, you must not let your feelings – like jealousy – cloud your judgement. Good night, my friend."

He walked away heavily into the darkness.

"I *will* find the answer," Bresciano muttered. "I know it was someone who had reason to hate or fear poor Jamie and I will prove it. I will!"

Whatever Abraham might say, he had uncovered a

motive, a powerful motive. Corporal Jones had said an outgoing deserter could have tried to murder Jamie to escape detection, well, so could an incoming spy do the same for the same reason. Now that he had found his motive he was able to admit, to his shame, that Abraham had been right about one thing. His original insistence that the Walloons should be considered as suspects had had no basis other than his envy of Robert's privileged position where Bianca was concerned. But that had been before. It was different now. Now he was being objective. And he had one new fact to work with. Pascal had said quite casually that they had been based near Willis's. What had Robert been doing last Thursday? And last Friday? And the other two, naturally.

It had grown late, the communal meal would be over, but by going round to the back of the Barracks he might be able to find Cookie-Will. And find him he did and was given a hunk of sour bread spread with rancid grease, 'for Sparrow's friend,' Cookie-Will said. It gave Bresciano one more thing to be grateful to Jamie for, and he thankfully accepted the sort of food he would have scorned in the past. Then he helped the cook put the last pans away before taking the rough road from the Barracks to Willis's.

It seemed steeper tonight. From the clear sky, the crescent moon, a pallid goats'-cheese moon, lit his way as he toiled upwards above the final huddle of the huts of the poor in the euphemistically named Buena Vista. A few scattered trees stood like spectres guarding the road, and when he reached the hidden entrance to his track to the cave, he thought how much had happened since he had walked there in the morning.

Now that he thought of it, the day had been unreal, like the sort of dreams that fall short of being nightmares but prevent you from resting. Mrs Weston, hurrying him out the back of her quarter, so vulnerable, possibly in danger, her conversation disjointed by fear of discovery. And the horrors Pascal had recited in his precise voice. Horrors he found coming back to him in the dark. Even Abraham with his talk of that woman, her life ravaged by sorrow, her mind deranged. Images associated with them took possession of his imagination and he was unable to dislodge them.

Even once in his hut, after he collected his few possessions ready to move out the next day, he could not rid himself of what he had seen and heard and he sat up half the night, not wanting to close his eyes.

*　*　*　*

"Everyone ready to move in half an hour!" Sergeant Connor's voice roused him.

He got up sluggishly, but thankful to be leaving the hut, and went out into a scene bathed with light from a blue sky across which small clouds far above were sped on their way by sharp, high winds. Even the daily cannonade that had originally made him shudder he now welcomed as a sign of normality. Wednesday, a week since he had joined up: it was a new day.

The men bustled around getting ready to leave, except for a small number who were to remain behind keeping a lookout. The elevated position of their camp offered a fine vantage point. These were the men less fit to do heavy work, some already complaining about the sore gums that indicated the onset of scurvy.

"I don't know about you, Busyano. You're no damn use to me with that hand of yours." The Sergeant swung away from him and lined the rest of the men up before he inspected the huts.

There was a gap in the ranks – Tom again – and the men moved closer to each other to try and cover for their missing comrade, though there was little chance that it would escape the Sergeant's notice. Nor did it: there was a roar of anger from Tom's hut and the Sergeant emerged with a half-eaten pig's head carried at the end of a wooden stake and dragging some bedding behind him:

"Tom Tennant! You haven't done a bloody thing I said. Your hut's a disgrace and this…" he threw down the pig's head, "is beginning to smell. I want you here in front of me – now!"

A silence fell on the camp and the men shifted uneasily away from each other to leave the original gap in their ranks. No point in trying to protect that fool, Tom, now.

"He's not here, sir." Corporal Jones spoke up.

"Any of you misbegotten lot seen him?" The Sergeant glared balefully, his eyes raking the ranks.

"He wasn't in our hut last night, Sarge," an ingratiating voice spoke out.

"Not been seen since he come along eatin' that fresh meat yesterday."

"You're right there!"

"That's right. Told me 'e'd been told to work up at Princess Caroline's battery."

"Didn't come down with the rest of us to the Line Wall."

There was anger and envy in the voices. Where they had been willing to cover up his absence a moment ago, their grievances now swung them in the opposite direction.

"I'll have his bloody hide!"

But before the Sergeant could take that or any other action, a small boy came running up from Buena Vista calling out in Genoese and pointing back the way he had come. He ran full tilt into the Sergeant and began pulling at his sleeve.

"Now what? What you shouting about? Get away!"

The boy's shrill voice repeated whatever it was, excited and self-important. Bresciano drew in his breath.

"Anyone understand him? You, Busyano, what is he gabbling on about?"

"He says... he says there's a soldier down there fallen down the slope and he looks dead."

CHAPTER X

The boy, recognising him as a fellow local and for that reason less frightening than the other soldiers, whirled round and pulled urgently on Bresciano's hand, trying to drag him down the hill, his voice rising excitedly as he elaborated on the dead soldier. Bresciano held back briefly until the Sergeant's gruff, "Don't just stand there, you fool, find out what he's trying to tell us!" released him, and he allowed himself to be led down the hill. Sergeant Connor and Corporal Jones followed with the other men.

Halfway down the hill the boy turned aside and guided them through a mass of high bushes which fringed the road. An almost sheer cliff loomed above them, and half -way up, on a ledge almost as precipitous as the cliff itself, something that looked like a huddle of clothes, or a uniformed figure, could be seen lying motionless.

"I was looking for food," the boy said, "there's nothing to eat at home and my small brother and the other one, the baby, are always crying so I came to set a rabbit snare up here and when I looked up, I saw his arm sticking out over the edge, so I called him and he didn't answer so then I aimed a stone with my catapult – I can sometimes catch a sparrow with it – and I hit him, but he still didn't move. So I went up to get you lot."

"What's he saying?" The Sergeant, who had just emerged from the bushes, snapped at Bresciano, "Why can't he talk in Spanish? I can make some sense of that." He appeared to resent the fact that Bresciano might know something he himself did not.

"Only that he's hungry, sir."

"He took his time, didn't he? What else?"

"His brothers are hungry too so he came out looking for something to eat and he saw the body. He says... he thinks whoever it is... is dead."

"Is he sure of that? How can he tell? Did he go up to it?"

"No, sir. He just fired at it with his catapult and hit him, hit him hard by the sound of it. He says the man did not move."

"Could be dead then. Hmm. A badly wounded body presents difficulties. Easier to get a corpse down."

The Sergeant's pragmatism shocked Bresciano. Why, the man sounded relieved.

"We'll need scaling ladders. I suppose we can get them from the Barracks," Corporal Jones looked at the slope dubiously.

"I doubt that we've got anything big enough for this," the Sergeant said. "We can go and look and come back later. No hurry if he's dead."

"Wait. There's an easier way." Bresciano, anxious not to dismiss the possibility that the man was simply unconscious, had been studying the rock-face and now recognised the cliff: at the top of it was the cave he had visited the previous morning and he knew that at some point the track leading up to it passed close to this lower ledge, which could be reached from it by a scramble across a rocky scree.

"What's that, Busyano – are you acting the know-all again?" The Sergeant was scornful and irritable. "We've wasted enough time. We should have been down half an hour ago."

"I know this area, sir," Bresciano said earnestly. "I grew up around here. There's a path up near the camp and from there I think I can get across to that spot, and lower the... the... body down on ropes."

Connor looked at him: "Use your head – not on your own, you can't. Look at you. Do all that with only one hand?"

The Sergeant saw the men looking at him expectantly and came to a decision. "Jones, you go with him back to Willis's and get ropes and canvas while you're about it, and take Talbot with you as well. Then see if Private Bressiano can really take you to that spot. We'll be at the foot of the cliff, so you can lower the body down to us: and don't slip or expect us to catch you if you fall! Oh, and you, Malone," he lowered his voice as if not wanting to be heard, " take this boy down to Cookie at the Barracks and get him something to eat."

Bresciano and Jones, together with Talbot, a wiry man, returned to the camp at Willis's and once they were armed with ropes and a canvas sheet Bresciano led them, retracing his steps of the previous day, pushing his way though the bushes and on to the path with Jones following slowly and Talbot moving with the casual confidence of a tight-rope walker. After all these years, Bresciano could not remember exactly where to turn off. He had to stop several times and peer through the bushes, and Jones said doubtfully,

"Are you sure there's a way to that place?"

Bresciano who was beginning to doubt himself, replied firmly. "I know the way is along this path. I was born here. We played near here nearly every day when we were children."

But now, once he had cut and pushed his way though the scrub and on to the scree, it was to find that time and minor landslides had made the slope unsafe and he lost confidence as he struggled to keep his balance, dislodging small stones that tumbled and bounced down to where the Sergeant and the rest of the party waited.

At last, there it was – closer to the cave than he remembered – an even steeper slope of loose stones. Hampered by his sore right hand and his fear of heights, he moved uncertainly and as he stepped on to the loose stones which led downwards toward the lower ledge, he almost slipped. Jones, just behind him, placing his feet carefully, reached out to Bresciano and held him back.

"Are you all right?"

"I'm sure I will be as long as I don't look down – I think."

"No. That's enough. We can see our way clearly. You've done your job. Now let us get on with it. Wait here."

As he carefully worked his way round Bresciano he remarked, "You must have some mountain goat blood in you, Mr Bresciano. I was brought up on the Welsh mountains, and I'd have thought twice about playing around this sort of slope when I was a boy!"

"It wasn't that I wanted to – I just had… a friend who was absolutely fearless, who dragged me along everywhere." Then, remembering that Bianca had showed more favour to

Jones than to him, he said no more and was glad that he had not mentioned her name.

Jones moved away with Talbot, each steadying the other from time to time as the stones rolled under them and threatened to send them down the slope and over the cliff. Stubbornly, Bresciano chose to follow but was forced to stop, his mouth dry and his head swimming. Vertigo: and no shelter to be had. He crouched down, making himself look straight ahead, and clung as best he could to a stunted oleander. Talbot had moved confidently forward and was now standing on the small sloping ledge.

There was the body, lying face down on the rocky ground. Jones approached more cautiously and turned it over.

It was Tom, and there was no doubt that he was dead. Bresciano saw enough to make him catch his breath. Tom's skull was split open and his torn and tattered uniform was stained with clotted blood.

"It's Tennant, Sarge. He's dead right enough." Jones called out.

With infinite care the two men lifted the stained and broken body from the clean white limestone slope on to the canvas they had brought with them. Then they tied the limp form up in the canvas and lowered it carefully over the edge of the cliff, inching it down to the group below.

Bresciano had not liked the man, but as he watched the corpse being lowered, an inert mass, he was surprised at the degree of distress the scene caused him. Tom alive had been either obstreperous or filled with alcoholic bonhomie. It seemed impossible that there was nothing left of that now – just a mangled corpse. The task was done and as Talbot and Jones made their way to where he was crouching, Bresciano crawled backwards to where the path was firmer, before standing upright.

"Poor sod. His clothes still smelt of rum." Talbot viewed the event pragmatically.

"Strange." Jones muttered.

Bresciano did not think it was strange at all. It was clear to him that Tom, having discovered the quiet cave when he killed the ape, had returned to it – a secret place where he did not need to share whatever he had – and drunk himself silly on the rum bought with his new-found wealth. That gold chain and bottles of rum. Had he been stealing from the other men? From one of the houses left empty when the civilian population was encouraged by Eliott to leave? Tom had had the money to buy rum enough to make him blind drunk and had then staggered over the cliff to his death.

He thought, "If I'd dared to look down when I was up there digging out the palmettos, I'd have been the one to discover the body."

It was a disturbing thought.

* * * *

By the time they had made their way back to the Blue Barracks, Tom's body had been laid out on the cot in the improvised mortuary where Jamie had been placed a few days earlier. Talbot enlivened their return with details of Tom's injuries. In addition to the crushed skull, there were fearsome lacerations on his arms and body, the result of the fall, from striking projecting rocks as the body plummeted down the cliff, Talbot said authoritatively. At the Barracks Bresciano was glad to part company with him as they were directed to one of the dormitories where the rest of the men were stowing away their few possessions.

"Here," the Sergeant called him over, "what were you doing up there on your hands and knees while the other two went for the body?"

Bresciano felt what a ridiculous figure he must have cut while the other men did the dangerous work.

"Corporal Jones told me to stay. I'm a bit... clumsy, sir, and I get dizzy with... it's called vertigo."

"I know what it's called! So why did you volunteer, you fool?"

Bresciano blinked nervously. "I thought it was quicker. He might just have been unconscious, still have been alive."

Sergeant Connor grunted and looked at him fixedly, "A good soldier faces danger, but doesn't take stupid risks. Remember that. Well, now you better get down to Captain Weston and do some safer work there."

But there was still no sign of the Captain and the fair copy of the inventory still lay prominently on the desk. The young orderly sitting in the office, full of his own importance, would happily have set this gangling new lad a task, but deemed it wiser to play safe: he knew that he would be ultimately responsible to the Captain for his actions and dared not take risks.

Bresciano went out into the passage with a light heart – neither the Captain nor the Sergeant had assigned him any duties so he was free to go. He looked around the store-rooms again, but was unable to find any more lemons. When he went to the kitchen, his friend the cook had nothing to give him.

"That young boy the Sergeant sent, fancy that! – Antonio his name is – 'e's eaten up all the scraps I 'ad left over."

Oh, well, Bresciano thought, at least someone hungry had got the benefit of the miserable leftovers from the men's meal. And the Sergeant called Bresciano by his real name – or near enough – for the first time. Perhaps he was beginning to accept him, though his talk of 'safer work' in the office rankled. And as for sending young Antonio down... perhaps there was some kindness in the man.

Then he remembered that Sergeant Connor was one of his prime suspects.

*　*　*　*

Outside the Barracks he paused, wondering what to do next. His investigations had ground to a halt and he was completely at sea. He found himself speculating idly about Tom's last actions. Killing an ape for food had surely been a desperate act. The large males were known to be vicious fighters among themselves and had been known to attack humans. Perhaps the creature had already been wounded. The cave had been empty when Bresciano went in so Tom must have dragged the ape's body elsewhere to cut it up. Why bother to do that? Then a thought struck him: where were the remains of the ape? He remembered stories he had heard, that the bodies of dead apes were never found because their pack mates spirited them away through a secret tunnel for burial in their ancestral home in Africa. No, that was just a fanciful myth, a silly idea, but there was still something wrong there and he could not put his finger on it. Something was missing from the picture: the battered body on the ledge, the bare white limestone slope... what else?

Corporal Jones, he now remembered, had thought there was something strange about the body when they had found it. Or had he seen something? Had the ape's body been down there somewhere? Why should it? But Jones had gone down to the town on some errand, and the Sergeant and the rest of the men were off to work on the defences to the south of the town. Bresciano decided to go down to the town himself. He could go and see how Lucia was. And he might also find Jones; he had a feeling that the Corporal could provide him with information which could help him to make better sense of things.

He walked briskly downhill and as he passed the Westons' house, he noticed that it seemed silent and deserted. There was not even the sound of harpsichord music to be heard. He wondered if Mrs Weston was all right; and what was happening to Captain Weston? Were he and Lieutenant Black still under arrest? Would they really have fought a duel if information had not been laid against them? Could that have been done by Mrs Weston? Or had it been a case of indiscreet talk reaching the Governor's ears?

Bresciano stopped and looked back at the house. He pulled at his lip and shook his head. "Terrible," he muttered, "A duel could have been to the death. Killing each other in cold blood like that!" Bresciano decided virtuously that it was a form of licensed murder. The Captain and the Lieutenant were men prepared to resolve their problem through violent means. Dangerous men. Yet surely General Eliott would have to release them soon: he could hardly spare the services of two officers while Gibraltar was under siege.

His questions were soon to be answered. As soon as he turned into Waterport Street from Bell Lane, he caught sight of a familiar figure in front of him.

"Abraham!" he called.

Hassan turned round. "Giovanni, I was just on the way to your house to leave a message for you: I heard that you were working at the Barracks with Captain Weston, so, knowing you…"

"Knowing me? What do you mean?"

"I would be willing to stake money on the chances of your taking French leave to carry out these investigations of yours while the Captain was not around, so I thought I had better warn you."

Bresciano was alarmed. "Warn me? About what?"

"Only that the Governor released Captain Weston and Lieutenant Black yesterday afternoon at some stage, so you'll have the Captain after you if you haven't finished your work for him."

"Oh, that's all right. The work is finished and sitting on his desk waiting for him. But what happened? Didn't Eliott punish them?"

"I'm told he has reprimanded them most severely. And he's not a man to brook insubordination lightly. This time, though, he appears to have limited himself to telling them to settle their differences peacefully and to save their energies for killing the enemy, not each other!"

Bresciano digested this information. "The General seems to be a very humane man."

"Indeed he is. And very shrewd with it. Do you know that he pardoned that – that deserter, the one I was helping to interrogate, and sent him back across the lines?" Abraham was big with news, delighted to have been involved in the affair, "In fact it was a clever idea, as well as being humane, because he has been primed with incorrect information about our ..." he stopped abruptly, embarrassed. "I should not have said that to you – to anyone."

Bresciano nodded sympathetically. "I can be trusted, Abraham." And he grinned at the idea: false information about what? The state of the defences most likely, which 'information' should work to Gibraltar's advantage if the Spaniards swallowed it. He was impressed. "General Eliott is certainly the sort of leader we need in this situation," he began.

But Hassan interrupted, anxious to move the conversation into other channels, "What about that German madman who somehow wandered into the garrison about a month ago? Didn't you hear about him? He was full of wild stories about his adventures. He claimed to be a Prussian Baron, and that he had the plans for a cannon which could fire all the way across the Straits to Morocco. He must have sounded convincing enough because he managed to get an audience with the Governor, who told him he had no quarrel with the Moors, and had no wish to fire cannonballs at them. Then, as he could make no sense of the man, for all that the general speaks fluent German, he gave the poor fellow – Munchausen, that is his name, I think – into the hands of the doctors, who treated him for his mania with bleeding and cold showers. The usual sort of thing. They say he is very much calmed now and he is to be sent to the mainland under a flag of truce. Goodness knows what tales he will tell *them* there. Whatever they are, I'm sure he'll give the Spaniards something to think about!"

The thought of a cannon to be fired southward at Morocco in defence of a fortress that was being besieged to the north by Spain made Bresciano laugh out loud.

The two friends parted. Bresciano had obtained from Hassan unwitting confirmation that a supposed deserter could indeed be a spy. Furthermore, if even a madman could get into the fortress, anyone coming from the mainland had to be treated with caution: he had been right to think the Walloons were definite suspects. He had to investigate 'Rob-air' as soon as possible.

Once he had all the information, he could discuss it with Abraham, whose opinion he had come to respect. Of course, there was also what's-his-name to consider – Jean Pierre, the cipher in the group. And Pascal, the quiet one. But how was he to carry out his task?

"Yes!" he cried out. He had a perfect opportunity while his hand healed: he would claim that he was collating information on all those working with the Artificers – civilians and Walloons alike. He tested the idea out, addressing a pile of cobblestones: "I am recording information on all who are now involved with the Artificers. It is for… administrative purposes. I am working directly under Captain Weston…"

His hand flew to his mouth. The Captain was on the loose and here was he, wandering merrily round the town! He had to get back on duty immediately! He hesitated a moment for he was only minutes away from his house. Five minutes would make little difference. He could always claim that he had gone in search of the Captain.

At home, things seemed to be better. Lucia was sitting out in an armchair, and her pocks were definitely drying up.

"See, Giovanni, I haven't scratched even one of them, even though they itch terribly, but they are getting better, aren't they?"

Her brother was happy to agree with her.

"And tell me, what happened to your hand?"

Inspired by Abraham's tale of the mad Prussian, he invented a tall story about how, unaided, he was building great walls all round Gibraltar, so that the enemy would break their heads against them if they tried to attack, and was rewarded by her giggles of amusement.

In the kitchen, he apologised to his mother for not bringing food, but she said that Giancarlo had been able to buy some vegetables and had even caught some fish, so they were not going hungry. It was, he realised, not exactly true, for the small fish he saw ready gutted on the table would hardly have satisfied the appetite of two adults in times past, let alone a family of five, but it was food and it was fresh.

"Of course not!" his father boomed, appearing at the door. "It is my duty to provide for my family – not that your contribution is not appreciated, boy!"

Bresciano was about to take offence at being called a boy again, but he saw in time the twinkle in his father's eye. Giancarlo was just trying to needle him, and he knew better than to rise to the bait.

"Has João recovered, then? Were you able to go out with him?"

His father shook his head. "No, I had to take old Gavarone again, and he's no help – more of a liability; he's really too old for the work, but as I said, he can do with some money these days."

"Lieutenant Drinkwater was good enough to call," his mother said. "A nice young man. He spoke to me about how he was enjoying the books, 'a real life-saver', he said, and how a town like Gibraltar should have a library. He wanted to ask my permission to lend my books to another officer. I gather he had asked you already, but wanted to get my consent formally. He spoke very highly of him, and I agreed, of course. Is it not strange that someone as gently spoken as Lieutenant Drinkwater should be thirsting for the Spanish attack to start 'so that we can see some action'? That is what he said. And here are we saying a nightly rosary to stop any such thing happening. He complains of boredom while we think of nothing but where the next meal will come from. These young men wanting books and war – it does not make sense to me. Is that what you want too, Gianni?"

"I don't *want* war. I simply feel it will… it might come."

"And have you met this Lieutenant Black?"

"Not yet."

Bresciano felt he was being given another avenue of investigation. Drinkwater was passing on the books to Lieutenant Black so there might be an opportunity to talk to Black at some time, using the books as a pretext.

"Can you stay and talk to us a while?" his mother said.

"I had better get back to the Barracks. The Captain could return at any moment and expects to see me there. He is very strict."

He left his house hurriedly, turned up the nearest alley and ran straight into the Captain.

"Ah," he said, saluting, "ah… Sir!" He felt as if the blood had drained down to his feet.

"Did you complete the work I set you?"

Bresciano nodded, wordless.

"And why are you not at the Barracks?"

"There was no one to… tell me what to do next, so I came to look for you, sir."

"To my house?" The voice was quiet.

"No sir, no. No sir. I was going… I thought… King's Bastion might be…"

"I may need you tomorrow." The quiet voice silenced him. "Now I have other matters to attend to."

He turned on his heel and Bresciano leaned against the wall, his legs trembling. What a fool he had been! Even his excuse was foolish. He had been going away from the King's Bastion, not towards it. Thank goodness the Captain had failed to notice.

Nearly a full day free! He would make good use of it, starting at the King's Head. He made his way with some trepidation, with no idea what Bianca's reaction would be when she saw him, but he had the feeling it would not be pleasant. She was not there, but the other barmaid greeted him loudly and with a suggestive wink.

"Come here, big man, and transact some important matters in my vicinity!"

His face burned as she echoed his pompous speech of the previous day, and he looked around, expecting the jeering chorus of soldiers which he was becoming accustomed to. But there was no one else in the bar. No, there was someone; as his eyes became accustomed to the gloom, he saw that Corporal

Jones was sitting in a dark corner, staring into his mug of ale.

Trying to speak lightly, he said to the woman, "I'm sorry, Carmela, you're not fortunate, er... you are out of luck again. Just give me a mug of ale, please. Now I have to speak to my corporal." Then he added lamely, "I'll pay tomorrow."

"You know where to find me, lad." She served him the ale with a knowing smile that made him swallow hard, and he took his ale to the corner and sat next to Jones.

"What's the matter, Bresciano? You look very thoughtful."

"I was wondering about something you said this morning. You used the word 'strange' about Tom."

Jones looked at him and said briefly, "Finding Tom disturbed me." He was reluctant to say more.

"But you must have seen many dead men before."

"No, it's not that. It's just that when I saw him, I thought... never mind what I thought."

"There was something strange, though." Bresciano prompted him.

"Yes."

"His death might not be quite what it seemed," Bresciano put the words into his mouth.

"Yes. I didn't want to say anything after the Sergeant's reaction when you suggested that Jamie had been murdered, I'd rather keep my mouth shut and stay out of trouble. After all, it was only a small thing when all's said and done."

Bresciano stiffened. He had begun to feel uneasy about that incomplete picture of Tom's death, but he had cried wolf before and he tried now to be circumspect. Keeping his voice even, he said:

"Corporal, you can tell me. I'm nobody. Was it something you saw that made you think that way? Was it a dead ape?"

Jones looked up at him, startled. "No. Nothing like that. It was Tom's clothes – you could smell the rum on them, even his breeches."

"But Tom was a drinker."

"That's right, he was a drinker, and drinkers don't pour rum on their clothes – they pour it down their throats!"

"He could have spilt some as he fell over the cliff."

"There was no bottle that I could see anywhere. And in any case, his uniform... why, I tell you, even his trousers smelt of rum. That couldn't have happened accidentally."

"You mean... do you think... that someone pushed him over the cliff after soaking his clothes with rum to make it look as if he had fallen over while drunk?"

Jones shrugged uneasily, and Bresciano continued, as he finally put the events of the previous few hours together in his mind in some sort of logical order. "I hadn't thought of that! I was wondering about what I had failed to see, something I've just made sense of: he had terrible injuries, but there was no blood!"

"There was enough blood on his clothes."

"Yes, there was a lot of blood on his clothes, but nothing on the ground! Those white stones! What if he was killed before he went over the cliff?"

Jones looked at him and said slowly, "Bresciano, I don't want to be involved in this. These are all your ideas. Is that clear? Is that perfectly clear?"

"Perfectly. I won't mention your name."

"That you will not!"

"But I must find out what happened to Tom – and to Jamie."

"As long as you realize that you are on your own." Jones nodded, and returned to his ale.

Bresciano sat there thinking. What a fool he had been! There was no ape; there had never been an ape. Tom had not killed an ape for food. His extra meat ration had come from – of course! – from the pig's head. Hadn't Aunt Maria mentioned that a pig's head had been sold for a pound? That meant that the blood in the cave had been Tom's blood. It was Tom, not an ape, who had been brutally bludgeoned to death in the cave. Then he had been taken to the edge, soaked in rum, and thrown over.

His mug of ale remained untouched. He was not even aware of Corporal Jones leaving the tavern. All he could see was a shadowy figure in his mind, a dangerous presence.

Tom had been murdered. And Jamie too had been murdered. It could not be a coincidence: the two deaths had to be connected in some way. Someone had wanted them both dead.

Who had killed them? And what could be the motive for the double murder?

CHAPTER XI

Bresciano drained his mug and got up, studiously avoiding the barmaid as he left and trying to ignore her ill-disguised amusement.

A few simple facts were what he wanted, something that would stop his mind going round in circles, something that no one could dispute. Take the possibilities to explain the source of Tom's newly-found wealth: had there been any thefts in the camp, or at the Barracks, or even in the town? Even if he learnt of any thefts, how could he be sure that Tom had been the thief?

"For goodness' sake," he muttered, exasperated, "how difficult can it be to resolve such a minor question?"

The only consolation was that two solid facts remained: there was the gold chain Tom had got for his lucky bullet and the pig's head, which the Sergeant had found and all the men had seen. That had been real enough, and in these days of few supplies of fresh meat, it was more than likely to have been the one sold for a pound. And the rum! Tom had been drinking it for days. That was a fact too. The inevitable conclusion was that Tom suddenly had money to spend. He had acquired money, and it must have been through theft or looting, for surely Tom had not been the sort of man to salt away a small nest-egg by saving out of his meagre fourpence ha'penny a day. And if he had, it made no sense that he should spend it all at once in such a profligate manner.

Bresciano stood at the door of the tavern and sighed gustily: if he succeeded in finding an answer to these questions, it would still only be a drop in the ocean, leaving all major matters unresolved.

And while he considered the question of Tom's affluence, he realised that someone could have killed Tom for whatever money he had stolen or saved. But if theft were the motive for his murder, it could have no connection with Jamie's death for Jamie had had even less worth stealing. The deaths had nothing in common, except for…

There was the sudden sound of nearby laughter and the loud voices of men released from work and seeking what social life the tavern afforded.

"If it isn't Bianca's old, old friend!"

Robert de la Tour's laughing voice cut across his thoughts and Bresciano turned, annoyed at being interrupted in his musings, though they had not been leading him anywhere.

"Giovanni, old fellow, do not just stand there! Come back inside and join us for an hour or two. Work is done and here we are, Jean Pierre and myself, with our wages and a thirstiness upon us!"

A slap on the back and an arm round his shoulders and he found himself back inside the tavern.

Bresciano was unreasonably annoyed at Robert's misuse of the language. If he was going to employ the bonhomie of the very British, very upper-class 'old fellow', why did he throw in that inept use of 'thirstiness'? And that declamatory 'work is done'! As if he referred to some Biblical event. Why the grand manner?

Bresciano had already begun to develop a degree of pedantry which would remain with him for the rest of his life. As he had nothing concrete against the Walloon, he needed to find a reason – any reason – to justify his irritable reaction to the tall young warrior, so he settled on Robert's infuriating fluency in a language not his own. Furthermore, he disliked his slight accent and the emphatic way he enunciated his r's. A French trait, perhaps?

But the most galling thing of all was that the Walloon looked like a soldier, bore himself like an officer, and had a worldly and raffish air that threw into relief Bresciano's coltish movements and youthful uncertainties. And though he needed to speak to Robert and get information about him, he wanted as little direct contact with the man as possible. A ridiculous situation.

Jean Pierre, a man of few words, jingled the coins in his pocket and his face split into a grin. "Drink and food," he said, his English pronunciation execrable.

In these days of repulsive rations, money went on food when you could get it. Bresciano realised that he too had money due to him, money he would give his mother.

"I am afraid I can contribute nothing. I have a family to help support," he said.

"What scruples are these? We ask only for your company, my stout fellow!"

Bresciano winced at being addressed so.

"We are agreed then? You shall be our guest. They have come by some better food today – some local merchants keep back supplies till the prices rise enough to satisfy their greed, eh? So the delectable Bianca informs me!" He winked knowingly.

Bianca – certainly delectable – had scowled at Bresciano's entry and smiled encouragingly at Robert by contrast. Jean Pierre seemed content to sink into the background.

The buxom Carmela served them, ignoring Bresciano in her eagerness to please Robert and, once more, Bresciano became unreasonably annoyed. Where he had been anxious to escape Carmela's clutches, he now resented the absence of her unwelcome advances as she vied with Bianca for Robert's attention.

"Tell us about how you came into Gibraltar," Carmela unwittingly saved Bresciano the need to initiate the subject. "I was not present when you spoke of it before. Come on and tell Carmela," she pouted.

"But I have told you already!" Robert protested, his Spanish almost as fluent as his English and imbued with a similar accent that appeared to exercise a fascination for women at least, for Bianca now stood at his elbow and also encouraged him.

"You told us nothing! I had to ask Jean Pierre here to explain how it happened, and he wasn't much help!"

Jean Pierre grunted and settled down to drinking his ale.

"Go on, lad, how'd it 'appen?" one of the Artificers present joined in as a chorus of rough male voices was added to the pleas of the women. "And speak in a Christian language so we can understand you!"

"All right! All right! I surrender to *force majeure*! I will tell you." He drank deeply from his tankard before launching into his narrative: "For us it was simple and we were fortunate because we had planned it well. You see, before we arrived there was a failed attempt that we were told of. It was early this year…"

He turned to Jean Pierre, "*Quand ont-ils nous dit que nos compatriots avaient subi le terrible désastre?*"

"*Janvier*," Jean Pierre emerged from his ale.

"Yes, this past January." His face became grave. "A party of six of our countrymen was pursued as they fled towards the safety of the fortress. It was well past sunrise and though they ran like the wind, only three survived unscathed. The one they took alive was hanged the next day – a corporal, charming fellow, so I'm told. Another they killed. Yet another they left for dead. Your people rescued him later, but his injuries were appalling. They had used bayonets, swords and rifle butts on him, and he didn't live long."

There was a silence in the tavern, what had begun as a light-hearted chance for entertainment had now taken a serious turn.

"How… why did you… how could you take such a risk?" Carmela's eyes had filled with sympathetic tears.

"What we heard helped to strengthen our resolve." He drained his tankard only to find another pressed into his hand.

"Go on, lad."

"There is little to tell. We arrived here at the Spanish lines in late November, no it was…" once again he turned to his friend, "*Quand sommes-nous arrivés ici?*"

"*Le quinze novembre*," Jean Pierre supplied.

"Of course: the middle of November." He smiled, "How would I manage without you, Jean Pierre?" Then he addressed his audience, "He is a marvel with anything to do with numbers! So, to resume my tale, we soon had heard the story. Within weeks Pascal planned to escape, but at night. What could we do? We could not let him go alone: a man needs to draw courage from friends."

There were mutters of agreement.

"We escaped, wriggling on our bellies on the ground like worms. We each started off from a different point to divide any pursuit there might be. It was a night with a fair moon so we could see our way, but it was also a night of some cloud that obscured us part of the time. The ground was wet from the recent rains, which made our progress slow. As matters turned out, poor Jean Pierre had the worst of it. Someone must have spotted movement near the ground and took quite a few shots at him. And in the dark I had strayed too near him for comfort because several stray bullets came my way. I think they may have taken us for rabbits or hares. Pascal managed better: he told us how he was lucky enough to find a shallow trench to crawl along, lucky devil! Well, it was almost light by the time we felt safe enough to stand up and stagger towards the safety of the city walls."

He stopped suddenly. "So there you have it! We wriggled and wriggled away from the tyranny of the French yoke and the arrogance of the Spanish Dons! A toast to freedom and to the wonderful English!"

The laughter was back in his voice as he raised his tankard, and the triumphant end of his tale was greeted by some applause and a few appreciative remarks of approval.

Bresciano was silent. However Robert might dramatise the narrative and then make light of his own escape, there was no denying the danger he had courted to get into the fortress

The food came, a thin stew in which floated a few meagre pieces of old Spanish black pudding, a little potato and the odd sliver of onion. As he spooned it up hungrily, Bresciano reflected on what he had heard and concluded, albeit reluctantly, that being a spy involved courting danger. Nevertheless, the fact that Robert might be brave did not mean he was innocent of the heinous crime of spying. It galled him to admit Robert's courage till he realised that a spy would have arranged with his masters that there should be no pursuit. Of course! It had not been a question of courage, but of a cunningly contrived pseudo-escape. The thought cheered him up. He knew himself to be facing no hero, but simply a devious man.

They progressed from the stew to another tankard of ale, which Bresciano refused, anxious to keep a clear head, and then the clay pipes and cigarillos came out and talk once more became the order of the day. He seized his opportunity.

"I feel bad about asking you for information after such a pleasant evening, but now that I am no longer working with you down on the city walls, I have been put to some clerical work. It is very tedious. I work in a small room by myself writing all the time. Sometimes I barely take in what I write. Ridiculous records which I am certain no one will ever read!" He was pleased with the way he was presenting his subterfuge. "And now I have to collect information about anyone working with the Artificers. Do you mind answering a few questions? Just very boring, very bureaucratic stuff."

Robert leaned back in his chair and nodded.

"I need to know where you are quartered."

"As from yesterday morning we are at the Blue Barracks, in a basement area. It is dry – more so than our previous dwelling!"

"Where was that? Just for my records."

"A smelly goatherd's hut above your temporary camp."

"I see, and when...? As you can see, I'm not very good at this sort of work. I lack a logical mind!" Bresciano smiled, pleased with himself, "I should have begun by asking when you arrived in the fortress."

"Let us see. Today is Wednesday and we have been here over a week so I am almost certain it was a Monday. *Nous sommes arrivés á Gibraltar...c'était lundi dernier, n'est-ce pas?*" He turned to his silent friend, who nodded. "There it is: the Monday past. I should have remembered because it was the day after the church service. They are very keen on religion on that side of the lines! At least the priests and commanders are. I went along. I had no desire to attract unwelcome attention to myself. As for Pascal, he went piously ahead, though he managed to slip away very soon. And Jean Pierre acted sick, out of sheer idleness, but all he got for his pains was to be made to dig a new latrine!"

Damn Robert! Once he got the bit between his teeth there was no stopping him. Bresciano managed to check the flow of talk.

"I see. So you came in on Monday and you moved up to the hut immediately?"

"No. We escaped on Monday night but only arrived Tuesday morning. Then we were held till the evening. We all had some information to give and Pascal had written down details of the new Spanish battery we had been working on. I can tell you that we have been lucky to escape with our lives from there: your cannon fire is costing the Spanish dearly. I think that was what decided Jean Pierre to escape! Only a few days before we…"

"Thank you so much," Bresciano said hastily, "I may need to check the details again once I have written my report for Captain Weston, before I hand in the good copy. So let me get things clear in my mind: shall I say you went to the hut on Wednesday?"

The tavern had been steadily filling up with men, and the noise level had been rising so that Robert had to raise his voice to be heard and Bresciano almost missed his last words.

"No, my good fellow. We went up on the Tuesday night itself, Jean Pierre and I. Pascal followed shortly after. It was dark by the time we were directed up to the hut. In fact, carrying the blankets and bobs and bits we had been issued, we might not have found it without the help of a slip of a lad, an Artificer, who pointed us in the right direction."

Bresciano stared at Robert.

"A slip of a lad," he echoed, his mind racing.

"Yes, and a strange one, too. He told us we would be safe up there because there was a small angel living close by! We were certainly safe enough – safe, but wet. The angel didn't stop the rain coming in through that terrible roof!" There it was again, that amused tone of voice that always charmed his listeners. "Still, the lad was a helpful fellow. He even went back to help Pascal. I'm only sorry I missed their meeting – Pascal with barely a word of English and the lad telling him enthusiastically about our own private angel! I know what Jean Pierre had to say about any angel out in that weather: it made me laugh, '*Pas un ange – c'est un canard céleste*'." He translated for the others, and Bresciano laughed on cue, but it *was* funny to imagine a celestial duck. Perhaps there was more to Jean Pierre than appeared. "And you began work with us immediately? Thursday? Friday?"

He was having trouble containing his excitement – he had established a connection between Jamie and the Walloons! But he had asked too eagerly, before he had thought things out so his questions had everything to do with the attempt on Jamie's life and his murder, but nothing to do with any imaginary record for Captain Weston. Robert looked at him in surprise.

"You are very keen on your 'tedious work'! I see that thorough records are in truth to be kept. Well, Wednesday we were free. Jean Pierre slept up at the hut. Pascal said he wanted to see the old Moorish castle, I think he is a man who finds ruins interesting, and I came to find where the taverns were!"

"I see. Work on Thursday? Yes?"

"That is correct. Will you have another drink, my friend?" He stood up, ready to take their tankards up to the counter where Bianca waited. "I do not need to ask Jean Pierre if he wants another! Ah, what a joy it is to have some money to spend, even such a small amount as a soldier can command."

"No, thank you. I shall have to be going."

There was no way now that Bresciano could ask about Thursday evening and Friday late afternoon without causing suspicion. He bit his lip and looked away from Robert and the sight of Bianca's welcoming smile as he approached her.

As he prepared to leave, his eye fell on Jean Pierre who was smoking with a vacant look on his face. That was his man, Bresciano thought. It would be a matter of getting him on his own and asking him a few questions about their whereabouts on those crucial days. He would then confirm the answers with Pascal. For the present he would content himself with speaking a few words directly to the man, enough to establish friendly contact.

"*Bong soir, mon ami. Je vais maintenant a… au le… Blue Barracks. Je suis un peu fatigué. Ton ami, Rob-air, est très… bon homme, eh?*"

"*Oui, c'est vrai.*"

Bresciano smiled and shook his hand warmly, leaving Jean Pierre looking puzzled at this unexpected sign of bonhomie.

Outside the King's Head he saw Emiliana across the road, in the arms of a fat man – Murch – and his anger at her for the lies she had told Bianca evaporated. It was a sad way for a woman's life to go. Emiliana with her drinking and probably with no work now, for he did not believe her tale of the Captain finding her work in a respectable household; nor her praise for Captain Weston helping her – followed as it was by her complaints about 'two dollars' not amounting to anything. Her bitter words came back to him: 'Sometimes it doesn't pay to know too much.'

It had been staring him in the face. And before Robert had accosted him outside the tavern, he had been making his way towards the truth, one truth: what the two murders had in common was unexpected money. Jamie had been able to purchase good wine and Tom had had enough money to spend on what were luxuries for a private. That alone linked the murders – money. And what of Emiliana's two dollars? They had probably come from the Captain to buy her silence. Buying silence, that lay at the root... of what?

He tried again. Like Emiliana and Jamie, Tom had been getting money from someone – but why were they giving it to him? It could only be to buy *his* silence. Tom had been blackmailing somebody! What secret could Tom have known that was deadly enough to drive someone to murder him? What secret could poor Jamie have known to pay for it with his life?

But Jamie had thought of everyone as his friend, he would never have threatened... Bresciano paused: Jamie could *unwittingly* have betrayed a secret, whereas Bresciano could imagine Tom becoming greedy, demanding more, threatening exposure. And in the end must have pushed the victim too far and paid with his life. His lucky bullet had not helped him. Emiliana had been right – it hadn't paid *them* to know too much. And if the Captain had bribed Emiliana to pay for her 'discretion', it began to look as if the Captain's *modus operandi* was to attempt to buy a person's silence before killing him. Immediately he was aware that there was a major flaw in that thought process, a flaw he had not identified. And there were gaps in his reasoning. He was not worried: he decided, with the optimism of youth, that matters were becoming clearer.

Certainly the Captain with his Thursday and Friday card games up at the Barracks would have been virtually on the spot to murder Jamie. And that made him a clear suspect. Just as certainly as Robert – all the Walloons – were suspects. How Sergeant Connor fitted in to the picture was still unclear, but he was another person with motive and opportunity. Now he, Bresciano, self-appointed investigator of crimes, only needed to discover where Lieutenant Black had been, and Mrs Weston, he supposed, must be investigated, if only to be cleared of blame. Things were definitely becoming simpler.

He had the certainty that the deaths were linked so, after

that, all he would need to know was where they all had been when Tom was killed up by the cave.

His euphoria vanished. With a feeling of despair he faced the fact that he had no idea when precisely Tom had been killed. Furthermore, if what he thought about Captain Weston was true, then Emiliana's life was in danger! He knew little, had achieved nothing and was as far from the truth as he had ever been.

Slowly he trudged away from the tavern and back to the Barracks. He found himself pausing outside the Westons' house. The door opened and a wedge of golden light spilt out into the gathering darkness. There were two women held in it and Bresciano felt his breath quicken at the thought that one was Mrs Weston, that elusive and fragile creature. But it was Lola's portly form that emerged, leaving the other woman within – a tall, lean female who seemed to be either giving or receiving information before bidding Lola a curt good-night in broken Spanish and snapping the door shut. From where he stood Bresciano heard two bolts being shot inside the house. It made his scalp crawl: the beautiful princess locked in a tower and guarded now, not just by plump friendly Lola, but by a witch.

What was it Emiliana had quoted the Captain as saying? 'She won't be alone for long'? She was assuredly not alone now. The Captain was ensuring that she was watched over day and night by Lola or by the Witch, apart from whoever else he might have recruited – those prying eyes that Mrs Weston had feared. How far could jealousy drive a man? That duel. He had found himself condemning it roundly, but what about his own father and his three duels? Why did he consider those different? Perhaps it was because Captain Weston was a grown man, a captain, a person used to military discipline, whereas his father had been a rash youth.

"What are you doing here, son?"

His father had come up to him and had been watching him as he had stood observing the scene unfolding at the door.

"Papa! Er... I am on my way to the Barracks and I stopped a second."

"To catch your breath? You? A fit young man? Or was it for a glimpse of the lovely Lola?" He teased him.

"I don't know what you are talking about."

"You do know, Giovanni. You would not be a man if you had failed to notice the beautiful *Scignoa* Weston. Even I, at my age, have noticed her. She is not a woman to pass unremarked in a small place like this. But you are well advised to admire from a distance."

"Oh, you heard about the duel?"

"Of course. There is little enough to talk about in the town, so a duel is big news."

"Papa, I wondered if you could tell me... no, never mind."

"You want to know why I fought in Genoa? I will tell you. You are old enough to know the truth. The first time I was eighteen, like you, and I was drunk and I fought a good friend who was also drunk. First blood was drawn and our other friends, who fortunately were not so drunk, stopped us."

"What did you fight about?"

"The next day none of us could remember except that it had something to do with our taste in clothes. The second duel was more serious because I was sober and was accused of cheating at cards. And the third time it was over a young woman. My rival was not a good swordsman and... I was fortunate that he survived, but that was when my family disowned me. You see, my rival was the son of a nobleman and the woman whose honour I was defending – at her instigation – was what the English call 'a prime article'." He saw his son's attempt to look knowing, "She was a kept woman who had come from the local brothel and had risen in the world. She was very lovely, very graceful and, I realised later, totally without scruples or morals. You see, Giovanni, a woman can drive a man to great foolishness. But, once more I was lucky because if I had not come to Gibraltar, I would not have met your mother."

"But..."

"Mrs Weston is a dangerous woman to know. Keep away, Giovanni. I am serious." He walked away, his parting words stung Bresciano, "You are still very green. You are wet behind the ears, boy."

It was not said unkindly, but it was spoken with the confidence of an older man, a father to his son, a man of the world to an innocent, and Bresciano bristled visibly. Why should his father assume that he knew everything there was to know? Could he not see that there was a world of difference between a lady like Mrs Weston and the woman he had fought over?

He arrived at the Barracks in an angry mood and was glad that Sergeant Connor and the men on the southern defences had not yet returned. In the dining area a group of men were clearing their plates and he waited till only Cookie-Will remained, for he was in no mood for jokes and banter. The cook was happy to serve Bresciano with a meal, while he chattered away about his dream of opening a pie shop in Gibraltar when the siege was over.

"I make a good pie, I do, when I've got the meat to fill it with! I'll leave the Artificers an' find meself a nice plump local lass, an' we'll serve meat pies and ale – an' you'll always be welcome in our pie shop, lad!"

Bresciano listened with half an ear, wondering idly whether Carmela would make a suitable wife for Cookie – she certainly qualified as plump. And though he had other things to occupy his mind, it was pleasant to sit here relaxing; his exertions by the cliff had caught up with him and a rest was welcome. After half an hour the men still had not returned.

"Must be encamped near their work," Cookie-Will was resigned. "I'll 'ave to serve this same muck up tomorrer an' it'll taste even worse then."

"Have you always been a cook in the army?"

"Nah! I started off as a soldier, but there were too much killin' for my likin'. So I got meself into the cook-'ouse instead."

"How can you tell when somebody died?" Perhaps Cookie-Will could help with finding out about the time of Tom's death.

"When 'e stopped breathin'!" Cookie-Will laughed till his three chins shook.

"No! I mean, when you find a dead body, how can you tell when he died?"

"Most dead bodies I seen 've bin on the battle field." He gave the matter his full attention as he passed his hand over the stubble on his chin. "Funny that. Sometimes they was limp when it 'ad all just 'appened. An' sometimes, when we 'ad to wait to collect the dead, it were a different tale. Stiff as a board they'd be. Awful – lyin' there all twisted and stiff like wooden dolls. Been dead for hours. And 'ere's a strange thing. I first found this out when we found me great aunt Hermione one night lying dead in 'er yard. We reckoned she'd fallen there that morning after church. It were a Sunday and she 'ad 'er prayer book in 'er 'and."

"And what was odd about that?"

"Nothin'. The old girl was a great one for prayer. It was 'er being stiff that were strange."

"How?"

"'Acos she weren't stiff at all!" Cookie-Will had clearly told the tale on more than one occasion and relished the surprise element he had built into it over the years. "And then we found as she 'adn't been to church neither that morning nor to evensong. So we worked out she must've been dead for over a day. And I found since that it's the same with the bodies we got off the battlefields. We'd 'aul away to get these rigid corpses moved, sweatin' over it – specially when there was three or four tangled together and mangled like you can't imagine – and if we could 'ave waited to the next day, the job would've been that much simpler. That's it, you see: first you're floppy, then you go all stiff and then you go floppy again."

Bresciano was feeling queasy at the cheerful recital, but he needed the information:

"So you can tell exactly when a person died from the way the body is?"

"I 'spect a doctor can. I can't. All I know is wot I seen. I tell you, some of them corpses would turn your stummick. Bits missing and blood everywhere. Right then, want these last scraps of pie? Though I wouldn't call it pie, meself."

But Bresciano was hurrying out of the door towards the fresh air.

He had established one thing, however vague: Tom's body, that limp form Jones and Talbot had wrapped in the tarpaulin, must have been dead over a day if Cookie-Will was to be believed. He tried to conjure up what he had seen in the cave the previous morning: the ground caked with blood. That was it! Caked with blood meant the blood had had time to congeal. And when Tom's absence had been discovered in the morning they left Willis's, the men had clearly not seen Tom since Monday lunchtime when his supply of fresh meat had made his presence a memorable source of envy. After that no one had seen him. He had stayed in the area, claiming to have work above the camp, while the rest went down to the city walls. He could have been killed any time that Monday afternoon. The body had not been found till today, Wednesday morning. Was it long enough for the stiffness of death to have vanished? Perhaps he would ask Dr Coll; he might know.

By the time he got into his cot in the Barracks, he found that the Artificers had returned; but not even the smell of unwashed bodies, the presence of the ubiquitous bed-bugs nor the snorts and snores and flatulence of the other men could keep him from sleep.

*   *   *   *

He woke suddenly and sat up in the dark. He had been dreaming and desperately tried to remember before the image faded. Yes, a ridiculous dream: there was the angular Aunt Maria with a pig's head, drinking from a bottle of rum and shouting at him: 'Giovanni, it *does* pay to know too much sometimes!' in Emiliana's hoarse, drunken voice. He did not believe the pseudo-mystic rigmarole of dreams that Nonna Lucrezia espoused, aided by her strange pack of cards, but he did find that his dreams sometimes were like shadows of his ordinary life.

There was only one thing that he could think of, one of the ideas that had eluded him earlier: two murders, however closely linked, did not necessarily spring from *precisely* the same reason. Why little Jamie had been killed was still unclear to him, but perhaps Tom's death was easier to explain. He could have seen someone enter the hut just before Jamie was killed and decided later that the person he had seen was Jamie's killer.

From what Bresciano had learnt of Tom, he could see that, rather than tell anyone in authority, he would have used the information to threaten to expose the murderer. He had certainly been in the area – he had come running with the others behind Sergeant Connor. If Tom had tried to blackmail a murderer, it was not surprising that he had ended up a victim himself. But who was it that Tom had been blackmailing? And who had the opportunity to kill him?

Captain Weston and Lieutenant Black had been in

custody – no, Abraham had said that the Governor had released them that afternoon; either of them could have done it. The Sergeant? He could not see Connor agreeing to pay blackmail, even as a preliminary to killing the blackmailer; he would surely have taken immediate and violent action if Tom had tried to blackmail him. What about Robert? He knew that the Walloons had been quartered near Willis's – any of them, he supposed, could have had the opportunity to meet Tom by the secret cave on the pretext of paying him more money, and then brutally despatched him and thrown him over the cliff, hoping that the death would be assumed to be the result of a drunken accident. And now that he thought of Robert, it struck him that Robert's insistence on not having money made it more than likely that he *was* in funds!

He groaned with frustration in the dark. Anyone could have done it except, he assumed, Mrs Weston. Then he remembered his father's words about the woman, a graceful and unscrupulous woman, and a duel fought 'at her instigation'. Could Mrs Weston have egged the Lieutenant on to commit the crime which would protect their guilty secret – if they had one! What about Jamie's death? He was sure that the two murders were linked, but this did not help. He had the same suspects, and as far as he could tell, it looked as if they might all have had the opportunity to commit both murders.

He was getting nowhere. The grey light of dawn was just beginning to come in though the window and he was still wide awake.

He tried to remember Jamie's rambling chatter. Discounting his 'angels' and other obvious flights of fancy, his recurrent theme had been his 'friend', who was going to take him back to Scotland and give him a job as his ghillie. So the friend, if he had existed outside Jamie's imagination, was a Scotsman. But Bresciano had failed to pursue this idea because he knew that there was no Scottish regiment on the Rock, though there were, no doubt, some Scottish soldiers in the other regiments. Why, General Eliott himself was a Scotsman!

But no Scottish friend had turned up to pay his last respects after Jamie died. His suspects were not Scottish – he was sure he could have picked up a Scottish accent even in the educated tones of the Captain and the Lieutenant. Perhaps the 'friend' was imaginary after all… but why had Jamie said that he had to keep the friendship a secret or bad things would happen…?

Bresciano fell back into a dreamless slumber and was woken after seconds, or so it seemed to him, by the orderly he had met in Weston's office, who was unceremoniously shaking his shoulder:

"Wake up, lad, wake up! Captain Weston is back, and he wants you. And it's in a rare old mood he is, too. I'd jump to it, if I was you."

CHAPTER XII

Bresciano tumbled out of bed in a panic at the thought of what Captain Weston might want of him and why he was in a bad mood. Was it Bresciano himself who was in Weston's bad books? He might have discovered that Bresciano had been roaming the town when he should have been finishing his work at the Barracks or, and Bresciano grew cold at the thought, the Captain could have found out about his visit to Mrs Weston. He stood, frozen, his breeches halfway up his legs – but it was useless to speculate. Hurriedly he dressed, ran down the corridor and stopped outside Captain Weston's office, trying with little success to straighten his uniform and smooth down his hair.

He knocked tentatively and the unemotional voice responded, "Enter."

Bresciano stood in front of the desk, his eyes fixed on the floor, and waited for the Captain to speak or for his wrath to break, but there was silence and he risked a quick glance up at the man. Weston was not looking at him, but at the papers on his desk. Bresciano could see that it was his inventory that the Captain was perusing. A bad sign?

Eventually the Captain looked up, and said coldly, "You write a decent fist, Private."

There it was, approval that sounded more like a reprimand because of the tone in which it was given, but approbation nonetheless.

"Sir!" Bresciano waited, staring straight ahead. On the wall behind the Captain hung a small oil painting depicting a wild scene of craggy, snow-capped mountains, with a stag drinking at a brook.

Captain Weston handed Bresciano two sealed letters.

"I want you to deliver these letters, Private Bresciano. The first is the more urgent. You are to take it immediately to the Surgeon Major, Dr Baines; you will find him in the Naval Hospital. When you have delivered it, you will take the second to Captain Lord Manners, on *HMS Agincourt*. You will wait for an answer, a written answer, and return here." He hesitated, then added, "If I am not here, leave it with my orderly; *he* will bring it to my quarter in Governor's Street. Have you understood?"

He spoke slowly, as if to ensure that there would be no confusion about his instructions and Bresciano was offended at being treated like a fool.

"Go now. I may need you again this afternoon."

Bresciano took the letters, saluted, and left.

His long legs took him rapidly down the hill to Southport Street, past the small piece of waste land that had once been a thriving stables and out of the South Port towards the Naval Hospital. The day was sunny, but cool, and he made good time. As he strode along he found himself counting the oleanders at the roadside, as he had done as a child – counting but never touching them. Nonna Lucrezia had filled his mind with tales of how his hair would fall out if he did and how oleander blossom could be used to cast spells. The trees continued to flourish for they were indeed poisonous and even during the cold weather people would not take them even for firewood. Pretty trees with scented blooms, everything about them poisonous, from twigs to twisting seed-pods. It made him think of his father's words about beautiful and dangerous women.

He paused, something stirring at the back of his mind. Something about the Captain. Closing his eyes he attempted to conjure up the scene in the office that morning: his own fear, the picture on the wall, the Captain's usual dismissiveness... He opened his eyes. That was it. When the Captain had handed him the letters, he had not been dismissive. He had been, what was the word to describe his manner? Bresciano had felt it as disregard for an ignorant private, but that was not it. Had the Captain been pensive... wary... tired? None of the words helped him define what he had sensed and misinterpreted as condescension.

But he now had the impression that the Captain's impassive exterior had been hiding some tension, or some deep emotion, but he could not tell what it was. Perhaps it was linked to his detention by the Governor. That must have been a bitter experience for a man of his rank. Bresciano shrugged, surprised to find himself feeling sympathy for that stern man – a man who expected urgent letters to be delivered promptly! Drawn out of his wool-gathering by this thought, he resumed his walk at a brisk pace.

At the hospital gate the guard directed him to where he might find Dr Baines.

"He'll be in the smallpox ward. Not as crowded as it was, but bad enough! That's the place you want, at the far end, just afore the Devil's Tooth."

Bresciano could see the ominously named landmark the soldier had indicated, a sharp spur of limestone looming over the building. As he passed the other buildings, he heard a sharp agonised scream. He shuddered to think what might have caused that and when he pushed open the door of the building and stepped in, he found himself translated abruptly from the bright, clear December day into a long gloomy room, where his senses were assailed by the stench of corruption and the moans of the sick. Men, women and children were lying in beds crowded one against the other. Some lay ominously still. Three men stood in the middle of the room. One was obviously a medical orderly. One of the other two, probably the older man, must be Dr Baines. He was an elderly man, a tall lean figure with thinning grey hair, and he was dressed in the style of years gone by. He walked heavily, with the assistance of a cane, and he looked tired and harassed as he moved along what Bresciano thought of as a nightmare ward.

Stifling his nausea, Bresciano approached the group and addressed himself to him.

"Dr Baines? I have a message from Captain Weston, sir."

Baines took the letter, opened it, and looked grave. Then he pushed it into one of his capacious pockets with a sigh, a man tired of trying to bring comfort where no comfort was to be had.

He addressed himself to his companion. "I must go to the town at once. Please continue with the treatments, Dr Rogers.

Do what you can for these poor souls."

Bresciano followed the doctor out and Baines asked him: "Will you be returning to the town with me?"

"No, sir. I have another message to deliver for Captain Weston – to Captain Lord Manners at the New Mole."

"Ah, yes." Dr Baines shook his head sadly. He looked out towards the small harbour, formerly so busy and now sheltering only a single frigate and a few small boats. "He would be wanting to arrange passage home; it will not be easy…" he muttered, then his voice trailed off as he recalled the presence of this young enlisted lad. Baines sighed and called for his horse.

Handing Bresciano his cane, he mounted with a degree of difficulty, shaking out the skirts of his coat. A sharp wind had sprung up, sweeping the last few leaves on the ground into the air where they chased each other before falling back, and Bresciano noticed that among them lay what he realised was Captain Weston's letter. He picked it up and held it out to the Doctor, but Baines had trotted off briskly and even as Bresciano ran after him and called out his name, the wind whipped his words away and he was eventually left, breathless, with the paper in his hand.

Slowly he looked down at it. It was private. All letters were. Privacy had to be respected. He straightened out the now-crumpled sheet and was guiltily aware that he was allowing his eyes to linger on the page as he prepared to fold the paper. Forcing himself to look away, he hurried back into the hospital and left the letter with the porter he found on duty.

Back once again outside the hospital, he took several deep breaths of the fresh winter air. Whatever his reasons had been, Sergeant Connor had been right after all. The Naval Hospital was not a place where anyone who was not *in extremis* should be sent. Then he began the short downhill walk to Rosia Bay – a cove held within small sheltering cliffs – and then continued along the rough track that led to the New Mole.

But it was the Captain Weston's letter that occupied his mind. He knew he should have averted his gaze as soon as he realised what he was seeing, but he had not.

"I only thought it might help me to solve the murders of Jamie and Tom," he muttered to himself. "And I did not read it properly." He spoke defensively.

The letter had been quite short and he had indeed not read it, but he had seen enough. The dislocated words demanded attention. There was the tantalisingly incomplete sentence he had seen, 'she only succeeded in causing superficial scratches, which Mrs Bickerstaff, whom I have employed to...'; and the alarming, 'even between us, we cannot guard her'; the damning, 'she becomes cunning' and isolated words about 'vigilance'. Finally there was the cryptic end of the letter with some reference to 'the woman I still love'.

He was left with nothing but questions. Had Mrs Weston attacked Mrs Bickerstaff, her new jailer? Or had she struck out at the Captain? Was it aggression or self defence? Did the Captain equate jealousy with love that he could write those final words? Did they refer to his wife or to someone else, to another woman he had loved and still loved – an earlier love? Had this been an arranged marriage that had now turned sour?

This put a different complexion on matters. The dour Captain Weston now appeared to be a more complex and even a more sympathetic character, but he and Lieutenant Black were still unknown quantities. And so was the enigmatic Mrs Weston. Bresciano needed to make sense of their emotional triangle. Unless he did so he would never establish whether – or, indeed, if – any of them had had the motive and opportunity to kill both Jamie and Tom.

Meanwhile, there was his errand to Captain Lord Manners. He soon found himself in New Mole Parade, one more open parade ground in a military town, and walked down from there on to the New Mole.

Captain Manners was easy to find. Bresciano asked the first sailor he saw for *HMS Agincourt* and got a short reply:

"It's right in front of you, youngster. Just follow your nose!"

Loftily ignoring the possible reference to his prominent proboscis, Bresciano took the man's advice, and soon found himself on the ship's gangplank.

"Message for Captain Manners!" he called out uncertainly, and a fresh-faced midshipman, far younger than Bresciano, came up.

"Cap'n *Lord* Manners, you mean!" he said reprovingly.

"I have a letter for the Captain which requires an answer."

The boy took the letter and motioned to Bresciano to follow him down the ladder into the bowels of the ship. Bresciano ducked in time to avoid hitting his head on the lintel and walked behind the midshipman to the Captain's cabin.

Captain Manners was bending over a chart of the Bay which was spread out on his desk. He took the letter from the lad, broke the seal, and read it, then threw it down. Without even looking at Bresciano, he grunted:

"No ship going to England this week. Tell your master that I will inform him if the situation changes."

"I believe he wants a written answer, sir, sealed I'm sure."

"Damn your eyes, boy! I'm busy." He glared at Bresciano. "He told me to…"

Manners snatched up Captain Weston's letter and scrawled a few words across it and sealed it carelessly before tossing it to Bresciano.

That was it. Bresciano was dismissed. On the way up, fuming at the assumption that he was a mere servant, he bumped his head on the exit to the deck and reflected that compared to Manners – what an inappropriate name for the man, Lord though he might be! – Captain Weston was a model of civility.

Bresciano walked back to town on the track which ran by the Saluting Battery, now reinforced with extra cannon in case of attack, and through the South Port into Southport Street and then along Church Street. As he neared the Spanish Church, he saw a slim figure in a red cloak approaching him. He groaned. It was Bianca, and he was in no mood to listen to another tirade from her. There was no escape; he braced himself for another verbal onslaught.

But Bianca was in a surprisingly conciliatory mood. "Giovanni, I am glad to see you!"

At least that was a better beginning than their last encounter. Bresciano relaxed a little.

"I wanted to tell you that I'm sorry about the other day. I have been talking with my mother and she admitted that she blamed you unjustly. She said… well, she had been drinking already when you came along. Although you did bring her more wine! You must not, Giovanni. You know how things are with her now." He realised that this admission shamed Bianca and he instinctively took her hand in sympathy. "And I made her tell me what had really happened. I'm sorry, Giovanni, I know it wasn't all your fault, and I was... angry... unfair to you."

Bresciano's mood lifted, and he said awkwardly, "No, forget it, Bianca. It was just a misunderstanding of no importance between friends; and we are old friends, aren't we?"

"Oh, yes!" Bianca smiled, and raising herself on tip-toe she kissed him on the cheek. Bresciano glowed, and then remembered his investigation.

"Bianca, do you think that we could go, go together, and speak to your mother? I must know what is really happening inside the Weston house – please, for Jamie's sake."

Bianca cast her eyes to heaven, "Is that all you think about?"

"Yes... no... Bianca, I have to know who was responsible for Jamie's death. He was my friend, and yours too, I think. And someone has killed him. And there's Tom as well!"

He saw her frown and before she could protest further, he hurried into a quick explanation of all the strange circumstances of both deaths that could not be explained easily. She listened, more amenable to his ideas than she had been formerly, for she too had noticed Tom's sudden affluence and been suspicious of it.

"But, surely, even if you are right, it can have nothing to do with the Captain and his wife!"

"I don't know that. Mrs Weston seems to have caused a lot of gossip and Jamie innocently used to tell those stories about her. He may have made the Captain or Lieutenant Black angry, and..."

"Oh, all right." Bianca capitulated. "I've got a few minutes before I'm expected at the King's Head."

They walked up the side street to Emiliana's house. She was in, and for a change she was sober. Bianca, as always, went straight to the point.

"*Mamma mia*, you have to tell us. What is happening with Mrs Weston?"

Emiliana tried to resist. "I – I promised not to say. The

Captain paid me."

"Yes, with wine to make you drunk!" Bianca said bitterly.

"And two dollars... only two dollars!"

"Well, that may be enough to buy your silence where others are concerned, but I am your daughter. You must tell me at once. It is important!"

Emiliana, never the most strong-willed of women, caved in when faced with her daughter's determination.

"The Captain was angry because he found out that the Lieutenant visited his wife when he was not there."

"What happened between Mrs Weston and the Lieutenant? Was there any – you know!"

"Well, you know what men and women are." She tossed her head and looked away.

"*Mamma*, did you actually see anything?"

"Not to say 'see', but I'm no fool, am I?"

"I want facts. What exactly happened between her and that lieutenant?"

"All right! All right!" she snapped, annoyed at being forced to tell the unvarnished truth. "Nothing that I ever saw. But when she expected him, she dressed up special, she acted like a little girl, dancing around. And then when he came, they would sit down – and talk and talk."

"About what?"

"How should I know?"

"*Mamma*!"

"Oh... about books, just about books! And she sang for him and he... well, he looked at her with a hungry look – as if he would suck the soul out of her."

"But did they *do* anything?"

"Don't be a fool, girl. What could they do with me there? But afterwards, when I was not there – ah, who knows!"

"What is Mrs Weston like?" Bresciano put in.

"She is a stupid woman. Sometimes she was singing and dancing, and playing music on that – thing she has, and sometimes she would lie down on her bed, or even on the floor, crying! I think she is afraid of her husband."

"Was he violent towards her?"

"That I saw, only with his voice."

Bresciano recalled the cold, cutting tones of the Captain.

"But did he hit her? threaten her?"

"I said already, never that I saw." Her manner was sullen. The truth was not as dramatic as her lies, but she made the most of it. "Mind you, when I came in the morning, she would have bruises on her arms, her face, and she never told me how she got them. I say he beat her, as any husband would to a wife who went with another man!"

"You never yourself saw him do anything to her, except speak to her?"

"Have I not said so? Sometimes he would call the doctor – the English doctor, or Doctor Coll – who would look at her, and they would talk, the doctor and the Captain, very quietly, so she could not hear, and nor could I. Not that I ever listened!"

"Mrs Weston – what did she say to you? Did she speak to you?"

"What, that stuck-up cow? She only spoke to me to give me orders. Only when she saw me talking to that poor boy, the one who died – I was just giving him a drink of water, out of kindness – and she said that I must never speak to him again because he was spreading gossip about her, and he would have to be dealt with. That's what she said. That was one day after the Lieutenant had been there!" Emiliana finished triumphantly.

Bresciano felt himself grow cold at all that this implied.

"Was that when she told you that you must go?" Bianca asked.

"Yes, but I went back the next day: it was the husband who employed me! But she must have told the Captain something, because he called me and said it was better that I go, and he would give me a present if I did not say anything about what went on in the house. And I have kept my word. Only to you, the daughter of my heart, have I spoken of it!"

"Have you seen her since?" Bresciano inquired.

"Only once. I went to the house to ask the Captain if he would give me more... if he would give me my job back, and before I got there I saw her with her cloak walking up the hill – toward the Lieutenant's house!" Emiliana finished spitefully, adding, "why should she go up there at that time on a Friday? There was nothing up there – no shop, no friend of hers to visit... not that she had any lady friends... nothing! She never went out much before, except to church. If you ask me, I think she was going to the Lieutenant, to run off with him, and the

Captain caught them!"

Further questions elicited nothing of any importance except the fact that Emiliana had only worked at the Westons' for three months after her predecessor – Mrs Weston's old nanny out with them from England – had died. And it became clear that Emiliana knew little enough and that most of her ill-natured accusations were founded on the slenderest of evidence at best and only on spleen at worst.

As he left the house with Bianca, Bresciano thought about what Emiliana had said. To sift through what he had heard was confusing. Those last remarks of hers had smacked of rancour rather than truth. Furthermore – they made little sense: where did you run away to in a besieged town? The only thing he had learnt was that Mrs Weston had been out on the Friday when Jamie was murdered. Were her injuries self-inflicted in an attempt to gain the sympathy of her lover? Bianca broke into the confusion of his thoughts. They had reached Waterport Street.

"I have to go to the King's Head now, Giovanni. Will you come with me?"

With a start, Bresciano remembered that he had to report to Captain Weston.

"No, no, I must report for duty."

Again she gave him a quick peck on the cheek and said, "Well, maybe you will come to see me this evening."

With that she was gone, and Bresciano stood there looking after her, with his hand on his cheek.

"Well, well, Giovanni! The fair Bianca seems to be in a friendlier mood towards you today!" Abraham Hassan had come up behind them and must have seen Bianca's fond farewell.

Bresciano actually blushed. "She... she's been a good friend for a long time – since we were children," he protested.

"But now you are not children any longer. I do not know about the young lady, but your feelings are more than just friendship, are they not?"

Abraham was stating what they both already knew and Bresciano did not answer at once. Bianca was permanently on his mind. He wanted her. The old affection and closeness and love of their childhood friendship was still there, but now he knew that he felt for her as a man does for a woman. He wanted her. What he felt might be lust; he could not pretend otherwise to himself. At times he ached for her, which was why she could hurt him so when she flirted with other men or when she was angry with him.

"Ah, Abraham, what you saw meant very little," he sadly spoke the painful truth, "it was just that she realised that she had misjudged me when we last met and she was apologising."

"And what an apology!" Abraham said with a grin, then quoted. "'A woman of worth who can find? - for her price is above rubies.'"

"What was that?"

"It's from the Book of Proverbs, in the Bible."

"'A woman of worth.' Why do you call her that?"

"Think of it: I find that few women, or indeed men, have the courage and honesty to admit their mistakes, let alone make generous amends as she has done!"

Bresciano digested this in silence as they walked together towards the Blue Barracks. As they approached the hill leading to the building, Hassan turned away and Bresciano said,

"Wait, Abraham, I have just remembered: on the wall of Captain Weston's office there is a painting of high mountains with snow on them, and a stag drinking. It's not... it does not look at all like the rolling Devon moors which my mother always delights in telling me about. I liked the look of the place, though – wild but quiet. Do you know where in England that could be?"

"How could I?" Hassan was amused, "I've never been to England and I haven't seen your picture. But from what I have heard, the highest mountains are not in England but in Scotland."

"Scotland!" Bresciano's enthusiasm rose. "And the Captain's first name is Andrew! That is a Scottish name, isn't it? My mother taught me that: 'St George for England, St Andrew for Scotland.'"

"Don't know much about your saints," Hassan remarked.

"But if the Captain is Scottish, couldn't he have been Jamie's 'friend' who offered him employment when they returned to Scotland?"

Hassan smiled. "Giovanni, you are doing it again – making bricks without straw. I don't think, from what you've told me, that the Captain is anyone's friend, let alone the friend of a demented Artificer. And I will warn you once again, don't interfere in the lives of officers or you'll be in real trouble!"

With that he left and Bresciano, his enthusiasm hardly dimmed by his friend's cautionary words, made his way cheerfully up the hill with his long stride.

Captain Weston was not in his office. Bresciano sought out the orderly, who was in the kitchen enjoying a mug of ale with Cookie-Will. The orderly was pleased to be in charge and informed Bresciano loftily that the Captain was tied up with Dr Baines and would not be back for a couple of hours. He took Captain Manners' message and smoothed the now-crumpled sheet disapprovingly.

"You are to deliver it to his quarter – Captain Weston's instructions," Bresciano hesitated and then asked casually: "That picture on the wall of the Captain's office – it's his, I suppose – it's of Scotland, isn't it? Is the Captain a Scotsman?"

"I believe his mother was from Scotland. Why do you want to know, anyway?"

"Oh, just curious," he felt excited and tried to sound uninterested, "he doesn't sound like a Scotsman."

The orderly stood up, ready to leave: "That'd be because he proba'ly went to a proper English school to learn to speak proper English like a Christian." He obviously had little love for the Scots.

"'Ere, lad – Giovanni – 'ave a bite to eat. I'll lay odds you've 'ad nothin' today, and you wasn't at breakfast." Cookie-Will handed Bresciano a bowl of some thin soup and a hunk of bread. "It tastes like sawdust, this bread, but better'n nothing, eh?"

Bresciano nodded and ate gratefully what he was given. With the orderly's departure Cookie-Will slipped some boiled rice into Bresciano's bowl with a conspiratorial smile.

"Cookie, why is it that…? Well, it seems to me that a lot of soldiers seem to dislike Scotsmen." It worried him because if it was so, he might have to consider most of the Garrison as suspects for Jamie's murder.

"Don't you pay no 'eed to wot 'e says. Wot does that orderly know – jumped up little pipsqueak? It's like everythin' else; some like 'em and some don't. Far as I'm concerned, I like a man, not his country. Take our Guvner Eliott. A Scot 'e is and none the worse for it. Best man for this job. Not that I like him, mind you, but you got to respec' the old bugger is wot I say."

Bresciano grinned. He dismissed his fanciful idea of having half the garrison as suspects and tried to link what the orderly had said to what he had learned today. Had he discovered a crucial link with Jamie? Jamie's 'friend'? It seemed possible. The Captain's family would be well-off no doubt. They could afford to employ a ghillie – whatever that was!

But it had been Lieutenant Black, looking like a thundercloud, who had stalked into the tavern in search of Jamie. And Mrs Weston might well have run to him on that black Friday. And Emiliana had said that Jamie must 'be dealt with' for spreading gossip.

But was Emiliana misquoting or lying? The problem lay in that, while Bianca was his urgent reality, Mrs Weston was a charmed figure, a princess in a tower who might turn out to be the witch herself. Whichever she was, he was slipping, without being fully aware of it, into the same role that Lieutenant Black had assumed.

So Bresciano made his way out of the building thinking that if he had no more immediate duties for the Captain, he could risk going home briefly, or he could take the opportunity to try and see Mrs Weston. And then he could go to the King's Head to see Bianca. His heart lifted as he recalled how she had kissed him – only on the cheek, of course, but twice! He knew it might mean very little, as he had said to Abraham, but it gave him hope of better things to come.

Approaching the Captain's quarter down a narrow lane, he found himself moving aside into a deep doorway at the sound of hoof-beats behind him. Round the corner came two men and Bresciano caught his breath and pulled back into the shadows. Could it be Captain Weston? He could not afford to be seen by him in the vicinity of the house.

He breathed a sigh of relief. The two officers who rode past were unknown to him. They trotted past the house and into the Green Market.

"Now what?" he mumbled and stood undecided, pulling at his lip and frowning.

There was always the back yard. He might catch a glimpse of something from over the wall. Perhaps Mrs Weston might be there. Slowly he made his way round to the back of the quarter, looking askance to see if anyone was watching him. He had felt compelled to find out more about the ethereal Mrs Weston, but now that he stood by the wall, he was uncomfortable as well as nervous. Looking into other people's lives made him feel like a Peeping Tom and he did not relish the feeling.

The yard was empty, but the back door to the house was open. Suddenly Mrs Weston stood framed in the doorway, looking anxiously back over her shoulder. In her hand she carried a lighted oil lamp, a pointless exercise given that the sun still shone. Perhaps she had been down into the cellar. Did these quarters have cellars? She turned her head and he ducked down.

He heard her footsteps, barely audible even in the quiet of the yard and raised his head slightly. She was moving towards a corner where lay a pile of kindling and some firewood under a tarpaulin – a dangerous place to carry near-naked flames. Was she going to climb over it and out of the yard? Again she looked back and he raised his head to see her better. She caught sight of him, started guiltily and came towards him. She seemed to glide.

"Galahad!" she whispered with an uncertain smile.

Bresciano felt as if he had swallowed his Adam's apple.

"I knew you would return. Shall you stay this time?"

He shook his head wordlessly.

"Perhaps you are wise. They will all be here today, soon, very soon!" Her face darkened.

Again there was a clatter of hooves outside. But this time they stopped outside the house. Bresciano heard the front door opening and the murmur of voices as at least two men entered. The Captain and Dr Baines?

"Frances! Frances, my dear!" It was the Captain's voice, sounding urgent. He was not a man to be kept waiting, as Bresciano knew.

"Go!" Her face twisted into a grimace of fear, or was it hatred?

He felt her hand brush his face, a gossamer touch, as she whisked herself round.

Then he was crouching down and running down the alley and threading his way up several dark lanes and away from that quarter with its secrets, for he had still found out nothing. Eventually he made his way into the open. As he stepped out into the sunshine, a stentorian voice behind him bellowed:

"Private Busyano! Where the devil do you think you're going!"

It was Sergeant Connor.

CHAPTER XIII

"Sir!" Bresciano's voice caught in his throat.

"It's been three days since you twisted that damned hand of yours and you're still bloody swanning round the garrison like some fine lady of leisure! Get yourself to Dr Baines or one of his assistants – a proper English doctor, not one of your local quacks – and let's have you back with your detachment where even someone as useless as you is needed. These damned dark nights! One of those Spanish gunboats came close to shore and made a breach in the wall at South Bastion last night and I need every man I can get."

"Yes, sir."

"Well? You only twisted it. No permanent damage…" He hesitated. "You didn't… gouge a piece out, did you?"

"Sir?"

"Don't you understand what I'm saying? Gouge, gouge! How do you say that in Spanish? Or did the injury affect your brain as well as your hand?"

Bresciano looked blankly at the Sergeant.

"Er… *arrancar*, I think…"

"*Arrancar*, eh? Right. That's… what I thought." The Sergeant gave him a calculating look and Bresciano felt it was the Sergeant whose wits had gone a-begging so he simply waited, bewildered, wondering what the next question would be.

"Don't just stand there gawping at me. Move! Move!"

Bresciano turned and fled, slipping as he rounded the corner and hitting his injured wrist hard against the stone wall so that he let out a squeal of pain. Would he have to go all the way to the Naval Hospital to be seen, he wondered. He encountered Cookie-Will and asked him.

"You're in luck, lad. I've just come from seeing Dr Rogers for me bad knee. He's doing a sick call in the infirmary here."

Dr Rogers was finishing his clinic and about to leave when Bresciano presented himself.

"You're late for sick-call, Private!"

"Sorry, sir. Sergeant just told me I had to see you. He wants me back on duty."

But when the doctor examined his wrist, it looked as inflamed and was as painful as it had been two days before. Unlike Dr Coll, the military man was silent as he strapped up Bresciano's wrist, limiting himself to a grunt of satisfaction when it was done.

"Should I go back to work now, sir? Sergeant Connor needs the manpower... and Captain Weston is also expecting me to be available..."

"Indispensable, are you?"

Bresciano shook his head.

"Four days before you do any physical work. If you do, you will end up with a weak wrist that may take weeks to heal properly."

"But the Sergeant said..."

"And I said what I said! My orderly will give you a note for your sergeant. Now get out of here. I have really sick men needing my attention."

It was as well, Bresciano thought as he set off in search of the Sergeant, that he had not gone to Dr Coll: the Sergeant would certainly not have accepted the order for four more days' rest from a civilian. The thought reminded him that he needed to see Dr Coll in order to check out what Cookie-Will had said about the rigor that affected the dead. But first – the Sergeant. And the interview proved as unpleasant as he expected, with the Sergeant accusing him of malingering and of pulling the wool over the Doctor's eyes, of gorging himself on unearned rations, only stopping short at questioning his legitimacy.

But the Sergeant had, in fact, seen him slip and heard his cry of pain so he had almost expected to find himself short of a man yet again. First Daft Jamie, then Tom and now Bresciano for the second time. Those three. An unlikely trio.

The Sergeant's eyes narrowed as he considered what linked them together. Bresciano was too often present when... certain things happened or were discovered. Too damned often.

Trudging back to the Barracks, Bresciano stopped outside Dr Coll's house and, with a quick glance round to make sure he was not observed, knocked and slipped in quickly when the maid opened the door.

"Why in the name of all the saints does a lad like you want to know about dead bodies?"

Bresciano muttered something about having laid a wager with someone in an argument.

"It is morbid, that is what it is. At your age you should be thinking of life, not death... though with all this smallpox around, and now it's the scurvy scourging the town... but what you need is distraction, not dwelling on such things. Find yourself a nice young woman to give your thoughts a healthier direction. That is my advice. Brooding over macabre issues can lead to nervous ailments of the mind – melancholia, even madness!"

"Yes, Dr Coll, but, about this wager..."

"Oh, very well. Nothing about the matter is as yet scientifically clear; however, in my long experience in this honourable profession, my observations point to several things: the warmer the conditions, weather or room temperature, the sooner the rigor passes and the corollary is equally the case: the colder the conditions, the longer it will take for the rigor to pass. Then there is the size of the corpse, with the degree of corpulence also affecting the outcome. I hold a theory that a woman's constitution, being frailer than a man's, is more subject to the onset of rigor mortis, and from that very weakness, the rigor, once it has the female corpse in its grip, may last longer. Not that I will state this categorically, you understand. And I had an interesting case once of a tall, thin young man – not unlike you, my boy – whose body was not found for three days..." the Doctor's bass voice rumbled on cheerfully. For a man trying to discourage a 'morbid' interest in the subject, he was growing more expansive by the second.

By the end of his extended monologue, Bresciano was left with enough information to hazard a near-informed guess as to the time of Tom's death. The point on the ledge at which Tom's body was found was sheltered by low rocky outcrops on either side so that, with the sun shining, it became a small sun-trap. Tom had last been seen on the Monday. By Tuesday morning the blood Bresciano had discovered in the cave had coagulated to form a dry crust on the ground. Tuesday had been a warm day with the sun breaking through the clouds late in the morning, and the night had been unusually mild.

The body had not been found till Wednesday. Time enough for the rigor to have set in and then left the body? Bresciano pulled his lip and frowned. "Tom was murdered at some time after lunch, some time early on the Monday afternoon," he stated firmly in the face of his uncertainty. Perhaps Tom had been killed shortly after he had dined royally on pork and rum, that act so much resented by his companions. The very thought of such rich fare made Bresciano both hungry and queasy. Would his stomach ever again be able to digest more than bread and slops concocted out of what in the past would have been leftovers to be fed to their neighbour's pig?

Captain Weston had returned to the Barracks and greeted Bresciano icily after checking his timepiece.

"Most of the day is gone. How do you account for this dereliction of duty?"

"I... I... I'm afraid I slipped and hurt my hand again. Sergeant Connor sent me to the Doctor and Doctor Rogers has told me to continue with light duties. I could do some more clerical work for..."

"When I require your advice I shall inform you of it."

"Yes, sir."

The silence lengthened uncomfortably and Bresciano resisted the temptation to shuffle his feet.

"Go to Corporal Warner. I want a precise record of his stores. You will check his inventory against the stores he holds. Any discrepancies must be recorded and reported. You work slowly, but you are thorough. You will start immediately to compensate for the time lost."

Bresciano thought guiltily of how much time he had spent on his own concerns while the Captain had been away and he felt his stomach knotting with tension.

"As for Corporal Warner, it would be opportune to remind him of the penalties for theft. I will not tolerate any irregularities. You will so inform him."

"Yes, sir."

Bresciano flushed, saluted almost smartly and walked out. He breathed heavily, feeling as if the Captain's eyes were burning a hole in the back of his jacket. Theft again! Those lemons he had taken that he had wanted to think of as justifiable pilfering. It was theft! What would happen if someone found out what he had done? And who on earth was Corporal Warner? He hurried to ask Cookie-Will.

"Bless your 'eart! You want Corporal William Warner."

"Where do I find him? I have to check his stores."

"Right 'ere in front of you! I wasn't chris'ened Cookie-Will, you know." He laughed.

"Oh. The Captain says he won't tolerate theft. He was in a real... he sounded... and I... I wondered if..."

"Don't you worry none about it. Always on about that 'e is. No one pilfers my stores – 'cept me!" He laughed again and dug Bresciano in the ribs, "Wot's the use of being in charge of the food if I can't keep a bit back for me friends? That man lives in a world of 'is own! Not surprising, is it? That wife of 'is must be a proper 'andful, woo'nt you say? An' 'ow am I supposed to 'ccount for rotten meat crawlin' with maggots so bad that I 'ad to get rid of it?"

His virtuous indignation held more than a hint of mockery. He lit a lantern and took Bresciano by the arm and led him through the back of the cavernous kitchen, down some steps and along a dark passage to his store-room. The smell of the past summer's rotten cod still lingered faintly in the air, but what made Bresciano almost recoil was the chaos. Barrels of flour and rice littered the room and almost blocked their passage, and a quantity of sacks, none with more than a meagre quantity of potatoes and a few other vegetables, lay in haphazard heaps on the floor. The meat, high enough to challenge the most insensitive nose, was stored away from the rest, and on shelf upon shelf were stored a mass of boxes and an assortment of jugs and tubs, half empty or without contents at all, stacked without any attempt at order. It all appeared to dance in the uncertain light cast by the lantern.

"Not very tidy, is it?" Cookie-Will said with satisfaction. "Be honest, now."

"I... suppose not, no. How do you know what you have? And how do you decide what you need?"

"That, young Bresciano, is simple: I know I got precious little an' I know I can't get no more of any of it – and the Gov'nor knows it an' cuts the rations again and again. We're down to half a pound of rotten beef and a couple of ounces of rancid butter a week for each of the men now, and there'll be no more rice when this has gone," he slapped one of the barrels viciously. One good thing, though: we've run out of that salt cod – thank Gawd for that! We're still getting a pound of salt pork each a week, and all them measures I'm given includes the weight of the maggots! An' if nothing gets 'ere from England, an' nothing slips through from Minorca or Morocco soon, I don't know what we're going to do, I really don't an' that's a fact." For a moment he looked dejected and it was easier to see how the skin hung slackly on him, like clothes too baggy on a body that had once been much rounder and more firm. Cookie-Will, Bresciano reflected, had not taken as much advantage of his position as others might have. Then Cookie brightened, "Now, what do you say about checking my stores?"

Bresciano baulked at the idea and was unable to hide his disapproval of Cookie-Will's huge untidiness. He had never seen anything quite like it before.

"You don't see it, do you? It's called stra'egy, lad. Captain came in a week past, gave me a right wigging, then walked out fast as 'e could. Stands to reason. So I put a few things on the shelves an' move the bins around a bit an' then let everything go back to this." He waved a hand to encompass his domain. "But you won't find much dirt 'ere, and it's nice an' cold an' the food keeps better. An' as for rats, I got a way of dealing with rats. My guardian – Angel – sees to that."

As he said the words, there was a movement behind some of the sacks and Bresciano blenched. There *were* rats. And prayer was of little help.

"Come 'ere my Angel." Cookie-Will clicked his fingers and a small dog emerged from behind the sacks, wagging a stump of a tail. "Best ratter on the Rock of Gibraltar – a stray. Found 'im chasin' a rat one day: 'e got it in seconds, killed it 'afore I could blink an' ate it up in no time, an' 'im little more'n a puppy then. Been in charge of my stores ever since, 'aven't you my Angel?" He took the dog's muzzle and shook it affectionately. "What 'e catches, 'e eats and 'e never touches the rest. But don't you tell no one about my Angel. Our sainted

Guv'nor said no new dogs was to be kept while we got this siege. Likes cats 'e does." He gave the dog a valedictory pat on the head. "Now," he became business-like, "we got to see about checking these stores, eh? Captain doesn't understand nothing about it. Know what 'is allowance of food is? We gets two pound of rice a month an' 'e gets four – or we used to, until it ran out, excep' for what Cookie has 'idden away for 'is mates. You gets ten ounces of butter a month an' 'e gets forty. You're taller than 'im an' I'm a lot fatter, or I was, so we need more than 'im, but 'e's an officer, so there it is: they get it all, the officers. I'll leave you to check my invent'ry, then 'e can't say as I 'ad anything to do with it. It's over there on that barrel, with a pencil – and don't you go upsetting my organization too much!"

He left, Angel retired to his bed and Bresciano was left to make what sense he could of the situation. For over an hour he struggled to account for items on the list, getting colder by the minute till he felt chilled to the bone. Eventually he was forced to abandon the attempt. The flour, like everything else, was kept in a variety of bins and jars and even in some sacks so that every time he wrote down a figure, he found himself forced to change it within minutes. Without being familiar with the 'organization' he would never be able to check anything with the thoroughness his tidy soul demanded.

It made him feel helpless, and he sat down on one of the empty boxes, shivering and looking around in despair. It was as bad as his investigation with facts and guesses and suppositions accruing, clinging to each suspect like barnacles, obscuring the real shape of things. Sighing, he turned his attention back to the stores and decided that the best he could do was limit himself to sketching a plan of the room and recording all the scattered places where the main foodstuffs were stored. Then, the next day, he might begin to come to grips with the chaos and tackle the exact quantities involved. Halfway through his self-appointed task he stopped.

"That's what I have to do!" he said and, using the back of the paper, he abandoned his work and began to list his suspects and their motives before trying to recall where each one had been at the time of the murders. There were considerable gaps in his information, but it did give him a sense of direction. "The mist of unknowing is lifting to reveal the landscape!" he pronounced importantly, just as the sound of the sunset gun gave notice that the evening meal was about to be served.

The paper, carefully folded, went into his pocket and he picked up the lantern and made his way up. Tomorrow he would bring a blanket with him and – damn Cookie-Will and his cunning – he would get everything done as soon as he could. Then he might manage to pursue his suspects while keeping well out of the Captain's way.

In the dining room Cookie-Will waved to him with his ladle, a look of mischief lighting his face and Bresciano frowned, then remembered the lemons and raised his hand in greeting: who was he to judge? Supper was soon over. Though some men tried to make the food last as long as they could, Bresciano ate quickly, glad that it was at least piping hot, swallowing without chewing, getting it down as quickly as possible in order not to taste the flavour or feel the texture of the small pieces of meat that constituted his ounce and a half a day.

It was dark outside the Barracks, but he went out, wanting to be alone, and sat on a low wall below one of the windows, reflecting on the way his investigation was progressing by fits and starts. 'Progressing' was too strong a word, but he now had a wealth of information that he had not had a week ago. His main difficulties were deciding whom to trust and knowing what was important. He pulled his legs up onto the wall and hugged them, then stared into the darkness.

A lantern glowed ahead of him. Someone was coming towards him up the hill from Governor's Street. Surely not Captain Weston? Before he could decide whether to sink back into the darkness or spring to attention, he heard the welcome sound of Hassan's voice.

"What are you doing out here? It's cold and you look frozen."

"I am, but I wanted to be on my own a while."

"I know what you mean. At home I have a small room which I shared with my two brothers, and now I sleep in a large dormitory, but it is cramped. There are dozens of us and there are the snores, and then someone shouts in his sleep, and the smell of unwashed bodies and the..." he wrinkled his nose, "you know... people breaking wind. Some do not seem to care. And the indestructible bed bugs. So this evening, when

I was sent to deliver Garrison Orders to several barracks, I was actually glad enough to be out and about."

"How is the affair of that man you mentioned. The one you helped with, as interpreter?"

"Gone. Sent back. And you should not be asking! What about you? How is the great investigation? Have you made any advances?"

"You don't take me seriously, do you? But the second death makes things much more serious. No one has linked them, but I am positive that they are related. Tom Tarrant's death... "

"What are you talking about? I heard about his accident, but..."

"That was not an accident." Bresciano hugged himself against the cold.

"Come on, Giovanni, not again! What is your theory now?"

"I am talking about facts, not theory. Tom's clothes still smelt of rum when we found him. His clothes, mind you. So would you say he had been pouring it over himself instead of drinking it? That does not make sense. And it's not just me saying it. One of the men who recovered the body, a corporal, confessed that it was a suspicious circumstance, but he wasn't going to raise any sort of alarm about it – he wants no trouble. Someone wanted us to think Tarrant had fallen over in drunken confusion, lost his balance, slipped... something like that. And though there was blood on his clothes, there wasn't any to speak of on the ground and..."

"So what does that prove?"

"It would prove very little, but I happen to know where there was a lot of blood. Enough blood to have come from the sort of injuries I saw on Tom, including blood on a jagged stone that he had been attacked with – I'm sure of it."

He had captured his friend's attention and went on to explain everything he knew about the cave, Tom's sudden wealth and his ideas about blackmail. But he kept names to himself.

"You may be right," Abraham Hassan found himself reluctantly agreeing with his friend, but spoke in a worried tone of voice, "but be careful, I say, Giovanni. After all, if there is any... any real possibility that someone has killed twice, what is to stop him killing a third time? And that third victim could be you. Have you thought of that?"

"I will be careful. But no one knows that I am investigating so I'm safe."

"Well, let me know if anything happens." He shivered. "Now, if we stay here talking much longer, the question of safety will become academic. We shall both freeze to death. I am going inside now. This is my last delivery. I think I am ready to get to bed, even in that dormitory of mine."

They walked into the building and above them a window closed quietly, but the figure of a large man remained standing at it. After some time, Sergeant Connor turned away frowning. Since that lanky Gibraltar recruit had joined the Artificers, he had brought little but disturbance into the Sergeant's well-controlled life, and the Sergeant did not like having his life disturbed. He spoke reflectively to himself, with what could have been a hint of regret:

"He's a downy one, that one, but he may find out that it's not always good to be too clever."

*   *   *   *

In the dormitory to which he had been allocated, Bresciano lay sleepless, all too aware of the sounds that filled the night. It had been easy to sleep when it had only been Jamie and himself, but now he appreciated how Abraham Hassan felt. His fastidious soul revolted at the smell of sweat and unwashed clothes; and the snores and noises made sleep difficult. Time might reconcile him to it, but not tonight. After what felt like several hours of tired misery, pulling on his jacket and taking his blanket with him, he slipped out and slowly walked the length of the dark corridor outside. There were a couple of benches that he had seen earlier. They would be no harder than his rough pallet in the dormitory and at least it would be quiet.

But others had had the same idea and when he arrived, groping his way in the dark, he found himself driven away by the irritable groans and curses of the two shrouded bodies already occupying the benches. Undecided, he wrapped the blanket round him and turned towards where he knew he would at least find a few sacks to keep out the chill of the flagged floor. It took time and some resolution to find his way up to the storeroom where he had found the lemons, but it was simply one more shadowy and empty room with nothing to betray him. A warm glow of moonlight shone comfortingly in through the large window. With a sigh he finally lay down. He crossed his hands behind his head and stared upwards.

The warm glow of moonlight shifted and changed. Shifted and changed? It did not make sense.

It would be at least a couple of weeks before the next full moon. Sergeant Connor had complained about the dark night – that was why the gunboats had come close to shore and fired on the city walls under the protection offered by clouds shrouding a crescent moon. There was no full moon. Hastily he stood up and went to the window. There was a good view of the rooftops below and of the houses beyond. There was also a fine view of a conflagration near the Green Market.

Appalled, he blundered out of the room and back down the way he had come, knocking against walls and doors in the dark and, for a few minutes, incapable of thinking clearly. He remembered his father's tale of a fire in a theatre in Genoa: the fire had killed no one, but the panic and chaos had led to people being crushed to death. There was nothing but confusion to be gained by shouting for help, but he knew he must raise the alarm – but how? Who would know what to do?

There was bound to be a duty officer somewhere near the entrance. He headed down the stairs. Along the ground floor corridors there was enough light from a couple of lanterns for him to see clearly and he began to run. Corporal Jones and a second man he had never seen before were on duty.

"It must be two in the morning – what are you up to, Bresciano?"

"There's a fire near the Green Market! Something is blazing!"

He gasped out his news to them and, without waiting, ran out and down the hill towards the blaze. An occasional light shone from one house or other, but the streets were thick with shadows and the darkness was menacing. Below, near the city walls, not a single light was shining. Then it was there – and what he had seen from above became a beacon ahead of him as he raced towards the burning house. Chaos all around: screams, people running out of their houses, their faces painted a demonic red by the light from the conflagration. The air cracked and spat as an accompaniment to the twisting, leaping flames and the smoke billowing up. Someone was shouting above the noise, trying to bring order to the confusion, attempting to get the men to put out the fire.

Even before he had left the Barracks he had known in his heart what he would find. It was the Weston house that was burning – and where were the occupants? He pushed through the milling, fleeing crowd, forcing his way through towards the small row of houses that might soon all go up in flames – spreading it to the poorer wooden dwellings behind and then setting fire to the whole town. Captain Weston and the formidable Mrs Bickerstaff were outside the house, calling out and looking with desperation into the crowd. Mrs Weston was not with them.

Then came the sound of heavy running feet and the crowd was swept aside by several dozen Artificers, headed by Corporal Jones. Within a short time that seemed to stretch like an age – as if life was winding down to a state of stasis – the Artificers had been organised into two lines to bring water from the local pumps; the inhabitants of the threatened and other houses joined them carrying buckets and basins to be filled and thrown into the burning building.

It appeared to Bresciano that the highest flames came from the back of the house. The fire could have started in that yard where, only yesterday, he had seen Mrs Weston bending over the firewood with her lamp. What if she had done the same again? What if she had fallen and the lamp had slipped from her hand? What if she was lying back there in that inferno?

It was not his heart that sank. His whole being seemed to drain out of him. He had to find her! Before the frantic efforts of the men fighting the fire, the flames at the front of the house were beginning to diminish, but every moment counted and once more he forced his way through the bodies blocking his way, out through the crowd and towards the back lane. As he turned away from the street he saw the light of a lantern ahead of him, moving erratically up the wide sharply sloping lane that led upwards, known as Castle Street. It looked as if whoever carried it was lurching and staggering. Then the light went down to the ground, the single flame flickered before acquiring new life and spreading along the ground, a deadly pool of fire. That was when he heard her screaming as the hem of her skirt flamed.

He stumbled up towards her and reached her in a matter of seconds. With his jacket he beat the flames out. They had had little enough time for the flames to take hold of her nightdress, but he had glimpsed her ankles, red and raw. When he finally spoke to her, she failed to answer. She lay in a faint, a dead weight when he struggled to pick her up. He was clumsy with his twisted wrist and grateful for the help of an older man who had been aroused by the commotion. He walked carefully, the smell of her burnt clothes acrid in his nose and a stabbing pain in his wrist. It was imperative that he get her to Doctor Coll. And skirting the confusion and excitement of the crowd, for now that the fire was coming under control they were free to give rein to the animation that a disaster averted will give rise to, he made his way down.

Dr Coll, awakened by the noise, was opening the door of his house. He stood in his bare feet, wearing his nightshirt.

"What are you up to, Giovanni Bresciano?"

Why, thought Bresciano, did everyone suppose he was always up to something? Relief made him feel light-headed and he wanted to say, 'I am rescuing a maiden in distress.' Instead he held out his burden and simply said:

"Her house is on fire, but I think no one else was hurt. Her feet are burnt."

Dr Coll fussed his way into the smart front room with its uncomfortable furniture and laid her on the chaise-longue on which his wife spent much of her days.

"Stay with her. I shall need to get some ointment and soothing poultices for the burns, and laudanum in order to relieve her pain and stop her thrashing around when she wakes."

By the time he returned, Mrs Weston was moaning, recovering consciousness and, with it, an awareness of pain.

"My feet hurt!" She was like a child. "Please stop them hurting!"

"There, there, Mrs Weston. It is nothing to worry about. Surface burns only. Let us make you more comfortable. Drink this. Now bite on this – just a piece of strong leather. You will find it will help you bear the pain until the medicine takes effect."

He poured a strong dose of laudanum down her throat, instructed Bresciano to hold her hands, and then set to cleaning the burns and spreading ointment on them before wrapping them in bandages. As he did his work, Mrs Weston gripped Bresciano's hands with a strength that made him wince.

"Well, that should heal well. Not much harm done."

He soothed and reassured her as he worked. Her grip on Bresciano's hands slackened and the piece of leather slipped from her mouth.

"Sin must be burnt out. 'Everyone shall be burnt with fire'… the Bible… someone… said so…"

She spoke quietly, rationally, as if explaining a point of theology.

"The Lord is pleased by a burnt offering. The Bible says so too."

Then her eyelids sank and she slept. Bresciano was stunned. What ideas had that husband of hers been putting in her head? Was it a sin to prefer the innocent company – for innocent she surely was – of a quiet young scholar to that of her iceberg of a husband?

"Poor woman, poor, poor woman." Dr Coll looked down at her.

Then he became conscious of Bresciano, also looking down at her. Her hair was spread out like a halo. She had long lashes that now rested on her cheeks, casting a light shadow. And it was clear that all she was wearing was her cotton nightdress. Dr Coll looked round and found the blanket his wife always used when she lay down and, with a reproachful look at Bresciano, he quickly covered the sleeping woman.

"So, now you know." He spoke with severity. "And you will be discreet."

"Um."

Bresciano was glad to oblige and to be discreet, if he knew what he was required to be discreet about.

"You have met the lady before? More than once? I saw you enter the house recently."

"Yes. And another day she was carrying a lamp… it was daylight, but it was lit. She said that she was going to the cellar…" he improvised.

"Precisely, the Weston house has no cellar. So now you know. Not the first time, as I believe you've guessed." The

Doctor motioned a bewildered Bresciano out of the room and across to the kitchen. "Here," he spoke more kindly, "you look as if you might do with some medication yourself." And he handed Bresciano a small glass of brandy. "Drink up, lad, small sips. I do not believe in swallowing drink fast. The digestive process will not take kindly to it. Sit down. You are sure no one else was hurt? Very well." He sat opposite Bresciano and sipped his own drink.

"It is a tragedy. I have suspected how matters were for a long time, but had little to do with the family and interference is something the English do not relish. I am a man of few words, as you know."

Bresciano kept a straight face.

"It was the stairs that first alerted me to it. Too many falls. And the scratches on her husband's hands – and on his face once. A picture began to emerge."

Bresciano sat up and leaned forwards. Here it was. The Doctor might well have further evidence of the Captain's brutality.

"It may well be a family trait. I have known such cases where weaknesses in the family line become compounded by the passage of time, by a childless condition or by a fall or some violent concussion. There have certainly been contusions of a violent nature over this past year."

"Yes…?" Bresciano held his breath.

"Hysteria in the female." Dr Coll spoke with episcopal authority. "Yes, hysteria in the female is common enough. The word itself comes from the Greek '*hysteron*' – that's the womb, you know, so it is clear that only women will suffer from it, and it is commoner in childless women, like this poor lady. Sometimes it is attended by nervous spasms or delusions. Occasionally there is violence which, as it were, turns inwards. Such was the case with a young woman of my acquaintance. Before your time, but you may have heard your parents speak of her. Her body was washed ashore four days after she abandoned her paternal home. A terrible tragedy for the family. When the delusion is upon such subjects," he lowered his voice, "they are capable of inflicting violence on others, but it frequently leads to attempts at self-destruction."

Bresciano attempted to reconcile what the Doctor was saying with his own ideas of the Captain as a violent husband,

and the two trains of thought met like opposing currents at sea, so that his mind felt like a whirlpool sucking down any sense he had. "Ah!" He tried again, nodding as if he knew what it was all about. "So?"

"Only this past week I was able to turn Mrs Weston's mind from such an act." He paused and sipped his brandy appreciatively. "Let me see. It must have been on the Friday in the afternoon. I met her hurrying up Castle Street. 'Why,' I asked myself, 'is she taking this route?' You must know, young Bresciano, that there is nothing in that area for a respectable young married woman, a lady like her. There are the Barracks, a number of poor local dwellings, some young officers' quarters and a couple of houses... well, the sort of houses soldiers sometimes frequent." He cleared his throat. "I went up to her and gently led her back. It took me a while to persuade her. The most important factor in such cases is not to alarm the subject. She was carrying a knife, which I was able to take from her, and she told me that... well, no need to go into detail, we both understand what she intended. Self-destruction, you see. A need for expiation. An interesting phenomenon."

He finished his brandy and looked severely at Bresciano.

"You should not have asked so many questions. It is, after all, none of your business. I shall send a message to Captain Weston. He is a very... a man whose privacy is of the utmost importance to him so I shall tell him that she wandered into my house, injured. Your name shall not be mentioned and I am certain that she will remember little of this tomorrow. We must, above all, be discreet and save that upright man from shame. Discretion, young man!"

"Yes, Doctor. You may count on me."

He walked out into what was not yet dawn. That came late at this time of year. But he felt incapable of sleep. He began to make his way down to the Line Wall, where he sat, feeling the cold seep into his bones as he looked out into the Bay and pondered on what he had learnt that night. It was a confusing process which involved him in the painful admission that he had been completely wrong about some things, but at last some things were clear. The Captain, however unpleasant a person he was, might be a murderer, but he was not guilty of assaulting his wife. Rather, it was she who had inflicted injuries on him, wittingly or unwittingly. That beautiful fragile woman was dangerous. His father had been right. She was seriously unbalanced in her mind. It was even possible that she had set fire to her own house and it was only thanks to his fortuitous intervention that she herself had not been badly burnt as she fled the scene of her crime.

It made sense of some things Emiliana had said about Mrs Weston dancing one moment and weeping the next, of irrational behaviour. It was almost too much for him to assimilate. Nevertheless, he forced himself to remember everything Dr Coll had said and one fact served to console him. Mrs Weston had gone nowhere on the afternoon of the fateful Friday when Jamie was murdered, because the doctor had intercepted what appeared to have been a suicide attempt. She was innocent of any direct participation in that death. Truth to tell, she now appeared incapable of collaborating effectively in any scheme. She was… even to himself he would not speak of madness… she was not normal. And he visualised her as she had been in his arms – quiescent, like the beautiful maiden of a fairy tale. His fancies about truly being, as she had called him, a Galahad, were interred in the harshest manner

As for the Captain, he recalled the letter he had delivered to Dr Baines with its references to vigilance and guarding and his wife's cunning. It explained Mrs Bickerstaff – employed to prevent any attempt by Mrs Weston to take her own life… or that of her husband. Bresciano was now able to consider that those final words in the Captain's letter which surely referred to his wife – 'the woman I still love'. And that love could be a possessive love. Such a love as would express itself savagely in defence of what the Captain saw as his property, his honour, his… and there was one elusive idea that evaded his attempts to formulate it…

Bresciano's mind was incapable of further thought. He walked back to the Barracks and finally slept.

CHAPTER XIV

In the morning Bresciano woke early and hardly refreshed, having slept ill yet again. Down in the kitchen the clattering of pots and pans announced the start of Cookie's day. The sight of Bresciano's lanky form seemed to please him and he offered him some oatmeal for his breakfast.

"Sorry – there's not much today, lad. Still, I picked all them weevils out for you meself, I did! An' I'll get you a cup o' small beer from my private stock, to make up for it. Thing is, they've billeted them Walloonies on us – and no more rations issued, o' course! We'll just 'ave to make do."

Bresciano accepted the small cup of beer with a word of thanks and drained it in a draught. It helped to wash the tasteless oatmeal down.

"I'd better get on with that inventory, Cookie, or the Captain will be after me."

"Bless you, lad, we won't be seeing Captain this morning. There was a fire in his house, didn't you hear? He'll be busy all day sorting that out. I tell you what – you just take it easy, and Cookie will… just tidy up a bit an' set out all the stores for you to count later. I need a little time to… put them in order, like."

He gave Bresciano a gap-toothed grin of complicity. Both of them knew what Cookie-Will was up to. He had already hidden all the unauthorised food he had and would simply make it easier for Bresciano by presenting him with the stores that he wanted him to count – incidentally ensuring that Bresciano did not go rooting around for potential hiding places.

"Any road, you should be going to visit that little sister

of yours. Can't be too careful with that smallpox. You'll be wanting to know how the little lady is," Cookie added.

Bresciano caught his breath guiltily; he had meant to go and see Lucia yesterday, but with all that had happened it had slipped his mind. She had seemed so much better, but what did he know of medical matters; what if she had had a relapse? He would take advantage of Cookie's offer and visit his family. But he had nothing to take them.

"I don't suppose…" he said hesitantly.

Cookie smiled. "I don't 'ave much, but you can't go and see the little lass and not take her anything." He looked around to make sure they were still alone, then produced a small earthenware pot from the recesses of a cupboard. "Molasses!"

"Molasses? What are they?"

"It's like 'oney – but it comes from the sugar-cane, it does."

Bresciano removed the cork and put a finger inside. He licked his finger appreciatively.

"Lucia will love this, Cookie. I am really grateful to you; but – how did you get it?"

Cookie laughed, his jowls quivering. "Last week, the Governor's cook was sick an' they sent for me from the Convent. So I went to 'is kitchen and boiled 'is vegetables for 'im, an' came back 'ere – and when I opened my pack – wha' a surprise, there it were! I can't imagine 'ow it got from the Guvnor's big jar into my little pot, an' that's a fact."

Bresciano withdrew his hand from the pot as if it had stung him. Again he was complicit in stealing food – and now from the Governor, no less! If Murch had been flogged unmercifully for a lesser crime, what would they do to him if he was caught?

"Cookie, I don't really know…" he said doubtfully.

"Take it, boy, take it. And don't you worry. I never take enough for no one to notice. That's the secret, see? Greedy folk always gets spotted. Not me. An' the little lass needs it more than you or me or the Governor."

Bresciano nodded reluctantly, and put the pot into his bag. For Lucia, for his family, he would risk anything, he decided. But the feeling of guilt persisted.

When he knocked on the door of his house, it was Lucia who opened the door. Her face was still covered with crusted spots and she moved slowly, but she was smiling.

"Mother went with the Nonna to market to see if she could buy some food, so I'm in charge of the house," she said importantly. "And Aunt Maria is in church praying for food." She added, frowning, "What would manna taste like? It sounds very boring in the bible."

"Lucia, it's wonderful to see you up!" He picked her up and swung her round till she screamed with delight. "I'm sorry, I should not have done that. Shouldn't you be resting?"

"Oh, I feel so much better now, thanks to the 'magic' lemons you brought, that Mother said I could get out of my bed to open the door if you came. Have you brought me any more lemons, Giovanni?"

Bresciano could not stop smiling. It was wonderful to see that Lucia was so well now.

"Better than that – I've brought some magic honey!"

They went into the kitchen and Bresciano opened his bag and took out the pot. He removed the cork and commanded. "Put your finger in!" Lucia obeyed wide-eyed, and her brother said, "Now, lick it!"

Lucia squealed with joy. "It's better than honey, it's... it's really magic!"

There was a knock on the door, and Giovanni said,

"Lucia, get back into bed now. I'll answer the door."

Lucia pouted, but obeyed. To Bresciano's surprise, he found Lola, the Westons' maid, on the doorstep. She looked distressed and flustered.

"Ay, Giovanni, I came to speak with Señora Eleanor, your mother."

He stepped aside to let her in, saying, "My mother is out, but she should be back soon. Come in and rest yourself – you look upset."

Lola followed him into the kitchen and collapsed into his mother's chair.

"It is true, Giovanni, I am upset, my heart is beating so fast, and I wanted to talk to your mother about it; she always gives good advice."

"Your heart? Should you not see a doctor?"

"No, no. It is this crazy English family I am working for – you know, the Güestons."

"Can I help in any way?" Bresciano said, seeing a golden

opportunity to further his investigation.

Lola looked at him doubtfully. She knew Giovanni – he was only a boy. Bresciano stood straighter, hoping that she would see him as a soldier, an adult in whom she could confide. He must have succeeded, because she burst into speech.

"Mrs Güeston, she is ill," Lola banged her temples with her hands, "sick in here, *está mal del coco*, she is not well in the head and the *Capitán* employs me and *una inglesa* – Mrs Bigstuff – so we look after her day and night. And last night I was there with Señora Güeston. Ay! She was all the time moving around, but it was time for me to go so when Mrs Bigstuff arrived, I went to open the door and I explained that the Señora is very crazy all day. And I saw the *Capitán* coming down the street and I waited to tell him also, and that was when she escaped from me and set the back rooms of the house on fire with a lantern, and she ran out into the street like a crazy woman. I ran too, but I did not find her and then, the Lord be praised, soldiers came and put the fire out before the whole house was destroyed. When I came back, she was again in the house, lying in her bed, half conscious – I don't know how she got back – and Dr Coll had bandaged her poor legs. The *Capitán* was very angry with me for letting her do all this, but while he was shouting – no, he does not shout, but his voice makes me frightened – while he was blaming me, his wife… no, I shouldn't be telling you this, Giovanni…"

Bresciano smiled at her and patted her arm awkwardly. "Lola, you know me – I will tell no one. And my mother always says to Aunt Maria, 'It will do you a lot of good to unburden yourself'."

"That is true, Giovanni; you are a good boy. Since I saw you, my *palpitaciones* are better." She clutched her ample bosom, obviously relieved at being absolved of indiscretion, and continued.

"Can you believe it? She got out of her bed with her bandages and everything and threw herself down the stairs! I think she has broken her arm this time. I went to call Dr Coll again, but after that I left. I may have left for good. I'm so upset, Giovanni, I don't know what to do. I do want to help them, but my nerves…! And every day she is worse. And with so little food I feel tired all the time and I cannot control her, she has such strength. I don't think I can stand it!"

She burst into tears, and Bresciano put his arm round her shoulder uneasily, trying to console her. He noticed Lucia's head poking round the door and gestured her away. He was relieved that his rôle in rescuing Mrs Weston had not been noticed, but could not help reflecting with regret that as an unsung hero, he remained a man of no importance. Lola had stopped sobbing and began sniffling and he reached out and gave her a clean tea towel.

"And the Captain, when she fell down the stairs, he was with you? Do you think... is he mad too?" He asked tentatively.

"I told you. He was with me downstairs and... mad? No. The *Capitán*... no. He is not very *simpático*; he is dry like a piece of wood, but he is not mad. But she will drive him mad, because he loves her."

Lola was in full flood again. "Yes, he loves her, and he tries to protect her, but what does she do? She bites him, and scratches him like a cat, and she throws things, and says dreadful things to him. I suppose he is a good man, good, but so, so..." she struggled to express herself, "so... stretched, like a string that is pulled so tight that it will snap if you pull it any more!"

Lola sank back in the chair, exhausted by her own eloquence, and then got to her feet and said, more calmly, "Thank you, Giovanni, I will come back later when your mother is at home. Maybe she will advise me about what I should do – should I stay and try to help the poor lady?"

Bresciano escorted her to the door and as he closed it, Lucia emerged from her bedroom.

"What was all that about, Giovanni? Lola seemed to be so upset!"

"She is all right now. Come on, if you go back to bed, Lucia, I'll tell you a story that I am inventing about the siege."

He would follow the advice he had given Lola. It would help him to talk, he thought. Perhaps he could get the strange events of the past few days straight in his mind.

Lucia, more tired than she wanted to admit, went back happily to bed in her darkened room, and Bresciano sat down on a stool beside her. He told his story as a fairy tale, told her about an important soldier and his sick wife, and the fire, and then her questions drew him on to talk of the others he had met since joining up – the men in his unit and the Walloons. He kept the gorier details out of the narrative, but although she was drowsy, she kept asking questions.

At length she said sleepily, "I don't like a lot of those people – and I'm glad they are not real."

"What don't you like about them?" Bresciano asked.

"Well, the fat man is greedy, the Sergeant is angry, the Captain is angry and cold, and his wife sounds mad…" Her voice trailed off, and Bresciano thought she had gone to sleep. Then she added, "And those Wa…Walloons…"

"What about them?"

"They're all bad, aren't they? They must be because they promised to fight for the Spaniards, and then they ran away. That's a bad thing to do, to break a promise."

Bresciano struggled to find an answer to that, but then realised that he had no need to; a soft snore announced that Lucia had gone to sleep. He remained sitting by the bed until the sound of the front door opening announced that his mother and Nonna Lucrezia had returned.

Bresciano endured Nonna's embrace and squawks of delight at his return, and then, disengaging himself with difficulty, he kissed his mother, who said:

"It is good to see you, Giovanni, but look, there was nothing in the market except these few green leaves – I think they are kale. It is difficult to say, they are so limp – but I have one or two potatoes left – I can make a soup, perhaps. Father is out fishing again from the rocks at Europa Point. Thank goodness he has abandoned the idea of taking out the boat. It is far too dangerous with those Spanish gunboats coming ever closer to shore. I can only hope he'll bring something back this time."

Bresciano gave his mother the pot of molasses. "It is a present from the cook in our barracks," he said hastily, lest his mother should again suspect him of stealing food for them. "But you must tell no one that he gave it to me. Lucia has tried it and she loved it. She's so much better, isn't she? I think she will make a full recovery."

"Oh, Giovanni, you are a dear boy!" Eleanor said, and kissed him again.

Bresciano took his leave soon after, pleading the need

to get back to work, before his mother should try to get him to stay to share their little store of food. But when he left the house, he turned his steps towards the Line Wall. It was still early and he wanted to think about the Westons and the events of the previous night. He sat on the low wall and looked out toward the Bay. It would remain a favourite spot with him all his life. There was little enough to see: a white mist had rolled in over the water, and he could see no further than the small waves which lapped at the base of the wall.

"Good," he said aloud to himself. "No distractions."

Now, what was he to make of last night's events, and Lola's outburst this morning? It was clear that Mrs Weston was a severely disturbed woman. But her violence was aimed at herself – and at anyone who tried to impede her attempts at self-destruction. Furthermore, Dr Coll had provided her with an alibi for the Friday when Jamie was killed. The only possibility that remained was that she could have incited Lieutenant Black, who might be besotted with her, to do the deed – after all, had she not said according to Emiliana, that Jamie 'had to be dealt with'? And where had she been on the Thursday, when the first attempt had been made on Jamie's life? But, on the other hand, Emiliana had proved seriously unreliable in thinking Weston a wife beater and had been forced by Bianca to admit that she had invented rather than witnessed events in that disturbed house.

He took out his list of suspects and lightly drew an uncertain line through Mrs Weston's name.

Captain Weston might love his wife, as Lola had said, but perhaps he was not such a good man as she thought. He *was* like a rope stretched to snapping point, and when he had sent Bresciano with the letter for Dr Baines, he had communicated a powerful feeling of tension – such forcibly suppressed emotion could be the result of an honest man having turned to murder. First eliminate Jamie who was spreading scandal about his wife, then murder Tom Tennant, blackmailer. Captain Weston with his Scottish antecedents could conceivably have been Jamie's 'friend' – if such a friend had ever existed.

He looked back at his list. Next to Lieutenant Black's name was a blank. He had a suspect that he knew nothing about. It was ridiculous! So the two officers remained suspects, although, he admitted to himself, the scholarly Lieutenant seemed an unlikely one.

Sergeant Connor, Bresciano thought stubbornly, was still a strong possibility.

Certainly, he could not be Jamie's 'friend'. He was not Scottish, – he hated Scotsmen, but Jamie's 'friend' might just be a red herring, one of the many imaginary creatures that had peopled Jamie's confused world.

The Sergeant had certainly had the opportunity on both occasions that Jamie had been attacked, and there was the matter of the defective musket, too. What could his motive have been, though? Perhaps it was revenge on a Scotsman – any Scotsman – for his father's awful murder, with the added bonus that he would be getting rid of a useless body, someone who impaired the efficiency of his unit, someone who had provided an excuse for the men to voice their anger against the Sergeant. Was it a strong enough reason to commit murder, even for a man of fiery temper? By this point Bresciano was once more indulging in playing devil's advocate against himself. Recalling what Corporal Jones had said, he imagined how the Sergeant might have become deranged by grief at the loss of his wife and child, but would that make him resurrect his old, old grudge against the Scots? And where had the Sergeant been when Tom was murdered?

"Revenge is sweet," he muttered, pulling at his lip, remembering the Italian saying so often quoted by his father, "and it is a dish best served cold." But there was that date Jones had given... the Rebellion of '45. That was over thirty years ago. How cold could revenge get and still serve as a motive? Unless it were revenge on a large scale, or revenge in the mind of a deranged man. After all, the Sergeant had seemed decidedly peculiar the last time they met.

Who else was there? Robert. Yes! Robert had been based near Willis's Batteries at the time of the attack on Jamie and later when he was murdered. If he was a spy and Jamie had somehow come to know about it, he could surely have murdered him in order to ensure his silence. But how could Jamie have been a danger to him? Unless – unless he were a man that Jamie knew and had recognised, perhaps from Scotland. Bresciano began to feel a fraction more hopeful, because in that case, the loose-mouthed boy would have been an ever-present danger, and would have had to be eliminated if Robert were to avoid discovery. Robert spoke English well for a foreigner, very precisely, as foreigners sometimes did – but that might just be a ploy to avoid revealing a Scottish accent.

Bresciano sighed; it was still all rather far-fetched. If Robert was a spy, he had not had the opportunity to do much spying. When he was not at work, he spent most of his time at the wine-house – and that particular wine-house was not the sort of place where state secrets were bandied about. No, he went to the wine-house to see Bianca. There was the nub. Bresciano had to recognise that he didn't really think that Robert was the murderer – he just *wanted* him to be the one.

His mind wandered from his investigation, as he visualised the soft curves of Bianca, and her voice – when it was not making fun of him, of course, which was sweet and melodious…

"Giovanni!"

Bresciano started. It was her voice: it was Bianca. She had come up behind him silently. He turned, and she placed a kitchen pot wrapped in a cloth on the wall, then she jumped up beside him. "What are you doing, sitting here on your own?"

Bresciano suppressed an urge to embrace her. He had decided to take Pascal's advice and let her make the running – and there it was – she had come to him.

"I was just thinking… about Jamie, and what happened to him."

"Oh, Giovanni, can't you forget that?"

"No, I can't. I was fond of him, and I think you were too."

"But what can you do? What can any of us do?"

"I can find out who killed him, and prove it, and take the proof to – to the authorities. To General Eliott if it is necessary!" Bresciano said stubbornly.

Bianca smiled. "You have always been like that, Giovanni. You are pig-headed and you are enjoying trying to solve a puzzle, aren't you? I remember when I used to call you out to play, sometimes you would not come, because you were playing chess with your father. Oh, well, when you are ready to play, call me!"

Before he could react to her saucy invitation, a dark

shape loomed through the mist in front of them. There was a flash of light and the now familiar hiss of a shell whistling through the air. He flung himself on Bianca and they landed in a heap behind the parapet, with Bresciano on top. The shell flew over their heads and buried itself in the wall of the debtors' prison opposite.

There was a sudden silence, as if the world held its breath, followed by a deafening explosion that shattered the air around them as the shell burst – flinging debris, rubble and splintered wood through the air in a cloud of mortar dust.

Then came a further roar of cannon from King's Bastion driving the gunboat away.

Bresciano was coughing helplessly. Had Bianca been hurt? He could feel her trembling underneath him.

'It must be the shock,' he thought: women were frail creatures unsuited to the savagery of battle.

Then he realised that she was shaking with laughter.

"Oh, Giovanni, my hero!" she giggled. "If the cannonball didn't kill me, then you will, with your weight!"

Before she got up, she kissed him lightly on the lips. Bresciano, shaken, but still mindful of Pascal's advice, made a supreme effort not to respond in kind. Instead he turned away and said,

"Look, it was a Spanish gunboat creeping in on us under the mist. The guns of our King's Bastion have hit it: see there, it's ablaze!"

The thick mist was suffused with an orange glow as the gunboat was consumed by fire, and they could hear terrified cries as the Spanish sailors flung themselves into the sea, soon to be captured.

The moment of tenderness was over. He stood up and dusted off his uniform. "I must go back to the Barracks," he said. "There is work for me to do there."

"If you are going past my mother's house," Bianca said, "could you take this soup to her? She is staying with my aunt Marta, who lives opposite her, because she is not well. I think she may have bronchitis, and she doesn't eat enough, and drinks too much, so I asked Marta to look after her for a few days. I cooked this in the tavern for her. It's a good thing the shell, or you, didn't knock it off the wall and spill it!"

She handed Bresciano the pot, and left. Bresciano crossed

the Parade and started along Waterport Street towards Marta's house. His early fear that Emiliana's life might be in danger, as Jamie's had been, was laid to rest temporarily. At least, he thought, if the Captain went looking for Emiliana at her home to do her harm, he would not find her.

When he knocked on the door, there was no answer. He waited for a minute and then pushed the door open and went in. There was no sign of Marta. The single room which was her home was dark, and the air smelt musty. From under a pile of bedclothes in the corner came a faint groan.

"*Scignoa* Emiliana?" he called out softly.

There was an upheaval under the covers and a head emerged. A voice croaked:

"Leave me alone. I am dying!"

"*Scignoa*, it is I, Giovanni Bresciano. I have brought you some soup from Bianca."

Emiliana struggled to a sitting position. "Ah, Gianni, you are a good boy to come and visit a poor old friend who is dying."

She blew her nose loudly on the sleeve of a voluminous and filthy nightgown and broke into a paroxysm of coughing.

"Shall I open the window so that you can have some light?"

"No, no! Do you want to kill me? That is how I became ill – I somehow fell asleep on my doorstep last night, and the cold air…"

"How unfortunate." Bresciano spoke neutrally, realising what had happened. Emiliana must have been so drunk that she could not make it to her bed, and had caught a chill as a result. "Shall I leave the soup here and leave you to rest?"

"No, wait!" Emiliana suddenly became more animated. A predatory hand reached out to a table by the bed and grasped two letters.

"These are letters from the *teniente* Black which he gave me for *Scignoa* Güeston, which I… I forgot to give her."

Bresciano took them. "I see. Do you wish me to return them to her – or to the Lieutenant?"

"No… no. It is only that I cannot… I cannot see well enough to read what they say, and if I knew, perhaps I could tell the *Capitán*, or the young *teniente*, or the *Scignoa* and they would give me… a small something to recompense me for my… trouble. You understand?"

Bresciano almost threw the letters back at her. It was clear enough. She was illiterate and she wanted *him*, Giovanni Bresciano, to tell her what was in those letters so that she could use them for the purposes of blackmail. Then the thought came to him that if he knew what was in those letters it might help him to understand what was going on between the Lieutenant and Mrs Weston, every crumb of information in that area was important. To read them for that purpose would surely be justifiable, he tried to convince himself. He put the letters into his pocket and said,

"I will read them where there is more light and when I have time. Now I must go to my work."

He turned on his heel and went out of the door, pursued by a wail from Emiliana. "Gianni! You will bring them back and tell me what is written in them?"

He did not reply, but strode off up the hill toward the Blue Barracks.

When he arrived he found Jean Pierre standing in front of the Barracks, staring intently at the façade of the building – stone blocks covered by the wash of blue which gave the Barracks its name. This might be the moment to engage him in conversation and get some more information about Robert. Before Bresciano could speak, the Walloon turned and saw him.

"The front of this building has twelve hundred and forty eight stone blocks." He spoke his own variant of Franco-Spanish that he had adopted to make himself understood in the Garrison.

Bresciano stared at him, nonplussed for a moment. Jean Pierre, always ready with a date when Robert asked him. Was he like one of his childhood playmates, big Giacomo, who was more than a little simple-minded, had never even learnt to spell his name, but if you mentioned a date, could instantly give you the day of the week on which it had fallen? Not that Jean Pierre was stupid, but he certainly seemed slower than the other two Walloons.

"That's interesting, Jean Pierre," he said heartily, "Jean Pierre," he said expansively, in his best French, interlarded with Spanish. "Why don't you come down with me to the kitchen? Cookie may give us something to eat and then you can help me to count all the stores for the Captain – you will enjoy that, yes? And afterwards we can go down for a drink somewhere where the wine is better than at the King's Head and you can tell me all about your experiences in the Spanish army."

He would take him to a wine-house which was not frequented by the other two, the Mermaid Tavern, and this would give him a chance to interrogate the man undisturbed.

As Jean Pierre pondered this offer, his eyes still fixed on the façade of the Barracks, Bresciano observed with dismay the figure of Captain Weston approaching him up the hill. His uniform was rumpled and there was a smudge of soot on his forehead, but there was no mistaking the look in his eyes.

"Private Bresciano!" he rasped. "I have already had occasion to warn you about carrying out my orders promptly! Why are you wasting time talking to this foreigner when I instructed you to take an inventory of Corporal Warner's provisions?"

The man was almost rigid with an anger that was totally disproportionate to the offence he was dealing with and Bresciano found his mind going blank.

"Well? Well?"

Bresciano saluted, twice.

Then inspiration came: "I have, sir, virtually completed the work. However, the stores are scattered and er... difficult to quantify. Corporal Warner," he took a deep breath, "has explained that he uses a variety of containers so that any possible er... putrefaction is contained in the individual containers and does not contaminate the food supplies contained in other containers..." he winced mentally as he heard himself parroting these excuses, "and that is why I have – just this moment – stepped out to seek the assistance of this foreign gentleman who will check my figures as he has a talent for numerical work..." He had run out of breath and of ideas.

"The façade has twelve hundred and forty eight stone blocks, twenty eight windows, fifty six shutters and eight of those need new hinges." Jean Pierre said solemnly, as if on cue.

CHAPTER XV

"This man is a fool," the Captain glared at Jean Pierre who returned his look blankly.

"Twenty-two buttons," he said, looking over the Captain's uniform.

The Captain's eyebrows rose, his nostrils flared and Bresciano closed his eyes and suppressed a groan.

"And," said Jean Pierre, waving a hand towards Spain, "Ninety-nine guns and fifty mortars. Many thousand cannonballs. I could not count those."

The Captain's expression changed. "This man should be giving this information to the Town Major, not checking wheat, pease and salt beef stores!"

Jean Pierre looked at Bresciano for enlightenment and, when the Captain's words had been roughly translated, his face was split by a wide grin and he said that he had already done so on the day he arrived.

"In future, Private Bresciano, you will not take it upon yourself under any circumstances to make any decisions whatsoever about what work is to be done or not done, and by whom. That is for your superiors to determine. Do you understand?"

"Yes, sir."

"Very well. I will authorise this man to assist you today. He can collect a letter of authority from my office when he has finished helping you and he will present it to the corporal or sergeant in charge of his work unit. After today you must manage on your own. You may take him with you now. And you are to waste no more time."

He turned sharply on his heel and walked into the Barracks. Bresciano blew out the breath he had been holding and told Jean Pierre, as best he could in French, what his new task was to be for the day, before following the Captain into the building.

Cookie-Will was not unduly put out by the arrival of Jean Pierre, and escorted them down to the store. He even found two old blankets, to keep out the bone-chilling temperature of the cellar. Before leaving them he said he would help them along by explaining his systematised chaos. It was a simple enough method of organising stores using letters of the alphabet for different parts of the cellar and odd or even numbers for the shelves. Cookie-Will could lay his hands on any items, as he was pleased to show them. And each container had been marked with lines painted to indicate quantities.

"Why didn't you show me this when I started?" Bresciano was aggrieved.

"I dunno as I can say – 'abit of being cautious, I s'pose. But I jes' decided that if we work together and the Captain sees as 'ow everything's 'counted for, then 'e'll leave me alone to get on with me cooking without sticking 'is nose in my business. An' I'm grateful to you for saying as I keep my stores all over to stop any rot from spreadin'. You got a brain in that 'ead of yours, lad."

So what had seemed impossible to record the day before now became a simple matter of tedious clerical work. Jean Pierre calculated and counted contentedly, while Bresciano recorded. And when Cookie brought them each a hunk of bread spread with a smear of fat, together with a mug of ale, they sat out in the yard at the back and ate in companionable silence. There was enough sunshine reaching the corner of the yard where they sat to make them want to linger. Once the bread was gone, they made the little ale left last as long as they could.

It was a heaven-sent chance for Bresciano to investigate. The conversation lurched along in a mixture of French and Spanish with Jean Pierre throwing in the occasional English word, always with a wide grin which went with pride of achievement. Amid the trivia of what was said, certain facts stood out for Bresciano. The first came as a shock.

"We… almost caught when we began our escape. Pascal

started first. Then five minutes for Robert and five for me. Not all together, you understand? But a guard came and looked at us. Robert, he took his knife and…" he swept an arc across his throat with an imaginary knife. "We are safe. He is very quick. Good soldier. If he does not finish off the guard… only Pascal would have got away."

Bresciano digested this information with a look of horror. Robert the charmer, the courteous, the life and soul of the tavern when he had a tale to tell. Jean Pierre mistook horror for disbelief.

"It is true. He does the same before. He has to kill sometimes like that. Very quick. And we all crawl to get to Gibraltar. They shoot, but they do not see us, I think, only movement. Thirteen bullets for me."

"And several for Robert?" Bresciano remembered Robert's account of their escape.

"No. Only one. No danger for him, about thirty yards away."

So, thought Bresciano, Robert would lie even about something as trivial as that.

Then Jean Pierre was talking about their hut above Willis's when they arrived.

"And on Thursday night?" Bresciano prompted him.

"Pascal is sick. He has bottle with opium. His stomach. It hurts sometimes. He sleeps. Robert and me we go to see the pretty Bianca. People get us drink. I go back late to the hut."

"You alone? What about Robert?"

"Robert goes out before. He has 'good business' to do, he tells me."

"And was Pascal in the hut… er… was he better?"

Jean Pierre shrugged, "It is late, eleven may be, and he is still sleeping. The bottle of opium is empty. When Robert comes I am almost asleep." He reflected for a moment, "The tavern is good. Warm. Better than the hut. We go next day."

"Yes, I saw you there early," he certainly remembered; he had gone to impress Bianca during the time they were allowed for lunch. He had meant to talk about his investigation and had had to listen, instead, to her praise of the Walloons and watch her smiling at Robert.

"I remember you push us as we go out."

It was a statement of fact, not an accusation, and

Bresciano was embarrassed to recall how he had deliberately jostled the Walloons as they all left the tavern.

"Twelve people in the tavern. In the afternoon when we finish work... twenty seven people. We go back again after work. Pascal he says he goes to better place, less noise. Near the church. You know it?"

"Yes. It is a good place."

"Me, I go to the King Head – I like Bianca and Carmela, but Carmela is not there."

"And Robert?"

"He stays with me."

Bresciano's face fell. Jean Pierre was giving Robert an alibi for the Friday afternoon when Jamie was killed.

"He stays with me fifteen minutes. Then he goes."

"Ah!"

"Then he comes back."

"When?"

"An hour. He is looking happy. Then we stay longer and Carmela comes and she makes some soup and we eat. I like the King Head. One day Robert and me we will have a tavern together. Robert says we do it when we finish the siege. Robert is very good cook. He is always good – with women, with a knife, with stories." He drained the last drop of his ale and stood up. "Now we go in and count more stores."

And Bresciano had to shake himself out of his bemusement. Robert had no alibi for either day and Robert was an expert killer and a fine cook. It made confused sense at best. He followed Jean Pierre who was clearly eager to return to work and by the afternoon the work was almost done. Jean Pierre pulled out a large hunter watch and flipped open the lid.

"We working for four hours and sixteen minutes," he announced, and snapped the case shut, putting the watch back in his pocket lovingly.

He went off to collect the Captain's authorisation for the work done and Bresciano arranged to meet him later at the Mermaid Tavern. He still had questions he wanted to ask.

It was only then, when he put his hands in his pockets, that he remembered the two letters Emiliana had given him. He had too much to think about and too little to make his thoughts cohere. Thoughtfully he made his way towards the

South Port. Beyond the gates was Lieutenant Drinkwater's favourite spot which Bresciano appropriated and then, feeling like a usurper, abandoned. A little further down, in a sheltered hollow under a tree, he sat on the ground and took out the letters.

He read them with distaste at himself, not at the contents, which were the work of a very young man, a youth of little more than his own age. They were respectful and spoke eloquently of worship rather than lust or even love. She was ethereal, a princess, a figure of myth and he was no more than a humble squire or troubadour, singing her praises and ready to do noble deeds in her name for her greater glory. He wrote of a book of poems by Marvell that he would lend her, praised her musical talents to the heavens, and regretted the need for secrecy in their brief meetings. The second letter carried a mundane postscript which Bresciano read with real interest:

"Do not concern yourself about that young James MacFarlane. I believe it is not he who is to blame, but those who twist his words. Nevertheless, this situation must not be allowed to continue unrestrained. I shall speak to him. I am persuaded that a degree of sternness will suffice to silence him. He is no more than an innocent whose wits have gone a-begging. But that his idle words should have caused you a moment of pain has angered me intensely – that you should be so traduced!"

Bresciano re-read the passage. It did not sound like the thoughts of a man bent on murder. Could he have met Jamie? And could Jamie at his daftest have precipitated a crisis of anger in the Lieutenant? The only certain thing was that it confirmed one of Emiliana's many suspect statements. Emiliana! He could not return the letters to her. Far better to hand them to Bianca, who seemed the one person who could keep her mother in order.

He put the letters away and made to rise when he heard voices above. He recognised Drinkwater's distinctive drawl and another voice he had heard once before – Lieutenant Black's. Bresciano sank back: the Lieutenant was unburdening his soul to his friend, and Bresciano became an unwitting confidant.

"There is no way in which I can communicate with her and I have heard such rumours about her condition since the night of the fire as to provoke in me the greatest fears for her health and her safety. I am at my wits' end."

"Be wary of rumours," Drinkwater's voice betrayed nothing, "I have heard that Mrs Weston escaped unscathed, that she broke her arm as she fled, that her hair took fire and that she broke both legs. No! I do not aim to alarm you, but to reassure you. It appears to be in the nature of rumours to grow wildly inaccurate. It is a phenomenon I have observed without understanding it."

"But have you heard anything that may be true?"

"All I know is that Dr Baines cannot have been called in – he is dealing with some bad cases of scurvy in the Naval Hospital and a minor new outbreak of smallpox at Rosia and has been living in a quarter up there while the emergency lasts."

"I see. That is reassuring. He is, after all, Mrs Weston's physician. It would indicate that anything Mrs Weston may be suffering from must, necessarily, be of a minor order." The Lieutenant's relief was tempered with distress. "I feel helpless in the face of her sufferings."

"Ah, yes. It is the siege that is also to blame. We are all trapped in this smallest of areas – a military garrison clinging to a massive block of limestone with nothing to distract us; unpalatable food at best, and a total lack of activity. War, at least, gives a man something to do. It provides one with a noble purpose in life."

"But when I think of that frail creature at the mercy of... I am sorry, I should not be saying this."

"Do not be concerned about me. I am all discretion. I believe you will encounter few people who like the Captain, much as he is respected for his military and administrative skills. But I have heard it said that he has always doted on his wife. Also that she suffers from a degree of melancholia – so Mrs Green remarked to me one day, and Mrs Green is an eminently sensible woman. I have also heard that he is arranging to send her to England, to her family, who will care for her."

"Are you sure? Then it may be as well. I tell you, I cannot carry on like this. I will miss her damnably, but it is a relief to know that she will be safe. It has been so disheartening to feel... thwarted... to know that I have been powerless to alleviate her suffering... all I could do was watch. Do you know that Thursday past I could not bear to join in the usual card party with friends in case Captain Weston was there? Instead I went and stood opposite his quarter. I listened to Frances... Mrs Weston... playing on the spinet and singing – such sad songs... I must have stood for two hours, till I heard the sound of weeping. I had to suppress an impulse to go to the house and demand entry. And then a light went on upstairs in what I imagine is her room, and I waited till the light was extinguished before I left. When I passed the Blue Barracks I saw that the card party had broken up."

"They never break up till ten or eleven. You must indeed have waited for hours outside the Westons'"

"And it was as well that I had abandoned my vigil. Among those leaving was Captain Weston and I instinctively pulled myself back into the shadows to avoid his sight. It made me feel wretched! The act of a coward!"

"I would rather call it the act of a rational man. What purpose would you have gained in provoking him in any way? You have done nothing wrong, and I should advise you to continue to avoid him. Bear in mind what occurred the last time you faced each other. That duel of yours could have been the end of everything for you and, personally, I was shocked that the Captain should have accepted a challenge from you: why, he can give you twenty years! A man does not fight a young lad."

"I fear I offered him unforgivable offence. I struck him. I was aware that the fault was mine so I had determined to delope."

"My dear Charles, you really have not been using your head. You may have decided to acknowledge your fault by firing into the air, but he may equally well have been determined to hit you – and he is a fine shot."

"You are right. I know it. But what my head and my heart say are at odds with each other."

"Come along. There is little point in dwelling on all this. As my sainted aunt used to say, 'What's past is prologue.' We have a fortress to defend."

They left and Bresciano climbed back up to the road deep in thought. Lieutenant Black had given Mrs Weston an alibi for Thursday night and established that he and the Captain had both been abroad at the time of the attempt on Jamie's life.

"*Amigo!*" a voice hailed him.

Pascal, presumably returning from the city defences beyond the South Port, drew level with him.

"What are you doing down here? I presume no physical effort yet with that bad hand?" His Spanish was fluent, if a little stilted.

"No. I am working with Captain Weston…"

"You are keeping records. Robert told me. He says you are very thorough."

"Well, it is boring, but I have to do it well. The Captain is very strict."

He had already lied to Robert about recording the arrival of the Walloons; now he needed a lie to check their whereabouts on Monday when Tom was murdered. He cast about in his mind for something that would justify his enquiries and there was nothing significant about Monday except Tom's murder. He decided on a reasonable lie:

"Yes, now he has given me more work, new work. First, I have been checking food stores," that, he thought, sounded innocuous, and would be confirmed by Jean Pierre. "And now I have to find out about a theft…" he was improvising, "a theft of a length of rope, a lot of rope."

He stopped, the lie had come easily, but how to elaborate it?

Pascal looked confused.

"I think it may be…" inspiration came, "someone who wants to desert and plans to go… to climb down the eastern escarpment. So I feel a bit stupid asking people like you who have just come into the fortress." His lies were flowing freely. "Why should you want to leave again? But you don't argue with Captain Weston. The man is impossible!" Lying sent his pulse racing, but Bresciano realised that he was enjoying the excitement.

"Ask me what it is you are enquiring about."

"Well, the rope went missing after lunch on Monday, at… er… the Blue Barracks."

"After lunch on Monday? From the Blue Barracks?" Pascal stared ahead, a frown creased his forehead. "Yes, of course, you wish to know if I was near the Barracks. At that time I was doing nothing! I was directed up to Princess

Caroline's Battery and our corporal did not come even though Sergeant Connor had ordered me and several Artificers up there. I cannot... vouch... that is the correct word?... for the others because he took Jean Pierre and Robert off with another group. So, you see, I spent the early afternoon waiting for someone to come and tell us what to do! The wind was strong up there and we each went to find a sheltered spot as best we could. We waited and waited. I even dozed off! A ridiculous waste of time."

"Thank you, I feel foolish asking these questions."

"Sometimes we have to do things that do not please us, but they must be done. A war – or a siege – forces certain tasks on us." The expression on his face darkened.

Bresciano thought of Robert efficiently dispatching that guard on the night they escaped.

"Yes, but much of it is dull and not at all heroic."

"So, you want to be a hero? You have someone you want to impress?"

"No!"

"You are young. Me, I just want to come out of all this alive. Ah, I leave you here. I have arranged to meet a colleague who plays chess. I feel my mind grows stagnant in this place."

And he was gone. Bresciano continued down towards The Mermaid where he found Jean Pierre waiting for him in what was the basement of an old building near the now badly-damaged debtors' prison – so much time seemed to have passed since he had sat opposite the prison on the wall with Bianca before the gunboat had fired and he had attempted to save her life. So much time since she had kissed him. He sighed as they sat down at one of the grimy tables, sticky with the ill-cleaned grease spilt from many a cheap dinner in the past. A large tankard for the Walloon and a small measure for himself was all he could afford. He had not bothered to even think of collecting his wages, for what little he earned he wanted to spend eventually on nourishment for Lucia.

Life had acquired new meaning – or had lost its old meanings – depending on how you looked at it. Each day dragged into the next with the same discomfort and constant awareness of hunger; each day saw faces more drawn; each day physical tasks became harder to carry out.

"Soon it will be Noël," Jean Pierre informed no one in

particular.

It was true, December was more than half done, but no one was in a situation or mood for celebrations.

"The worst Noël I have ever had." Bresciano spoke sadly, but he thought of past Christmases without nostalgia, for they seemed to have nothing to do with his life now. They belonged to someone else, to a boy who dreamed of glory and who knew nothing about hunger and nothing about killing.

"Perhaps extra rations?"

"There aren't any, are there?"

Jean Pierre shrugged and drained his tankard. "No women here. Not good." He stood up, ready to leave, to join Robert at Bianca's tavern.

"Wait! I have some information I need for Captain Weston. It's about where people were on Monday after the lunch break. It appears that there has been a… "

But Jean Pierre had no curiosity about why the information was needed and he answered willingly.

"We went with the Sergeant down to the wall outside the town. South Bastion you call it. We work there all day."

"All the time?"

"No. The Sergeant leaves us when we sit down to lunch. And Robert is anxious to get away then, and takes his chance – but he comes back soon – seventy four minutes." He took out his watch and tapped it proudly. "It tells very good time. I am glad I took it before we left camp. It belong to a Frenchman. Yes, Robert was gone one hour and fourteen minutes, and me and everyone else, we eat and rest. Hard work building walls."

"Thank you."

Bresciano stared at his drink morosely. He felt very much alone. Whatever he did or discovered was solely his responsibility, and he felt ill-prepared for what loomed ahead, for slowly he had begun to reduce his suspects, and then he would have to take action somehow. Jean Pierre was clearly out of the picture. Mrs Weston was no murderess. Even the Lieutenant appeared a less than likely suspect though it must not be forgotten that he had no proven alibis for the days in question. And Pascal had been out with a work party when Tom was killed, sick when there had been the first attempt on Jamie's life and at his preferred tavern on the evening of Jamie's murder. That left Robert, the Sergeant – both away that lunch hour when Tom was murdered – and the Captain, who could have been anywhere.

All he had was what he now termed evidence by default. He could conjure up motives and he knew where some of the people were or were not at the relevant times, but he had not a single shred of evidence to link anyone to the crimes. The key he had found outside the hut had been evidence, but it pointed to no one in particular. The knots on the rope used to hang Jamie were evidence too, but once more... fishermen's knots... and not one suspect with any naval connections, except himself... and he was not a suspect...

His meanderings, he thought, were becoming ludicrous. He wished he could organise his thoughts better. Well, he would have to do his best.

The truth was that he was woefully ill-equipped to fathom out the mystery of the two murders; he was young and inexperienced, and he lacked any authority to interrogate his suspects.

He rose abruptly, leaving his drink untouched, and walked out. He wanted nothing so much as a long walk away from the town and away from his wretched investigation, but it was already growing dark and, with all the lights near the harbour soon to be extinguished to afford the enemy gunboats no identifiable targets, he was forced to make his way slowly back to the Barracks where an unpalatable supper would eventually be served and where he would while away the time making a neat copy of his inventory for the Captain.

*   *   *   *

Two hours later, his work almost done, he joined the other men who were crowding into the dining hall. Their talk, the sound of stools and benches being moved around, the grating noise of cutlery scraping on tin plates and the voices raised in laughter or complaint soon turned the cold hall into a lively place, and Bresciano found his gloomy mood gradually lifting, leaving him tired, but more hopeful. Jean Pierre waved him over and Bresciano joined him willingly before realising that it meant also joining Robert.

As matters turned out, he was soon pleased enough that Robert was there, for talk had turned to the ships, so long awaited from England, bringing supplies of food and equipment for the beleaguered garrison.

"It is an easy run from England to Gibraltar," Robert spoke authoritatively. "When I served on board a merchant ship…"

His voice was drowned as a bell rang, a sign that they must clear the room, and Bresciano cursed to himself. Robert in the navy, the merchant navy!

Once the tables were cleared and the pipes had come out, the conversation continued. Tobacco was running out, as was rum, and it was rumoured that Eliott had demanded supplies of both commodities for his garrison. Some scoffed at the idea of the commander interesting himself in such minutiae, till it was pointed out that before the siege began he had requested new kettles for the troops as such items were not available locally.

Fortunately someone wanted to hear what Robert had to say about the sea voyage from England… how long should supplies take… when had the last ship sailed through the Spanish blockade? Robert was easily persuaded to talk of his maritime experiences. He estimated that for the journey from England two weeks should be enough. He himself had done it in a frigate in less than that. He spoke of currents and winds and the difficulties of getting past the Spanish ships at Punta Carnero. He certainly seemed to know what he was talking about. And from that sea-route it was logical to talk about the tobacco trade with Cuba, the seductiveness and availability of Cuban beauties who liked men with light hair and blue eyes.

There was soon a small circle round Robert, eager to hear something new.

"Is it true that you were brought up in a shat-oh?"

"Wot's a shat-oh?"

"A froggie castle, you ignorant fool!"

"You a prince or something, Robert?"

"No, no." Robert laughingly held up his hands in protest, "In France and the Low Countries, we have small *châteaux* that are no more than large fortified houses. Do not be imagining a mighty castle. Not in the least. And you do not have to be of royal blood to live in one."

"A duke or something like that, eh?"

Robert waved a disclaiming hand, "It was a small place

and my parents were ordinary folk really – except that we had a nanny from England to teach us children to speak English. But I grew tired of that sort of life with too many servants doing everything. I wanted to see the world, so I ran away to sea! I was looking for adventure and excitement. I actually wanted to become a pirate. But my parents found out and chased me and took me back home. I was only eight!"

There was laughter and approval at this sally. Robert was a bit of a lad – he told a good tale – he provided good entertainment. But Bresciano could not rid himself of the image of Robert calmly and efficiently slitting a man's throat; and Robert tying those fishermen's knots with the rope that hanged Jamie.

Suddenly Jean Pierre said in very broken English, "Robert iss a… *très bon* cook. The Baron… he say… *ça*."

Robert's eyes turned on him coldly. "*C'etait une petite histoire, Jean Pierre, ce n'est pas vrai, d'accord*?" And turning to the rest, he smiled, "I told him a joke and he thinks it is the truth."

"Can't see you cooking for no one!"

"So wot 'appened after that – when d'you go to sea properly?"

Bresciano moved away and sat in a window embrasure, trying to put as much distance as possible between himself and Robert. That was an ugly look he had given Jean Pierre – it boded no good for the man. Would he one day slit his throat as well? Away from the circle of soldiers avid for entertainment, Bresciano tried to weigh what might be true in Robert's narrative. Perhaps he had been brought up in a *chateau* – as a child of one of the servants… perhaps the son of that English nanny! And he could have worked in the kitchens as he grew older. The Baron – probably the real owner of the *chateau* – had perhaps complimented him on his skills. Bresciano refused to believe in Robert as gentry or the scion of some minor nobility. He had lied about having been in a cavalry regiment and about a bullet nearly getting him – no – 'several bullets' was what he had claimed. The man was a charlatan, no better than that Munchausen that Abraham had told him about who had been packed off to Spain – except that the German could be forgiven his fantasies as the products of insanity. Robert had no excuse. He was a liar. He was also a cold-blooded killer.

Bresciano might have moved away from the group, but he could not blot out their voices. Some sort of argument had broken out and Robert was being asked to arbitrate. His laughing voice reached Bresciano:

"No, my friends, I will not take sides. I say nothing – I will save my breath to cool my porridge, as you English say!"

Bresciano sat frozen. He felt the hairs on his arms stir. He had only heard that expression before on one person's lips, and in a broad Scottish brogue, at that: Private Ferguson, that childhood friend who had amused him and Bianca with his crude jokes, had used it and had had to explain what he meant.

It was a Scottish saying.

That nanny could have been Scottish. Robert would have known about ghillies.

Had he found his murderer?

CHAPTER XVI

Bresciano left the mess hall with Jean Pierre, who glanced back darkly at Robert, who was still holding court at the table. Jean Pierre muttered obstinately: "The Baron said he was a good cook. Robert told me so himself. He was not joking! I don't argue with him – when he gets angry… it is bad."

Bresciano went thoughtfully to the store-room: Robert was not a man to be lightly crossed, if Jean Pierre was to be believed. And of all the people Bresciano had questioned so far, Jean Pierre was the one with least to hide, who said what he thought with a minimum of words. It was one more mark against the 'charming' Robert. Considerably cheered by the thought, he retrieved two eggs that Cookie had given him, wrapped them carefully in his spare shirt and put them in his pack. Then he made for the Barracks gate. Before he got there he was pulled up short by the sight of Sergeant Connor standing in the doorway, feet apart and arms akimbo.

"Private Busyano, come here!"

Bresciano made his way towards him apprehensively and saluted.

"Sir?"

"I hear you're checking… things for Captain Weston."

How on earth, Bresciano wondered, did the Sergeant manage to make a simple enquiry seem threatening?

"Yes, sir. He has asked me to make a full inventory of the stores – I already did the blankets and lamps and… things… and now it's food, you know, because of short rations… very important we know exactly what we have, to make it last… an accurate record… flour and meat and… everything…"

He babbled. The Sergeant had the ability to demoralise him by his mere presence, and now he was looking particularly intimidating.

"Only foodstuffs? What about this rope you say has gone missing? Did Captain Weston ask you to look into that? Amazing that the rope disappeared only yesterday and you were on to it immediately."

Bresciano hesitated, confused. The Sergeant had obviously somehow come to hear of his conversation with Pascal, and his improvised claim that some rope had disappeared. And now it appeared that some rope had really gone missing.

"Er...no, sir... er... Sergeant." He cast around desperately for some innocuous explanation. "It was only that... when we were checking the stores, Corporal Warner remarked that he thought some rope should have been there, and it wasn't...." He could only hope that he could rely on the resourceful Cookie-Will to back him up if the Sergeant decided to check.

The Sergeant stared at him fixedly in silence till Bresciano felt that he had to say something, anything, to break the tension. He opened his mouth, but no words came; this was even worse than his encounters with the acid Captain.

"Listen here, Busybodyano. I shan't warn you again." Sergeant Connor brought his face close to Bresciano's and his voice was quietly menacing. "Stick to what you're ordered to do, by me or the Captain, and don't shove that great nose of yours into what doesn't concern you, or it will be the worse for you... much worse!"

He dismissed Bresciano with a jerk of his head and watched, his eyes narrowed, as Bresciano turned on his heel and stumbled off, made clumsy by fear.

Once out of sight, Bresciano breathed more easily as he made his way slowly toward Waterport Street wondering why the Sergeant was so concerned with rope. Even if the rope had really disappeared, why should the Sergeant...? He surely wasn't planning to desert, not the Sergeant! Then Bresciano reflected that even if Robert had become his favourite... he corrected himself mentally... his *most likely* suspect, the Sergeant was still by no means in the clear. Jean Pierre had been quite definite that Sergeant Connor as well as Robert had left their working party on Monday when it had broken up for lunch, and the Sergeant had not returned till late afternoon when they had finished their work, so he had had even more time than Robert to meet Tom by the cave and kill him.

His possible motives for murdering Jamie were still unclear. Bresciano could not quite bring himself to believe that a hatred of Scotsmen in general could drive a man to kill the inoffensive Jamie, but given the Sergeant's threatening demeanour only minutes before, it began to seem possible that Jamie – breaking lanterns, spreading gossip in good-natured ignorance, being a thorn in the Sergeant's flesh since that musket had blown up – could have driven the Sergeant to irrational and murderous action. And what if Jamie had innocently said something about the Sergeant's late wife? Bresciano knew that this was wild supposition, but the possibility certainly existed.

Robert now, was a different matter; of course he was. He could have ample motive to commit murder. An efficient killer, and a liar to boot! One more potential spy, like Abraham's. And, Bresciano was convinced, there was now a definite Scottish connection linking him with Jamie! He hesitated. There was something wrong with his reasoning there, but he could not quite put a finger on it.

He recognised again in himself the wish that Robert should be the guilty party, and had to admit, reluctantly, that a better case could be made against Sergeant Connor.

When he reached the door of his house, he could hear a commotion inside, and he had a sudden fear that something was wrong – perhaps Lucia had suffered a relapse? The door was unlocked and he thrust it open and burst in.

The noise was coming from the kitchen. He could hear his father's booming voice, and – thank heaven – the sound of laughter from Lucia.

He found his family clustered around the kitchen table, and looking over the black-shrouded shoulders of Nonna and Aunt Maria, he saw what they were looking at admiringly – an enormous gilthead bream which stared back at them, glassy-eyed, from the table.

Giancarlo looked up at him. "Giovanni! See how your father can provide for our family. Never have I caught such a fish before. It must be the biggest *dorada* ever caught in the Bay! We will eat well tonight," he said with deep satisfaction.

Bresciano made appropriate noises of admiration, then

kissed the womenfolk and opened his pack.

"I'm afraid my contribution isn't so great, but it will help. Here are two eggs which my friend the cook has given me."

His mother took them from him. "That is wonderful, Giovanni. I will beat them up with some milk for Lucia. It will help her to regain her strength – she is so thin after her illness."

Lucia pulled a face, and Eleanor added, "Now, you can take that scowl off your face, young lady. I'll put some of the molasses you liked so much in it, and maybe even a little drop of brandy! Giovanni: you will stay and have some fish with us."

Bresciano shook his head. "No, it will be too late by the time it is cooked, and I must return to the Barracks. I only came to bring you the eggs."

The thought of fresh food for a change was very tempting, and he had to stop himself from saying more.

"Nonsense. I will save you a piece, and you will come tomorrow." Eleanor spoke firmly. "I would not enjoy it if I knew you were not sharing in our good fortune."

He left and made his way back to the Barracks through the dark streets. It had been an eventful day, and he was tired. He had time to reflect, as Friday drew to a close, that it was a week since Jamie's murder. A whole week had passed. He closed his eyes and was asleep within seconds of lying down on the hard bed.

* * * *

He woke early, and was down to breakfast before the working party had risen. He found that he was so ravenously hungry that the thin gruel which was all that Cookie-Will was able to provide tasted good. The other Artificers arrived for breakfast, bolted their food and left for King's Bastion, led by Corporal Jones. Bresciano was glad to see that the Sergeant was not there. Only Murch remained at the table, toying with the remains of his gruel.

Murch had been Tom's friend, Bresciano thought. Here was an opportunity to find out more about Tom and his new-found wealth.

"Are you not going to King's Bastion today?" he asked tentatively.

"Nah," Murch grunted. "Doctor saw me back, said it was

festering 'cos I hadn't kept it clean. How can you keep clean in this cess-pit, I ask you? Put a poultice on and put me off work, he did – but just for the one day, the miserable sod!"

"Er…." Bresciano considered how to proceed. "I just wanted to say, Mr Murch, that I'm sorry I was such a fool as to try to blame you for poor Jamie's death. I'd be grateful for the advice of an old soldier like you…"

"Yer seem to be doin' all right. Off duty for days on end, you've been!" Murch was unwilling to unbend.

"It's just – that I'm new to all this soldiering business, and an experienced man like you, you must have been on many campaigns, you've seen proper fighting… a real hero… you could advise me on how to get on…"

Murch unbent a little in response to Bresciano's flattery. "Aye, that's true, I know all the tricks of the trade, I do! Things you don't learn in no books."

"I feel very ignorant, and my money just seems to disappear. I don't know how others manage. I mean… some soldiers seem to be able to lay their hands on a little extra cash – look at your friend, poor old Tom."

"Tom! Don't talk to me about Tom! I'm sorry he's dead, I s'pose, but he were a greedy swine – 'ad money for extra food and drink, and did he share it with his mates? 'Course he didn't, and much good it did him!"

Bresciano wondered whether Murch would have been ready to share if he had been in Tom's place, but he only said: "Where did he get his money from, though?"

"Dunno! He never told me nothing – just made a show of it – waved it under our noses, he did. P'raps he got lucky, gambling. Tom liked a flutter, he did. I like a bit of a wager meself, too, but we never did win much, worse luck."

"Gambling? Hasn't that been forbidden by the Governor?"

Murch snorted. "A lot goes on round here that the Governor don't know 'bout. Why, the biggest gamblers are the officers – even old high-and-mighty Weston. What the Governor don't know don't hurt him!"

This was promising. Tom's affluence was still a mystery and was more likely to stem from blackmail than from gambling, but any information about Captain Weston, and perhaps about Lieutenant Black, might be interesting.

"Is the Captain a big gambler, then?" Bresciano probed.

"Well, I did 'ear from his batman that he dropped sixty quid last Thursday at the big game in the Major's quarters. Left early and in a bad mood, he said, and didn't return to his quarter until late evening. The batman wasn't best pleased about it. He had a little ladybird lined up and by the time he arrived she had gone off with one of them Walloons! And on Friday, he didn't turn up for the usual afternoon game till near evening, or so his man said."

So Weston's movements were unaccounted for during the time of the first attack on Jamie, and on the day of his death. Bresciano felt a surge of excitement. The Captain had been free on the Monday when Tom had been killed – hadn't been locked up over the business of the duel till later. And the same applied to Lieutenant Black, of course.

Perhaps Murch knew something about him.

But Murch had less to offer here. Yes, he knew that the Lieutenant gambled – they all did, didn't they? But he only played for low stakes, and not often, he had heard.

"Why'd you want ter know about gambling, any'ow? You fancy a flutter yerself?" he said eagerly, seeing a possible goose for the plucking.

"No, I'm no good at cards," Bresciano said hastily. "I do play chess, though."

"Chess!" Murch said, in a tone of disgust, rapidly losing interest in Bresciano. "Hey, Cookie," he shouted toward the kitchen. "You got a morsel of decent food for a poor starving man?"

There was an answering roar from the kitchen. "Nothing for you, you fat pig! You've stolen enough already to keep a battalion in provisions for a month, you 'ave!"

This was obviously a familiar battleground for the two men. Bresciano left them to it, and went to his storeroom to continue with the inventory for Captain Weston.

Two hours later, he laid his quill down with a sigh of relief, and rubbed his aching hand across his chest. He now had well over half of the inventory recorded neatly for the Captain to see. All the dry goods, flour, beans, peas were now accounted for. Thanks to Cookie-Will's ingenuity, the only discrepancy that the Captain could pick on was a missing bag of flour, which had been left out in the rain by the baker who delivered it and been ruined.

"I could've hidden that one, too," Cookie had confided to Bresciano, "But it always pays to let 'em have something to find and grouse about!"

But the Captain seemed abstracted, and did not even question the loss of the flour. He merely grunted "Good work; but be sure to give me the rest of it by tomorrow."

Bresciano went back to the dormitory and decided to take a rest from the tedious work of the inventory. He could finish that in the evening and have it on the Captain's desk at dawn. Instead he pulled out the list of suspects he had prepared. Tom's death must have occurred about midday on Monday, shortly after the man had gone missing, if Dr Coll's information was correct. He knew that Robert and the Sergeant had left the work party at that time, Robert for an hour, the Sergeant for longer; the Captain and Lieutenant had been free, but he had no idea of any of their movements after that. Who could he go to for information? Abraham would possibly be spending the Sabbath with his family and he did not wish to disturb him.

He decided to walk down to the centre of town. Perhaps he would bump into Lieutenant Drinkwater and make discreet enquiries about his friend Lieutenant Black. Then he would drop in to see Lucia and his mother and – his mouth watered at the thought – there would be a piece of *dorada* waiting for him there.

Waterport Street was almost deserted. He walked the length of it and back, and then up and down Church Street, and met no one. He turned down towards the Bay and as he approached the sea wall he spied a seated figure, his head bowed over a book.

He could hardly believe his luck: it was Lieutenant Black. Bresciano approached him diffidently.

"Excuse me, sir. I could not help seeing that you are reading one of my mother's books. May I ask whether you are finding it… er… satisfactory?"

It was not the most adroit of self-introductions, he told himself, but he need not have worried. The Lieutenant's eyes lit up at his words, and he replied,

"Indeed it is, Private… er… er… I am most grateful to Drinkwater and to your good mother for kindly allowing me to read her books. The only unsatisfactory part of it is that I will finish this one all too soon. Do you think – would your mother have any more books that I could borrow? I find myself in great need of reading matter; reading is a great distraction. It takes my… one's mind off other… concerns."

Bresciano smiled in relief. The 'concerns' that were on the Lieutenant's mind did not need to be spelt out. "Indeed she has, sir. I know that she has another book by the author of the one you are reading – *Amelia*, is it not? – entitled *Tom Jones*, and one with another lady's name in the title, *Clarissa*, I think…"

"Wonderful! I have read *Tom Jones*, of course, but would gladly read it again, and the other I have not read, although I have heard excellent reports of it."

Their conversation was interrupted by the approach of another officer. It was Lieutenant Drinkwater, who said jovially:

"My dear Black; I see that you have discovered my private librarian; but we must really ration your reading before it impairs both your eyesight and your chances of promotion! You know that Colonel Ross is not at all pleased with you on that account. As I hear, on Monday when you were supposed to report directly to him at noon, you were by the South Port with your nose in a book. And you were there when I went by shortly after. And there you remained for a further hour and a half as I well know – because I was with you."

They seemed to have forgotten Bresciano. Black smiled ruefully, and Bresciano said diplomatically, "I must leave now, gentlemen, but I will see to it that Private Hassan gets the books I mentioned and delivers them to one of you."

Drinkwater called after him. "I saw you first, Private. Just make sure that I get the books before Black!"

As Bresciano left, he thought exultantly that at least he had eliminated one suspect: Lieutenant Black could not have murdered Tom if he had been in Drinkwater's company on the Monday for about two hours after midday. If he could somehow eliminate Captain Weston, too, then there would be only Robert de la Tour and Sergeant Connor to consider. Could he work out a plan which would induce one of them to give himself away?

Meanwhile, he needed to talk to the Walloons again. He had not seen them at breakfast and was not sure where they had been assigned to work today. There should be a duty roster at the Blue Barracks.

On his way back to the Barracks he called in to his home. Lucia was out in the patio, trying ineffectually to catch sparrows.

"They won't stay still, Giovanni!" she complained, laughing at her own efforts.

"Leave them alone, Lucia," he advised. "They aren't any good for food, anyway."

As soon as Giovanni entered, Eleanor had started heating up a portion of the fish which Giancarlo had caught. He tried to escape, claiming that he was not hungry, but she put it firmly in front of him.

"Giovanni, don't you think I can't tell when you are lying," she said firmly. "I can see that you're starving. Eat it up, now. You don't know where your next good meal is coming from."

He sat down reluctantly, but the aroma and the taste of fresh food was too beguiling. He wolfed it down; it was delicious. He had forgotten how good his mother's cooking was, when she could obtain decent food to prepare. He sat back when he had finished.

At his request, his mother gave him the books for the officers, and he made his way up to the Barracks. He went round the back and slipped in unseen by the door leading to the kitchen.

Another hour's work produced a fair copy of the inventory of oil, butter, salt and rum for the daily ration. Now he had only to record the stocks of small beer, salt pork and other meats. He could complete that in the evening. Meanwhile, armed with the list he had just made, he went down to the office and gave it to the clerk. Surreptitiously, he looked at the daily roster and found that the Walloons had again been assigned to work at South Bastion.

He was taking serious risks in leaving his work on the stores, but he had begun to think that he was nearing a solution to the two murders and he was impatient of delay. It was Saturday and he felt that unless he resolved matters soon it would become more difficult with the passage of time.

Once more he left by the back entrance and started down the hill. He still had not decided how to approach the problem of Robert. To give himself time to think, he decided to detour towards the King's Head, thinking that he might see Bianca and possibly get some information out of her about the Walloons. He promised himself that he would continue to be formal and distant, as Pascal had advised. He thought that the tactic had been particularly effective at their last meeting… they had virtually embraced – he had shielded her from danger – and had then walked coolly away. He was playing his cards well for once.

It was still early and Bianca was taking down the shutters before opening the wine house.

"Good morning, Giovanni," she said cheerfully. "I'll be open in a moment and then you can have a drink."

"I do not drink so early in the day," he said loftily. "Not before the sun is… on top of… er… over the yardarm. In any case, I have… important work to do."

Bianca giggled at his attempt at the nautical phrase, and took the shutters into the bar-room. He followed her in, and she went behind the bar.

"Well, if you don't want a drink, then what *do* you want?" she asked.

Bresciano leaned over the bar, and tried to look commanding.

"I have been charged with investigating… certain matters," he said – impressively, he hoped.

"Oh, not the death of poor Jamie! You're not still going on about that, are you?"

"That investigation is still – proceeding. But I have also been asked to look into the movements of certain civilians and recent entrants to this fortress on Monday last, at midday, related to… to the theft of some rope… and – and the security of the Garrison!"

"That sounds very impressive, Giovanni," Bianca said, half-seriously. "But you are looking a little odd." She cocked her head to one side and studied his face. He looked to be in some discomfort. "You seem – as if you are uncomfortable. Do you have a touch of colic, perhaps? If so, I have some gin here to settle your stomach. You can have it as a medicine, even if the sun isn't over the… whatever it was!"

Bresciano put his hands down on the bar and leaned forward, trying to look severe.

"I do not have colic!" he raised his voice involuntarily

in his irritation, and tried to regain control of himself. "I am conducting a serious investigation, and I would like to ask you some questions – about those Walloons of yours!"

Bianca stared at Bresciano. Maybe he didn't have colic, she thought, but his expression was stormy. Was he... angry?... sad? She asked herself. He looked more miserable than severe. It was a look she remembered from childhood when something upset him and he refused to give in to tears. That was it, she decided – he was suffering from melancholy, dwelling too much on the death of poor Jamie and his sister's illness.

She smiled at him, hoping to cheer him up, "Giovanni, I didn't thank you for going to talk to my mother. Whatever you said to her certainly made her happy. I haven't seen her so cheerful for a long time – not when she was sober, anyway!"

Bresciano felt a pang of guilt at this point. Emiliana was happy because she thought she would be able to use the letters she had filched to get money out of the Westons. He had better not give the letters into Bianca's care, as he had originally planned.

Bianca tried again, misinterpreting his guilty look as more melancholia. She changed tack, and laughed out loud, recalling to Bresciano their encounter with the gunboat by the Line Wall.

"Oh, Giovanni, I can laugh about it now, but I was frightened the other day – and I was excited at the same time – isn't that strange? I think I felt better because you were with me, and you did try to save my life, didn't you? You are definitely my hero."

Her voice no longer had its usual teasing lilt; there was real affection there. She stepped out from behind the bar and came towards him, putting her hand out to take his. Bresciano was filled with exultation. God bless Pascal – his advice had worked! Now was the time for action! He leapt over a low table that separated them, caught his foot on the edge, and fell headlong into Bianca's arms.

Bianca, still laughing, held him up to steady him, but all the pent-up frustration of the past months that Bresciano had suffered now got the better of him. He wrapped his long arms fervently around her and tried to kiss her passionately. Her mood changed.

"Giovanni, what do you think you're doing? Let me go! Have you gone mad?"

But Bresciano had gone too far to draw back now – he attempted to find her lips with his and only succeeded in reaching first her ear and then her chin as she tried to wriggle out of his grasp. Her hair, which had been tied up in a workmanlike bun, came loose. Bresciano, seeing her flushed cheeks and long flowing tresses, was overcome by an almost savage desire to possess her and made a grab for her as she tried to get away. Unfortunately, his fingers caught on the hem of her bodice, and pulled it partly loose.

By now Bianca was beside herself with rage. With one hand she held up her bodice, and with the other she dealt Bresciano a stinging slap on the cheek.

"Giovanni, you fool!" she screamed at him. "So you are investigating the Walloons, are you? My Walloons, as you call them. Well, let me tell you where at least one of them was this Monday – Robert! He came here for a drink at midday, and – and he stayed with me for two hours. Two hours! Not here in the bar, but in my room, do you hear, in my room! He knows how to treat a woman. Do you understand me, you clown!"

Bresciano was aghast. His Bianca, with that popinjay. How could she? All reason fled and he shouted back at her words that he would never have said in his senses:

"Why should I be surprised? Like mother, like daughter!"

This final insult was too much for Bianca. She grabbed a pot and flung it at Bresciano, and it clanged against the door as he made an undignified exit. Bianca's bodice had come loose as she released it to throw her missile, but Bresciano was no longer there to appreciate the charms which were all too clearly revealed or to hear her shouts of "Giovanni, you pig! I never want to speak to you again!"

Bresciano stumbled though the streets, barely registering where he was going. It had begun to rain, but he did not notice. What he thought of as Bianca's betrayal, with Robert, of all people, was too hard to bear.

Then he stopped stock still in the street, and uttered a loud groan. It was worse, even worse than that. Bianca had not only betrayed him, but she had given the despicable Robert de la Tour an unshakeable alibi for the murder of Tom Tennant!

CHAPTER XVII

All he wanted was a hole to crawl into. Nothing mattered – not his investigation nor his family nor his life in the regiment. Bianca submitting to Robert's caresses. Worse than that – Bianca encouraging them, inviting them. The blood in his veins was turning to ice and he found himself shivering uncontrollably. He leaned against a wall and slowly slid down to the ground where he sat, hugging his knees, his head buried in his arms. Less than a fortnight ago he had walked into the tavern proudly, eager to show off his uniform, certain of impressing her. Bianca! Bianca!

He did not know how long he sat in his misery, conjuring up images of Bianca and Robert in bed, in each other's arms, touching, laughing, laughing at him, tearing at each other's clothing, sinking into each other in a frenzy of desire.

He flung back his head and howled: "No, no!"

It was torn out of him, like a deep-rooted plant being pulled out of the soil savagely, and with it went his boyish illusions of Bianca lying gentle in his strong, sheltering arms. She wanted none of him. She had given herself to that... that practised, professional lover – to a vicious murderer... to a man he despised, reviled and... envied desperately.

The quaking feeling in his stomach gradually subsided and he stood up uncertainly. Impossible to believe that it was still only mid-morning. He felt old, as if he had lived too long, as he walked wearily back to take up his duties in the Barracks, walking in through the main entrance and past Weston's office without a care for himself. The thought of company repelled him. Solitude was what he needed. Down in Cookie's store-room he would be alone with his misery and, avoiding Cookie whom he heard singing cheerfully and tunelessly in the kitchen, he made his way down to where he settled down to the last list with his blanket wrapped round him. It presented few problems and he found himself working automatically – writing words and figures, but unable to shake off the images of Bianca and Robert.

There was a bottle of some strong spirituous liquid on one of the shelves and he reached out for it. Every item he wrote was followed by a swig from the bottle. It burnt as it went down his gullet and he welcomed the discomfort. By the time the list was completed his writing was beginning to grow erratic and he was having to screw up his eyes to see clearly. Cookie's dog Angel emerged, moved tentatively towards Bresciano, and stared at him.

"She called me a s-swine, a pig." Bresciano said thickly.

The dog wagged his stump of a tail and moved closer.

"I shaid she wass no better than her mother!"

Angel licked his hand.

"It was a terrible thing to s-say. A terrible, terrible thing. Robert is a devil, but she'ss an angel!" He stroked the dog's rough coat. "An' you're an angel too!" he laughed weakly. "Jamie saw angels. Poor, poor Jamie, poor Sparrow. It's not fair! He was murdered."

He began to weep and Angel moved closer to him.

"I'm so tired. I'm hungry again… all the time… it'ss cold."

He sank down to the floor, his head on a sack of rice and the blanket partly covering him. Angel curled up in the crook of his legs, glad of the extra warmth.

And there it was that Cookie-Will found them, both snoring gently, when he came down an hour later.

"'Ere, wake up! You'll catch your death down 'ere. My God! You're like ice! Get up lad."

Bresciano attempted to sit up and felt a wave of nausea that made his head swim. He began to gag and Cookie-Will forced him to sit up and handed him an empty bucket.

"Get yourself out to the yard and don't you mess up my store-room! And 'ere was I thinking you was a gentleman! Get yourself out there before I throw you out."

Clumsy, ashamed and as sick in his stomach as in his

soul, Bresciano staggered out, shivering, followed by Cookie and Angel.

Five minutes later, penitent and shaken, Bresciano raised his head: "My mother kept some fish for me. I've thrown up the best meal I've had in weeks! And... she called me a pig and she was right!"

His misery spoke for itself and Cookie-Will, with rough kindness, pushed his head under the yard pump and dowsed it with cold water. Then he wrapped his head in his apron to dry it and sat him down in the only sunlit corner of the yard, finally wrapping the blanket round him. Angel joined him with a proprietary air.

"You jes' sit there and wait for me. Understand?"

A few minutes and he was back with a steaming bowl. "It's nobbut hot gruel, but it'll make you feel better. What was you thinking of? That was rum you drank, you fool boy. The cheapest. Gut-rot, that is. Now you drink that gruel and tell Cookie all about it."

So Bresciano, gradually thawing physically and emotionally as Cookie fussed over him and forced him to have his gruel, poured out his sad little tale, beginning with the morning's disastrous encounter with Bianca and ending with Jamie's death.

"It was awful. He was only like me, young. It would have been different if he had been an old man. It isn't right, is it? And he was murdered. Someone drugged him and hanged him."

"Do you know wot you're saying, lad?" Cookie was horrified.

"He was murdered as sure as I'm sitting here."

And Bresciano told Cookie-Will about all the circumstances surrounding Jamie's death, and succeeded in convincing him that there had indeed been foul play.

"And the awful thing is that I am beginning to think I'll never discover who did it to him. You know, when the Sergeant cut him down, I took Jamie in my arms. I thought he was still alive. I thought he was trying to say something, but when I put my ear to his mouth there wasn't even a breath. He was dead."

Bresciano closed his eyes and laid his throbbing head against the wall, grateful for the winter sun on his face.

"Poor Sparrow! Poor little lad," Cookie said sadly." One minute you're alive and the next you're dead. Life's a bugger. And if only he'd been alive, 'e could of told you who done it, couldn't he? Well, there it is. My goodness, with all this I nearly forgot – the Captain wants the rest of the invent'ry. That's the trouble with being efficient, people 'spect you to work. You'll 'ave to learn to be a bit stupid! Now I've wasted enough time on you, you young fool!" And he bustled off, brushing Bresciano's thanks aside with a wave of his podgy hand.

As his head settled into a dull ache, Bresciano opened his eyes. He pulled out his crumpled list of suspects and straightened it out on his knee. He might never know who had killed Jamie, but he knew who had not. Not Lieutenant Black, for whoever killed Jamie had also killed Tom to shut his mouth, and Drinkwater's alibi cleared the Lieutenant specifically of the second murder and therefore – by implication – of the first. And it could not have been the ethereal and unbalanced Mrs Weston. Certainly not the obsessive Jean Pierre who had always been in the company of others at the relevant times. And Pascal – either sick or in that tavern or with a working party at Princess Caroline's Battery – could also be eliminated. And, whether he liked it or not, just as he had done with Lieutenant Black, he had to clear Robert of blame. Bianca – oh, Bianca! – she had seen to that! He set his jaw at the thought: it was the hardest pill to swallow.

That left only the Captain and the Sergeant.

"The Sergeant - Oh my prophetic soul!" he muttered Hamlet's words.

When he had read *Hamlet* with a tutor his mother had found for him, he had found it hard to sympathise with a hero who took so long to get anything done. And here was he, Giovanni Bresciano, intent on revenge, or at least on unmasking Jamie's killer, being as useless as Hamlet. All Hamlet did was set that trap for his uncle – creating a situation where his uncle would betray himself and all *he* had done was eliminate…

Angel, suddenly alert, stood up, his body rigid. Then he leapt into action. With four bounds he crossed the yard and seized an unwary rat by the scruff of the neck. A violent shaking and, with the rat's now limp body hanging from his jaws, Angel disappeared with his prize.

Bresciano stared after him. Bless the dog and bless Cookie for his chance remark, and bless Hamlet!

He had the answer to his problems. As Cookie had said, had Jamie spoken, he would have been able to identify his murderer. Who was to know that Jamie had not done precisely that? He could have muttered something disjointed… a few words… partly unintelligible… cryptic… which had only begun to make sense now. Bresciano frowned and rubbed his nose. It wasn't convincing enough. He had to make it somehow credible. Well – he felt fired with purpose – he had to think of something so he *would* think of something. And once he had, he would set a trap. He had to get the murderer to betray himself. That done, he would pounce, like Angel.

To his surprise, he began to feel angry: he was tired of picking up mere snippets of information; tired of trying to make sense of people's motives; tired of the hole-in-the-corner business he had engaged in as he tried to investigate while he was expected to work; and tired of being harassed by superior officers. He could spend more time trying to check the Captain and the Sergeant's alibis – but the more time that passed, the less people would remember and the smaller his chances of uncovering the truth. He would have to act now… even if he had to set himself up as bait!

There it was… an idea coming to him fully formed. All he had to do was polish his story of Jamie's dying words, let both his suspects learn about it, and then make sure they knew where he would be – alone – at some particular time, in some isolated spot.

"Eureka!" he shouted, and then had to nurse his aching head.

So it was that eventually and with a relatively light step that he made his way up to the Captain's office and handed in the final page of the inventory. Taking note of Cookie's worldly wisdom, he had made a note of a bottle of rum which he claimed he had dropped and smashed.

"An honest man," the Captain said dryly. "It will, nevertheless, have to come out of your wages. I see your writing deteriorates at the end. You are not used to the work of a scribe."

Bresciano wanted to protest at this slur on his calligraphy, on which he prided himself, but he prudently held his tongue.

"You look unwell."

"Something I… ate, sir."

"It will not stop you working. You can report back to your usual working party tomorrow. I have no further use for you."

Bresciano marched out, reflecting on the fact that a murderer could look as ordinary as the Captain. If he feared him it was because of his acid manner and cold eyes, not for his capacity to inflict bodily harm. He paused in the passageway and decided that there was more than enough time for him to lie down before the evening meal. And it was with a sense of relief that he went up to the empty dormitory and stretched out in his cot, his feet sticking out over the foot of the bed, and slept, as Nonna would have said, like one of the blessed.

He awoke to the sound of the working parties returning. His headache had gone, but his mouth felt dirty and dry and he needed a long drink of water. He took his last few coins from his pack and slipped them into his pocket, then, tearing off the lower part of his page on suspects, he penned a note, disguising his handwriting and addressed it to the Captain. This too he tucked away.

Down in the kitchen he begged some food off Cookie-Will, claiming that he was on duty that night and would miss the evening meal. Cookie looked hard at him before handing him two slabs of bread and a piece of pork – a piece that looked fractionally more appetising than their usual fare.

"So where'r you off to?"

"Special duty. Er… guarding munitions. I will see you in the morning."

Cookie looked after him, half disbelieving, then turned to his pots and cauldrons with a sigh. It was hard to conjure up meals out of the stores he was allowed. What he wouldn't give for some fresh food – good meat, potatoes that weren't sprouting tendrils a foot long, and plenty of eggs. His one chicken, kept well hidden, had been laying erratically since November. He paused in his ruminations and looked at the doorway through which Bresciano was just disappearing: that boy was up to something. He had looked pale, haggard, but with an unsettling gleam in his eye.

And outside the Barracks Bresciano realised that his

idea of talking to Abraham might be foiled: it was still the Sabbath. Well, he reasoned, surely talking to a gentile on the Sabbath was permissible? He tried to remember at what time the service at the synagogues took place and which synagogue Abraham favoured. It would be a matter of luck as he did not even know if Abraham would be off duty.

Fortunately, he struck lucky at the Flemish synagogue on the Line Wall, just opposite the King's Bastion. The afternoon service appeared to be over, and a number of the faithful came out and stood around, greeting each other warmly. It was one of the limited occasions when they met these days. Bresciano was struck by their ravaged aspect. With salt pork being one of the few commodities available, the Jewish inhabitants were clearly suffering greater hardship than the rest of the beleaguered community of the fortress. And though their generosity was proverbial, they now had little to offer one another. Finally Abraham came out, putting away his prayer shawl and replacing his skull-cap with his military headgear.

Bresciano waved to him, moving through the crowd eagerly. "I'm so glad I've caught you. Can we have a quiet word?"

"Giovanni, you are waiting for me? You are fortunate. I have been on duty all day. Even Sabbath obligations have to wait during these uncertain days. Now, what is it you want?"

"I need to consult you about a plan I have: then I will have everything sorted out within hours!" he was tense with excitement.

"Come away from here. I do not know what you are talking about, and I cannot say that I trust you. You are looking a little wild."

"That's because I... because things are falling into place. I have now eliminated nearly all my suspects."

"I am pleased to hear that. But what do you mean by 'nearly all'? Does this mean you are still determined to continue with your enquiries?"

"No more enquiries. I have found out all I could."

"So your investigation is at an end." Abraham sounded relieved. "Now tell me how I can help you. Not another wild goose chase, I hope!"

"No. I hope you don't mind sitting out here," he indicated a pile of cobbles stacked against a wall, but I don't want to be overheard."

Abraham said nothing, but looked at Bresciano warily.

"I am left with two suspects and I need your help to trap the guilty party into betraying himself."

"Giovanni!"

"No, please listen to me!"

He began by telling his friend the good news – the names of all the people he no longer suspected. Then he outlined his scheme. First he would make sure the Sergeant knew that he would have the murderer's name by evening, then he would slip an anonymous note into the Captain's house. Thus both his suspects would know where to find him if they wanted to silence him or buy his silence. Abraham looked at him in disbelief.

"You are crazier than this Hamlet of yours! How on earth do you expect to capture someone whom you suspect of being a killer twice over?"

"I shall not be alone, I hope."

"Who else is going to be stupid enough to help you?"

"I was hoping you would."

"What!" Hassan was aghast.

"There won't be a problem – you will be hiding and I shall be acting as bait and we will both be armed."

"I refuse to have anything to do with this wildcat scheme of yours. How dared you drag me into this? You've let yourself become obsessed with this investigation. And it is still nothing but supposition on your part."

"Well, then, if I'm wrong, no one will come to this rendezvous and that will be the end of that."

"But if there is the remotest possibility that you are right…"

"That is why I need you there to help me."

"No! If you are right, you can go to some superior like your Colonel."

"And who will believe my word against that of the Sergeant or the Captain? I only have evidence that could point to anyone – that stool that was too low, the key by the side of the hut, the drugged wine, those knots…"

"Yes, what about those knots? The Captain was not in the navy, nor the Sergeant as far as you know."

"I know, but I've realised that it's a red herring – after all, I'm no sailor, and I know how to tie them!"

"You have no proof against anyone, Giovanni. No proof at all, not a shred of evidence."

"There is evidence enough to indicate that both Jamie and Tom were murdered. The evidence is in the odd circumstances – think of what I've told you about Tom's death and the bloody cave and the bloody rock used to kill him and..."

"And all those circumstances, however odd, could point at anyone!"

"No, don't you see? They point at only a small number of people, and I've cleared most of them, but without specific proof..."

They argued and wrangled back and forth till Hassan tired of the whole matter and stood up, ready to leave.

"No, Giovanni, I will not help you to get yourself killed. That is my final word."

"Then I shall go alone. And if I die in the attempt, well... you are not to feel badly about it. I know I've asked too much from you."

It was blackmail: they both knew it.

"I could kill you myself, Giovanni!"

"Then you will help me?"

"Tell me where and at what time." The words came savagely and reluctantly, but they came.

*　　*　　*　　*

The argument left Bresciano tired but exultant. What was left to be done would be easy by comparison. First, find the Sergeant, who would probably be having his abstemious mug or two of ale at one of the taverns.

And so it was. There sat the Sergeant on one of the settles at the tavern opposite the church. Bresciano braced himself, his heart beating fast, and shuffled in. He had an inane grin on his face and he made sure his eyelids drooped heavily. That was what drunks looked like. Now all he had to do was slur his speech and get near the Sergeant.

At the counter the tavern keeper eyed him disapprovingly, but Bresciano, his back to the Sergeant, managed to sound sober enough to buy himself a drink of ale. The rum he had drunk earlier seemed still to lie in his mouth and his gorge rose at the thought of anything to drink, but it was all in the line of duty, he thought.

Looking amiably foolish he moved to where the Sergeant was viewing him coldly and set down his drink with the exaggerated care of a man whose senses show signs of betraying him. Then he sat down and forced himself to take a sip from his tankard.

"Good evening, s-sir," he said slowly. "Thish is a fine, fine, fine place."

The Sergeant said nothing.

"It'ss better than the other places. Much, much, much better."

The Sergeant was staring at the wall behind Bresciano.

"I've met someone who s-speakss Gaelic."

That brought the Sergeant's eyes round to him.

"It'sh important, because I don't speak Gaelic. No. I don't."

"And why is it important?"

"Sh!" Bresciano leaned over confidentially. "Shecret! Very shecret. Poor Jamie MacFarlane's dying words were in Gaelic, but I didn't realise their importance at the time." His speech had become too fluent as he concentrated on getting his point across, so he threw in a small hiccup and took another drink from his mug.

"Jamie said nothing. He was dead when I cut him down."

"Not dead. Whishpered in my ear. Couldn't understand him. Shtands to reason. He spoke Gaelic, that's why."

"And what did he say in Gaelic?"

"Shecret! But if you ashk me, told me who killed him, oopps!" he clapped his hand to his mouth.

"And?"

"My new friend shpeakss Gaelic. Going to ashk him. Meeting him tonight when he comess off duty. Only thought of it today! Shilly me!" he attempted a giggle which sounded odd even to him. "Nine o'clock. There'sh a piece of waste ground jusht before the South Port. Got trees there. Mustn't tell anyone," he held up a stern finger. "Shecret!"

The Sergeant looked hard at Bresciano, then fixed his gaze once more on the wall, but this time he was frowning. And Bresciano, his task completed, slouched away and into the evening.

After a few seconds the Sergeant followed Bresciano to

the door and stared after him.

The Captain was next on Bresciano's agenda. Bresciano was pleased with the note he had penned, his writing disguised, sloping backwards instead of forwards, the letters printed, and the message terse:

"I know about MacFarlane and Tennant. You were seen on both occasions. I shall be at the old stables inside the South Port tonight at nine. If you value your safety and my silence you will meet me there."

Suddenly he stopped short as he realised that there was no point in slipping the note under the door unless Weston was at home. Hadn't someone told him that Saturday was his card night at the South Barracks? That was more than a mile away, far outside the city walls. Well beyond the town. How would he get there and deliver the note without being identified? How – but the problem was resolved for him by the sight of the Captain striding down the hill towards his quarter. The Captain had seen him, and Bresciano decided on a bold stroke. He went up to his superior officer, saluted smartly and handed him the note.

"What is this?"

"I do not know, sir. A man delivered it at the Barracks after you left and said it was of the utmost urgency." He almost barked his message out, toneless and brisk.

"What man?"

"A civilian. I did not recognise him." He knew better than to say too much.

"Describe him."

"A short man. He spoke English well. Wearing a cloak and hat pulled down low."

"Very well; you may leave."

Bresciano saluted again and walked off smartly, hugging his success to himself. Everything was working out well. It was an omen! Now all that remained was to collect his musket and some shot and make his way towards the town gate to be at the patch of overgrown waste land well before nine o'clock. As he had advised Abraham – it would never do to arrive after his murderer!

He avoided the mess hall and headed straight for the dormitory, where he had left his bread and meat, and sat down on his bed, eating hungrily. There was a large clay *tinaja* – a water container – in a corner of the room with a tin cup placed on the lid. He drank thirstily and then lay back in his bed, revising his plan mentally. And it was only then that he found himself questioning Bianca's statement. She had said – no, she had screamed out to him – that Robert had been with her for two hours. But Jean Pierre with his passion for numbers had been quite clear that it had been an hour and fourteen minutes. That meant that, if he believed the disinterested evidence of the obsessively accurate Walloon...

He sat up, confused. If Robert only had a little over an hour unaccounted for... It still was not clear. An hour and a quarter gave him time to murder Tom. But that time spent with Bianca still gave him an alibi. She said they had been in her room. If they had made... if they had been in bed... He felt woefully ignorant. How long did it take to...? The tone of his reflections disturbed him and brought back all those shameful and shaming pictures to his mind. He forced himself to try to clarify his thoughts. Perhaps Robert had carried out the 'act' quickly and then hurried away to meet and kill Tom.

That must be what happened. Bianca had been mistaken – no, she had lied to him about how long she had spent with the loathsome Robert. It could be that she had done it to hide the humiliating fact that he had just had his will of her and had then promptly walked out, his desire slaked... or perhaps it was to hurt Bresciano, to pay him back for what she must have seen as his violent attempt to force himself on her. And all he had wanted was to hold her and kiss her! Well, Robert, the man most likely to have killed Jamie and Tom, was firmly back on his list of suspects.

He cursed Bianca's false alibi. It was too late now to form a new plan that included Robert. He would have to go through with tonight's charade, for that was all that it was likely to be, but at least Abraham would be pleased! No danger for either of them tonight. Besides, it would serve to clear the ground of all suspects except Robert – and he would spring the same trap on Robert tomorrow! That would teach Bianca a lesson when she found her precious lover was a spy and a murderer.

By the time he reached his conclusions he was in better spirits. Tonight would see the end of his tortuous investigation one way or another. In the unlikely case that the Captain or the Sergeant was guilty, he would have his answer. And in the more likely event that no one arrived at the rendezvous – he would have finally homed in on one man – Robert!

The sound of tapping on the window-sill brought him out of his reverie. Heavy raindrops were falling. It did not matter. He jammed his hat firmly on, wrapped himself in his coat, and slipped the musket under it. Then he walked down the stairs and out of the back gate unobserved.

His mood was now euphoric. Everything would be resolved tonight.

CHAPTER XVIII

Abraham Hassan shifted uneasily in his chair as his father recited the blessings on wine, spices and the lighted candle, which marked the end of the Jewish Sabbath and the beginning of a new week. He dutifully sniffed the spices – a few cloves, almost odourless by now, jealously guarded and kept from week to week, for who could find more spices in these days of blockade? He held up his hand to the light, sipped the wine, then kissed his father's hand.

"I must go now," he said reluctantly, kissing his mother and his sisters.

"His father raised his thick eyebrows. "Why? Have you secret knowledge that the Spaniards will invade tonight?" he enquired with heavy sarcasm. Abraham knew better than to answer him, but the womenfolk looked appealingly at him.

"Stay with us for a little while, Abraham," his mother begged him.

"I cannot. The Colonel has ordered my attendance to – to write down his report to the Governor." The lie did not come easily. Again he silently cursed Giovanni for his folly, and himself for agreeing to be part of it; and now he was forced to lie to his parents!

Taking up his hat and his musket, he left the house. It was raining heavily. Clapping the hat on his head, he turned down Church Street in the direction of the South Port. Perhaps if he arrived early he would be able to dissuade Bresciano from his quixotic scheme.

He had only gone a few paces when he was confronted by the short, stocky figure of his sergeant.

"Where d'you think you're going, Private Hassan?"

As Hassan hesitated, the sergeant continued: "Well, it doesn't matter, because there's only one place you're going tonight, and that's to Casemates Barracks. There's another deserter to question, and the Colonel needs your Spanish. He wants you there at eight o'clock, sharp, mind you – that's ten minutes from now, so jump to it!"

The sergeant was standing squarely in the middle of the street. There was no chance for Hassan to get to the South Port to warn his friend that he could not be there to help him. Glumly, he turned northwards. The sergeant, waiting only to see that Hassan was on his way, strode off into the rain.

Hassan trudged unhappily through the muddy street in the direction of Casemates Barracks. He was furious with himself, and even more so with Giovanni Bresciano. How dare the man presume upon their friendship by expecting Hassan to back him up in his crazy schemes? And now he would be on his own there near the South Port waiting to catch his supposed murderer. Ridiculous! All he would catch in this weather was pneumonia, and serve him right! At least the Colonel's summons had turned his lie to his mother into truth, he comforted himself, although he was aware of the fallacy of his argument.

He walked on steadily, but his conscience was not at ease. Suppose there *was* a murderer after all, and he was not there to protect that stupid Bresciano when he confronted the killer? But what could he do? There was no time to retrace his steps and go to the South Port, even if he were not intercepted by the sergeant on the way there.

Then he remembered that he was only a few paces away from Irish Town and the King's Arms, where he knew that Bianca, Bresciano's childhood friend, worked. If he spoke to her, she would surely be able to dissuade Bresciano, or at least to send someone to see that he was all right. He cut down a side street into Irish Town. At the door of the wine-house he hesitated momentarily and looked around, hoping that no one he knew would observe him entering. Then he squared his shoulders and went in.

There were only one or two customers in the room, and to his relief, Bianca was behind the bar.

He approached the bar and said; "Miss Bellini, is it not?"

"That's right. I'm Bianca Bellini, but what's it to you?

Can I serve you some wine? We don't often see your people in here – it is Mr Hassan, isn't it?"

"Yes, yes, I'm Abraham Hassan, but I didn't come for a drink…" he hesitated, "I wanted to talk about Giovanni Bresciano."

He thought that Bianca had stiffened as he mentioned Bresciano's name, but she said neutrally,

"Oh, yes, and why should you want to talk to me about him?"

Hurriedly, he told Bianca about Bresciano's wild plan to catch the so-called murderer, and how he, Hassan, had been supposed to help him, but was called away on duty.

Bianca said nothing, frowning at what she mentally classified as a farrago of Giovanni nonsense.

"I thought, that as he is your friend, you would be able to find someone to help him instead of me or even better, to convince him to give up his mad plan."

Bianca was silent, then said, reluctantly, "Yes, he is my friend."

Hassan realised that he would get no more out of her, but he could not spare any more time to convince her that action was necessary to save Bresciano from his own folly. He could only hope that she would take his plea seriously.

"Please do what you can to help him. I must go now, my Colonel is waiting."

He left the bar and was jostled as he went into the street by two Walloons coming in. He continued on his way to Casemates, to find that the deserter whom he was supposed to interrogate was a bumpkin barely articulate enough to give his own name. The Colonel's attempts to gain information from this simpleton were doomed to failure, but the Colonel was a stubborn man; and it was two hours before he let the deserter – and Hassan – go.

* * * *

Bianca stood behind the bar and watched Hassan leave. She was glad that she had not shown her anger at Bresciano to a relative stranger. But as Pascal and Robert came up to the bar, her self-control snapped.

"The fool! The stupid, stupid fool!"

"I trust it is not me or Pascal that you are referring to!" That was Robert; but the swagger in his voice made it clear that he could not conceive that anyone could possibly think *him* a fool.

"No, it is not you, Robert. It is that idiot Giovanni Bresciano. Apparently he says he will soon 'know' who killed poor Jaime! Some nonsense about Jamie's dying words in Gaelic that he has finally found someone to translate for him, so he's off to that sprawl of waste ground by the South Port to get the name of the murderer! Or to meet the murderer himself for all that I could make out. And we all know Jamie killed himself, didn't he? Oh, Giovanni's as much of an idiot as poor Jamie was. He won't catch any murderer – all he'll catch is his death of cold!" She spoke in Spanish to make sure both men understood her.

"Yes, indeed, he'll catch his death – in this weather. But forget him, my little Bianca. It is cold here too – perhaps you and I can go to your room and get warm together – yes?" That was Robert, with his ready smile.

But Bianca was in no mood for dalliance and she ignored his unsubtle efforts at seduction and turned to Pascal instead.

"What do you think of Bresciano's behaviour? What should I do?"

"He is a well-meaning lad, but a little deluded, *non*? Leave him alone – he will come to his senses when he's spent an hour or so in the rain," Pascal replied dully, and then groaned and clutched his belly.

"You are looking pale, M'sieu Pascal; are you not well? Perhaps a little brandy?"

Pascal waved the offer aside. "No, no. It is that damned gut-ache I always get. I already had a brandy and it made it worse." He looked at the slate on which the owner of the bar always scrawled whatever food was available. It was blank. "Do you have any soup tonight? That sometimes helps the pain."

"No, look at the slate, we haven't made any tonight – Carmela couldn't find any food to make it with. But you could try the Mermaid."

"I will go. If there is nothing to be had there, I must go back to the Barracks – I still have some opium there: enough to help me sleep until the pain goes away."

He left, and Robert stayed behind to concentrate on conquering Bianca. But she was silent and unresponsive to his blandishments, and he soon gave up, drained his glass and left, saying that he would go and see how his friend Pascal was.

A tall figure rose from behind a table in the shadows at the back of the room, and followed Robert out.

Bianca busied herself with collecting empty glasses and tankards and rinsing them out in the basin underneath the bar, but her mind was not on her work. She was uneasily aware that she had let Giovanni down – and in spite of his recent behaviour, he had always been her friend and, despite her anger, she valued that friendship.

*   *   *   *

Bresciano stood miserably under a tree which gave him scant protection from the driving rain. Around him the undergrowth was thick and ahead of him more trees obscured his view of the road. He felt he had not chosen his rendezvous too wisely, but was consoled by the fact that no one was likely to come.

His musket was primed and loaded, but how to keep the powder dry? He tucked the barrel under his coat, uneasily aware that it was not a very safe thing to do, and settled down to wait.

The wind was rising. He heard a rustle among the nearby trees and peered around in the dark. Had his quarry arrived, or was it Hassan hiding there, ready to come to his aid if necessary? The wind dropped slightly, and he could hear no more; it must have been the wind.

How long had he been there? An hour? Two hours? He shifted uncomfortably yet again, and wished that he was back at home – or even the inhospitable Barracks would have been a great improvement. It was getting late. No one would come now, surely, and his great plan would have come to nothing. Hassan had been right – where the devil was he, anyhow?

He looked toward the road. Someone was coming along it, a dim figure barely visible in the murk. Was this his quarry? The figure did not look like Sergeant Connor – it must be the Captain – or perhaps it was Robert, after all! Bresciano swallowed hard and took a deep breath, then, trying to control his fear, he stepped forward. But as the shape came closer and acquired definition, he realised that it was Pascal.

This was a nuisance. If one of his suspects appeared now, he would surely be put off by seeing a companion with Bresciano, and go away.

"Pascal!" he hissed.

The Walloon looked up.

"Mr Bresciano: what are you doing here in such a dreadful night? Surely they have not set you to guard the trees!"

"No, no – I am waiting for someone – for a friend – a girl friend." He improvised. "Please go away – if she sees you, she will not come."

"But why should Ah go away? We're friends, are we not?"

Bresciano realised, with a start, that they were not talking in their usual Spanish. Pascal was talking English – and in a way that reminded him of… of something…

It is difficult to change horses in midstream at the best of times. Bresciano was tired, his earlier euphoria had given way to weariness and he failed to assimilate the situation that now faced him. He had invested too much in Robert as his prime suspect to change his mind so suddenly. He was bewildered: why should Pascal sound like… like Jamie?

"Why? Where? How could…?"

His uncertain questions withered into silence and his eyes widened with horror as realisation came to him. He tried to pull his musket out from under his coat.

"Dinna try it!" Pascal snapped. A pistol had appeared in his right hand.

"You – you were Jamie's 'friend'? You are… Scottish?"

He spoke bitterly. He felt deflated; disbelieving still the evidence before him – all his fine investigation had come to this, that he had failed miserably to uncover the truth.

"Yes. Ah'm afraid he recognised me – his father used to mind ma father's sheep. I didna want to kill him – Ah did try to keep him sweet wi' promises, but he was a bletherer – Ah couldna trust him to keep quiet, so he had to go!"

"But why…?"

"Why did I come here? Tae pay back the Sassenachs for what they did to ma kin. That story I told you – it wasna' the

French that did it – it was the Sassenachs, curse them, and it was many years after Culloden, only five years ago – and they did it to ma family – it was ma dog they blinded – ma ain faithful Connie – she knew me when I came, though she couldna' see me - she licked ma hand, and died! A've waited a long time for this! Now, Ah'll get ma revenge and kill that renegade Scot, Eliott – he's the ainly one saving this midden of a Rock – wi'out him, this place will fall to Spain, and ye'll all be dead meat!" Pascal's voice was rising with increasing excitement, and his accent became more and more like Jamie's, but the gun in his hand continued to point unwaveringly at Bresciano's chest.

"Ah'm afraid Ah shall have to kill you first, though," he added more calmly.

"You – you'll never kill General Eliott." Bresciano tried to keep his voice from quavering. He must try to keep Pascal talking. Surely Hassan was nearby, and would take action to save him! "He's well-guarded…"

"I'd hae got him the ither day, if that crazy woman had known how to aim – Ah gave her the musket, and told her what to do, but she missed, the stupid crummie. But he rides round alone every eve on his white horse, and he always tak's the same road. Easy enough to pick him off wi' a musket or a pistol!"

"And Tom – you killed Tom, too."

"Aye, it was hard enough to kill Jamie, a Scot and an innocent, but Tom – a Sassenach and a right worthless one – he tried tae blackmail me – said he'd seen me go into the hut to hang puir wee Jamie – it was a pleasure to brain him and throw him off the craig! And now …" The barrel of the pistol jerked upwards.

Abraham, Abraham, where are you? Bresciano silently implored his friend to appear, but there was no sound except the wind in the trees. He must try again to gain more time.

"I thought that Robert…" he began.

"Ah, Robert! Yes, you wanted it to be Robert, didn't ye, because he was cutting you out with yon pretty lassie; but Robert – he's naught but a blowhard fool and a braggart – all those tales he tells of his great house in Flanders – he was surely but a kitchen-boy there who ran away and was caught and pressed into the Army. Now he tells everyone that he was the bairn of the owner – and I think he has come to believe it!"

"But Jean Pierre? He said you were at the tavern the evening Jamie was killed." Bresciano said desperately.

"That one! He believes everything you tell him – unless he can count it and prove you wrong! If Ah tell him Ah'm sick wi' a gut-ache, he believes me. If Ah tell him Ah was in the tavern of the gentry, he believes me. Only if Ah tell him that there are a million stars in the sky will he count them to prove me wrong!"

Pascal was sounding almost affable, and Bresciano began to hope that he might relent and not kill him. As he came to terms with Pascal's guilt, he saw in his mind's eye, Pascal struggling to keep his grip on a block of limestone and remembered his cry, "Someone, help!" before he had reverted to French. And he recalled Robert's account of their escape from Spain:

"No one shot at you when you left the Spanish lines to come to Gibraltar!"

"'Twas all arranged. And now Ah have that rope hidden awa' and Ah shall be gone back to Spain – where I shall be a hero on ma return. " He stated the fact with no evidence of satisfaction, "but what matters is that Ah shall have had ma vengeance."

Then his voice changed again: "Enough blatherin', ma friend Bresciano. It's time to end it!"

Bresciano could see Pascal's finger tensing on the trigger, and cried out "Wait! If you shoot me, the shot will be heard and you will be caught!"

As if in answer, there was a volley of cannon fire from several Spanish gunboats in the Bay, and an answering volley from the Rock's batteries. Pascal smiled.

"You see, ma Spanish friends and your English friends are helping me. Naebody will pay heed to a single pistol-shot while that noise is going on! Goodbye, laddie. It has been a pleasure knowing ye. Under other circumstances I think we could hae been friends."

Pascal backed away, his finger tightening on the trigger. There was a roar, and Bresciano clutched at his chest.

CHAPTER XIX

His hand gripping his chest convulsively, Bresciano felt as if his soul was draining out of him and thought, "So this is what it is like to die. This is the end."

It was painless... but as his hand jerked over his chest, he found no blood, no wound and he watched in amazement as Pascal, a look of bewilderment on his face, fell to his knees before pitching head-first to the ground.

Out from the bushes rose the figure of Sergeant Connor, a smoking pistol in his hand.

"Close your mouth, Bresciano, and try not to look more stupid than you are. You look like a fish that's just been landed."

After the explosion and the cannonades that had ripped the air apart, the silence that followed made the night seem hollow.

"So what the hell have you been playing at?"

But Bresciano had sunk to his knees and was being violently sick.

The Sergeant looked at him distastefully and waited till the paroxysms were over before hauling him to his feet.

"You bloody fool. You could have been killed. You and your drunken act at the tavern. Who did you think would believe such a performance? And next time you want to act the drunk, just remember that if you stagger out of a tavern, you don't suddenly recover your balance and speed away once you've got outside."

Bresciano looked at the figure on the ground and back at the Sergeant: "But... but... I thought..." How was he to say what he had really thought?

"I think I know what you thought!"

The Sergeant glared at him, determined not to betray his relief: if he had not arrived when he did, the lad would have been dead. It was not pleasant to be thought a murderer by a young whipper-snapper like this one, but Connor was honest enough to admit that he had paid scant attention to what Bresciano had said about the first attempt on Jamie's life, and it could have looked as if he was trying to cover up a crime. If he had looked beyond the raw recruit's long words and first foolish accusation of Murch, he might have saved not one, but two lives. He might call the lad a fool, and worse, but the young recruit had been right about Jamie – and about Tom Tennant. Connor kept his eyes fixed on Bresciano's face till the younger man dropped his eyes and stared at his feet.

"You are a fool, Bresciano, but you are one of my men and I look after my own. You and your bloody questions. Couldn't keep that great nose of yours out of things, could you?"

"How... how did he..." he pointed to the body on the ground, "How did he know I would be here? I never let *him* know... I only..."

"Got yourself more suspects, have you? Perhaps the Captain? Or the Colonel? Or Eliott himself?"

Bresciano closed his mouth, feeling himself grow even colder than he was at the thought of the problem he would face if the Captain ever realised what that cryptic note he had handed him was about.

"But how did he, Pascal, find out...?"

"Ask young Bianca at the King's Arms. She can tell you."

"Bianca?"

None of it made sense to Bresciano, but before he could ask more questions, the silence was shattered by a hallooing as a group of men burst through the bushes, led by Corporal Jones, who managed to salute and gasp,

"Are we too late?"

And within seconds the sound of heavy footfalls announced the arrival of a second group which included some Artificers, several local men and a roisterously drunk Jean Pierre. It was led by an agitated Abraham Hassan.

"Bresciano – so... no one came to your wretched rendezvous?"

The secluded place was now alive with people milling about, calling out, asking questions, wanting answers as they stared at the body of Pascal – and the whole event was acquiring the character of a farce. It was only the presence of the Sergeant that held things together.

"Just a nasty accident, nothing to fuss about like a lot of chickens. Two of you men," he raised his powerful voice, "pick up the body and take it to the Blue Barracks."

"How did you know where to come?" A confused Bresciano asked Corporal Jones.

"Bianca asked me to see that you were safe."

"Bianca!" There it was again.

"Right," the Sergeant's voice cut through the hubbub, "the rest of you can stop gawking and leave here. It's all over and done with. Nothing more to see. Go! And as for you, Bresciano, you have a report to make. Now get away from here," then he lowered his voice, "and keep your lip buttoned about that murdering traitor! Not a word about the truth to anyone, you hear? We don't want no panic among the men."

And as he watched Bresciano scrambling off after the others, the Sergeant permitted himself a smile as he reviewed the events of the evening.

*   *   *   *

For Bresciano there were questions from the other men: what had happened? Who had killed Pascal? And, beginning to feel exhilarated at the thought that it was all over and that he had – albeit by accident – done as he intended and found Jamie's killer that he might pay for his deed, Bresciano found himself improvising fluently: remembering that the supposed Walloon had been a chess player, he said that he had arranged to meet Pascal about... an unusual chess set that was owned by a local man who was anxious to sell it – someone must have heard them talking about it about it – Pascal was carrying some money – when Bresciano arrived he heard a shot and was just in time to see Pascal on the ground and someone rifling through his pockets. He had given chase, but the man had got away – no, he hadn't seen his face.

Corporal Jones looked at him curiously, but kept his counsel, as did Abraham Hassan. The rest of the men, who had come out on an unspecified mission that had promised some excitement and a break from the monotony of their lives, were disappointed at Bresciano's tame tale, though a few offered to try and find traces of Pascal's killer. Bresciano, feeling light-headed with relief, said solemnly:

"You'll never catch Pascal's killer. How would you recognise him? Even I can't say who it was."

Together they made their way back and Bresciano, eager to see Bianca, headed to the King's Head. He needed to know whether he was indebted to her for the attack on his life or for his deliverance or both. But his plan was frustrated as the Sergeant caught up with him,

"I want you at the Barracks, now. We'll sort out that report of yours."

They marched off together in silence as the other men fell back. And in silence they arrived at the Barracks where the Sergeant took Bresciano into Captain Weston's empty office.

"Sit down at that desk. Take a paper and pen. I want you to write down all that you noticed about the deaths of James MacFarlane and Tom Tennant that made you suspect foul play. Everything about that, but nothing else. You understand? This is a report, not a bloody novel. I shall be back in half an hour and you better have it ready when I return."

Bresciano sat down miserably and wrote out all the suspicious circumstances that had added up to that supposed suicide and the later supposed accident. He only left out his own attempts to clear or inculpate the people he had thought were involved. Reduced to a report, the efforts of the past two weeks looked pathetically short on paper. He was finished by the time the Sergeant returned.

"Now, I want to know about this evening's events. You haven't written those out, have you? Good. Begin."

And Bresciano began uncertainly, "I had been unable to discover who the... guilty party was so I decided to set a trap. I made out that there had been some dying words of Jamie's in Gaelic..." He made his recital as brief as he could, stumbling over it as he came to the awkward part, "so I let... it be known... I told er people... where I'd be... so that... well, the guilty party," he felt himself blushing, "would go to find me and... would try to kill me. But I had asked a friend to be there to back me up! I don't know why he was so late!"

"A friend, was it? I'm surprised you have any friends. I heard this Pascal talking about murdering Eliott so you can leave that part to me. Now, is there anything else?"

Bresciano had expected far worse than this and decided to risk trying to recruit the Sergeant's help; after all, things could not get any worse:

"The worst thing… this is really the worst… is that I gave the Captain a note about the rendezvous purporting to come from a stranger I had met."

"'Purporting' was it? My God – you suspected the Captain? Are you insane, boy? What on earth did the Captain have to do with Daft Jamie? I doubt he even knew him. Your imagination is dangerous. I can't believe what you're saying." He looked at Bresciano in disbelief. "So what did the note say?"

Bresciano cringed as he recited the message he had written. It sounded like a particularly lurid extract from the Newgate Calendar.

Connor said nothing. Bresciano waited for his wrath to fall, but the Sergeant was lost in thought.

"Pick up that pen and write what I tell you." He began to dictate: "This night – give the date – I set a trap for the killer. I let it be… known that I would be at – say the place and the time," the Sergeant watched as Bresciano wrote and the only sound in the room was the scratching of the pen on the paper. When it stopped, the Sergeant continued, "I felt it would be dangerous to be alone so I arranged for a friend to help and… informed the Sergeant of my intention," Sergeant Connor raised one eyebrow, which gave him an almost satanic look, "and sent a note to Captain Weston – and you can put your purporting in there – in… the hope of making him curious… er… curious enough to come and provide further support. Then sign it clearly with your name and rank."

As Bresciano wrote the last blessed sentence that would save him from everything bar a tongue lashing for stupid presumption, the Sergeant walked out and called one of the guards. Bresciano waited miserably: perhaps a night in the cells? Just to let him cool his heels? There was a long silence that stretched out painfully till the guard returned carrying two tankards of ale which he handed to the Sergeant, who put one on the desk in front of Bresciano.

"Drink up. I'll just read this to make sure you haven't said something stupid."

And Bresciano, feeling reprieved for the second time that night, drank gratefully, watching the Sergeant's immobile face. Eventually Connor looked up and considered Bresciano thoughtfully.

"It makes sense when you put it all down. Do you remember that story Pascal fed you about his family being killed by the French?"

"How do you know that, sir?"

"I was in the settle behind you at the tavern. I know enough Spanish to pick things up. It was the part about the dog's eyes being gouged out that made me realize that I knew the story. It happened in Scotland when I was back there a couple of years ago. Atrocities committed over the years." He looked past Bresciano, "I have reason to hate the Scots." Then he looked back at his mug and said reluctantly, "Some of them probably have good reason to hate *us*. That tale he told you made me curious about that Pascal. He was no Walloon. I've been keeping an eye on him. Tonight I saw him leave The King's Head when he heard of your plan from Bianca. I followed. And I've been keeping an eye on you too. That conversation you had with a friend of yours – that other Gibraltar lad who also joined up…"

"Abraham Hassan?"

"I was going to close a window when I overheard you one night outside the Barracks. I wondered what hare-brained ideas you might be hatching. You and Pascal! As if I didn't have enough to do."

"He had given me an alibi… and I believed him."

"You're too quick to trust people. Always get someone else to back up what you've been told. Anyone can lie."

"I should have sought corroboration," Bresciano said bitterly.

"That's right. Corroboration. You do like your jaw-breakers!" He stood up, "Well, you've given Eliott the best present he could have hoped for this Christmas. I'll just add a line or two to this report of yours… just to 'corroborate' what you've said and say what I overheard Pascal saying tonight. You are dismissed."

And Bresciano, gulping down what was left of his ale,

was finally free to get down to The King's Head to see Bianca.

His arrival at the tavern was greeted with mock cheers.

"Scared away the thief, 'e did."

"Now we'll never know 'oo dun it!"

"He's a right hero."

Behind the counter Bianca stood, a stricken look on her face. She took off her apron and threw it down after a hurried word with Carmela and came towards him. She took his hand and dragged him out into the street.

"Bianca, I'm so sorry about what happened earlier. Truly sorry. It was an accident." He blurted the words out, but Bianca barely heard him as she rushed to apologise to him:

"Giovanni, I'm sorry! You might have been killed and it would have been my fault." She held his face in her hands and stared at him as if wanting to memorise his features. "You've been right all along and I've been stupid."

"Oh, no. It's me, I've been so... jealous."

"Of Robert? Him! I've found out that he's been playing me off against Carmela!" She spoke without heat. "And when I told you he had been with me in my room for two hours – I lied, it wasn't true. I just wanted to hurt you. I am so, so sorry! And if I hadn't been angry with you I wouldn't have gone on about your plan tonight with Pascal and Robert hearing every word – but I didn't know...! It was David... Corporal Jones who took it seriously when he came in. He told me to say no more and took some men off after you. And when he returned, he told me what had happened. Can you ever forgive me?"

Instinct took over from caution and he bent down, pulled her towards him and kissed her, a trifle inexpertly as the first kiss missed her mouth and landed on her nose. But the second time he found her lips with his. It was an intoxicating experience which he repeated again and again, growing more agitated and amorous. He was aware of her body pressing against him and pulled away suddenly.

"I'm sorry," he mumbled.

"Why?"

She put her arms round his neck and raised herself on tiptoes to kiss him back with a great deal more expertise than he had demonstrated. Then her hands strayed to his chest. He gulped.

"Bianca! Bianca!"

"Don't say anything. Come with me."

She took his hand and led him away from the tavern, away from the disreputable Irish Town and across Waterport Street towards the room she rented, small and sparsely furnished. Once inside she lit a candle.

"Come here, Giovanni, and take off your shoes and socks and that jacket. It's wet, and so are you. Just look at your shirt. You'll catch your death! Take it off."

And as he obeyed her, she removed a pin at her breast that secured her shawl. Then her hair was released from the hairpins that had secured it and it tumbled over her shoulders. By the time Bresciano was left standing in his breeches, she was there in front of him wearing nothing but her shift. He simply stared. He could make out the swell of her breasts under the cheap cotton material and he found himself breathing like a man who has run a wild race. He ached for her with a violence that shook him.

"No!" he groaned – it was too much to bear.

And then she was in his arms, murmuring endearments in his ear, and he picked her up, wincing a little as he took her weight on his weak wrist, feeling her bare flesh against his chest, and carried her across to the bed and lay down with her.

They came together with more haste than passion because for him it was a desperate coupling and for her, an expression of loving generosity as she showed him how to accomplish what he had dreamed of in his frustrated innocence. And when it was done and he felt spent, she offered him a more tranquil union and guided his inexpert hands over her body so that he experienced a different fulfilment in shared pleasure.

*   *   *   *

When he awoke, it was to the insistent but distant sound of early gunfire on the Sunday morning. She still lay beside him, her breath warm on his chest, her eyelashes shadowing her cheek and her tumbled hair about her shoulders. Her shift lay on the ground and he carefully covered her nakedness with the blanket that had slipped down to her waist.

They would have to get married! He was a man of honour. His parents would learn to accept her. They had always liked her as a child, even at her rebellious worst. She was not like her mother! That he should ever have said such things to her! They would marry and she would not have to work in a tavern for a living. He wanted to make love to her again and again and again. They must marry as soon as possible. Then her eyes opened and, even in the dim light of dawn, he noticed how the hazel was flecked with green and gold. Why had he never noticed before?

"What are you thinking, my Giovanni?"

"That you are beautiful and... and that we will get married. I want... I want you do me the honour to be my wife." The words felt foolish the moment he spoke, almost pompous.

She turned to lean up against him, shivering slightly now that she was awake, and pulling the rough blanket up to her chin.

"I love you, Giovanni. I always have. But not like you love me. No, be quiet," she stopped his protests, "listen to me. I will always love you. And I don't want you to forget me – not ever."

"How could I? I want you to be there always."

"I told you to listen. You have to hear what I have to say. It is simple. If Gibraltar was a big city like those I've heard people talk about – big cities like London or Cadiz... or if it was a big country like Wales or Spain or England... then things would be different."

"What are you talking about? What has all this to do with us? Why the geography lesson?" He felt exhilaration rising inside him like great bubbles of laughter.

"Be quiet, Giovanni for goodness' sake, just keep your mouth shut!"

This was so much like her usual self that he laughed delightedly.

"I am serious. In a big place we could get together and marry or not marry and people would not care; they would not even know us. But here I am Emiliana's daughter and I will be till the day I die. 'The daughter of that drunk' – I've heard them say it. And, 'That slut from the tavern.' And I've heard worse from some of our sainted ladies outside the church. I have sharp ears. So how could I marry you? They would call you a cuckold before we'd been married a month."

"I don't care," panic sharpened his voice, "I don't want

to lose you!"

"Don't talk of losing me! I don't belong to you or to anyone. But I *will* marry and get away from this place."

"Yes, yes! I'll take you to Devon, to my mother's people! I'll support you."

"Oh, my sweet Giovanni! You are eighteen years old and earning fourpence-ha'penny a day, and all I know how to do is serve in a tavern and clean. Did I not say I loved you? I would not let you marry me and ruin your own life."

She ended the conversation by moving off the bed, picking up her shift and slipping it on. Then she dressed in a business-like way.

"Marry me!" he jumped out of bed and tried to embrace her.

She disengaged herself briskly: "I cannot marry you. I am going to marry Corporal Jones."

"What? You can't!" He was stunned and fell back a step.

"Oh, but I can – and I will. He has proposed several times and I have decided to accept him. We will marry here and he will send me to England on the first ship that leaves the fortress. We will go to Wales when he is done with the army and raise sheep on his father's farm."

He was horrified, disbelieving, "So why did you let me… why did you make…?"

"I don't know. But when I thought that you might have been killed, and through my fault, it felt as if someone had pulled my heart out of my body. And when I saw you, and when you kissed me – I wanted you to make love to me. I wanted you last night just like you wanted me. And I'm glad we've been together. I don't regret it. It was good. Oh! Don't look at me like that. Just think…" she struggled to find a way of showing him how unsuitable a match he was proposing: "just think what your mother would say if she knew about last night. What would she think of me? And – you may as well know, if you haven't already realised it – this has not been the first time for me. There have been others, two others. One died and the other left me – oh, it doesn't matter who."

"But I love you!"

"Even that will pass. I know. I'm not going to argue with you. My mind is made up. And think, Giovanni, think: if we married and people talked and one day you were less in love –

then you might remember last night, and the other two men… and you would say, 'like mother like daughter.'"

"Never! I was just so jealous and so angry yesterday. I wanted the words back as soon as I said them. I would cut out my tongue before saying…"

"I know I am right. We both know I am not like my mother, but you might think it, even if you didn't say it. I am right."

She handed him his clothes and opened her small window. The sky was opalescent in the dawn. And she leaned out, breathing in the morning air and looking away while he dressed, sensing that he would be more embarrassed to be seen dressing in the cold light of morning than he had been when he had undressed the night before.

She felt him standing behind her and, without turning round, spoke her farewells: "Goodbye, Giovanni. I think it will be better if you stop coming to the King's Arms. It will be easier. Just remember that I have loved you… in my own way."

And when he had left, she sighed and cried a little and smiled a little.

Bresciano made his way back to the Barracks, his footsteps dragging and his eyes bleak. Why had she accepted Jones? Why not accept his honourable proposal? He was willing to marry her! No, that was wrong: he wanted to marry her. He wanted to make love to her every day of his life. The desire to feel her body next to his was so strong that he almost turned back. His steps took him towards where Emiliana had been staying and, with disgust, he remembered the letters she had given him. It was her fault that Bianca wouldn't marry him. He strode up to the door and knocked hard and long, drawing a protest from the neighbours.

"Wake up Emiliana! Get up!"

He heard her voice inside raised in complaint and waited as she drew the bolts.

As the door opened he saw her, a bleary-eyed slattern, and his heart bled for her daughter.

"Those letters you gave me said nothing. One was… about food supplies and the other was about… medicines. I threw them away." He thrust his hand in his pocket and felt the letters, crumpling them in his fist.

Then he turned and walked away, leaving her looking blankly after him.

* * * *

At the Barracks, from which he had been absent without leave, he retained enough sense of self-preservation to make his way quickly to the dining room where he would wait for the rest of the men to come down to breakfast. There he sat at one of the long trestle tables and rested his head on his arms. And when Cookie-Will shook him, he said nothing about Bresciano's suspiciously reddened eyes, and just handed him a mug of a thin excuse for coffee and a thick piece of bread with a bit of lard smeared carefully across it.

Bresciano was glad enough to drink the coffee, but as the men clattered into the dining hall, he pushed his untouched bread towards greedy, stupid, innocent Murch. And here it was that the Captain's orderly found Bresciano, still nursing his mug and ignoring the good-natured chaffing of his colleagues.

"You are wanted in the Captain's office," he stood smartly to attention and then dropped his self-important manner as Bresciano rose reluctantly, "'Ere, what 'ave you been up to?"

Outside the Captain's office stood the Sergeant who roughly straightened Bresciano's collar and rumpled jacket: "Get in there, Private."

In the room the Captain was by his desk and a heavily built officer stood at the window with his back to the door.

As Bresciano entered the man spoke quietly to the Captain, "Your request is granted. I have personally told Captain Lord Manners to comply with it with despatch. The winds being favourable and God being willing, he will shortly sail for England with dispatches. He may initially have to sail into the Mediterranean to take evasive action, but your wife should reach England well before the spring."

Bresciano coughed discreetly. "Private Bresciano reporting, sir." He was uncomfortably aware that he had overheard the tail-end of a private conversation.

The man at the window turned and Bresciano recognised the thin lips and the heavy parrot-beak of a nose of General

Eliott. His heart sank and he closed his eyes: a court martial! Surely nothing less would have brought the Governor here.

"So, you are the man. I believe I may owe my life to you, sir. I thank you, and I congratulate you on as pretty a piece of deductive work as I have seen."

And the great man extended his hand which Bresciano, his eyes flying open, stared at foolishly till he felt the Sergeant prodding him in the back.

"Sir!"

"There have been some minor irregularities, it seems, which, on this occasion, we can all agree to ignore." He addressed himself to the Captain who seemed to swallow his spleen as he nodded. "I am sure, Mr Bresciano, that I can trust your discretion. This affair is not for the ears of the general public or even of the garrison. The Sergeant here will secure the silence of the few others who know."

Bresciano stared ahead, wondering what would come next. Eliott was observing him measuringly with shrewd eyes. Then he spoke:

"Do you by any chance know Second Lieutenant Holloway?"

"I have met him, sir, in Lieutenant Drinkwater's company."

"Good. I believe that, in addition to his other duties as staff officer to the Chief Engineer, he is at present acting adjutant of the Artificer Company. A man like you might be of use to him. I shall so inform him. I believe you will find that work more congenial than that which you are at present engaged in." His mouth relaxed into something like a smile. "You may leave us now, Private Bresciano."

"Yes, sir. Thank you, sir." Bresciano gulped, saluted and turned, making his way out into the passage in a daze.

"We won't be needing you today, lad. Take yourself off." The Sergeant saw him out of the building.

Bresciano left and as he walked, he pondered on what he had heard in the office. Mrs Weston was to be sent back home, presumably to her family. And the Captain had agreed to 'forget' Bresciano's rash and 'anonymous' note. All had ended as well as could be expected.

He made his way home reflecting that he could tell no one of the success of his self-imposed task, nor of the congratulations of the great man, but then, except for the 'puzzle' he had set his father, and the 'made-up' story he had entertained Lucia with, he had never confided any of it to his family. It was as well. Better that nothing should be known either of his investigation or of his unsuccessful love. A thought brought him up short: in his anxiety to cast Robert as the villain, he had failed to note that a man who had lived his life out in Belgium – Scottish connections or not – would never have been recognised by poor Jamie. It struck him forcibly that, whatever Eliott might say, he had everything to learn about conducting an investigation objectively.

He resumed his walk and on his way he was amazed to hear sounds of jubilation in the street. Had the people somehow heard of Eliott's deliverance from an assassin's bullet? Impossible. Was this Sunday a particular feast? Why were the bells ringing?

And the answer came soon enough. The *Speedwell*, her sails swelling under a favourable wind, was a brave sight as she approached the small harbour of the beleaguered town, having lived up to her name and evaded Admiral Barceló's watchdogs at Punta Carnero. A ship would mean supplies of some sort! And as he hurried to his parents' house, he saw shutters thrown open in shops now normally closed for all but an hour or two a day, and goods that had been impossible to find now displayed openly. Some dastardly shopkeepers had hoarded scarce goods to force the price as high as it would go, and now, faced with the possibility of new supplies, they were anxious to move and sell their old stock before the *Speedwell's* cargo was unloaded! He stopped a moment to watch the *Speedwell* swinging in to anchor safely.

Food. There would be more to eat. And there would be two ships returning to England, ships that could take civilians anxious to leave the town while they were offered the opportunity. The unfortunate Mrs Weston would leave on Captain Manners' frigate, and with the *Speedwell* – its mission completed – also returning to England, there would be room enough for Bianca... Bianca Jones... to get away to safety.

A short two weeks ago he had joined the Artificers, anxious to be seen as a man. So much had happened. He had held a dead friend in his arms; he had turned thief for little Lucia's sake and would live with the remorse that caused him as long as men in the garrison suffered from scurvy; and he had solved two crimes after a fashion and lost his virginity. He was more of a man than he had been. But he thought that perhaps what made him a man was more to do with accepting the confusion of his life rather than with acquiring any certainties… for he had none.

People, crying with relief or excitement, jostled him as they ran out into the streets and down to see the *Speedwell* at anchor. It was the twenty-first of December and everyone was suddenly glad to think of Christmas: it would be celebrated as best they could. Hollow-cheeked and with deep shadows under their eyes, they ran along the street, rejoicing.

He found the door of his house open. Inside Aunt María and Lucia were alone.

"They've gone down to the harbour. Your father wants to see what food has come in and what is to be had," Aunt María's gaunt face lit up with pleasure at seeing him.

"Look, Giovanni, I've got a sparrow!" Lucia held out her cupped hands, in which she held a sparrow. "It was lying on the ground. Someone must have hit it with a stone or something. I think he was just dazed. He is all right now." She stroked its head gently with her forefinger, and the little bird trembled in her hand, feathers ruffled. "But he is too pretty to eat. And, besides, Papa thinks there will be proper food for us in the ship that has arrived. I shall keep him as a pet. What shall I call it? All I need is a cage."

Bresciano smiled at her with relief. She was well on the way to recovery, and the smallpox rash looked as if it might heal without scarring. He forced himself to speak a little sternly:

"No, Lucia, some creatures should not be caged."

Lucia pouted a little, and Bresciano thought of Bianca's words. She did not belong to anyone. And he thought of poor Jamie MacFarlane:

"I'll tell you what, Little Lu: let's call it Jamie, and let it go free."

THE END.

Due out Winter 2011

THE PEARLS OF TANGIER

A Bresciano Mystery

When Bresciano went off to Tangier on family business, he expected nothing worse than having to deal with an aggrieved sister and an emotionally volatile Aunt Maria. The last thing he expected was to be thrown in gaol the day after he arrived and then to be landed with the investigation of a murder and a serious theft.

To complicate matters further he is faced with an elopement and an abduction that has him breaking the law in a savage country where being a British subject will not protect him.

*   *   *   *

Bresciano looked around. The quay was busy with people in a wide assortment of costumes – European, naval, a couple of wealthy Arabs with flowing robes, sweating porters wearing ragged *bombachos* – baggy trousers gathered at the knee – and many others sporting the simple hooded *jellabahs* that reached down to their feet. He saw a couple of them bearing down on him.

"I take you; you come for me; you want good *fondouk*? Very clean, very cheap, Take you to *Zocco*, to market, you buy, Yes? You want camel?" A hoarse voice at his elbow was addressing him in mangled English and Bresciano's scowl evaporated as he looked at the ragged urchin eagerly pulling at his sleeve. As well have him as a guide as anyone else, and he waved the men away.

"No, I do not want a camel or anything else. I just want to get to the *fondouk* of Madame Joanna Sciavone. Do you know where it is?"

"I take you; you come for me; you want good *fondouk*? Very clean, very cheap…" the litany began again.

"No. Just take me to where I said. I simply want the *Fondouk* Sciavone." He spoke firmly.

The urchin made a sound of disgust and spat at a skinny cat slinking past, missed and wrinkled his nose. "*Fondouk* Sciavone?" He threw out his hands and spoke like a person who could not believe his ears.

"Yes." Bresciano descended firmly into pidgin. "You take. I come for you," and remembering his Lingua Franca, he added, inaccurately, that the owner was his aunt. He also held out a coin, just out of the lad's reach, as a further inducement.

The deed was done……

* * * *

And the next day, meeting up with his friend Abraham Hassan, everything began to change.

…..an altercation behind them made Abraham look up. A group of armed men dressed in the Emperor's colours were pushing their way through the dispersing crowd. Fine striped turbans, bright baggy trousers and leather waistcoats made them striking figures, and tucked into their wide cummerbunds were long curved daggers. And as they forced their way through unceremoniously, they were calling out in Arabic. Abraham raised his hand to them.

"What on earth is going on?" Bresciano asked in some amusement. He had never imagined his friend with contacts in the palace.

"I can't tell, but they are asking for someone who speaks English and Arabic."

It was all he had time to say before the guards descended on them, their leader speaking rapidly in Arabic, the incomprehensible words sounding harsh in Bresciano's ears, and seized them both roughly.

Bresciano felt himself gripped firmly by both arms, the leader of the guards snarling incomprehensibly at him. He could see that the same was happening to his friend Hassan who was struggling against his captors.

"Abraham, what's going on?" he hissed.

"They are looking for an interpreter to go somewhere into the interior with the English doctor from Gibraltar who is to treat the prince. I'm sorry, Giovanni – it's all my fault: I was stupid enough to attract their attention. I can't do it – I must return to my Rachel… she's not well. I am pretending not to understand them – you do the same." Hassan's face was pallid.

"But I don't know any Arabic." Bresciano said, confused.

At that moment, Hassan, panic endowing him with unexpected strength, tore himself free of the grasp of his captors leaving them holding his jacket, and darted down an alleyway at a speed which belied his figure, shouting "Run, Giovanni, run!"

The two guards who had been holding Hassan made after him as he disappeared around a corner, and the men holding Bresciano momentarily loosened their grip on him. Seizing his opportunity he struggled loose and tried to follow his friend, but his attempt was foiled by one of the guards, who extended a slippered foot and tripped him up. Bresciano lost his balance and fell to one side; his head hit the wall of the alleyway with a crack, and for a few seconds he watched the world spin round him before it darkened into nothing…

Sam Benady's family settled in Gibraltar in 1735. He is a paediatrician and amateur historian and has worked in, among other places, Bristol, Jerusalem, and Gibraltar – where he ran the Child Health Services almost single-handedly for over 20 years, having to cope with, among many other things, a serious epidemic of meningitis.

Mary Chiappe: teacher and journalist. Her forefathers came from Sicily and her foremothers were peasants from Andalusia – with gypsy blood somewhere along the way. A brief foray into politics made her Gibraltar's first woman minister at the age of 25. She resigned to do what she really enjoyed – teaching.

Photos © Pedrito Guzmán